"A ... [illegible]

"Funny and touching . . . delicious, delightful!"
—Edith Layton

"You'll have a decidedly winning hand with the House of Cards."
—Romance Reviews Today

"Barbara Metzger knows how to mix a dash of the ridiculous with her tried-and-true romantic instincts."
—*Romantic Times* (top pick, 4½ stars)

"Metzger's gift for re-creating the flavor and ambience of the period shines here, and the antics of her dirty-dish villains, near villains, and starry-eyed lovers are certain to entertain."
—*Publishers Weekly* (starred review)

"The complexities of both story and character contribute much to its richness. Like life, this book is much more exciting when the layers are peeled back and savored."
—*Affaire de Coeur*

"A true tour de force . . . Only an author with Metzger's deft skill could successfully mix a Regency tale of death, ruined reputations, and scandal with humor for a fine and ultimately satisfying broth . . . a very satisfying read."
—The Best Reviews

"[She] brings the Regency era vividly to life with deft humor, sparkling dialogue, and witty descriptions."
—Romance Reviews Today

"Metzger has penned another winning Regency tale. Filled with her hallmark humor, distinctive wit, and entertaining style, this is one romance that will not fail to enchant."
—*Booklist* (starred review)

ALSO BY BARBARA METZGER

Queen of Diamonds

Jack of Clubs

Ace of Hearts

The Duel

A Perfect Gentleman

Wedded Bliss

The Hourglass

BARBARA METZGER

A SIGNET ECLIPSE BOOK

SIGNET ECLIPSE
Published by New American Library, a division of
Penguin Group (USA) Inc., 375 Hudson Street,
New York, New York 10014, USA
Penguin Group (Canada), 90 Eglinton Avenue East, Suite 700, Toronto,
Ontario M4P 2Y3, Canada (a division of Pearson Penguin Canada Inc.)
Penguin Books Ltd., 80 Strand, London WC2R 0RL, England
Penguin Ireland, 25 St. Stephen's Green, Dublin 2,
Ireland (a division of Penguin Books Ltd.)
Penguin Group (Australia), 250 Camberwell Road, Camberwell, Victoria 3124,
Australia (a division of Pearson Australia Group Pty. Ltd.)
Penguin Books India Pvt. Ltd., 11 Community Centre, Panchsheel Park,
New Delhi - 110 017, India
Penguin Group (NZ), 67 Apollo Drive, Mairangi Bay,
Auckland 1311, New Zealand (a division of Pearson New Zealand Ltd.)
Penguin Books (South Africa) (Pty.) Ltd., 24 Sturdee Avenue,
Rosebank, Johannesburg 2196, South Africa

Penguin Books Ltd., Registered Offices:
80 Strand, London WC2R 0RL, England

First published by Signet Eclipse, an imprint of New American Library,
a division of Penguin Group (USA) Inc.

First Printing, March 2007
10 9 8 7 6 5 4 3 2 1

To Laura, for letting me,
and in memory of Hero,
who sat beside me for every word.

CHAPTER ONE

He was sick to death of his job. No, he was Death, or one of them, anyway. Collecting the departed was too much work for just one man. Why, a good influenza epidemic could keep a legion of death dealers busy for months, to say nothing of wars and famines. Besides, the Grim Reaper's minions were not exactly men anymore. Most hardly remembered their own mortality. Not so Ar Death. He recalled being Sir Coryn of Ardsley, and he recalled all of his sins in the brutal battles they called the Crusades. He ached to make amends, to atone, to end his labors among the aged and the ailing, the injured as well as the innocent.

Unfortunately, one did not simply resign from being Death, any more than one refused to die. Who would do the wretched job if they could be lawyers or politicians instead? Only the basest, cruelest, most heartless of souls would apply for the positions. Ar once had a heart as well as a soul, and he sorely missed them.

He could not go to His Grimness and beg to be excused, not with so many stains on his earthly record. He'd only land in a worse place. Visiting Hell was one thing. Ar did not wish to live there, or be dead there, as the case may be. Visit he would, though, for in Hell lay his only chance at rebirth, redemption, and retirement. Elysium, Nirvana, Asgard, Tir-na-n'Og, all knew him. None held hope for a Final Ferryman. Ar could have stepped through the Pearly Gates, but no one gambled there. That left the Devil.

The Great Hall of Hell was hot and smoky and echoed with eternal screams. After over half a millennium spent on the job—and centuries devising an escape—Ar was used to the sounds and smells, as well as the revolting bones Satan constantly tossed.

"Epsilon, is it?" His Evil Eminence asked, peering through his red, reptilian eyes at the cloaked figure before him. The Letters of Extinction, whose names were taken from every alphabet ever known on earth, were hard to distinguish, especially in the Stygian gloom.

"No, sir. I believe you mean Greek Rho, who is taking care of a shipwreck in the Aegean. I am English Ar, at your service."

"Mine and everyone else's," the Devil grumbled, jealous as always of losing a single soul. Then he grinned, showing pointed teeth, and tossed the bones from one clawed hand to the next. "But you'd play a game of chance, eh, just among friends?"

The Devil had no friends. And he cheated. But Ar was desperate, and his plans were ready. He had studied the current times, the societies and economies, and made arrangements. Ah, the things one could accomplish by giving a clerk time to say his farewells.

"Aye," he said. "A quick game or two. There is a large military engagement pending. I'll be needed."

"The usual stakes?"

Old Nick liked to have his sinners sooner rather than later. He thought it a great joke that Ar Death was willing to play for gold and gems. What could a Final Debt Collector want with earthly riches, and where could he spend them?

Ar waved his hand, or what would be his hand if he had a body. "Not this time. Today I'd wager on returning to life."

Another hooded figure—Aleph, Ar thought, a Hebraic Harvester—left the table, muttering about the coming confrontation. Ar did not know if he meant the war on earth or the Devil's fury at Ar's effrontery. Instead, the walls shook with Satan's laughter. "Life? When you, better than anyone, know how fleeting it can be?"

Ar nodded. "Even so. I would try to be a better man this time."

"You are what you are, fool, for all eternity. We all are, without change. Besides, you will never beat me." He spilled the gruesome, gleaming bones out onto the table and grinned at the winning pattern shown. "Losing means you will have to do my bidding forever. A quick shake of the hourglass, a few souls lost in transit, so to speak."

Ar took a deep mental breath, having neither lungs nor airway for inhaling. If he won, he'd gain mortality. If he lost, he'd still be Death, coming just a bit sooner to the Devil's disciples than expected. In truth, he was always earlier than anyone wanted. As for stealing innocent souls from Heaven, that was impossible. Ar was merely the enforcer, not the judge. He nodded. "I agree."

"A bet! A bet!" a gremlin shouted, hopping up and

down. Satan swatted at the small creature, who scurried to Ar's side, clinging to his cape.

The game commenced. Ar lost the first round, and Satan drew smoke crosshatches in the air with a taloned finger. "So many sinners, so little time."

But then Ar's luck changed. Smoke poured out of Old Nick's ears. He shook the bones harder. Ar still won. The smoke marks faded; the Archfiend's grin did, too. He cursed his lucky, spell-ridden saint's bone, to no avail. Of course not. Ar had switched the relics with a monkey's remains.

No one cheated Death, not even the Devil.

The very ground trembled with bloodred rage. The demons writhed; the wraiths withered. The trembling gremlin at Ar's side dug his claws into Ar's hooded cloak. The former warrior stood tall. "I won."

"You won life, for all the good it will do you." Satan snatched the hourglass pin from the front of Ar's cape. "Six months. I give you six months to find this symbol of your employment, now the symbol of the missing piece of yourself. Find it, find your humanity. If not, you will be my minion forever."

Before Ar could claim foul, Satan tossed the pin, and Ar, out of Hades.

Smoke. Screams. Heat. Oh, hell, he was back in Hell.

Ar got to his feet. Feet? He had feet? He did, and hands, to feel for a face, a body, blessed ballocks! He even had clothes under his own cloak, thank goodness, and thanks to the saint whose ensorcelled bone still rested in a hidden pocket there, along with Ar's cache of documents and bank deposits.

"I am alive," he whispered, marveling at the very act of breathing.

"Alive! I'm alive, too!" The gremlin was hopping up and down nearby.

Ar frowned. "Not for long. You'll be burned at the stake or shot on sight." The shin-high creature was slimy, dark as a cinder, with a forked tail and horns. No one could mistake it for anything but a denizen of the Dark. They'd suspect Ar, too, if he was seen with the beast. "Go. Get back where you belong."

"But I'm alive!"

Ar looked around. He was on a muddy field, in the obvious aftermath of a monstrous battle. Sudden bursts of spectral light told him his former comrades were at work, telltale flashes of life candles being extinguished. "Find a Dead Letter to carry you back. I thought I saw Spanish Ese."

"No. I breathe. I fit. See?" The gremlin twisted around.

"I see a monkey, you flea brain. What would a monkey be doing at a war?"

The gremlin became a goat.

"You'll be cooked at the first campfire. Now begone before you ruin my chances, too."

A large black bird flew to his shoulder and pecked at his ear. "I help find the brooch."

Ar had forgotten about the hourglass pin that every Alphabet Agent wore. He slowly turned, noticing smoldering fires, piles of bodies, fallen horses, shattered cannon, and mud as far as he could see. "Damnation, how am I to locate the wretched thing here?" He well knew he had far more than a trinket to find. Where was he to start, seeking his soul?

In the distance a few men were moving around, turning bodies over to find their friends. No, they were cutting off silver buttons, stealing what they could from the dead soldiers. Was this what he wished to be, some poor scrap of humanity, grubbing through his allotted time?

No. He would be better. He *could* be better. The man he had been, that ruthless Sir Coryn, had at least been brave. Now he would temper valor with wisdom. He pledged to behave nobly, honorably, with kindness and generosity, knightly traits from a time long forgotten, long forsworn. If he could not find his own salvation or the bauble, at least he could do some good with his six months and the fortune he had amassed.

First he had to discover who won this battle they would call Waterloo, which language to speak, what currency to use.

The nearest soldier to him was driving a cart, trying to reload his pistol with one arm. The other was bandaged and hanging limply, in a ragged uniform that had once been scarlet. An Englishman, then.

Ar walked closer until he could call out: "Doth the King's Army taketh the day, friend? That is," he hurriedly corrected, "did England win?"

"They say we did," the man answered. "Heavens be praised."

Ar touched the papers in his right pocket for reassurance, instead of his left, and said, "Amen."

"Although not without terrible cost, my lord."

"I claim not your liege—" Ar started, but then he realized what the wounded, weary soldier must see: fine boots and rich apparel, clean hands unsullied by combat. He nodded. "A sad day, victory or not."

"And for the poor horses." The man wiped at the tear

streaks down one filthy cheek with his good hand. "My job is putting the blighters out of their misery and collecting the saddles to send back to the families before the scavengers get everything." He scowled at the crow on the nob's shoulder.

Now Ar realized that the screams he heard were from the wounded mounts. The injured soldiers and officers had been carted off, leaving the dead for later. He had no idea what powers remained to him, if any, but he had to start his new chivalrous life somewhere. Let him begin with the animals. "Lord Ardeth at your service."

The soldier gaped at the fine gentleman's offer to help. "Gawd, now I seen everything."

Not by half, he hadn't. "I always liked horses," was all the instant earl could think to say. "And I have a way with hurt creatures. Perhaps I can calm them, or help get a few on their feet so we can lead them to a veterinary."

"It's a dreadful piece of work," Sergeant Campbell warned.

Lord Ardeth took up the soldier's pistol, having studied one of the weapons after the last battle he'd been assigned. Death did not bother him. It was life that was terrifying.

They managed to save a string of horses, not the stalwart destriers used for carrying armored knights into battle, but brave chargers nevertheless. Ardeth rode a handsome black stallion named Black Butch, whose owner would not be riding again, ever. He had the fallen hero's name, to send compensation to his family.

The sergeant and the earl led their small herd back to the cavalry encampment for water and doctoring. The master of horses almost wept in gratitude, and neither he nor his staff would soon forget the dark rider or Campbell's awed recounting of his lordship's uncanny skills.

After a hasty swallow of wine and a heel of bread—Ardeth had forgotten that a body needed sustenance and was growing light-headed—he insisted on taking Campbell to the field hospital. The sounds and stench and suffering were too much like Hell for him to enter, yet had he not just vowed to serve his fellow men?

He gladly bypassed the areas of amputation and cauterization. "Your arm needs cleansing and stitching, nothing else," he told the sergeant. They stepped into a field of cots and pallets and threadbare blankets laid on the sodden ground, all filled with wounded, waiting soldiers.

"Great gods." In all his years, in famine and flood, Ardeth had never seen such devastation. Did he really want to be part of a species that could wreak so much havoc on its own kind? Then he saw the telltale flash of a life winking out. He narrowed his eyes to spot one of his former workmates leaning on a staff, watching a surgeon at work. One of the Cyrillic letters, he thought, wasting time. "Get on with it, Zheh," he shouted in Russian. "Can you not see how many men are in agony?"

More than half of these poor souls would die of blood loss or wounds gone putrid or fevers that would rage through the hospital, Ardeth knew. Better to end their suffering now. "Move!" he shouted, this time in English. Any man who could walk or crawl got out of the way of the tall dark figure in his flowing cape. Ardeth ignored the mortals in favor of the specter they could not see.

Another light flashed. "*Dah*, fine for you to give orders," the Slavic terminator muttered. "If some of us would do our jobs instead of dreaming what cannot be, then others of us would not have to work so hard. *Nyet.*"

Humility came hard to one such as Sir Coryn of Ardsley or Ar of the Afterlife or Lord Ardeth, but the earl bowed. "My apologies. Having a short span of time shortens one's temper, it seems."

A surgeon in a gore-specked apron came over to see what the stir was about. His lips curled into a sneer at the sight of a well-dressed nobleman. "My men need laudanum, my lord, not fancy words and pretty manners. We are too busy for your sort here."

"But I have some experience with sickness," Ardeth said in a vast understatement. "And know ways of bringing peace without opiates."

"Like that Herr Mesmer, eh? I read of him."

"Something like that, yes. There are pressure points, sleep inducers, many other ways to relieve pain."

Campbell stepped forward. "I've seen his lordship with the horses. He worked wonders, he did."

"Very well, we can use whatever means the Lord, and this lord, can provide," the surgeon said, turning to get back to his endless-seeming stitching. "But the raven has to go. We do not need any symbols of death flapping around, scaring the men worse."

"He is a crow," Ardeth began, but the bird flapped up and down on his shoulder.

"I'm alive! Alive I am!" it squawked.

The surgeon and the nearby patients all gasped. First this stranger talked to the air in foreign tongues; then his—pet?—gave voice.

"He means Olive," Ardeth hurried to explain. "I almost managed to teach the featherhead his name. He sayeth—he says little else." The threatening look the earl fixed on the gremlin ought to guarantee that. "But he can wait outside if his presence upsets the men." To the crow

Ardeth whispered, "Go look for the pin. I'll be here a while, it seems."

Campbell had been relating to the soldiers and the aides what his lordship had done at the battlefield. Even the infantrymen loved horses, so they forgot what they'd seen, what they'd heard, and welcomed a well-breeched rescuer into their midst.

Ardeth got to work.

Hours later—he'd lost count of how many—he heard a commotion. A major was shouting at the surgeon, who was shaking his head.

"There are officers who need doctoring, I say."

"And I say I cannot spare any of my staff. They are ready to collapse as is."

"What of that man?" the major asked, pointing toward Ardeth. "He seems to be competent. His patients are not moaning, and his hands are clean, at least."

"That is Ardeth. His volunteering to help was a blessing."

The major walked toward Ardeth, not looking at the men he had to step between.

"We need you in the officers' tent."

"They need me here."

"A general is wounded, I say."

"Are your companions more worthy than the men who fought for them, then?"

The major straightened, although he still did not reach Ardeth's height. "They are officers and gentlemen."

Ardeth could not help noticing that the man's uniform was nearly spotless, with lace at his collar and cuffs. He knew the kind. "Were you in the battle?"

"Of course. I led my troops to their position before returning to headquarters for further orders."

"While you turned these so-called common men into cannon fodder, ordering them to keep marching to their deaths?" He rudely turned his back on the arrogant dastard.

"Ardeth!"

He turned back. The major had his hand on the sword at his side. Ardeth thought of melting the steel. Instead he stated, "That is Coryn, Earl of Ardeth."

Now the officer looked confused. "I have never heard of any such earldom, and I know my peerage."

Ardeth decided this was as good a time as any to begin spinning his web. "The title had been in abeyance until my grandfather was found. He was a third son, who went exploring the world, never expecting to inherit. His son, my late father, also had the wanderlust, so the College of Arms could never locate him, either. I have seen the Orient, Africa, and the New World, but never England. That is about to change. My bona fides have already been appraised and approved, so you shall, I swear, be hearing more of me, but not today, nor in the officers' quarters, either. Good day, Major."

The officer stomped away, only to return shortly, chasing a large black bird that settled on Ardeth's shoulder. The crow held a gold button in its beak.

"Thief!" Major Willeford shouted, almost stepping on the foot of a sleeping soldier.

"And a poor thief at that," Ardeth murmured. "That does not even look like an hourglass."

"An hourglass? Are your attics to let? It is a medal, by George. And I earned it!"

"Did you, now?" Ardeth passed it back to the officer, who frowned. Ardeth's hands and clothing were no longer quite so clean.

Willeford said, "You really ought to come with me to the officers' quarters. This is no place for a gentleman."

"Yet this is where I am needed most."

"You shall not succeed in England, you know, not with that attitude. Loyalty to one's own kind matters."

Ardeth had heard tales from the major's men. "The loyalty you showed your soldiers? You rode away on your horse when they were being cut down on foot. I think you do not wish me to speak to your superior officers after all, wounded or not."

Again, the major's hand was on his sword. "Are you calling me a coward?"

The earl did not answer. Instead he asked, "Are you thinking of challenging me? Do not bother. I shall not duel. Enough blood has been shed, and life is too precious, even yours."

The major's face turned red as he heard snickers from the wounded men. "Foreign scum like you will never be accepted in proper English society. My brother-in-law is the Duke of Sneddin. He'll see that you are rejected at all the gentlemen's clubs, refused invitations to the beau monde. You will be a pariah in the polite world."

"Did I forget to mention the fortune my grandfather amassed in his wanderings, or how my father tripled his wealth?" This was not such a non sequitur to anyone who understood how the aristocracy actually operated. "My own investments have returned a handsome profit also."

Major Lord Willeford spun on his heels. "You, sir, can go to hell."

"Ah, but I just came from there."

CHAPTER TWO

If she kept busy, Genie would not have to think about her situation. With any luck, she would eventually fall into the sleep of exhaustion and not have to think at all. With her luck, though, Genie decided, she'd only have nightmares about being left in the middle of a war with no funds, no family, nowhere to go.

That was no nightmare. That was real. That was her life. Imogene Hopewell Macklin was disgraced, deserted, disowned. Gads.

She wiped another injured soldier's brow, trying to think of these poor men crammed into the makeshift hospital instead of her own woes. Besides, if she stayed to help nurse the wounded, no one would ask why she did not return to where the officers' womenfolk were providing care in Brussels, or why she did not go back to her own lodgings there to grieve.

She was no longer welcomed among the ladies, she was too numb to mourn, and she had no lodgings.

Her landlady had panicked and fled, locking all the doors while Genie was out, tossing the tenants' belongings onto the street. Genie had no money to pay her rent anyway if the woman came back. She could not think about that, either, or her trunks left out for thieves and beggars to carry off what little she owned.

Here she was needed, at least. No one cared that she knew nothing of nursing. These men sought comfort, not cures. They did not mind that her hands were shaking or her voice was quavering. She could offer them water and listen to their prayers. She could write letters to their loved ones, and pen their last wills. What were her problems compared with theirs?

A selfish voice whispered in her mind that the soldiers had loved ones, that they had possessions to bequeath, addresses to send them to. And their wounds would heal. Her pain was inside, where it never would.

She must not think about pain, lest her thoughts skitter toward Elgin. The cad had not even had the decency to die in battle, a hero. No, he'd been caught the night before in the arms of another officer's wife, too drunk to defend himself, as usual. No, she definitely must not think about Elgin, either.

She almost laughed, despite her despair, because she had nothing left to fill her mind, not the past, not the present, certainly not the future . . . until the dark stranger strode into the crude hospital tent while lightning flashed.

He'd ridden a black horse, they said. Seeing his black cloak, the black bird on his shoulder, his dark hair and eyes, the men started to whisper about the Angel of Death. This man was helping, though, and standing up for the common soldier against a despised officer. Both actions were unheard of, especially for a titled gentleman.

His language bespoke breeding and education, albeit foreign; his apparel indicated wealth; his bearing denoted pride, confidence, power, everything Genie lacked.

Fine bones and a straight nose made him strikingly handsome, too, in an exotic way. No ruddy, round-faced English squire, he was tall and thin, with a pale complexion as if he seldom stepped outdoors, yet he lifted men with ease. His voice was no booming, blustering blare from the hunting field or the battlefield, yet everyone heard when he spoke. His hands were gentle, the soldiers said when he'd moved on, not rough and hurried like those of the surgeons' other assistants. The soldiers told her they felt honored that the newcomer had tried to relieve their suffering when he could have rested in luxury. Lord Ardeth was certainly no spoiled, pleasure-seeking member of the privileged class, perhaps because of his distant upbringing, Genie supposed. She had been among the *ton*, had met cabinet ministers and generals, a royal duke, and an Austrian prince. Lord Ardeth was like nothing she had ever known or heard of, so she found him interesting—at a distance.

The earl was fascinating—and frightening. He appeared as if the marble statue of a pagan god had deigned to step off his pedestal and into their midst, bolts of lightning in his hands. All-knowing and all-powerful, he seemed, stone hard and unyielding—in contrast to his kindness. The gods of mythology were a tricksy lot at best, and Genie would not like to be in Lord Ardeth's way when he recalled his dominion over lesser folk. Just like a godling, or like an earl, everyone was lesser, and he well knew it.

Genie shivered at the notion of confronting such a grand personage, despite the stifling heat. A woman had no defenses against such authority, no secrets. She chided herself for her fears. This was no ballroom where the hostess would perform introductions. Besides, what could her puny existence matter to such as the Earl of Ardeth, anyway?

Then he called to her.

"You there, mistress. I need help."

Ardeth had found that the living were far more grateful than the dying, who, more often than not, argued, cursed, and fought against their implacable fate.

Some of these men he could save. Others he could make comfortable. Campbell had been a help at first, like a loyal squire at his liege lord's side. The man was wounded himself, though, and anxious about the horses. Ardeth sent him off with a purse and the promise of a position after the army was done with him. Now he needed an extra pair of hands.

He'd noticed the woman earlier. She had caught his attention at first because she so obviously did not belong here. Better dressed and younger than any other female attending the wounded, she was neither nurse nor nun. As he worked, he watched her from the corner of his eye, speculating about her presence where no lady would dare to be. A camp follower? No, there was an innocence about her, an unmistakable refinement, a frailty no woman of the world possessed, no matter how good an actress. And the men treated her with courtesy.

Any female would envy the young woman's hair. Despite the scrap of lace covering her head, physical efforts had loosened the plaited bun behind her neck, so strands of red and gold curled at her cheeks and down her shoulders. Like sunset it was, like the molten heat at the center of the earth.

She had a tiny smattering of freckles, too, like gold dust.

He'd seen more beautiful women, of course, but not recently, and not as a man who could appreciate the soft skin, the rounded form, the graceful posture. Ardeth made himself ignore the female's looks. He was no lust-crazed libertine, even if he had been celibate for centuries. His body was barely flesh. He would not let it burn. For now, what was important was that the woman seemed competent and calm. So he called out to her.

"Me?"

"This man needs more help than I can provide on my own. Come."

She hesitated, proving her intelligence to Ardeth. He was no one an obviously gently bred female should know. "Pray, you, come."

Now she did edge closer, stepping to the opposite side of the cot from where he stood over a failing soldier, as far from the stranger as possible. "But . . . but the doctors said this man was beyond hope."

"Their hope. The sawbones need to expend their efforts most efficiently."

She stroked the wounded man's brow. "But his wounds are so extensive."

"His days are not done."

Neither were Elgin's, nor those of the scores of other fallen soldiers. "No one is ever ready."

"Nevertheless, every creature on earth has a certain allotment of time. This man has not used his up yet."

"How can you know?"

"I know. When the sand runs out, a life is over."

She frowned. "Then we can know when we will die?"

"Some of us." Six months. "But this is not the time for speculation. Do you have a strong enough stomach?"

Genie had cast up her accounts that morning. She'd had nothing to eat since, so was not in danger of losing another meal. "I can manage."

He lifted the sheet back. Genie caught her breath.

"You will *not* faint," he ordered.

She swallowed, hard. "I shall try."

And he tried to fit the man's intestines back into his abdomen, directing her where to press, when to hand him torn sheets and bindings.

"Surely he cannot live."

The earl glanced around as if looking for something she could not see. "He will!"

As if his saying so made it so, Genie thought, astounded at his lordship's arrogance. He might have a title and a fortune, but that did not give him the power of life and death. Yet the soldier still breathed. And the next hopeless case, and the next.

At some point—Genie had long lost track of the time, day or night—his man Campbell brought them a tray with hot tea and bread and cold meat. She shook her head no, but the earl did not listen, leading her outside the tent to a bench and commanding her to eat.

The crow flew down and dropped a shiny coin at Lord Ardeth's feet.

"Not even close," the earl said.

The large bird cocked his head and looked at Genie with white-rimmed black eyes. "I'm alive!"

She tossed a piece of her bread to the amazing talking creature.

"Say you're Olive, blast it!" the earl ordered.

The bird looked at the woman again, swallowed the morsel of bread, looked at Ardeth, and said, "You're alive, blast it."

Genie smiled. "Silly bird."

Not so silly. Her smile was so sweet that Ardeth had to smile, too, for the first time in eons. Now he really did feel alive, and more determined than ever to stay past his six months. "Go look some more," he told the trans-formed gremlin.

Then he tried to make the woman smile again, for the sheer glory of it, by saying they should have a proper in-troduction, lest the high sticklers find fault with his man-ners. "For I realize I do not even know the name of my able assistant. That is improper for your society, yes?"

She did smile at that, as if one of the fussy patronesses of Almack's was watching. "I am Imogene Hopewell Macklin, my lord."

No "Mrs." or "Miss" or "Lady," he noted, his curios-ity aroused. "I suppose your family calls you Genie?"

Her smile faded. "They used to." She sipped at her tea, closing the conversation.

When they had finished the meal—the best his money and Campbell's scrounging could provide from the offi-cers' quarters—he was reluctant to end the woman's rest. She seemed worn to the nub, with a look he'd encoun-tered far too often.

"Did you lose a loved one in the battle?"

Genie brushed crumbs off her soiled gown. Without meeting his eyes, she lied and said, "Yes."

He did not see a ring, but that meant little in such dire times. Her reticence meant more. "A husband? A brother?"

"Yes."

"How unfortunate. I am sorry for your double loss."

She still looked down. "Only one."

"You married your brother?" Surely Ar would have heard if English laws had changed so drastically.

"Elgin Macklin was my husband, but he told everyone he was my brother."

"I see." He did not see, not at all. Why would a man be ashamed to claim this fine young lady as his bride, but not as his kin?

Now that she had begun, Genie wanted him—someone, anyone—to understand. "At first we were posted to Canada, but then his family arranged a lieutenancy for Elgin on General Wellington's own staff in Portugal, a position of great honor. But the general did not approve of his junior officers being married, much less wedding without the army's permission."

"Yet you and Macklin did just that."

"There were . . . circumstances. A scandal, to be exact. We had no choice but to wed. My family washed their hands of us, so, again, I had no choice but to follow the drum with Elgin."

Bitterness crept into her voice as she continued: "When we got to Portugal, he was always going to tell the general next week, next month, but hated to be found in the lie. When I insisted, he swore he would make our marriage public after the coming battle."

"The gossip columns did not spread word of it?" Ardeth had read the newspapers every chance he had, to keep abreast of current events and customs.

"The families made certain of that. We had a quiet wedding and a hasty departure from the public eye."

"So he let people think you were brother and sister. Do many gentlemen take their kin into danger?" Some had ridden with the crusaders, but not many.

"If they had no one to care for them at home, yes. And no one suspected this confrontation would take place so close to Brussels, or be so massive. Why, there was danc-

ing last night. Or was it the night before? Many officers'
wives joined their husbands here. Other members of the
ton came to make it a festive social gathering. Most fled
home when the French threatened to overtake the city."

"But you stayed."

"I had nowhere else to go. And Elgin said it was safe,
that the British Army could not be defeated."

"He lied."

"He lied about many things," she said, anger in her
voice. "Our marriage, our finances, his gambling. At first
I understood. He wished to be married as little as I did,
and it suited him to be considered a bachelor."

Ardeth assumed the churl conducted himself as a single man, too. "Later?"

"I tried to be a good wife to him and I thought he became
reconciled. He was going to make things right, even if it
cost him his place on His Grace's staff, as soon as he could
get the general's ear. But then it was too late. He was dead."

"I am sorry."

"As am I. He might not have been the man I would
have selected for a husband, and he might have been
foolishly reckless—but he was too young to die."

"Everyone is."

She sighed. "I might as well tell you about my further
disgrace."

"You need not."

"You will hear about it as soon as you join the officers
or the diplomatic corps anyway." She had decided he
must be with the Foreign Office, to find himself in the
middle of a war. She sighed again before continuing.
"The major's wife came to console me, so I tried to explain to her. She accused me of fabricating the whole
story to protect my reputation."

He let his eyes fall to her waistline. "Again, you had no choice."

"I had no choice," she agreed, too weary to wonder how he knew about her pregnancy when she had realized it for herself only recently. Nothing was showing. "She said I was a light-skirt who was using my brother's death to hide my own sins. But I have my marriage lines and my ring. That is, they are with my trunks in Brussels, if they have not been stolen. The other Englishwomen turned their backs on me, as if I had seduced one of their husbands."

"Your family will know the truth."

"My father crossed my name out of the family Bible for bringing shame to his doorstep."

"Then your husband's family will take you in, especially if you bear their grandchild."

"Elgin's father is dead, and his brother is now Baron Cormack."

"Cormack should welcome you as a sister, then."

She shook her head, loosening more tendrils of hair around her face. "It is more complicated than that. You see, my sister was to marry Elgin, but she had her heart set on his brother, Roger, the heir to their father's title. She arranged for us, Elgin and me, to be compromised, although Elgin never believed I did not have a hand in it. And then she claimed I stole her own true love, so Roger had to wed her out of family honor. No, I cannot go to them."

"Your sister sounds like a woman I met once in He— Helsinki. She murdered her husband and chopped him up into little pieces."

"Oh, Lorraine would not kill Roger. He is her entrée to the upper echelons of polite society. Our father is a mere squire, not nearly grand enough to suit my sister."

"What shall you do?"

"I suppose I shall throw myself on the mercy of General Wellington, if he agrees to see me. Or beg in the streets, for I have no money," she finished with a weak laugh that turned into a moan. Suddenly all the sorrow and terror and horrors she had seen were too much for her. She was weeping, shaking, sobbing—in the earl's arms.

"Hush, my lady, hush." How ironic, Ardeth thought. He could finally comfort a grieving widow. He decided not to use any calming tricks; she needed to relieve her pain and fear. And he liked holding her.

When her sobs turned to hiccups and her spasms of heartbroken cries turned to whimpers, he stroked her back and said, "Do not fret, lady. Do not worry anymore. I will see that the general listens and the ladies understand. Your trunks will be restored, your accounts settled."

"You would do all that? Why?"

"Because it is the honorable thing to do."

She stepped back, out of his embrace, embarrassed at the scene she had enacted for him, a total stranger, and a toplofty one at that. "But you have not contributed to my problems. They are not yours to resolve."

"Ah, but knights always rescue maidens in distress."

"Not in this day and age. Further, I am no maiden, and you are no knight-errant."

"Are you sure? I do have a quest. No matter, I aim to be worthy."

"Of . . . ?"

He ignored her question. "Besides, I admire you. Few ladies would soil their hands as you did, despite your distress and your delicate condition. Few enough men could help as much. You deserve a cavalier, Mrs. Macklin, Genie. There's magic in your name, you know."

"I cannot grant any wishes, not even my own."

"Maybe, maybe not. Time will tell. Meanwhile, I shall make everything right."

She accepted the handkerchief he offered her, and blew her nose, not a very ladylike gesture, but a necessary one. Then she smiled again. "I thank you, and admire your confidence in return, but even you cannot move mountains. I fear my good name is hopelessly destroyed. No one will take me in or hire me. No decent man would accept my child, and no decent woman would permit me near hers. My family has betrayed me. I fear my situation is hopeless."

But at least five soldiers still breathed due solely to his skill. Heaven alone knew what he could manage with an earl's influence and money.

They were both right.

His gold rescued her belongings and secured better accommodations and purchased her a black gown. His title and haughty manner landed her an appointment with the general's aide to show her papers. She would be accorded whatever provisions the War Office made for its widows, and transport home.

Nothing could sway the wives, however. They were busy in the aftermath of the bloody battle, but so were their tongues. They had been deceived, and they were not going to be forgiving. Miss Macklin might be Mrs. Macklin, but now she had taken up with an unknown, unholy earl, with her husband, if such he was, barely cold.

Lady Willeford turned her back on Genie outside the general's office. Her husband sneered when he saw the earl at her side. Then he had to skip to the side when the black bird swooped down and snatched at the gold tassel on the major's right boot.

Willeford tried to kick the flying thief and ended up stumbling against his wife, who shrieked and slapped at him while the crow plucked at the boot.

"Tassels remind it of the whips in Hell," Ardeth muttered softly while the major and his wife gathered themselves.

Furious, Lady Willeford addressed Genie: "And Hell is where you shall find yourself, Miss Macklin. Or Mrs. Macklin. Or whatever you call yourself. I call you strumpet. You and your new protector shall never be welcomed among decent people. You are a disgrace."

Genie had not recovered from the hours spent in the hospital, or the shock of finding herself a widow, or of being befriended by an earl. She swayed on her feet.

"Do not dare to swoon," Ardeth ordered, his arm holding her steady. "You are not going to faint. You are going to show that she-witch the backbone I saw last night. Show her, for your self-respect and your future. And your son's future."

Genie closed her eyes for a moment, then raised her chin, absorbing his strength and his support. She showed more than her backbone; she showed her redhead's temper. "You dare call me names, madam, but you were not ministering to the men your husband abandoned on the field. You were here drinking tea. You stayed on at the parties when the brave young soldiers were marching into battle. You do not seek to understand my plight, only condemn it. So your opinion does not mean this much." She snapped her fingers. "Because you do not matter." Then she did what the major's wife had done before. She turned her back, giving Lady Willeford the cut direct.

Then that lady shrieked. "Spider!"

"Spider?" What manner of insult was that? Genie wondered, but the woman was batting at the air, slapping at her clothes. Ardeth was smiling.

"Did you . . . ?" Genie tried to ask.

He merely took her arm and led her farther away, saying, "Brava!" as they left the headquarters.

Genie was glad for his support; she was trembling so violently in reaction. "Brave but foolhardy. I am still scourged by scandal. Forgive me, but your assistance, however appreciated, only adds to my ruination. Everyone knows that there is nothing a highborn gentleman such as you could want with a poor widow of uncertain past. Nothing proper, at any rate."

Ardeth stroked his chin. "A wedding would be proper."

Genie stopped walking. "I beg your pardon?"

"Your reputation would be restored if you married me."

"May I faint now?"

CHAPTER THREE

"No, you shall not faint. I have seen you under fire. You are strong."

Strong? Genie did not think her legs would hold her up. Her brains and her body alike were turned to blanc-mange. As if he understood, Lord Ardeth led her to a bench outside headquarters. She sank down, because she could not run. If she could not faint, perhaps she should just throw herself under a passing cart. Here she was, alone in a foreign city, and her only . . . friend was this tall stranger of commanding presence and unknown past. He was handsome, for certain, in a dark, brooding, serious way, far unlike Elgin with his fair boyish looks and ready laugh. Lord Ardeth appeared to be older, perhaps thirty, or perhaps forty with his weary eyes, or twenty with his smooth skin. He was a puzzle, one Genie had no interest in solving. He had shown her nothing but kindness, yet she still feared him. With just cause, it seemed, for the earl had to be a madman.

"I must have misunderstood, my lord."

"No, you heard correctly. I am proposing marriage. Awkwardly, obviously, but marriage all the same." He was pacing in front of the bench in long, athletic strides. The crow took up a perch on a nearby railing, his head cocked to one side as if the creature was as confused as Genie.

"I realize that a maiden wishes to be wooed, but we have no time for ballads and bouquets."

Ballads and bouquets? Maidens? He definitely had been out of England too long, Genie decided, unless he had been locked in his family's attics, where no one could see their demented disgrace.

"It is the best solution," Lord Ardeth continued. "No one shuns a countess."

Genie was no longer worried about being ostracized by polite society. Now she feared for her very life. Thank goodness enough officers and soldiers were entering and exiting the building that she did not have to consider herself alone with a lunatic. The men were looking at them with curiosity, but surely one would come to her aid if she cried out. "Forgive me, my lord, but you do not even know me."

"Nor you me." Lord Ardeth waved one long hand in the air in dismissal. He had never met his first wife until the day of the wedding. "That does not matter."

He was worse than crazy. Wed a total stranger after a day or two of acquaintance? How could he think that a marriage could succeed that way? Genie had had a hard enough time accommodating herself to Elgin's quirks, and she had known him nearly her entire life. She firmly believed that women should know what they were getting when they gave their hands and their lives into some man's keeping. She stood up, hoping her feet were ready to carry her away. She would worry about her future later. "Thank you for the, ah, honor, my lord. But I am afraid—"

"Do not be. I would not hurt you. No one else would, were you my wife. Think on it, lady. What other choices have you? You said your family will not take you in, nor your dead husband's relatives. Would you seek a position, in your condition? No one would hire you, were you able to keep working. Or do you believe the British government will pay you a pension? Ha! My wife would still be waiting for six hun—"

"You have a wife?"

"If I had a wife, I meant. She would be long dead before the government thought to look after her. You and the babe would starve waiting for official promises to turn to gold."

He was right and Genie knew it. Still, marriage? She shook her head.

Ardeth watched the sunlight flicker through the reddish curls that were not hidden by her black bonnet. "Do not say no. Sit. Hear me out."

Against her better judgment, Genie sat again, clutching her reticule as if the paltry contents could bash in the earl's skull if he turned dangerous.

"I am rich," he began as if his apparel, to say nothing of the funds he had already expended on her behalf, did not proclaim his wealth and his generosity. "And I am titled. It means naught to me except that I will have entrée to all levels of society. As my wife you will be welcomed also."

If not welcomed, his countess would be tolerated, Genie knew, for such was the power of an earldom and money.

"I do not know if I can make your son heir to the earldom. Too many people will know the circumstances of your previous marriage and the dates."

"I might have a daughter," Genie put in, for the sake of argument in this absurd conversation.

"No, your child is a son."

Both the crow and Genie shook their heads. The irrational man believed he could read the stars, or whatever addled, impossible notion it was that made him so confident.

He was going on, as if there were nothing unusual about predicting births or proposing marriage to lost widows. "Someone would be sure to contest such an effort, although I believe he is legally my son if I am married to his mother at the time of his birth and I acknowledge him as mine. I will have to look into the law. Either way, he can bear my name with whatever authority it carries. I shall settle a goodly sum on him, and on you, of course. You would be left a wealthy widow this time, and soon."

"Soon?" The attics-to-let earl was not consulting any crystal ball, but again he sounded certain. She had seen him lifting the wounded soldiers, staying awake for hours with little sustenance or rest, yet she felt a pang at the thought of his weakness. "Have you a wasting disease, then?"

"Yes. That is, no."

The crow gave a loud squawk. The earl glared at him, on the railing. "No, I am not ailing, but my time is measured, in all-too-short hours and weeks." Reminded that his time was flying, he ordered the crow to fly, too, to keep looking.

Which did not reassure Genie in the least of his soundness, his mental soundness, anyway. "Um, how old are you?"

"In years or experience?" He turned and stared at her with his dark eyes, willing her to understand, knowing she could not. Now Ardeth was the one to shake his head. "I was one and thirty when I passed on—that is, when I passed my last birthday. It is enough that I am ancient in wisdom and I know marriage is the right thing for both of us."

"For both of us? I do not see how you can benefit."

"For one thing, I would gain the honor of a deed well-done, if only in my eyes. I could not leave a damsel unprotected, you see. That would be forsaking my vows."

"Are you a holy man, then?" That might explain his steadfast beliefs, Genie decided, and his selfless helping of the wounded soldiers when no other gentleman of his rank would attend to them. "I did not think such religious orders permitted marriage, though."

"I belong to neither cult nor congregation, yet my vows are no less sacred and binding."

"To whom? You made me no promises."

"To myself, like an oath of chivalry."

"Chivalry belongs in storybooks, with knights and white chargers."

"Black."

"Black?"

"I always preferred black horses."

Now the conversation had gone totally beyond Genie's control or comprehension. She stood again. "I will be all right. I have passage back to England—you heard the captain—and I shall find a solution on my own. You have been more than kind and have fulfilled any possible onus laid upon you by your, ah, code of honor."

He crossed his arms over his broad chest, an unmoving iron statue except for his black cape billowing behind him and a lock of dark hair lifting off his forehead. "No. Marriage is the only way of providing for your future."

Genie clucked her tongue. "Nonsense. You could simply ask me to become your mistress." She would not accept, of course, but such arrangements were made all the time, wherever there were needy women and wealthy men with other needs. She prayed that her situation never became that desperate.

His expression grew darker and sterner, if possible. "You insult both of us, and the memory of your husband. He wed you out of honor."

"Elgin Macklin wed me because my father threatened to shoot him."

"You will not become any man's whore! I shall not permit it."

Genie almost expected to be burned by the fire in his voice and the sparks in his eyes, like lightning that appeared in the sudden clouds on this clear day. She would not show how much his anger frightened her, though, so she raised her chin. "You are not my keeper, my lord. No one made you responsible for me or my morals. You might have consulted higher powers for your oath, but you did not consult me."

"Forget my vows. Common decency dictates that a gentleman look after those in need. Marriage is how I can accomplish that most expeditiously."

Genie did not care to be the object of his misplaced noblesse oblige. Expeditiously, indeed! "Common decency also dictates a year of mourning. If you speak of insults, Elgin's memory—and all of society—will be affronted if I wed without a proper mourning period." That should end the ridiculous conversation, Genie decided, if he cared about propriety.

"I cannot wait a year. Neither can your son."

"Daughter." The man might be an earl, but Genie was growing weary of Ardeth's arrogant manner.

He raised one black eyebrow and quirked his lip in what might have been a smile. "You would not wish your child to face all the gossip and scorn of society."

"I do not wish it for myself, either, but it is bound to happen, and to you, too, if you continue with this mad scheme. You would be tarred with the same brush of scandal."

Now he did smile. "Believe me, I have been painted with far worse."

"You do not understand. With my history, I shall never be considered fit for polite society."

"You are far more fit than I, Mrs. Macklin, yet I am not afraid to face your *ton*."

"I am not afraid."

They both knew she was lying.

"Then stop making your feeble excuses," he said. "If you are concerned about the physical side of marriage, I swear I shall not importune you with unwanted intimacy."

Quick color flooded Genie's fair complexion. She was so bemused by his lordship's outrageous offer, she had not even considered all the ramifications. Sharing a stranger's fortune and title was one thing; sharing his bed was another. Good grief, was she even considering such a preposterous proposal? The man was not in his right mind. She could not take advantage of his nobility, no matter how tempting. He'd saved countless lives in the field hospital, but she was not one of his forlorn hopes, even if everyone else had given up on her.

"My lord—"

"Ardeth," he countered. "Or Coryn, if we are to wed."

"My lord," she persisted. "You have been in the thick of battle and its aftermath. You cannot be thinking clearly. No gentleman of sense would make such an offer, and no lady of honor would accept."

"Are you implying that I am—what did that sergeant say?—cork-brained?"

Well, she was, but Genie was too polite to say so. "Of course not, only that you must be too exhausted to have given the matter your full attention. Aside from easing your conscience, for whatever personal reasons you might have, there is absolutely no benefit to you in such an alliance with an impoverished widow of blemished reputation, bearing another man's child. As a wealthy peer, you can seek a bride from the highest echelons of society, one with a rich dowry, an untarnished name, and great beauty. Why would you do anything else?"

He studied the gathering clouds, as if waiting for the crow to come back, or a divine answer to her question. Finally he turned to her again. "I have enough money, and I care not for the petty posturing of your so-called quality. Beauty fades, although yours is the kind that lasts and grows more attractive with time."

Genie blushed again, that he thought she was pretty. Elgin had considered her red-tinged hair too gingery and garish, her figure too slim, her nose too short. Then again, he had loved her sister, a rounded blond goddess of a girl.

Ardeth was still looking at her, as if he could see through her black gown, through her protests. "A woman's spirit, her heart, and her soul are what matters. I have seen yours, and you are a true lady. Helping you will help me atone for past sins, verily. You ask what other benefit I will reap. In return I ask your assistance."

Genie laughed, but without humor, trying to encompass his strength, his confidence, the very aura of power that surrounded him. The passing soldiers gave him wide berth and downcast eyes; the officers nodded respectfully, from a distance. Women simply stared, licking their lips like dogs at a butcher shop. This man could need nothing from anyone, and she said so.

"Nay, I do need aid in returning to your world. That is, to England. I do not know all of its ways."

She recalled that he'd told Major Lord Willeford of his family's living abroad. That might explain some of his odd turns of speech and manners. "You will learn quickly enough from the gentlemen at the coffeehouses and men's clubs."

"Pompous prigs and wastrels cannot help me find something I have lost. You can."

"Here, in Brussels?" Genie was prepared to search every square inch, in return for what he had already given her.

"I hope not. If so, I must leave it behind, for my affairs require me to get to England. My investments, my estate and inheritance, all need my presence, to say nothing of the College of Arms, confirming my succession to the earldom."

Genie was confused, a not-unusual state when dealing with Lord Ardeth. "But if you leave, how will you find your, ah, missing treasure?"

"I am not precisely certain what it is that I am looking for."

Well, that made things as clear as mud. "Then how can I help?"

"By letting me help you, if you can understand that."

"As your wife?"

"I suppose I could give you an annuity, find you a se-
cluded village here in the Low Countries to live where no
one will doubt one more British war widow, or perhaps
Wales or Scotland. I could hire a companion so your conventions are satisfied, and I could stay away so no one
questions our relationship or your morals. I understand
that comely widows are always subject to conjecture and
improper proposals, but you could have your babe in
peace and live a quiet life, unless you choose to create another scandal."

"I never set out to become grist for the gossip mills."

"Yet it follows you like flies to honey."

Genie took a moment to think about this new offer. "I
could repay you, eventually."

They both knew the impossibility of that.

Ardeth went on. "Aside from the dullness, you would
still be a fugitive in hiding. If anyone learned of your
past, you would be vilified. If anyone knew of my financial support, you would be deemed a fallen woman. I
would not be there to protect you from village louts, or
your son from suspicions of bastardy. You could not enter
the world you were born to lest someone recognize you.
Worst of all, you would be living more lies. Is that what
you want?"

She did not want to be beholden to anyone, but she did
not want to be left behind. The hours after Elgin's death,
before Lord Ardeth entered the hospital and her life, were
the most terrifying agony Genie had ever lived through.
Abandoned, ostracized, alone. She did not wish to face
that again.

"I—"

"A marriage license can remedy all of that. What is
mine would be yours. A home of your own—no, several

houses—that need a woman's touch. A fortune to spend on gowns and jewels and furs. Horses, yachts, whatever you fancy. Travel if you wish, charitable acts if you will. Protection from insult and provision for your son. A leading place in local society, a guaranteed position in London's beau monde. Just think, you could send Lady Willeford to—what is that place?—social Coventry."

"I would have precedence over my sister, wouldn't I? Her husband is a mere baron."

"A countess comes only after princesses and duchesses and marchionesses, and how many of them have access to such wealth? Or such a generous husband?"

"You make it sound so mercenary."

"But you would only be selling your presence—not your body, I swear—and only for a short time."

"How can I refuse? I know I should, but your offer is too tempting."

"Of course it is. I have taken lessons from the Devil himself."

He placed his hand over his heart. "I pledge my life, what I have of it, to your honor and your happiness." Then he knelt at her feet, head bowed, and kissed her hand to seal the bargain.

Which had to be the loveliest moment of Genie's life, until a double rainbow burst through the clouds.

CHAPTER FOUR

Sunrise and Genie's hair. After being in the shadows so long, Ardeth was drawn to them like a moth to the flames, or a miser to gold. He thought he could savor them forever. Unfortunately, he did not have forever.

He was even more determined now to stay here beyond his six months, no matter how much time he would have. For all its pain and misery and squalor, life was better than any of the alternatives. It was . . . alive.

The gremlin thought so, too. Even in his half sleep on the bedpost of Ardeth's grand bed at the finest hotel in Brussels, the crow muttered, "Alive. Clucking Hell. I'm alive."

Ardeth went back to staring out the window, a blanket around his shoulders. His body was not used to feeling the cold, it seemed. Or maybe the chill was due to another day dawning with him no nearer to finding the hourglass pin. He knew the blasted thing was only a symbol, only a ruse of the Devil's to make Ar waste precious time chasing a spectral illusion. He'd never find it, not if Satan did not want him to. But he could find his own humanity, and perhaps that would be enough to win the bet.

How many lives did he have to save? How much suffering must he relieve? How many coins doled out to the hungry, how many promises of work for the destitute and desperate? Ardeth had no idea, but he was making a start.

Marrying Mrs. Macklin was another step forward. He knew it was the right thing to do by the warming glow he felt somewhere in the vicinity of his heart. He had a heart that beat and pumped blood. Maybe it would thaw; maybe it would feel.

He felt something for the female, that was for sure. He might view her as a fragile waif needing rescuing, but his body—his healthy male body of when he died at thirty-one—recognized her as an attractive, appealing woman.

Od's blood, he thought, why could his body not have remembered all of its functions before he'd made that promise of a chaste marriage? Had he left his bedamned brains behind? As Ar Death he'd felt nothing for centuries. As Lord Ardeth he felt lust, rampant and raging, like a stag in rut—or a man denied for decades. Every time he saw the woman, his desire grew. Thank the gods for his concealing cloak. She also grew, more beautiful by the hour, it seemed, with rest and good food, with stylish garments, and without the terror etched on her face.

No, he could not take back his promise, not without putting the fear back in her green eyes. Besides, consummating their coming marriage would be dishonorable while she was grieving for her husband, useless piece of offal that he had been. Mrs. Macklin deserved time to mourn, time to grow accustomed to Ardeth. Six months was far too short a time.

Time, again, that precious commodity. He looked at his new pocket watch by the first light of day, wishing he could make the hands move more slowly. This was his wedding day. Tonight would not be his wedding night. Damn.

Marrying the woman was still the right thing to do. He had to travel to England, to claim his lands and accounts. There was no other way but marriage that he could do that while protecting her and the reputation she held dear. Giving her his name and a secure future was a good deed, a noble act, a self-sacrifice, even. Why, he would be giving up the chance to father a son of his own, one to carry on after him. That was what every man seemed to want, wasn't it? Of course he was not every man, not by half. No matter, the idea of wedding the widow felt . . . nice. Nice was another long-forgotten emotion he welcomed, especially since it was not nearly as uncomfortable as unsatisfied desire.

He'd bought her bonnets and shawls and laces when the shops reopened, just to see her smile. No, he told himself, he was not trying to buy her affections. That would be base, beneath him. The image of Mrs. Macklin, beneath him, was quickly erased. He did not want a woman's compliance out of gratitude.

Lord, it was going to be a long six months after he vowed his faithfulness. He pulled the blanket more firmly around his shoulders. Maybe he should find a young officer to wed her, a fellow of good birth but little fortune who'd be willing to have her for a price. The young man would swear to cherish her—or Ardeth would have his liver and lights—for far longer than the half year Ardeth had. A suitable marriage of convenience might be better for all of them.

Then the recent Reaper recalled her smile and knew he would not give her to another man. He could add possessiveness and jealousy to his rediscovered feelings, which might not make him a better man, but made him a more believable man. Ardeth could not help himself; Mrs. Macklin made him feel more alive. Just her name stirred him. Imogene Hopewell Macklin. Imagine. Hope. Well. A magic Genie. She was obviously meant to be his.

She needed him. He needed her. There were worse excuses for weddings.

The gremlin must have agreed with him, for the crow brought back a gold band yesterday and dropped it at Ardeth's feet. Many such keepsakes would have been trampled under the mud of the battlefield, or stolen from corpses.

"I sent you for the hourglass, you plaguesome creature."

"Pretty for the pretty, pigeon brain," the crow squawked back, flapping its wings in Ardeth's face.

No one was chasing the bird crying "thief"; no initials could lead to the ring's rightful owner. Most of all, the jewels in the vault of the earl's castle, now called Ardsley Keep, were far away.

"I suppose it will have to do, Olive."

"Stuff it."

Genie's first betrothal was a hurried affair, three weeks of calling the banns in front of her own village parish, where each and every congregant knew Elgin had been meant for her sister, Lorraine. This was a still-shorter scramble, although longer than his lordship wished. He was in a hurry to return to London and his inheritance, she understood. Genie would not mind leaving this scene of carnage, disgrace, and innuendo.

Not even the Earl of Ardeth could conjure a proper, legal wedding in so little time, however, locating a willing English cleric and a special license so far from Britain.

"Perhaps we should wait until we return home," she offered.

"No, people will talk. They are bound to, anyway, with my sudden appearance and reinstatement of the Ardsley family title."

To say nothing of his peculiarities, Genie thought, but did not speak aloud. He always wore his cape despite the heat of the day, carried a crow on his shoulder, and often spoke to empty air. He could put a pain-wracked soldier to sleep with a word and a touch, yet he never seemed to sleep himself. Genie chose to ignore the disturbing aspects. She had to, to preserve her own sanity. "I thought you did not care about gossip."

"For myself, I do not."

"If you are concerned with my reputation, staying at the same hotel and traveling with you, then we can hold the ceremony in a nearby church here and worry about the particulars later," she offered, still not certain of her fiancé's religious beliefs. For all she knew, he could choose to be wedded by a warlock.

"No, everything must be aboveboard, without question. I would have no one doubt the legitimacy of our union. As you said, there will be gossip aplenty without a mourning period, and again when the child is born too early to be of my blood. There would be more if we did not marry. Let no one think either of us is unhappy with the match. I would wed you in London's grandest cathedral, in front of the king if I could."

The king was almost as mad as Lord Ardeth.

Fearing that time and distance would let Genie doubt her decision, he kept her busy with visits to the wounded soldiers, calls on the consulate, and dress fittings when he found a seamstress willing to take up her needle again. He bought her gifts, gloves and books and candied sweets—almost like a real betrothal, almost like a man in love. He ignored the scandalized looks, the matrons' titters, the soldiers' snickers, so Genie tried to, also.

None of the officers' wives came to call on Genie, not to offer congratulations or condolences. Everyone wanted to speak with Lord Ardeth. When the earl was consulting with bankers and generals and surgeons and ambassadors, giving his advice and getting their cooperation for the wedding and the return to England, he made sure Genie was not alone. He knew she would fret herself into a panic. That panicked her worse, that he understood her so well, while she understood him not at all.

His man Campbell was full of praise for his lordship, but the sergeant could not explain where his new employer had come from, how he learned his healing techniques, or what a rich nob was doing in the middle of a war. The soldier had met the earl mere hours before Genie had, and Lord Ardeth had helped with the horses, which were Campbell's first love. Lord Ardeth was arranging Campbell's discharge from the army, and that was enough—that and a well-paying position and passage back home. He was to be the earl's man-of-all-work, footman, valet, and groom until they were home. Then he was to be in charge of filling the earl's stables. Campbell thought he must have died and gone to heaven, the way he kept grinning. Except Lord Ardeth wouldn't have let his man die, Campbell swore while he accompanied Genie on her way, on his lordship's orders.

Campbell's second love after horses, it quickly turned out, was Marie, the French maid Ardeth found to help Genie with her clothes and her hair. She knew all the latest styles, plus the best way to conceal Mrs. Macklin's growing condition. She also knew a good opportunity when she saw it. Of course she'd rather serve the master than the mistress, but Monsieur *le Comte* was not as generous with his affection as with his money. *C'est la vie.* Marie's former employer had fled back to France ahead of the advancing armies, so she was alone and without income. Brussels offered no such lucrative post, now that the British were leaving, so she was eager to accept whatever job Monsieur was offering. She was not as eager to accept poor Campbell's attentions. A mere sergeant turned gentleman's gentleman was below her standards, but he'd do—until they reached London and Marie could find a better beau.

Genie did not inquire too closely into the nature of her new maid's last position, but very much feared she was being cared for by a cast-off kept woman.

Besides Campbell and Marie making sure Genie was never alone, the crow was constantly flying overhead or tapping on Genie's window. The silly bird seemed to be making sure she did not run off rather than marry the earl.

"Alive, keep alive," she thought the crow cawed whenever the feathered forager dropped coins, buttons, or beads at her feet or on her bed.

"That's Olive," she said, trying to teach it. "Can you say Olive? And no, I cannot keep you. You are the earl's companion." She did feed the crow bits of fruit and cheese, occasionally dipping a corner of bread in wine, which he seemed to like even better.

"I love, I love," he cooed while she gently stroked his shiny black head.

"That's right—your name is Olive."

The night before the wedding, Ardeth escorted Genie to a dinner at the foreign embassy. She was dressed to the nines—in black—with lace and her only jewelry, a strand of pearls. She knew she was in better looks than ever, but not half as stunning as the man at her side. He made sure to introduce her to the dignitaries and their wives as his bride-to-be. One look from him, his hand possessively placed over hers on his arm, stilled any comments or criticisms, even when he muttered, "Shite" when someone spilled wine near her skirt, which stayed dry somehow. She was shown a deference she'd never experienced, not as younger sibling to an acknowledged beauty, nor as Elgin Macklin's second-choice bride, or his supposed tagalong camp-following sister. It was heady stuff, this being a countess. The effort required for her to act like a great lady, knowing they were all weighing her every word and action, was also terrifying, as if marrying Lord Ardeth weren't scary enough. She watched the sun rise on her wedding day, too.

For her first wedding, Genie had worn a girlish white gown. Her sister, Lorraine, had declared herself old enough to wear bright colors, so her worn muslin had come to Genie. She had carried a drooping bouquet of wildflowers she'd picked herself, a few of their petals dropping as she walked to the village church behind her angry parents. Her father was so disgusted with his younger daughter that he refused to harness his horses for the short distance. According to Squire Hopewell, stealing her sister's beau, kissing Elgin outside the assembly room, and disgracing his family name were bad enough without Imogene trying to lie and blame dear Lorraine.

The ceremony had been conducted during regular
Sunday services at her village church, and the bride was
the only one who cried, although the groom looked dis-
mal enough for tears. Elgin's eyes were bloodshot anyway, most likely from the three weeks of drinking he'd
done before shackling himself to his sweetheart's plain,
skinny redheaded sister. His neckcloth had been askew
and his clothes stank of stale wine. Lorraine, who should
have been weeping at the loss of her longtime love, was
too busy flirting with his older brother, Roger, back from
London for the nuptials.

Only the immediate families had returned to the
Hopewells' home for the wedding breakfast, Elgin's
mother sniffing in disapproval of both the Hopewells'
cottage and their conniving to trap Roger, who'd been
destined for a duke's daughter at the least. Now, because
the elder Hopewell chit had been denied her promised
parti, Roger was forced to wed a nobody. The fathers
were closeted to discuss marriage settlements. Imogene,
Elgin, and their sorry scandal would be sent out of sight,
off to war. The heir and dear Lorraine would take up residence in London after a fancy wedding.

Squire Hopewell had left the book room smiling. His
poppet would be a baroness someday. Roger, the future
baron, left the wedding breakfast with a serving maid.

What a difference between that miserable event and
Genie's second marriage. Now she wore a stylish black
silk gown, but with a white lace mantilla on her head. She
carried pure white roses, and she and her maid, Marie,
had arrived in an elegant carriage that was decked in
more roses. The ceremony was held at the British ambas-
sador's palatial residence, strewn with flowers, a violin-
ist playing softly in the corner. A reception would follow

at the hotel. The grand guests—foreign diplomats, generals, and local gentry—would dine inside, but common soldiers and servants, all those who could walk or limp to get there, were going to be served in the stable yard. Ardeth had declared it a day of celebration, of his nuptials and the British victory, a day to set aside the suffering and grieving, if only for an hour or two.

Sergeant Campbell was not the only grizzled veteran to wipe his eyes. Half the ladies present sniffled at the romance of the thing, and in regret that their own husbands did not measure up to Lord Ardeth.

This time Genie's formidable groom was magnificent, putting every other man—and the bride—in the shade. The earl wore formal dress, black satin knee breeches and tailcoat, with sparkling white neckcloth and waistcoat that set off his black hair and dark eyes. He smelled of spices and woods and scented soap, with a bit of smoke mixed in, most likely from a pipe, Genie guessed. He was tall and well formed—and he was smiling.

Today was also literal and figurative worlds away from Sir Coryn of Ardsley's first wedding. That one was held at his bride's father's drafty, mildewed castle. He'd ridden there in full armor against marauding bands, with his own troop of knights, vassals, and pages. Hot and sweaty, with no opportunity—or inclination, truth be told—to bathe, he'd knelt in the chapel next to his fifteen-year-old bride, who'd sobbed through the ceremony despite the chest of gold and jewels he'd brought as the bride-price. Everyone got drunk after, and a fight broke out among the two factions, instead of the alliance the marriage was supposed to cement. He did not remember what the girl wore. He barely recalled the color of her hair or her name, only that she sobbed throughout the days of their marriage until he rode off to the wars six months later.

What a difference an eon made, give or take a century or two. Today he was dressed in the finest garments money could buy, having bathed in oils from India with steaming hot water, and shaved not once but twice. He'd driven to a well-appointed mansion in a fine carriage behind highbred horses, to be welcomed by powerful, intelligent, unarmed gentlemen and their lady wives.

And his bride was radiant, without a hint of tears.

Too bad this union was not destined to last longer than the last one.

Everything was going well until the vicar asked, "Do you, Imogene Hopewell Macklin, take this man . . . ?"

Silence.

Did she know he was not truly a man? Ardeth shook his head. That was impossible. He had been facing forward, letting his mind wander to his plans for the reception and the coming trip. He hadn't been listening to the vicar's droning speech until the lack of it caught his attention. Why should he heed this stranger when he knew the holy vow he was taking, its rights and responsibilities, as well as the cost of forsaking it, better than any collared cleric?

Now he turned to face the bride. He'd thought Genie rapt in attention to the vicar, a slight smile on her lips. Now he recognized that smile for the same kind of frozen rictus he'd seen when he'd done his job, his former job. She wasn't . . . ? No, of course not. She was simply paralyzed with fear, poor puss, and he had no idea what to do about it, not with all these people watching. She was right to be afraid, by Hades.

He squeezed her hand, bothered that he could not tell

how icy hers was through their gloves. His hands were always cold anyway and could not have helped warm her. Damn, he cursed, then prayed that she would not change her mind now. Campbell, beside him, started to gnaw on his lip as the vicar repeated his question.

Marie, on Genie's other side as her attendant and witness, whispered loudly enough for half the guests to hear, "You'll never get a better offer, *chérie*," which served only to remind Genie that she was gambling with her life and that of her child on a man who moved in the highest circles and moved like a shadow, a man who looked like a paragon and spoke in paradoxes. She had no business being here, in this society, with this silver-tongued stranger.

"Of course you will get a better offer," Ardeth murmured to her. "You are beautiful and kindhearted. Any man would die to have you as his wife. Well, perhaps not die," he quickly amended. That was the whole point. "But I hope you will choose me, for I will spend what time I have being a good husband, I swear." He brought her hand to his mouth for a kiss on her glove. "Do not be afraid, lady. I would never let harm come to you. You believe that, don't you?"

She wet her lips and nodded. "Yes, I do, I think."

"And you believe that we are both entitled to the chance at finding some happiness in this life?"

This time she spoke louder, with more conviction. "I do."

Twenty witnesses let out held breaths, relieved that there would be no more embarrassing moments. Now no one would have to solve the awkward problem of that rotter Macklin's widow. Now no men would have to worry about their wives sighing over the elegant earl.

Ardeth thanked Heaven, Hell, and everywhere in between.

"I do, too," he whispered.

"Me three," came the squawk from atop the unlit chandelier, then another, louder squawk from the unfortunate turbaned lady sitting beneath.

CHAPTER FIVE

For all the differences, weddings had not changed a great
deal. Nor had the wedding nights, except that now no
one was expected to hang bloodied sheets out the window,
or consummate the union with witnesses present. The male
guests at the hotel fete still made raucous, ribald jokes, perhaps more so because the bride was no shy virgin.

Ardeth was offended. What kind of gentlemen spoke
so in front of a lady? He might have done the same in his
time, but had these puny people not learned better manners in all the years? He would not reprimand any of
them or order the innkeeper to stop pouring the wine and
ale that loosened even well-bred tongues. He needed their
goodwill back in England. Besides, taking umbrage for
such a small slight was a poor reflection of his own character, he decided. Instead, he decided to leave.

Genie was exhausted and embarrassed. She believed
that half the risqué songs would not be sung if she were
a real lady, born to the aristocracy. She hated the thought

of the earl realizing he'd married so far beneath him, and on the same day as the wedding. Leaving was appealing, but impossible. "We cannot simply disappear, my lord," she said with regret. "This is our party. We are the hosts."

"We are an earl and his countess, my lady. Have you not yet realized that we can do almost anything we wish? Watch."

He tapped his wineglass. It was a small enough sound, but everyone in the vicinity stilled. "Friends, my lady and I thank you for coming to help celebrate our wedding. Your good wishes are sincerely appreciated. As you know, marriage is a journey, an exploration of uncharted waters, learning which shoals are treacherous, which reefs offer safe harbor. We begin our voyage tonight. So we bid you farewell. Let the celebration continue."

The cheers were for the new bottles of champagne being brought out. The party would be more festive anyway without the groom's disapproving glares.

Instead of leading Genie upstairs to their rooms, Ardeth led her out to the carriage, where Marie sat up with Campbell on the driver's seat. Trunks were already strapped to the back and the roof, and Ardeth's black stallion was tied behind.

"We are not to spend the night here?" Genie asked.

"We travel to the coast, to the yacht I have hired to return us to England."

At her quiet "Oh," he took up her hand again. "Should I have consulted you? I fear I am not in the habit of asking another's opinion. I was right—we have much to learn about each other and being part of a pair. I have been solitary too long."

"No, traveling now is fine. In fact the celebration was growing far too lively for my taste."

Lively? Was that what it was? Ardeth had found death far more peaceful. He relaxed against the cushions, glad to be away. "At least we agree on that."

Genie fussed with her gloves. "I am concerned about the heirloom that you lost. Should we really be giving up the search?"

"Oh, I have rewards posted everywhere. If the bauble is close by, someone will find it and return the thing for the money I promised."

"Will they recognize it? I thought you were not sure of its description."

He unfolded a sheet of paper with a small picture on it, with the reward offer written in four languages.

"But it is just an hourglass. Our governess used one to time lessons. Surely that cannot be so valuable."

"The size is deceptive. The piece is actually a gold and glass brooch. Although the sands do shift, they do not keep accurate time as you know it."

Once again he'd managed to rattle her. "As I know it? Doesn't everyone mark hours and minutes the same way?"

"I have seen clocks of dripping water, sundials, and monoliths," he said, avoiding her actual question. "You might say this timepiece has a sentimental attachment far beyond its usefulness."

"I see. Was it your mother's?"

Coryn the boy had been fostered out to a brutal warlord at such an early age that he could not recall having a mother, although he must have. "No, it was a more recent acquisition."

Genie was still troubled. "But how will you know it from all the replicas people are bound to bring you in hopes of winning the reward?" She handed back the sheet of paper. "It appears easy to duplicate, especially if it does not work correctly."

"Nay, it is impossible to copy, and no one will part with its match. I will know the original. You must trust me on that."

It seemed to Genie that she had already taken a great deal on faith. What was one more irreplaceable hourglass that did not work? Her husband was definitely daft. She might as well humor him, Genie decided, so she asked, "Have you left the crow behind to search?"

Ardeth looked around, noticing for the first time that the gremlin was missing. "No, I have little control of the beast, ah, the bird. I am sure he will turn up."

He sat back and closed his eyes, ending the conversation and leaving Genie to wonder about a man who cared so much for a scrap of broken jewelry, and so little for his constant companion. She could not help wondering also what that meant for her and this hasty marriage.

Genie could not nap despite her weariness and the well-sprung coach. She sighed and wriggled around, trying to find a more comfortable position, which must have disturbed Ardeth. He rapped on the carriage roof, ordering Campbell to pull up, then got out and mounted Black Butch.

Now Genie had to fret that she had offended her new husband. If this marriage journey was a sea voyage, as he'd said, her ship was already leaking. Genie sighed again and gave up worrying. At least she was not hungry or homeless, and that was enough for now. She fell asleep this time, without Ardeth's dark presence to disturb her mind.

He came alongside the coach near dusk and tapped on the window. "I am sorry to awaken you, but we are near the harbor. We'll set sail in the morning, so we could sleep aboard the ship, but we will find more amenities at an inn. You see, I am learning, asking which you prefer."

Genie chose the inn, thinking that they were bound to have separate chambers there. Who knew how many cabins were on the ship? Who knew how committed the earl was to his promises?

Ardeth rode ahead to make arrangements.

At the inn he'd selected, he sent a rider back to direct the coach. Upstairs, he ordered baths, dinner, rooms for the servants, stalls for the horses. The innkeeper hurried to serve without even hearing his name or title, once he'd seen the earl's gold. Ardeth could have bought the inn for just a bit more.

His lordship chose a room overlooking the innyard so he could see the coach pull up. He knew this was no lawless borderland where women were held for ransom or worse, but he still worried. He was resolved not to fail in this simple test of being a married man.

He heard a tapping on the window and opened it to let in the accursed bird.

"Kiss the bride? Kiss the bride?"

Ardeth looked around at his solitary room, then at the door beyond which his new wife would be housed. He'd ordered wine and flowers for her, and a tray for her supper so she could rest. Alone, as promised.

"No."

The crow tried to quack from the windowsill.

"Dumb duck."

"Numb fu—"

Ardeth slammed the window.

Marie shook her head after she'd taken away the dinner tray, and helped Genie out of her bath and into her night rail. She chattered about the wedding guests, their clothes, their manners, and which married men had roving eyes. The French maid's own eyes kept straying to the connecting door between her mistress's room and the earl's. As soon as his lordship appeared, Marie could go on to find her own room in the attics, unless she decided to enliven Campbell's night.

The door stayed closed. Marie brushed Genie's hair again, rearranged the few jars and bottles on the table, and yawned a time or two in case her mistress missed the point.

Genie had not. "I think I will read in bed awhile," she said, dismissing the maid. "We make an early start in the morning, I believe."

"Me, I believe I have never seen such a honeymoon," Marie muttered on her way out the door, with a grim look toward the earl's chamber.

Marie might be a competent maid, and she might be the only female acquaintance Genie had in this place, and she might be—must be—far more experienced with men than Genie, but she was still the maid. Genie was not born to a house full of servants, but she knew better than to tolerate criticism of her marriage, particularly from a woman who was no better than a light-skirt.

Genie almost asked exactly how many wedding nights Marie had experienced—not how many beds she had shared with married men. Instead she merely said, "Lord Ardeth is not like other men." She ignored the older woman's grin, fervent nod, and crossing of herself as an afterthought. "He makes his own rules, and you had better obey them, especially about gossiping about your employers. Good night."

Well, Genie had experienced one wedding night before, and she knew what men wanted out of marriage. No matter what Ardeth said, he'd be here, sooner or later. After her nap in the carriage, Genie was not tired, not with thoughts like that battling in her brain. She owed Ardeth for rescuing her; the least she could do was be an acquiescent bride. After all, he was clean—she'd heard servants carrying out his bathwater—and sober. How bad could it be? She doubted the earl would hurt her, not when he was so gentle with the injured soldiers and his horses. Surely a wife rated higher than a horse? Maybe not. She had not, to Elgin.

Heavens, she ought not be thinking of Elgin on her wedding night. Then again, if he was watching from wherever his reckless, feckless soul had landed, let him see that another man appreciated her, that another man treated her like a lady. And that another man almost made her want to please him.

Almost.

Let neither Elgin nor the earl see her knees knocking together.

Genie pinched color into her cheeks, prodded steel into her backbone, and knocked softly on her husband's door.

"Yes?"

Yes, she was going in. Yes, she was going to offer herself to the scowling man who'd been staring out the inn's window. Yes, she was going to pretend to enjoy whatever happened. On the other hand . . .

"No. I mean, nothing. I just wanted—"

He pulled her into the room to see her face by the candlelight. "Is everything to your liking? Have you enough covers and coal for the hearth?"

She was already too warm, just stepping into his room with its blazing fire. He was wearing a thick robe and fur-lined slippers, despite the warm night air.

"Everything is fine. The room is lovely. The dinner was delicious."

"Then . . . ?"

She had no answer. Was he caper-witted as well as crazy? This was their wedding night and she was wearing a nearly transparent robe over her equally gossamer nightgown. Her hair was loose around her shoulders instead of in a neat plait, and she smelled of some exotic perfume Marie had produced. What did he think she was doing at his door? She licked her lips, thinking that moisture might make the words easier to pronounce, but he spoke first.

"I suppose you cannot sleep, either. Here, let me—" He reached over to touch her neck, the way she had seen him touch the severely injured soldiers, lulling them to a pain-free sleep.

She jumped back. "No, thank you. Whatever it is you do, I would rather not know. That is, I would rather you didn't." She need not have pinched her cheeks, Genie realized. They must be scarlet by now. "I mean, I am not tired at all after resting in the carriage."

"Ah."

"Ah" was as helpful as a cup of hemlock. "I thought we might—"

"Talk? Quite right." He led her to a chair in front of the fireplace, then leaned against the mantel. "We should speak of where you'd like to live, if you have an older woman you would like to invite to live with you as companion, how much—what do you call it?—pin money you will need. We were in such a rush I never thought to ask."

"Whatever you decide will be fine. I have no great needs, nor any female in mind. Perhaps one of your relatives?"

"I doubt you'd care to dig up any of them."

"Dirty dishes, are they? We have a few scoundrels and squirrels on the Hopewell family tree that we never mention, either. I suppose I am one of them."

"Scoundrel or squirrel?"

"Just unmentionable."

He smiled. "That will change. We are invited to the prime minister's house. People will speak of you, but only with admiration."

Genie doubted that, after her second scandalous marriage. "Thank you, but that is not what I came for."

"You want to speak of finances?"

"I do not want to speak at all." She was growing so warm in the overheated room, so near to the fire, that she started to undo the top button at the closure of her robe. While she was doing it, she decided to continue down the row of buttons. Perhaps he would get the idea then.

His nearly black eyes followed her fingers the way a castaway's eyes followed a ship on the horizon, his last hope sailing away without him. Ardeth cursed. He knew why she'd come, of course. If the martyred look on her guileless face did not tell the tale, her clumsy fingers fumbling with the buttons did. Like a nervous virgin, she had come to offer the only commodity she had. And if he took it, he'd be lost forever. He cursed again in several obsolete languages. Foul words were not going to solve his immediate problem, however.

He reached out to still her hand, wondering if he ought to send her to dreamless sleep after all. As wary as a fawn, she pulled back.

"Don't," he said. "Don't be afraid."

"You do things to people, influence them. Sway them to your opinion. I have seen you do it, at the dinners, today at the reception. Other times you know what they are thinking, what they need." She had hoped this would be one of those times. Sadly, it seemed not to be, and she ought to be glad. "I do not know how you do it, but please do not. I have given my hand to you, not my thoughts."

He took her hand and brought it to his lips, kissing the gold ring on her finger. She felt warm, vibrant, achingly woman. "You have given enough."

He was trying to tell her she did not need to continue, but the female was as stubborn as a mule.

"We were wed this morning."

One dark eyebrow rose. "I do seem to recall the occasion."

"It is our wedding night."

"One usually follows the other."

"You are going to make me say it, aren't you?"

He held his hands in the air as if to ward off blame. "I am not making you do anything. Nor am I the one who knocked on your door in the middle of the night. I wish to heaven you had not."

"Why?"

There was no subtlety to the woman at all. Perhaps she was right and she would not make a good politician's wife. Instead of answering, he said, "Go back to your room, Genie, where you will be safe from me."

"Why?"

Not why she would be safe, but why she would sleep alone on their wedding night. "Because I cannot."

"Oh, you *are* sick, then." Now her face was scarlet, and not from the heat. "That is why you do not mind about the baby, because you cannot have one of your own. I am so sorry to have reminded you, to have . . . you know." She tried to leave, but he held her hand.

"No, I am not lacking in that regard." Not judging by the fire in his blood or the bulge in his breeches.

"You do not find me attractive?"

Not judging by the bulge in his blood or the fire in his breeches. "I find you damnably attractive." He needed all of his mental strength to drop her hand and step back, away from temptation. "And that is the problem. I will be damned forever if I make love to you tonight."

"But we are married."

"But I gave my word. I could simply say I am tired or ill in some other way or too busy." He gestured toward the desk, which was piled high with papers. "I will not lie to you if I can help it. I want you. But I made a promise."

"To me, so it does not matter."

He looked away from her, staring into the flames in the fireplace. "To me it does."

"But I absolve you of your vow."

"I have sworn to be an honorable man, a man of my word, not governed by base urges and selfish motives. I have to be better than an ordinary man." Better than the man he was.

"You would be a saint?"

He laughed at the thought of what those lofty beings would do if he joined them. "If I knew how, yes. I am not that ambitious, however. It will be enough to be honorable, I hope. I will not touch you while you grieve for Macklin's memory."

"But I do not mourn him, except as a useless death. Do not think his was a noble end, fighting the French to keep England free. He died drunk in another woman's arms. A married woman, whose husband was wearing his sword, and who was sober enough to aim it true."

"Macklin is lucky I did not come to fetch him."

Her forehead puckered in confusion. "Did you know my husband, then?"

"No, but one of my . . . associates did. I pray he was delivered to the right place."

"But they said he would be buried here, with the other fallen men. There are far too many to transport home. And that way his family does not have to know the truth." She took a hesitant step nearer. "So Elgin is no longer my burden to bear."

"You bear his child."

"And I bear my own brand of honor. I wed you of my free will, and I will do my duty."

He slammed his fist into the mantelpiece, causing a vase of flowers to jump. He steadied it. "I do not want a woman out of duty! Or gratitude, or servitude. I helped you in the only way I could, without conditions or demands. That was what I needed to do."

"Then I am just another good deed?"

"You are my wife."

"In name only?"

"In respect and friendship, I hope."

"And the other part of marriage, the, ah, intimate aspect?"

"A woman should make love when she feels love. No other time."

Now there was a novel concept. If true, Genie would not be pregnant.

CHAPTER SIX

No baby? Then there would have been no need to marry Lord Ardeth. His theory was interesting, but with no relation to reality. In her experience, men took, women gave. That was the way of the world, not some pretty pipe dream.

Genie accepted the glass of wine that the earl offered, and asked, "But what about all the marriages of convenience, or the dynastic matches whose whole purpose is to provide heirs for thrones, titles, and wealth?"

He sipped at his own wine, savoring the taste after so many years without. "All matters naught, in the end. Elgin Macklin will not see his son. What of the French Louis, the English Henrys, or the Egyptian Ramseses? Where are they now?" He could tell her precisely where, but that was not the point. "Your own prince regent has no heir, despite his political maneuvering. England will survive."

"But what of those unions that merge fortunes? You

are a rich man yourself. Do you not want your flesh and blood to inherit your money?"

He shrugged. "I have already started making plans for the gold, establishing a fund for the widows and orphans of the soldiers we could not save. I intend to build schools and hospitals and much more. Do not worry—you will be well provided for, as I promised. There is enough left to do a world of good."

Genie was so amazed she almost dropped her glass. "You would give all of your money away?"

"Not your share, but yes. I will not need it when I am done."

"You are a very peculiar man."

He laughed, more at himself than anything else. "You do not know the half of it."

"You see things others do not." She touched her stomach. "You speak like no other man, think like no one I have ever known. Women should have choices. Money should be spent. Heirs do not matter. I know you have been in foreign lands, but I have never heard of a society with such notions. What are you?"

The crow had been sleeping on the bedpost, glossy head under one wing. Now the bird blinked and bobbed. "Reaper," he mumbled. "Reaper."

Ardeth scowled at the gremlin, which was now fluffing its feathers and going back to sleep. "The pest means 'reader.' I am a prodigious reader of varied philosophies. For all my studies, I have decided to be a man of honor, as I said. A man who is trying to find his lost soul, if that makes any sense."

"Don't you mean save your soul?"

"No, mine was lost long ago, with the hourglass. But I will find it. Then I will be free if I can make amends."

He seemed so noble to Genie, so selfless and honorable, she had a hard time believing anything else. "Were you were not always a gentleman, that you must atone?"

"A gentleman? I was never that." He looked at his hands with their nails that were now smooth and manicured, but hands that had held broadsword, battle-axe, and mace. "To my sorrow."

"Did you take lives?" she guessed.

"Too many to count."

"But you saved some. I saw that myself."

"Too few."

"Were you a mercenary, then, fighting in wars around the world? Is that how you became wealthy, selling your sword for gold?"

"I started as a warrior, battling for land and gold and influence. Then I became a kind of tax collector for those with far more power than I ever imagined."

"You have great inner strengths." Genie had never seen him weary or undecided. He seemed annoyed by the crow, but he never shouted or swatted at it, the way Elgin would have. "I cannot imagine anyone but royalty with more innate authority."

He brushed that aside. "I have nothing compared to those I served."

Genie did not believe him. She'd read of other lands, too, of czars and sultans and satraps. The Earl of Ardeth was surely more regal. Reminded of sultans, though, she thought of harems. "What about women?" Now that he was answering questions, Genie found she had many.

"To my regret I battled for wenches, too, and won many, whether they were willing or not. But I am long since done with rakehell ways, I swear."

"What of your first wife?"

"She was seldom willing." He could not remember the color of her eyes, only that they were always reddened from weeping. "Or did you mean to ask if I had other women then? In plain truth, I was neither a caring husband nor a faithful one for the short time I was wed."

"What happened to her?"

He honestly had no idea. "She died." He turned toward the window again, and turned the conversation. "Tell me, did you enjoy lovemaking with your Elgin?"

Genie coughed on a sip of the wine. "Gracious, that is not a proper topic."

"But my sins are?"

He was right. Genie owed him her honesty, and an explanation. "Elgin did not love me any more than I loved him. I became reconciled to our marriage. He did not." Genie saw no reason to delve further into her own past. It was the future that concerned her now, tonight especially. "You said a woman should feel love before, ah, consummating her union."

Now he came back to the chair where she sat, and looked down at her. "That was not precisely what I said. Are you by any chance implying that you feel affection for me?"

Genie did not know what to say. How to tell one's husband of half a day that he baffled her and bemused her, and sometimes made her blood run cold? Instead she said, "That was not what I meant. I was wondering if mutual attraction was enough to satisfy your conditions."

He knelt by her chair and took up her hand. "Are you saying that you feel a roaring, raging passion for me?"

Genie snatched her hand back. "NO!"

"Damn."

He did not seem to be angry or disappointed, so Genie

let her curiosity rule again. "Goodness, do ladies feel roaring, raging passions?"

"With the right lover, they do. It is called lust, one of the baser emotions among mortal men, and the most common."

"I am sorry if I led you to believe—"

He laughed. "I was merely teasing. Do you think I would believe you eager to share my bed when you shy from my touch like a skittish colt? Although I suppose I would not turn you down if you were panting and pleading. I am only human, after all." He chuckled again, but Genie did not see the humor.

"I made my vows, too," she said, "knowing that intimacy is part of marriage. I would honor my word the same as you."

"Without affection or attraction? I would not ask it of you. What I do ask is for your help, not out of duty or subservience or righteousness."

"You are an earl. What could I do to help you?"

"You can help spend my money, for one thing. You can point the way." He sat in the only other chair in the room, at the desk with all its papers. "You see all the decisions to be made? So come, Lady Ardeth, sit and relax, and talk of what is needed. You will know more than I about schools and foundling homes."

Despite her intentions, Genie was relieved to be excused from her wifely duties—although Ardeth was far more handsome than Elgin. Perhaps she was a tiny bit attracted to him after all, intrigued by his refined looks that hid great power. She wondered what else his clothing hid, and if his courtly manners would extend to that large bed that loomed behind him. She purposely turned her head to study the documents he handed her, and told herself she was delighted to be consulted about his charitable work and finances. Elgin never so much as showed her their accounts, nor did he spend a groat on anything but himself. And consulting was far more enjoyable than Elgin's conjugal visits had ever been.

After an hour of discussion and decisions, Genie felt like a partner, maybe not a wife, but a valued colleague in bettering other lives. Her husband might be a bedlamite as well as a benefactor, but she could not remember the last time she felt so content, with such a sense of accomplishment. "This is a much better way of spending one's wedding night," she said, then clapped a hand over her mouth, realizing what she had said.

Ardeth only laughed and took the list she was compiling out of her hand. "Fool that I am, I almost forgot. But it truly is our wedding night, when I should be thinking of my lovely bride instead of cold numbers." He offered her another glass of wine, but she refused, noticing how little he imbibed. The last thing he'd want was a wife turned wanton by the spirits, or made sloppy in her calculations, or falling asleep in his big, soft-looking bed.

"Maybe I should leave now. If we are to depart early . . ."

"The ship sails when we are ready, not before. But come, I want to know what you want for yourself, so I know how much of my fortune I can spend on good deeds."

Having a glimpse of the vastness of his wealth, Genie knew he was teasing again. She could not spend a tenth of it in her lifetime.

"What would you like most?" he asked. "Jewels? Artwork? Greenhouses full of exotic blooms? Tell me."

"I like the idea of turning workhouses into training places, where poor people can learn a trade."

"No, I mean for yourself, besides a new wardrobe, of course. You'll need one for the changing seasons, and your changing shape. We already have two houses, or is it three? I believe they are crowded with treasures, with a safe full of heirloom gems. But what else would you spend money on, now that you can? All I gave you as a wedding gift was a plain gold ring."

Genie had intended to give him her body. "I gave you nothing."

"Of course you did. You made me laugh. Now it is your turn."

She took a moment to think. Recently all she had wanted was to know that her rent had been paid, that the butcher would not refuse her credit. A new ribbon to freshen her old bonnet had been a rare luxury. Now she could have anything she wanted—anything money could buy, that was.

Ardeth was adding another chunk of coal to the already-blazing fire. "Surely you must have dreamed of something when you were growing up?"

Her parents' affection, her sister's friendship? Those he could not purchase for her. "I wanted a pony of my own, but always had to share with my sister."

"That is no challenge. I intend to fill the stables anyway. You may have your choice of the best-behaved mounts. What else?"

"Well, I once thought I would like to travel, but following the army cured me of that, I suppose."

He nodded. "Travel is not all it is cracked up to be, by Harry."

"I suppose you have seen all the sights, though, all the

marvelous places of the world. If I could, I'd like to see the Great Pyramids."

"No, you wouldn't like them. Sandstorms and locusts."

"The Alps, then. They are said to be awe-inspiring."

"Avalanches."

"India, with the colorful markets and the spice trade."

"The worst. Constant droughts, then constant floods. The same as Africa. Insects and epidemics. Besides, getting to any of those places is hazardous enough. Hurricanes, cyclones, shipwrecks galore, to say nothing of pirates and mutinies."

She had to laugh. "What about the moon?"

"No one has managed to die there. Yet. You will be far safer in England."

She was still chuckling, thinking he was joking again. "How is it you have traveled the world over and seen nothing but doom and destruction? Were you so busy that you saw nothing beautiful anywhere?"

Ardeth looked at Genie, with the firelight behind her making her robe more diaphanous than ever. He could make out the shape of her rounded breasts and the rosy glow of her nipples. Her red-gold hair was curling from the heat in the room, forming a shimmering halo around her delicate features. And her soft lips were turned up in a smile. For him.

"I do not think I have ever seen a more lovely sight than right now."

"Oh." Her smile faded. "You need not give me Spanish coin, you know, false flattery. That was never part of our bargain. And you have convinced me: I will be content to view the moon through the window, and think about visiting Scotland or Ireland." She started to rise.

"So you may give away another wagonload of gold to those who actually need it. Good night."

"No, do not leave yet. We have much more to discuss, like the houses and home farms. I know nothing of domestic matters."

"You are a great reader, you said. You will learn from books. And we have a lifetime to discuss the rest."

Six months was too short a lifetime to waste in sleep. "Please stay."

"It is late. Besides, it is too warm in here for me. I suppose you are used to hotter climes."

He simply shrugged.

Half of her wanted to stay, to hear his foolishness, to see that look of admiration in his ebony eyes. Her sensible half wanted to flee. Reason lost. "But perhaps you could open a window?"

Instead he snapped his fingers; the fire went out.

"It was only a silly parlor trick," Ardeth shouted at her retreating back. "Anyone can do it," he said to the door that slammed behind her. Then he cursed, long and loud, in scores of languages. He might have cursed all night without repeating himself; he knew so many foul imprecations and improbable suggestions. After all, few people had ever greeted his arrival with kindly welcomes.

Frustration was a new experience he could do without. Then he kicked the bed. "Damn." So was pain.

His anger had awoken the gremlin crow, whose head was turning, beady eyes looking for a way out or a place to hide.

"Don't say it," Ardeth ordered.

"Me?"

"Who else would dare call me a fool?"

"Me?"

"And I shan't have it—do you hear me?—impudence from a foul being that eats worms."

"Me?"

"I know I handled the woman badly. I do not need you to tell me. I was trying to impress her, that was all, like a schoolboy. Fool."

"Me?"

"I told you to be quiet. One more comment out of that pointy beak and I will get a cat."

"Meow?"

"That's right. A big, ferocious feline with long claws and sharp teeth. Not one more word."

So the crow silently squatted on Ardeth's pillow.

CHAPTER SEVEN

The rest of the wedding journey—an end to army life, an escape from despair, or the entry to real existence, depending on whose eyes the trip was viewed through—passed uneventfully.

Ardeth kept busy with the horses, his papers, and his increasing staff of couriers, information gatherers, and outright spies. He was planning his arrival in London and introduction to its society with the same care he had given sieges on enemy strongholds. He did not intend to fail. Too much depended on his acceptance. Now he was responsible for another's welcome back into the rarefied air of the aristocracy, where she would have to live after he was gone.

Genie had no intention of living among the haut monde, because she knew she would never be accepted there. She would worry about Ardeth's disappointment later, though, for now she kept busy with seasickness, motion sickness, morning sickness, and being sick at heart when they finally reached London.

Gracious, she had taken enough of a chance wedding a slightly mad stranger, but Ardeth was far stranger than that! She had married a monster, a freak. There was no other way of describing her befuddlement. Ardeth did not seem evil, just so different her mind could not comprehend his nature. She tried out the notion that he might be an angel. Heaven knew he was beautiful enough. Sometimes he talked in such otherworldly terms that she could not conceive of a real man being so noble, so wise, so learned. She had a hard enough time believing in angels coming to earth to work wonders, however, much less marrying pregnant widows. Besides, what did angels need with money if a simple miracle or two could better mankind? And no angel would pull a dagger from his boot to carve his beefsteak.

Her mind skittered to the idea that her husband—good grief, she was truly married to the man!—was a wizard, with a crow for familiar. But wizards were fairy-tale creatures, weren't they, ancient, with long white beards and pointed hats? Ardeth was far too virile for that. And he had no staff. Well, not that kind.

Perhaps he was a warlock, she speculated, for he'd spoken of killing. But a warlock would not marry in front of a priest, under a cross. At least she thought not, recalling tales of covens meeting at midnight, naked under moonlight. She would not let herself think of Ardeth without his clothes on, so eliminated black magic from her musing.

Which left everyday magic, then, if every day was a country fair or a ha'penny show. A wandering magician could learn tricks from many cultures, sleight of hand from hundreds of sources, even books. She'd heard of fakirs who slept on beds of nails, shamans who did rain dances, Gypsies who told fortunes, and mediums who spoke with the dead. She scarcely believed any of it, but she was not well-read or well traveled, so supposed such things were possible. And she had heard Ardeth himself shout that he'd performed a trick. So her husband was a conjurer? At the same time he was an earl? That was even harder to believe.

Unless he had pulled the earldom out of his hat, as a magician pulled out a rabbit, or a gold coin from behind someone's ear. His wealth could be as much an illusion. In that case the determined London newspapers would soon discover that none of his story was true, that he was a charlatan, a mountebank.

Did they hang impostors? What of their wives? She guessed they would be transported to Botany Bay at the least, which was better than being burned at the stake, she supposed.

At best his relatives would lock him in Bedlam Hospital, and condemn her for taking advantage of a poor deluded lunatic. Heaven knew what would happen to her then, for she thought any contract a crazy person signed could be declared invalid. Even wills had to be made with sound minds.

The sound she made was half whimper, half moan.

If her fears were not bad enough, they were magnified by her self-imposed isolation in the earl's London town house. She had no one to discuss her concerns with. She would not speak about her husband to the servants, not to gossipy Marie, and not to steadfast Campbell, who was so happy with the horses, he'd never hear a word of criticism of his master. As for the other servants, they were all in awe of the earl, and so correct in manners that they awed Genie. Why, she almost curtsied to the butler!

Even if the housekeeper were a friendly, motherly sort instead of a coolly efficient work of starch, Genie would not be so disloyal as to talk about the man who had rescued her and now had her ensconced in the center of Mayfair, with new servants to manage, new furnishings to select, a new wardrobe to purchase.

For the latter, Marie quickly discovered the correct modistes to patronize, and Genie quickly discovered that a countess did not have to be bothered with tedious fittings or waiting her turn in some shop. Linendrapers and dressmakers came to her, to her house, at her convenience. For the chance at dressing a countess, a courteous countess whose husband paid the bills promptly, one enterprising shop owner hired a young woman of Genie's height and weight, except for the baby, so Genie did not have to stand to be pinned and poked.

As a matter of fact, and a matter of choice, Genie seldom left the house. She told herself she was too busy, helping Ardeth, making a home for him. In truth she was too worried about facing society. If he was not denounced as an interloper, she would be. He'd discover she was not welcome in an earl's circles, that he'd married a pariah who could not attend the balls and such where he would meet other men of influence, to speak of his charities.

For herself, she could withstand the turned backs and sneers. She was not sure about Ardeth. With his sense of honor, he was liable to repay the insults by turning some disapproving dowager into a frog.

Genie giggled at the idea.

"Is something funny, my lady wife?"

Genie quickly got to her feet, spilling a few of the parcels she was unwrapping onto the floor. The carpet was so thick, nothing broke. "I did not hear you, my lord."

"Don't you think you could call me Ardeth or Coryn by now?"

"You call me wife."

"I like the sound of it. And your laughter. Have I told you recently?"

See? Magic. He melted her fears away with a few words. The room was warmer, the day brighter, because he was smiling.

"No," she said, but added, "You have been too busy," in case he thought she was looking for more compliments. "I have hardly seen you." That sounded wrong, too—the man betwattled her brain! "Not that I am complaining, of course, for I never expected you to dance attendance on me."

"Yet dance we shall. The walls of bureaucracy have now been breached. My claim to the title has been validated. My call to Parliament will be forthcoming."

"No one questioned your birth?" She wanted to say "sanity" or "peculiarity," but did not dare.

"I have proof of my legitimacy, if that was what had you worried, and my right to the earldom. That has been on record for decades. My signature has been accepted at the banks."

Someone should question the intelligence of those in charge, she thought, but said, "Then congratulations indeed!"

He took her hand and swung her around, right off her feet, in a mad whirl. "I have met with the foreign secretary, the home secretary, and the prime minister. His Excellency the prince is hosting a grand fete to celebrate the defeat of Bonaparte after all those years. I am invited. I shall learn to waltz."

"I thought everyone knew how to waltz by now."

"Not where I came from. Show me, lady wife."

So Genie hummed and counted the beat. Ardeth learned quickly, except that he wanted only to sweep her up and twirl her around, missing the boxes on the floor by inches.

"No, no," she said through her laughter. "The waltz is far more decorous than that. And your partner will become ill if you keep spinning."

"Are you feeling queasy? Shall I . . . ?"

She slipped from his arms and fussed with the twine on another box. "I am fine, thank you. You will do well at the ball."

"It would be a serious insult to refuse the prince."

Genie was catching her breath, and not just from the wild waltz. She had never been held so easily, with so much joy. "Of course it would. You must attend. The prince might listen to your plans to improve conditions of the poor instead of spending all his money on building palaces and pavilions."

"From what I hear, he will never listen. But others might. You will be expected at my side, of course. People are already asking about you, and I can only claim your weariness from the journey for so long."

She wrapped the string around her fingers, rather than meet his eyes. "I thought I would not attend public functions yet. In memory of Elgin, you know."

"Nearly everyone there will have lost someone in the war. They are celebrating that no more young men will be sacrificed."

"There is no reason to stir up more gossip," she insisted.

"Gossip lurks in every dark corner, like dust. Such it has been in every court I have ever visited, as well as every alehouse, washing well, and milking shed. The only way to defeat it is in the open air. Furthermore, the Russian prince will be there with his sister, and three Austrian princesses, I understand. Everyone will be talking about them, not you."

"I am not ready to go out."

"What, you have nothing suitable to wear?" He raised one dark eyebrow at the stacks of parcels in the small, cluttered parlor at the back of the house. There was even a crate in one corner.

"These are not mine! I would never spend your money on so much frippery."

He peered into one box, but saw only wrapping tissue. "Toys for poor children? Hats and mittens for the workhouses? I thought we discussed hiring a warehouse for that kind of thing."

"We did. These are your packages. They are all hourglasses." She led him to the connecting room, where shelf upon shelf was filled with the timepieces. Some were tiny, with enough sand to time an egg or a move at a game of chess. Others were so large they could have clocked a cricket match. Some were wood, some brass. A few were gold, or gold plated. Some of the sand was white, and some looked like mud dredged out of the river Thames yesterday.

"Campbell found a man to build the shelves," Genie told Ardeth. "Scores of hourglasses arrive every day through your agents, more so now that the reward notices have been posted in London. I have the names of all the senders, in case one deserves the money, but I do not think so, from your description. A few have clasps roughly glued to the backs, trying to make them into brooches, but Olive says they are not right."

"Olive?"

"I thought he would recognize the one you seek, because you sent him out looking."

"I sent him to get rid of the nuisance. That twit would not recognize his own pecker, that is, his own beak."

"Well, he does claim these are not alive, as if an hourglass could live and breathe. I thought he was saying they were not for Olive, not food, not shiny enough. Then he said they were not ours."

The former Dead Letter knew the former gremlin was saying "not Ar's."

Ardeth picked up a little one of the collection, surprised at its lightness. The real one, for all its smallness, carried the weight of the world, or so it had always seemed. He put this one down.

"I appreciate your efforts, but they are not necessary. I would know if the thing were found. I would . . . feel differently, I think."

Abracadabra again, Genie thought, her ebullience fading. "What shall I do with these? I'd think schools and hospitals would rather have clocks."

"We could melt down the gold ones, I suppose, or return as many as we can, with a few coins. The ones sent as gifts to curry favor require mere thank-you notes. But leave them for now. We need to discuss the prince's reception."

"I would rather not go."

"I know," was all he said, lifting an hourglass that had colored glass beads embedded in its bottom and top. It was garish enough for a bordello, if the wenches worked by the hour.

Lord Ardeth was not asking, Genie knew, feeling more trapped by his turned back and silence. He'd done so much, given so much, and asked so little in return. Now he was letting her choose her own path, confident she would choose the right one. She'd rather catalog the timepieces.

She could let him go off on his own, Genie thought. Ardeth had managed well so far. According to Campbell, the earl had won membership to White's men's club, which he accepted, and invitations to Jackson's boxing parlor, Manton's shooting gallery, and Antonio's fencing academy, all of which he refused. Genie wondered what he'd told the sporting gentlemen, for he'd told her he would not take up arms against a man, ever again, not even in play. The Corinthians ought to be glad Ardeth was not wielding fists or sword or pistol, for she'd wager he'd be a formidable opponent. As for White's, Genie knew her husband did not care to gamble, and never drank to excess since she'd known him. Again, she wondered what the other men thought, if they were already calling him the Eccentric Earl. As sure as the sins he would not commit, he was different from the rest of them, yet seemed to command respect wherever he went.

Most likely the tulips would admire his style. They'd all soon be wearing long black capes like his despite the warm weather, and putting on dark, mysterious airs, which the women would adore. The hint of danger, the slight scent of smoke, his unspoken past—and his wealth—would make him an irresistible challenge for the women of the so-called polite world. They would be less than polite in their pursuit, married or not.

Maybe she better go to the celebration, Genie told herself.

She owed him the protection of her presence. Besides, the earl had not been brought up in English society and might not know all of its ways. That was what he'd asked of her, wasn't it, her help in finding his place? His manners appeared perfect, now that he'd stopped eating with his fingers, courtly even, but what if he said something bizarre, like his muttering now about why anyone would keep a memento mori, a reminder of death. The hourglasses were only timing devices, for goodness' sake, and he had asked for them.

Genie decided she ought to go with him, to stop him, if she could, from advertising his oddities. Heavens, what if he decided to take his pet crow, or put out all the fires in Carlton House? Or start one.

"Very well, I will go."

"Thank you," he said, his rare smile returning.

Genie held up her hand. "But I will not dance. That would be too outrageous a flouting of the conventions."

"How disappointing. I was looking forward to a real dance with my wife."

Genie thought she might have liked that, too, despite her concerns, which was worrying in itself. Insanity must be contagious, like a putrid sore throat. Feeling any kind of attraction to Lord Ardeth now was bound to be more painful later.

"Prinny is known to adore crowds," she told him, "so I doubt there will be room for dancing anyway. Besides, I hear he keeps his rooms too warm for any strenuous activity such as dancing. Ladies have been known to swoon from the heat."

"Then I will be comfortable there. I do not understand this English penchant for cold, damp rooms and unlit fires."

"It is summertime."

"So what?"

Genie could not imagine Ardeth being uncomfortable anywhere. Wherever he was, he was in charge. Like now, when he was planning a dancing party of their own.

"We can hire an orchestra, serve champagne punch and those lobster patties that seem to be in fashion, and festoon the ballroom with silk swags and flowers."

"Appearing in public is in poor enough taste as is. Entertaining on such a large scale so soon after my husb— that is, after Elgin's death would be highly improper. No one would come anyway."

"Good. I did not mean for us to invite anyone else to our ball but the two of us. Would you like that?"

"What, hold a grand fete for you and me?"

"You in your prettiest gown, me trying to remember the steps. The musicians behind a screen so they cannot see my blunders or stare at my beautiful wife."

"Who is breeding, in case you have forgotten."

"And more beautiful for it."

She *tsk*ed at him, rather than let him see her pleasure in his compliments. "A private ball would be a silly waste." And the most romantic thing she had ever imagined. She could almost feel his arms about her, drifting to the music, with the sweet scent of roses in the air and no one to spout propriety. Then they could go upstairs— when he'd remember his oath of abstinence. "A total waste. Surely you have better things to do with your time and money."

He turned six of the hourglasses upside down, one after the other, to let the sands run out. "I am not sure anymore."

"Well, I am. I have much to do before the prince's reception. For one thing, I cannot go until I pay a duty call I have been putting off."

"I did not take you for a shirker or a coward."

"Sometimes avoiding unpleasantness is easier than facing it head-on. I owe my former mother-in-law the courtesy of a visit before I enter society. She never liked me, and she will disapprove even more of my hasty marriage, with good cause."

"You did what you had to do to survive."

"She would prefer that I had perished rather than cause another scandal, and will certainly tell me so. I brought home some things of Elgin's she might like to have, though, his sword and pistol, a pocket watch that might have been a gift from his father."

"Do you think she'd believe Macklin owned one of these hourglasses? You could tuck it in with his scabbard."

Genie ignored his efforts at lightening her mood. "I was hoping she would not be in town, but I had one of the footmen make inquiries." She sighed. "Lady Cormack is here, likely well aware of my return to England."

"You could send the trappings."

"Now that would be cowardly. Elgin's mother deserves an explanation of our marriage. The nature of his death will be harder to explain."

"Being run through by a jealous husband on the eve of battle? No mother wants to hear that. Lie."

"You are telling me to lie? You, who believes honor is everything?"

"Kindness is something, too."

She nodded. "I will ask if I might call on her tomorrow."

It was Ardeth's turn to cluck his tongue. "She is, what, a dowager baroness? When are you going to realize your place in this world? You are a countess, Lady Ardeth. If you wish to visit, you do. Otherwise, you ask her to call on you."

"That would be rude and arrogant."

"But effective. How can she berate you in your own home, with your new husband at your side? That would be ruder still."

"I thank you for the offer to stand beside me, but this is my duty. There is no need for both of us to suffer the lady's rancor."

He smiled, but without humor. "Do you really think I would let some nasty old beldam upset you?"

Heavens, with that look he might turn the woman into a pillar of salt, or have her be struck by lightning. "I have to handle this on my own."

"No, you truly do not. You are married now."

She was married before, and managed everything from finding rooms to fending off inebriated young officers who thought she was Elgin's sister and thus fair game.

Genie compromised. She sent her former mother-in-law a note inviting the older woman for tea tomorrow, if it was convenient, or to name a time for Genie to call on her if not. She was half hoping Lady Cormack would not reply at all.

Or that her personal prestidigitator could make the baroness disappear altogether.

CHAPTER EIGHT

Lady Cormack arrived promptly that afternoon. She arrived so promptly that Genie was not ready. She directed her maid to tell the footman to ask the butler to show her mother-in-law into the best parlor. That was how things were done in the great houses of Mayfair, instead of yelling down the stairwell, which would have been easier but quite common. The toplofty butler would have been shocked.

Genie was being rude anyway, she knew, keeping the woman waiting, but there was no help for it. She had been sick to her stomach, and still had butterflies after Ardeth's merry waltz. Then she wanted to dress perfectly, not like the frightened girl in a hand-me-down gown at her wedding.

She wore black. All of her new clothes were in dark colors. At least no one could say she was dressing like a fast woman, no matter how fast her remarriage had occurred. She wore her pearls as her only ornament other than the gold wedding band, with her braided hair tucked neatly under a black lace cap, except for a few red-gold strands allowed to curl down her shoulder. The gown itself was stylish without being dashing. The high waist concealed enough; the neckline revealed enough. She wore a black lace fichu at the low collar, again for propriety, and a fringed black shawl, because the short puffed sleeves left her feeling too undressed, too vulnerable to criticism, no matter their modishness.

Genie might have worn black, but Lady Cormack wore Black. From head to toe, fingertip to fat fingertip, she was a wide, walking coal heap with lumps to match. Her gown was high-necked and long-sleeved. Her gloves were black lace; her necklace was black jet beads. The only items not black on the woman were her hair, an improbable blond for her age, and her flabby cheeks, probably rosy from her weight and her wait. When Genie arrived, she had been eating bonbons, while inspecting the furnishings of the room and fuming.

She had grown a great deal stouter since the ill-fated wedding, and her face was more lined, with most of the lines pointing downward from constant frowning. On her head she wore a large black ruched bonnet trimmed in black ribbon streamers and black lace, with a knot of feathers at one side. Black feathers, they were. Shiny black feathers.

"Cawk!"

Just as Lady Cormack was about to greet Genie with a blustering scold, preliminary to the blistering one she had in mind, Olive swooped down from the drapery rod, shrieking.

"Mine," the bird cawed as he attacked the bonnet. "Mine!"

Genie did not know whether the crow was claiming
the feathers or defending his territory from what he per-
ceived as another crow.

"No," Genie shouted over the din, for Lady Cormack
was screaming as loudly as the bird, flapping her hands
in the air while Olive kept flapping his wings.

"Stop!" Genie shouted again. Neither one listened to
her. Olive kept pecking at the bonnet, pulling out feathers—along with lace and ribbons and a few blond hairs
with gray-brown roots. As furiously as the woman waved
her arms, batting at the bird, Olive kept diving and
shrilling in dismay.

"Mine!"

Maybe Olive thought Lady Cormack had killed one of
his friends.

"No! The feathers are not yours! And stop yelling."
The last was directed to the crow and Lady Cormack and
whoever else was listening, like the maid she could hear
screaming in the outer hallway. The maid was the only
one whose shouts might have done any good by fetching
help.

Genie did not want to hurt the earl's pet by swatting
him away, but neither did she want her mother-in-law
slashed by that clacking bill or raked by the grasping
talons or snatched bald. So she whipped off her shawl and
tried to throw it over Olive. She missed and tipped over a
vase that was likely worth enough to found another orphanage. She stepped over the broken bits, water, and
flowers, and tried again. This time she smashed a dish of
comfits to the floor. Her final try managed to knock the
bonnet off Lady Cormack's head. The shawl stayed
wrapped around the woman's face; the hat sailed across
the room, Olive in hawklike pursuit.

The bird swooped on the bonnet, cawing victory through a beak full of feathers. Then Genie's words finally penetrated his gamy gremlin brain, for the crow cocked his head and looked at her. "Not mine?"

"No. Not even close. You have all yours. And these never came from one of your brethren. Look." She picked up a feather from the floor—where Lady Cormack was now thrashing, trapped in the shawl. "See? The stem is white. These were pigeon feathers or ducks'. They were dyed."

"Dead?"

"Of course they were dead, but dyed black."

"Ar's?"

"No, not ours, either."

Olive turned his head from side to side to see from both eyes. "Ar lady?"

"No, not mine, either. And that should be my lady, not our lady. My lady."

Olive bobbed his head. "Mine."

"Silly bird, were you protecting me?"

Olive cooed softly. He might be admitting his error, or he might be choking on a bit of lace. Lady Cormack was choking on her own anger, sputtering and swatting at the shawl, trying to heave her hefty self off the floor. She slapped Genie's hand away when she came to offer assistance.

"That abominable creature is yours?" she wheezed.

Genie hated to claim the wretch, but she said, "It is ours, yes."

"Ar's," Olive said. "Alive."

"That's his name. Olive."

The maid from the hall finally had the courage to come in now that the shouting had stopped. She looked around and started weeping. She'd be the one to have to clean up the mess.

The housekeeper rushed in, saw a baroness on her back, a bird on a bonnet, a blubbering maid in the corner—and her mistress battling laughter. She promptly resigned. This was not what she was accustomed to.

The stately butler wheeled in the tea cart. He noted the shards of priceless pottery, the pieces of candy, the flower petals, and a peeress, all on the floor. Then he looked at his scandal-prone mistress, curled his lip, and wheeled the tea cart out again. His resignation would also be tendered before dinner. At least Genie could hire her own people now.

When Marie came in to see what the commotion was about, Genie said, "Take this upstairs and repair it." She tried to hand over Lady Cormack's bonnet.

"Why? It is ugly."

Lady Cormack gasped. So did Genie. Olive was too busy eating one of the bonbons to notice.

"Just do it!"

Lady Cormack started beating her fists and her feet on the floor. "I have never seen such a ramshackle household. I have never seen such unruly servants." Her voice trailed away as she said, "I have never seen . . ."

Genie's thoughts finished the sentence: Such a handsome, dignified, extraordinary gentleman.

Lord Ardeth had entered the parlor. He looked at Genie first to make certain she was unharmed, then whispered something to the maid, who jumped up and ran out. Before Genie could ask what he'd said—What if he threatened to grow warts on her nose? The story would be all over London by dinnertime—Ardeth raised Lady Cormack from the floor. Impossibly, he lifted her as if she were as light as one of the ruined feathers, and gently deposited her on the sofa. Implausibly, he'd kicked the broken china and fallen sweets under a chair at the same time. Then he bowed, with a cavalier's flourish.

"Welcome to my home, my lady. Coryn Ardsley, Earl of Ardeth, at your service. I apologize for any inconvenience. Perhaps some sherry?"

Her mouth was hanging open. "Well, I never."

"I seldom do myself, but the occasion seems to merit something stronger than tea. Do you not agree, madam?"

Genie was already pouring a decanter of brandy out into waiting glasses on a side table. To the devil with sherry, she thought, or tea. Ardeth took two glasses from her and handed one to Lady Cormack, again in a courtly manner that kept her speechless. He took a sip of his, gracefully sidestepped the puddle on the floor, and used his free hand to open the window. Then he sent a dangerous, dagger look at the crow.

"No wine?"

"No whining, no cawing, no making excuses. Go, or else."

For all his lack of sense, Olive knew enough to fly as fast as he could. Genie thought she heard a loud "Whew" as the crow headed for the rooftop, then his name.

Fortified, Lady Cormack recalled her outrage and reclaimed her tongue. "What was that abomination, and why was it in a gentleman's home?"

Ardeth said, "It is a spawn of Hell, sent to bedevil me."

"Poppycock," Lady Cormack said with a snort.

So much for the truth. Ardeth glanced at Genie over the top of his glass and shrugged. She wanted to handle the situation herself, his look seemed to be saying. So she could handle it.

"It is a rare bird," Genie said. "A very rare talking bird that Lord Ardeth brought back from . . . from the Indies."

"It didn't look like any parrot I've ever heard tell of."

"Oh, Olive is much rarer than that."

The baroness looked at the earl. "And he don't look tanned."

Genie replied, "They traveled by way of the Orient."

Since Lady Cormack had no idea that the Indies and the Orient were at opposite ends of the earth, she dropped that line of questioning. "They say he's rich as Croesus. Is it true?"

Ardeth merely bowed again. Genie refused to answer such an impertinent query.

"And that's why you married him without even waiting for my boy to be cold in the ground."

"That was not why," both Genie and Ardeth answered at once.

The maid came in at that moment, pushing the tea cart. She curtsied to the earl, smiled at Genie, and offered Lady Cormack a platter of small sandwiches, pastries, and biscuits before leaving the room.

While her mother-in-law was making her selection—several selections—Genie whispered to Ardeth, "What did you say to her?"

"Merely that I'd mention her name to that new footman if she behaved."

Genie was relieved, until he added with a wink, as if he was reading her mind again, "Or else I'll make her a love potion."

With a watercress sandwich in one hand, a lemon tart in the other, and half a slice of poppy seed cake in her mouth, Lady Cormack was ready to go on the attack.

"My poor little lamb. How could you shame our family name that way? And him."

Genie tried to stay calm and not lose her temper. After all, the woman had suffered a loss, even if she seemed to care more about her social standing than about her son. "I had no choice but to accept his lordship's generous offer. Please understand, I had no way to live, no funds, nowhere to go." When Lady Cormack simply crammed another bite of poppy seed cake into her mouth, Genie asked, "Would you have taken me in?"

Lady Cormack must have swallowed a seed wrong. She coughed.

"You never replied when I wrote you from Portugal, in desperation."

Now the dowager was turning purple. Genie handed Ardeth a cup of tea to bring her.

After a gulp and a demand for more sugar, which did not sweeten her tongue, Lady Cormack said, "You abandoned him, shameless adventuress that you are! Why should I consider you part of my family?"

Genie was shaking her head. "You know that is not the case. After we returned from the posting to Canada, Elgin abandoned me in Portugal when the first peace was declared. I wrote to you several times when he went alone to Vienna for the Peace Congress. If I had not found a position with a wealthy Portuguese family, teaching English to their sons and drawing to their daughters, I would have starved. You did not answer. For four years of our marriage, you did not once write."

Ardeth was looking furious. "You never said the dastard did that."

"There was no need to bring out all the skeletons from the closet."

No, Ardeth thought, skeletons did not like being disturbed.

"He was your husband," Lady Cormack insisted. "It was his right to leave you where you would be safe, instead of carrying you off to some heathenish country."

"Was it his right to go on to Brussels without me, still claiming to be a bachelor?"

Steam was coming from the tea, and from Ardeth, Genie swore. She quickly added, "One of the army wives who had befriended me sent a message that they were all going to the Netherlands. My employers graciously arranged for me to follow. I had no way of knowing Bonaparte was going to raise his army again and confront the allies there. I simply wanted Elgin to acknowledge our marriage, to make provision for me. He promised to, after the battle, but he never did."

Ardeth was up and pacing, reminding Genie of a hungry black panther she'd seen once at the Royal Menagerie. "I am sorry for his death," she told Elgin's mother, "and sorry I had no time to pay respect to his memory. But I had no choice. No one offered to help me except Lord Ardeth. Thank heaven for him."

She might thank Hell, instead. The earl had had enough. "Her rightful protectors had deserted Mrs. Macklin: her husband, her family, and you, it appears." He glared at Lady Cormack, who tried to shrink in her chair. "It was my duty as a gentleman to see your daughter-in-law to safety. Marriage was the easiest and quickest way."

"They say she is with child." The baroness tried to squint at the front of Genie's gown. "With my grandchild."

Genie said nothing.

"If you had told me that, Imogene, I would have sent funds. The barony needs a second heir. The boy your sister birthed is sick and puny. They doubt he'll live to succeed, and she is lax in producing another."

"I am sorry. About the boy's health, that is. I never knew any of that. My sister and I are not in communication. She returned my pleas for assistance unopened."

Lady Cormack ignored the fact that she had actually read the letters—sniveling rubbish, she'd considered Genie's difficulties, no more than the hoyden deserved—then ignored them. She was none too fond of her other daughter-in-law, either, and sorely aggravated by the heir's infirmity. She, herself, had produced two healthy sons for her late husband, and now she was about to see it all go for naught. "Bad lungs, the physicians say. There have never been weak lungs in the Macklin family or my own," she insisted, blaming Genie and her sister for the boy's lack of vigor. "Roger should have married the Duke of Eldert's gal. Good breeding there, *her* sister has five boys already."

She held her teacup out for more, then pointed to the brandy decanter, for more of that, too. "So another boy would be welcome. I could raise him up fit for the barony."

Genie was desperate. She could not let this fat female claim her child. "He—if it is indeed a boy—is not your grandson," she blurted without thinking.

Lord Ardeth casually held his fob watch up, as though he had somewhere better to go. "I claim the boy as mine."

Lady Cormack gasped. So did Genie. The dowager spoke first. "Ha. The child cannot be yours. They say you appeared after the battle, just days before your wedding."

Before Genie could say she'd meant that she would

never give up the child, not that it was fathered by another, Ardeth said, "'Sooth, I was always around."

Lady Cormack struggled to her feet, trailing crumbs. She pointed one sausage-shaped finger at Genie and shouted, "You were unfaithful to my son, you Jezebel! How dare you ask for money! How dare you show your face in polite society! I will tell everyone of your whoring with this . . . this interloper. No one knows his people, or where he got his gold. Dealing with the Devil, I'd wager."

"You'd win," Ardeth murmured. Louder, he said, "Here is an even surer bet: If you speak thusly of my wife, then I shall tell everyone of your son's death."

"No," Genie cried. "We agreed."

Lady Cormack sank back onto the sofa, needing another sip of the fortified tea. "What calumny is this, trying to ruin my son's reputation as a hero?"

"As you'd ruin my lady wife's as a gentlewoman." Somehow it was important for Ardeth to see Genie accepted, or all of his sacrifice—his freedom, his blood heir—would be in vain. He had sworn to make her life better, and his own future depended on his keeping his vows. No matter what happened to him, he needed her to carry on his plans when he was gone. Without society's nod, she would stay in the house or stay isolated at Ardsley Keep, her light dimmed by humiliation. Not Genie, not his wife. "She is above reproach."

"She is below decency! Your precious countess trapped my poor boy into indiscretion. Or did she tell you some taradiddle about that, too?"

"She told me of the circumstances surrounding her betrothal, yes."

"Did she tell you she stole Elgin out from under her own sister's nose?"

"She told me of being sent outside to find her sister's lost reticule, wearing Miss Lorraine Hopewell's distinctive shawl against the night, at that same sister's insistence. Did you ever listen to Miss Imogene Hopewell's side of the story?"

"What for? The deed was done. They were seen by everyone, thanks to her screams to draw attention."

"Not screams for help?"

"Pish-tosh. Past history." Lady Cormack tried to squeeze out a tear. "Now he's dead, my poor brave boy, because of her."

"My wife was not the one who sent Macklin to the army. I believe you and your late husband were responsible for that."

"We thought it best to get the dirty linen out of sight."

"No. It is best to wash dirty linen clean. Instead, your son rolled in the muck. He was never a proper husband to a young, innocent girl. He left her in the middle of a war!"

"My son was a hero," she persisted. "He died saving his men!"

"He died before the battle, leaving his men with no officer to lead them but a raw recruit."

"Ardeth, do not," Genie begged.

"She never listened to you or your pleas. She deserves to hear the truth for once." He turned back to the baroness, whose fat jowls were quivering in outrage. "Your son's men were slaughtered."

"That is a lie!"

"Do you want to speak to the woman whose bed he was in when her officer husband found them? That hothead died in the battle, at least, so the army was spared a murder trial and a court-martial."

"Another lie. I would have heard of such goings-on."

"I ensured that no one would. I spoke to the general, and I found the woman, who was left as destitute as Mrs. Macklin."

"Then you should have married that light-skirt."

"I was already promised to Imogene, who needed me more. But I do have that widow's deposition, and I paid for her return home, and her silence. She was nothing but a wanton, yes, but your son's wife was a real lady."

"If she never played Elgin false, then the child is a Macklin and belongs with us."

"Not by law. I consulted the best barrister in London. If an infant is born to my legal wife, and I do not renounce him, he is mine."

"Others know," Genie reminded him. He'd been sure his relatives would have heard, and would challenge any claims to Ardeth's title and estate.

"They will not speak of it."

Genie wondered how he was so confident, but she would not disagree with him in front of Lady Cormack. "The army tried to hush the scandal, and my sudden marriage gave everyone something else to replace that gossip, so they could ignore the facts. And so many men died then."

The baroness started to blubber in earnest. "You and your sister ruined both my sons. My Roger could have wed a rich wife with better breeding. My Elgin is gone."

Ardeth handed over a monogrammed handkerchief. "Cry pax, madam. I am sorry for your loss. And sorrier for the manner. I would hope the new baron and his bride have reconciled themselves to the match and find happiness with each other and their son. But I will not permit my wife's future to be destroyed. Nor my son's."

Genie looked at him with relief and wonder. He was really going to claim the boy. The child, that is, for she might still have a daughter. Her reputation was still blown to smithereens—she'd wedded less than a week after the child's father died, or had an affair with another man before that. They would discuss it later. For now, the babe was safe from Macklin clutches.

Lady Cormack could see that she had lost. She could not castigate the female while Ardeth was present, nor could she raise the next baron. Botheration, she could not even besmirch the harlot's name among her own friends. She did not doubt for a minute Ardeth's threat to expose Elgin's little contretemps. That would be a worse reflection on the family name and on Roger, who was seeking a cabinet post.

She stood again, this time headed for the door. She could not resist a parting shot, however: "You are a fallen woman either way, Countess." She spoke the title with a sneer. "No one will associate with you. You will never be accepted among polite society."

"But I never wished to be," Genie said. "I expect to live quietly at my husband's country property right after the prince's reception for the foreign dignitaries."

The last tea cake must have gone rancid, for Lady Cormack felt a pain in her gut. "The prince's?"

"Yes, we were invited. Shall I see you there?"

Not unless Lady Cormack could bribe or browbeat a coveted invitation out of someone.

"I shall not dance, of course," Genie went on, seeing her former mother-in-law's pained look.

"But she will be greeted with respect," Ardeth said, a statement and a warning. Then he excused himself a moment and came back with an hourglass in his hand.

"Please accept this as a token of our esteem," he said as he escorted the woman from the room. "And a reminder that life passes too quickly to be spent in regret and bitterness."

Lady Cormack clutched the elaborate gold and jeweled device to her greedy breast. "Oh, I agree."

And Genie agreed that was the perfect way of getting rid of the most garish, tasteless hourglass in the collection.

CHAPTER NINE

Dragon slaying—or dowager flaying—was fun, Ardeth decided. In fact, being alive was generally far more amusing than being Death. Other than the occasional grave joke, there'd been nothing to laugh about in his past existence. He'd thought this time, for his brief six months, he'd have to be equally as grim—see? He'd just made a Reaper pun. He'd set out to be moral, honorable, conscientious about being good to atone for being so bad. Perhaps, just perhaps, there was more to this humanity business than he remembered. Like now, with a sumptuous meal at his own table, warm candlelight gleaming off the silver utensils he remembered to use, and his wife's red hair, how could a man not feel lighter, freer, unbowed by bygone sorrows and worrisome tomorrows? He touched his heart and felt something stir. Maybe he was a little closer to his goal. Maybe he was just hungry.

With no butler, Ardeth had a footman set the platters on the table. He and Lady Ardeth would help themselves in privacy. Tonight would be the first time he and Genie had been alone in days, or taken a meal together. She had eaten nothing but dry toast in her bedroom in the mornings, and he had been gone on business for most of the days. Tonight's food was delicious, the finest he had tasted in centuries. He savored every swallow of sea turtle soup, prawns in oyster sauce, eel in aspic, and asparagus in lobster.

Genie's appetite was quite gone, her digestion too uncertain, especially after the tea with her former mother-in-law. The only reason she had come down to dinner was that she and the earl had a great deal to discuss that night.

She wanted to talk about the prince's coming fete, and how she would be a blight on Ardeth's enjoyment.

Ardeth was glad the woman was not so afraid of him that she was fearful of arguing, but the meal would have been far more pleasant, he decided, without their going over the same rough ground. To think that just a few weeks ago he could have touched her lips and silenced her, touched her head and have her forget ever seeing him. He would not, if he still could, for that would be an insult to her intelligence and independence. Then again, that way he could eat his meal in peace.

"Come, my lady, do not ruin the dinner with fretting. Have a bit of this excellent macaroni dish. I do not remember any finer." He did not remember any, period. Did they have tomatoes in his lifetime?

She would not take the plate, or the bait. "You've seen my own family's attitude. Others will be even less forgiving."

Ardeth reluctantly set his fork aside. "I still feel that self-interest will win out over snobbery. And we agreed, a prince's invitation is not to be sneered at. You will be formally presented as my wife, whether anyone likes it or not. You will just have to see."

"See? Are you blind? Our own housekeeper disapproved of me!"

He looked longingly at the platter of beef and Yorkshire pudding, untouched at Genie's end of the table. "Then I am doubly glad she is gone."

"But—"

"Enough, madam. We are sounding like an old married couple."

"Which we are not. We are barely married, by anyone's estimation."

He did not want to discuss that, either. The beef and Yorkshire pudding were not half as tempting as his wife in black silk, the tops of her snowy breasts showing over the low neck of the gown. Her hair was gathered at the back of her head tonight, with long reddish curls left to brush forward on her shoulders.

Gentlemen did not drool, he reminded himself, reaching for his napkin. He tried to get her to discuss who else would be at the fete, and precisely what constituted a formal presentation to royalty. "Remember, I do not know your world as well as I should. I need your assistance."

"You speak as if I was ever at court. A squire's daughter does not make her come-out at the queen's drawing room. I cannot help you. You have to understand that."

He understood fear. He'd seen it often enough. "You will help by being at my side. Furthermore, once you are acknowledged by the prince, my own relatives cannot show you disrespect when we travel to Ardsley Keep."

"I did not know you had family living there."

He'd prefer not to talk about that, either. He helped himself to a serving of stewed vegetables, not his first choice, but close at hand. The vegetables were like glue, from sitting. He warmed them a bit with a touch to see if that would help.

Genie ignored the steam suddenly rising from the bowl her husband held. "Are there many? How are they connected?" she persisted.

"Enough, and distantly. They are more caretakers and hangers-on than true family."

"Will they resent my child if it is a boy and you claim him, as you told Lady Cormack?"

He decided he liked potatoes better than carrots. He might like dining alone better, too, but a knight could not be rude to a lady. "I am not certain of their expectations at this point. Certainly they were aware of my existence and that I might have an heir of my own. We shall just have to wait and see about that, too. Do you want me to inquire about hiring a new butler or do you want to handle it?"

Genie had shredded her roll and moved the peas around on her plate to build a small green mountain. He could hire Beelzebub himself to be butler for all she cared. He'd told Lady Cormack that if he declared the babe his, the child would be considered legally his. The problem was, he'd also told Genie that he might not be around in six months, to make that declaration. The other problem was that he might not be around at all. How could she eat? "I would like a further explanation."

"I would like a serving of syllabub. Would you pass the platter?"

Exasperated, Genie got up and brought the dish to his side. "I shall leave you to your syllabub, then your port and cigars."

"I do not smoke cigars."

"A pipe, then."

"No."

She wrinkled her nose. "I thought I smelled smoke about your clothes."

Ardeth decided he'd been so used to the stench of Hellfire that he could not smell it on his person anymore. "I must have been standing too close to the fire. Getting warm, you know."

The house was so hot, even with all the windows open, that Genie had forgone a shawl. "You might need a better valet to air your clothes."

His clothes were all new. "Oh, the smell is fading with this warmer weather and my acclimation." As were his skills to influence people. Ardeth had been experimenting, where it would cause no harm, of course. That was why all of his favorite dishes were on the table at once. Cook was very susceptible. The departing butler was not, or the prig's wig would have caught fire. A bit of steam on the vegetables was all Ardeth could manage.

In a way the earl felt more like a mortal, that his plan was working; in another way he felt the waning of his talents as a frightening loss of power, of his identity. That was what he wanted, though, wasn't it?

That was why he needed Genie to come to the peace celebration, while he could still make sure she would be treated well, and she could make sure he did not douse any fires. Thinking she would be easier to convince on his own, without a speck of spectral doing, he rose from the table, too, to follow her out. A willing wife was more desirable than dessert.

"What do ladies do," he asked, "while the menfolk are left behind to indulge?" He already knew the men behaved like beasts in the field. It was ever thus.

"They gossip, or sit with their sewing, play at the pianoforte or sing—"

"Ah, music. Do you have a good voice?"

Genie laughed. "Barely passable. Do you?"

Ardeth had no idea. When had he occasion to sing? He'd heard the best—nothing could surpass the Heavenly Choir—but thought he might enjoy Genie's singing as he followed her to the music room. He already enjoyed watching her rounded bottom sway and the sound of the silk gown swishing as she moved.

She sat and played a few simple pieces at the pianoforte before beginning a country ballad she could sing.

Ardeth sat back and closed his eyes in contentment. How domestic, he thought, how simple, how lovely. How much she sounded like the crow.

Genie spent the next few days trying to hire new senior staff. If there was a guidebook on how to be a proper lady, she was positive, selecting perfect servants must rate a chapter for itself. She was the countess; it was her job to see that the household ran smoothly. Without that guidebook, however, she had no idea how to go on.

She had never hired anybody in her life. What few servants her parents had at the manor were chosen by her mother. During her marriage, Elgin's batman served as man-of-all-work, including the cooking. They had not been able to afford a maid, so Genie had taken care of her own needs and the cleaning. When she taught the Portuguese grandee's children, she was little better than a servant herself. Now she was expected—no, she expected it of herself—to produce reliable, honest, experienced staff. Her husband was busy inspecting sites for orphanages and veterans' hospitals, forming alliances for reforms in Parliament, and studying where the most improvement could be made in most people's lives. He seemed to enjoy walking the streets days and nights, seeing how all classes lived. Despite his offer, Genie would not bother him with nonsense that a real lady could accomplish blindfolded.

By the second day she wondered if those duchesses and viscountesses actually did don blinders and pick a name out of a hat. The task seemed impossible.

Campbell found a highly recommended placement agency, which sent scores of applicants for the two positions. Word of mouth brought scads more. She dutifully interviewed each, realizing that she should have hired a secretary first, to read the references and thin the lines of job seekers. A secretary could help with the hourglasses, too. The dratted things kept multiplying like rabbits, all needing to be cataloged for Ardeth's inspection, then returned, paid for, or shelved.

But she had advertised for a butler and a housekeeper, so Genie felt obliged to continue the interviews. None of the men or women seemed right. Most seemed pitiable, not hirable. She felt sorry for the ancient butlers, hard of hearing, bent over with rheumatics, who had been replaced by younger men. She worried about young men who would not be hired without experience, yet could not gain the experience without positions. Worse were the women who were displaced by the mistress's poor, unpaid relation, or dismissed when the master acted poorly.

Genie knew what it felt like to be out of work and out of money, so she listened. She gave a coin to each unemployed applicant, except the ones who felt themselves superior to her.

There were many of those, too.

Genie did not read the gossip columns in the newspapers. Why should she, when she knew so few people in town? Why should she when her own name might be there? Nor did she listen to rumors trickling from the servants' grapevine through Marie's backstairs cronies. Many of the job seekers must have.

One woman's nostrils flared when she stepped over the threshold of the hourglass room, where Genie was conducting interviews so she could arrange the timepieces between appointments. One would-be housekeeper would be affronted to work for a woman of chancy repute. Another wished to speak only with the master. As for the butlers, one started to inform her of his rules concerning proper conduct, as if she were one of the undermaids, and another told her he would not have come to such a house at all had there been other opportunities. A few smelled of spirits; a few smelled of unwashed bodies. A few could smell smoke and demanded the chimneys be cleaned before they slept in such a fire hazard. One seemed to smell money, and shifted his eyes from gold hourglass to valuable painting to priceless statue.

A few of the more qualified butlers acted as if they were interviewing her. Would the earl be coming back to London during the next parliamentary session? more than one asked. Genie knew they were concerned that if the house sat empty, they would receive no vails from visitors, no bribes from tradesmen. Most wanted to know if they were expected to travel to the—gasp—country with the family. If not, would they be paid their full salary?

Genie devised a winnowing process for possible, passable candidates. She asked the prospective butlers to introduce imaginary callers: a duke, a merchant, a female who would not give her name. Some could not understand the notion of playacting. Others felt such efforts were beneath them. Two announced that anyone without a title was not worth presenting; that would be a footman's job.

Genie felt more qualified to interview prospective housekeepers. After all, she'd had to maintain her own quarters for herself for many years now. Even in her mother's home, she'd had chores. So she knew when a house was clean. She tested the women by asking the formula for beeswax polish, and the best way to remove stains from upholstery. One refused to answer, or to work for a mistress who was going to "interfere." Another found the house too cluttered for her taste, with too many fragile pieces for maidservants to break, which could be laid at the housekeeper's door. Genie still felt guilty over the vase she herself had broken, so could understand the trepidations.

A tall, thin woman thought the hourglass collection was ridiculous and possibly blasphemous, although she did not explain how. A gray-haired matron declared them too hard to keep clean. Add a talking bird, an infant to come, and an earl out to reform the world, and the list of applicants grew shorter.

Marie was no help. She thought Genie ought to hire one of the young handsome chaps as butler—the one who had dimples and broad shoulders. Heavens, Genie'd be having to start a home for unwed housemaids with that one around. Campbell thought one of the women was a good candidate, until Marie caught sight of the pretty female and declared her bachelor fare.

"You do not want to give Monsieur ideas, *chérie*."

Well, she did, but not with a housekeeper. Genie still

needed to hire someone, two someones. She was too busy to organize carpet beating or washday herself, and too ill in the mornings. The footman who'd been promoted to underbutler was not dignified enough for such an eminent gentleman's residence, not when he could barely read the calling cards. Botheration.

The last applicant on the second day was a woman of about forty, forty long, cold winters. She appreciated that the house was kept warm, and admired the artwork and interesting collections. An impoverished lord's spinster daughter, she was seeking a position rather than end her days in the workhouse. Miss Hadley was well-mannered, well-spoken, and well used to gossip after living with a drunk for a father and a madwoman for a mother, both now gone on to a better place, she hoped.

Genie decided she was perfect—for a secretary and companion. Miss Hadley knew how to go on in society and could advise Genie. She had a neat hand, a good head for numbers, and tolerance for the unconventional. As she told her new mistress, growing up with a blind drunk and a bedlamite taught humility and patience. What Genie appreciated most was that Miss Hadley was honest. Her background might be public knowledge, but not to her prospective employer. And how could Genie hold the woman's birth against her, when her own child's parentage was going to be in question?

So Miss Hadley took over the hunt for the senior servants. Genie took a nap.

She did not know how long she slept before hearing a tapping on her door, the one that led to the earl's chambers. She sat up and quickly tidied her hair, feeling a surge of hope at this unexpected visit. Unfortunately, Ardeth seemed more embarrassed than amorous.

"My lord?"

"I'm sorry. I did not know you were asleep." With so much to see, so much to do, he could not imagine wasting an unnecessary hour in bed.

"That's quite all right. I need to get on with my day anyway. Did you require something?"

A lot, with her warm and rosy from sleep, her gown a bit disordered. He never thought he'd need a cold bath, but perhaps soon, if his lady wife made so tempting a picture. He turned his back, studying the painting on the wall instead. Flowers and fruit did not tempt him at all, thank goodness. When he was back in command of his errant urges, he said, "There is a strange woman singing among the hourglasses."

"Oh yes, that is Miss Hadley. She is marvelous and needs a position. I worried that I should consult you first—"

"Nonsense, if you like her, that is your prerogative. I like her voice. And her manner is neither toadying nor cringing."

"Nor haughty. I think she likes me, which is comforting."

Poor puss, Ardeth thought, so very alone and unsure that an upper servant's approval mattered. He had to change that. "Then we have our new housekeeper."

"Oh, Miss Hadley is not to be housekeeper. She is my secretary and companion. You thought I should have one, recall?" Genie went on to explain Miss Hadley's history and qualifications.

"I am doubly delighted. Not only have you found such a wise head to help and advise you, but now I can confess that I hired a couple to be butler and housekeeper."

Genie felt like a failure. Hiring the staff was one of the

few wifely duties Lord Ardeth let her perform, and she had failed. "Oh. How nice."

"On your approval, of course. You see, I went to visit Mrs. Smythe-Gardiner."

"The one whose husband skewered—"

"Yes, that one."

Genie wanted to ask what business the earl had with the Cyprian who seduced Elgin, but she knew a good wife held her tongue even if her heart was broken, along with the vows her husband had made.

Ardeth turned to look at the few bottles on his wife's dressing table. She needed no cosmetics, he thought, but he did like the floral scent she wore. He did not like how she did not trust him. "I'd heard she found a new protector and was leaving London. I wished to make sure that she had funds to get far away."

A large boulder seemed to lift off Genie's chest.

"I found her already gone with her house left empty, her small staff left with no pay. The Randolphs are a pleasant couple who kept the place tidy despite the circumstances. Randolph was properly butlerish, you know, all polite and uppity, until I mentioned our need for staff. I thought the man might kiss me. They have a son, horse-mad he is, but he knows his way around London for running errands and such. I thought that, having borne a child, Mrs. Randolph might be able to assist you with some of your discomfort. They like children, pets, and both country and city living. They would not gossip about their previous employers, and they had not helped themselves to any of the furnishings in lieu of their pay. The pair seems just what we require."

Genie did kiss him. It was a quick, impetuous hug and a smack on the cheek. Both of them jumped back.

Genie spoke first. "I am so sorry. I know you do not wish such familiarity."

"No, no. That was quite, ah, lovely." Lovely, hell. The painting on the wall was lovely. Genie's touch was luminous. When had anyone, ever, spontaneously embraced him? It was all he could do not to catch her to him, to feel her so close again. He tried to make light of the shattering impact such a small gesture had made on his equilibrium. "I must remember to bring home servants in the future. I thought to fetch flowers, but I can tell that you are happier with Mr. and Mrs. Randolph."

She was, and not simply because he had considered her needs. Besides having the chore completed so satisfactorily, she was relieved Ardeth had not gone to that wayward widow for dalliance. More, he had not rebuffed her own sudden show of affection, had not gone stiff and cold. Now she saw a glimmer of hope that they might have a real marriage one day . . . or one night.

That very night, in fact.

Genie was almost asleep when she heard the tapping again. She sat up and lit a candle, although her excitement might have brightened the room. How wonderful and scary and stirring at the same time—she'd shown her willingness and he'd responded!

She was wearing another filmy nightgown and thought about donning the matching robe, then thought better of it. She hurried to open the connecting door. No one was there. The chamber on the other side was dark and empty, like her hopes.

The tapping came again. Genie went to the window, which was open a bare inch, against the earlier rain and dampness. *Tap. Tap.*

"Olive?" She pulled up the window.

" 'Awk!" The bird sounded as if his throat was sore. He was wet and bedraggled, missing a feather or two, and trembling. " 'Awk."

"Where have you been, silly bird? I bet you haven't eaten in days. Heaven knows if you even know how to find food on your own." She fed him pieces of the biscuits left at her night table to help settle her stomach. "You know Lord Ardeth never meant to toss you out."

When she smoothed the dark feathers after drying him with a handkerchief, Genie found a gash in one of his wings. "Good grief. You've been in a fight?"

" 'Awk!"

"You mean hawk? A Cockney hawk? You poor ninny. You should not be out with those devils."

Olive bobbed his head. She was right. Better the devil you knew.

Genie felt foolish talking to the crow, but he seemed calmer from hearing her voice. "No, you should have come to me right away if the master was angry. Remember, mine?"

She thought the bird muttered, "Mine till death do us part," but a crow—no matter how much a mimic—had neither the intelligence nor the vocabulary for such complicated notions or phrases. "You could not have said that."

She was right. What he'd said, looking toward that closed connecting door, was "Mine till Death does his part."

CHAPTER TEN

The Randolphs arrived early the next morning, bags and baggage, son and old dog.

"Oh, did I neglect to mention they had a little bitch?" Ardeth asked after making the introductions.

Genie liked the Randolphs. They seemed eager to please, grateful for their new position, happy in the rooms assigned to them, and very close-knit. Servants had little enough security, and the couple had been left with no back wages, no pensions, and no letters of recommendation. Still, they appreciated that they had each other. Genie envied them that.

After helping with the bags, young Sean Randolph was sent off on his way to school, despite his claim that since he already knew his letters and numbers, he should work in the stables. As Genie took Mrs. Randolph on a tour of the house, the small, shaggy dog trundled along after them.

"Do not think she'll be underfoot, ma'am. She's fat and lazy and only likes her meals, her ears scratched, and a bit of sun for her naps. Our old Helen will sleep at the foot of the boy's bed, as usual."

Genie did not mind. Olive did. "Hellhound! Hellhound!" The gremlin remembered the fierce demon dogs and set up such a raucous noise that half the pigeons in London took flight.

Mrs. Randolph put her hands over her ears, and that same watering pot of a maid Susan started to weep again.

Ardeth hurried back from showing Mr. Randolph the wine cellar, prepared to defend his dependents from those slavering, snarling beasts. Helen was snoring.

The earl took the bird on his arm and looked him in the eye, one obsidian stare to another. "Do you wish to go back there?" He did not mean the wine cellar.

That sharp bill snapped shut with a click.

"The dog stays. You will be friends."

"Fiends?"

"Friends. Understand?"

"I—aye."

While the Randolphs settled in, Olive settled who was in charge. The crow learned to imitate Mr. Randolph's voice, making the poor dog sit, stay, and come, just for the devilish fun of it. After all, he was a gremlin at heart. He also taught the dog to share her food—or get pecked in the rump. And when Olive was weary, he rode on the old dog's wide back, patrolling the back garden against intruders and hawks, now that he had a protector.

Soon the house was cleaner, quieter, more organized—and frantic as everyone helped Genie prepare for the prince's rout. They all seemed to understand the importance of the countess's first public outing. They wanted to please their sweet new mistress and, more, their new master. One of his rare smiles or a word of praise made the work go faster, the load lighter. What made Lord Ardeth happy would make them all happy, it seemed. He had that knack, without trying, Genie thought. Heaven knew she wanted to please him, too.

Miss Hadley and Marie held endless discussions of gowns and hairstyles and accessories, almost ignoring Genie except for the hours spent teaching her court manners. Miss Hadley knew precisely how low Genie ought to curtsy to royalty and made certain Genie knew it, too, and how to rise up again without falling over.

Her spirits were already low enough. She had a fine husband—eccentric and often intimidating but kind, and not too obviously attics-to-let. At least none of the others seemed to notice that he was demented, or else they thought all noblemen spoke to ghosts . . . in several ancient languages. The magic tricks she ignored altogether.

No matter, Ardeth was her husband, and Genie was going to disappoint him. He was never going to desire her as a wife, she supposed, because he never came to her door again, or took meals with her. Now he'd see that she was unacceptable to polite society, which he did seem to desire. He'd realize what a bad bargain he'd made. Oh, he now had a well-run household, thanks to women far more experienced than she, but that was all. Genie had not been able to find his hourglass, although she scoured pawnshops young Sean knew of, in hopes that someone had found it and sold it for money. None of the stores had anything like the small brooch Ardeth had described. She could not even do that for him.

Worst of all, she could never be the lady he deserved. If she did not fall on her arse, she was liable to cast up her accounts on the prince's shoes.

Miss Hadley made her keep practicing her bows, and

Mrs. Randolph knew just the peppermint drops to settle her stomach. Sean offered his lucky rabbit foot, Olive brought her a pearl, Marie stayed up nights sewing instead of visiting Campbell over the stables, and a frustrated Campbell polished the carriage to a fare-thee-well, lest the countess's skirts get soiled. Even the weepy maid Susan did her share, questioning her new beau, the footman next door. She found out that *his* employers were invited for somewhat later than the earl and his countess, after their private audience. That information was as good as a jail sentence to Genie, who dropped another of Ardeth's Chinese dynasty vases from suddenly numb fingers. Susan started crying.

Meanwhile, Mr. Randolph visited the local pub to glean the guest list, so Lord Ardeth could be prepared. Soon the butler knew which general favored pensions for the veterans, which viscount owned collapsing coal mines he might be willing to sell. That information was as good as gold, the earl had said, so his agents could continue his work when he was gone. Randolph assumed his lordship meant gone to his country seat for the birth of his child. Ardeth meant Gone.

The servants feared livelihoods depended on that night. Ardeth feared lives did.

It was of paramount importance that he impress the aristocrats as one of them, so no one would ask any questions later. This was his chance to make a difference, to prove his worth. Damn, he was blessed merely to have the chance. Sometimes he felt like pricking himself, just to see the blood.

Genie had to take her place, too. When she took up life at Ardsley Keep, she would be the highest-ranking lady in the neighborhood, so the local society would have to accept her. He intended to see that Londoners had as little choice, no matter what tricks of manipulation he had to employ. He'd set the cat among the pigeons if he had to, or the crow among the prigs. See how blue their blood ran with a gremlin running amok. Genie was his, and none would turn their back on her, ever. Besides, she had to face her family or she would never be whole-heart. Her spiteful sister was going to be at Carlton House, he knew, along with her husband, Elgin's older brother, Roger, Baron Cormack. Ardeth did not tell Genie that. Too much information was dangerous.

She was nervous enough. He wanted to comfort her, to soothe her—not with mind touches, but with finger touches, hand caresses, back rubs. And more.

A lot more.

He had almost reconciled his vows with his desires. She was his wife, and she was willing. She was not mourning Macklin, and she was not indifferent to his own self. There was nothing sinful in a man's making love to his wife. That's what he told himself. Then he recalled that he was not quite the man she thought he was.

He might never be if he gave in to carnal instincts now, forsaking all noble intentions. He had deeper concerns, too. Ardeth did not know if he'd be able to play the gentleman in Genie's arms. After centuries without a woman? He could terrify her. Worse, if he lost control, he could harm her. That "little death" of sexual completion could turn far more deadly.

That would be just like the Devil, giving Ardeth his six months, then eternity to regret them. That's how long he'd feel guilty if he hurt his wife.

So he stayed away as long as he could.

*   *   *

Ardeth could not avoid, ignore, or pretend indifference to Genie on the night of the fete. He took one look at his beautiful, alluring wife coming down the stairs, and he almost rushed up those same stairs to carry her back to her bedroom, his bedroom, any room that had a bed. Hell, any room that had a carpet and a door. He'd tear that shimmery gown off her lush body, unpin her fiery curls, and make her his wife in deed. Just that first glimpse of the ruby he'd given her, right between her high breasts, and he'd been willing to take his chances—except for the chance of risking her life. That dread cooled his blood and slowed his breathing and stopped him from acting the moonstruck calf right in front of the entire household, it seemed, who had come to see Lady Ardeth off to her first grand party.

What a sight she was, in a gown of a gray so dark it was almost midnight, with black spangles shaped like tiny stars and moons scattered on the black lace overdress that hid her pregnancy. Her hair was gathered into a topknot, held with a star-studded diamond tiara. The ruby hung from a string of rare black pearls, reflecting the molten fire color of her hair. Ardeth wondered how he'd considered her merely comely at first, her nose too short, her skin too freckled. Not a hint of a freckle appeared now, not a flaw in sight. Her nose was perfect, held high with the assurance of a woman who knew she was in looks.

He'd seen scores of pretty women, of course, the most magnificent queens and courtesans of their times, too often struck down at the height of their beauty. They were usually vain creatures, worried over how they would look when they met him, as if he cared. He'd barely noticed, just doing his job.

He noticed now, every detail.

Lady Ardeth was not merely pretty. She was fearful, he knew, but her courage shone through, adding new dimension to what was on the surface. Add her selfless efforts to please and the glow of new life, and she was a masterpiece waiting for canvas and paint. She was perfect. She was his. But the child was not.

"Shall we go?" He stepped to the bottom of the stairs and offered his arm.

Thank goodness he was there, Genie thought, for she almost lost her footing, along with what little confidence she had, and the piece of toast she'd nibbled on earlier. The ruby necklace had arrived that afternoon, so she knew he must have thought of her, or how she would appear to tonight's audience, anyway, as if she were on show, like a mare at Tattersall's. But nary a kind word or compliment passed his firmed lips. No smile warmed his cold dark visage. He was as severe and forbidding as when she'd first met him at the field hospital, intent on saving lives and nothing else. Tonight he was bent on winning over the *ton* for his own reasons, and she knew she could not complain. She had a home and a title, a new wardrobe for now, a generous annuity for later. She'd signed the documents ensuring a safe future just this morning. She also had an escort certain to be the envy of every other woman there. Oh, and a diamond tiara that felt like the Rock of Gibraltar on her already-aching head. What more could a woman want?

The carriage ride seemed both interminable and altogether too short to Genie. Lord Ardeth sat across from her, careful of her skirts, if seemingly oblivious to her feelings. They did not speak until the coach drew to a halt behind a long line of others waiting to discharge passengers.

"I understand no one gets out and walks," Ardeth said. "What fools. They could be inside, enjoying themselves."

Enjoying? Was that what they were supposed to do? Genie would have stayed in the carriage all night, and liked it far more, but she stepped down when their turn came and raised her chin. She would take a leaf from Ardeth's book and look straight ahead, as calm as a countess, as haughty as anyone in the haut monde. She might not belong here by birth, but she was wedded to the position, gowned and jeweled for the occasion. She would make her husband proud. If he noticed her hand trembling on his arm, he did not mention it.

She was relieved to find theirs was not a private audience with the regent, as she'd feared. The foreign dignitaries were there, along with sundry allied generals, members of the cabinet, the prince's particular friends, and a few former mistresses. She knew none of them, and none looked her way until Ardeth led her to the prince at the attendant's nod.

Miss Hadley would have been proud of Genie's curtsy. The prince seemed to be impressed, grinning widely, but he was known to appreciate a pretty woman.

"Ah, Ardeth, we were wondering about your sudden choice. Great deal of talk, don't you know? Now we understand, eh?"

The earl made a careful bow, then frowned as the prince took Genie's hand in his and held it. And held it.

"And you, my dear," His Highness was saying to Genie, loudly enough for everyone in the antechamber to hear, "we have been eager to meet our latest peeress. Or should we say Peerless, eh?" He laughed, his loose jowls flapping, the myriad medals bouncing on his broad chest. His hangers-on dutifully chuckled and nodded.

Ardeth glared at Genie's hand, still encased in Prinny's fat fingers. He did not dare to cause them to shrivel or itch, not here. The prince ignored him and addressed Genie, this time in a quieter voice, meant for her alone. "We were not certain whether to offer condolences or congratulations. Hard choices, what?"

Genie did not know whether he meant his choice or hers, but he seemed genuinely touched by her plight, so she dipped her head and said, "Too kind, sire. Thank you for your understanding and your gracious invitation."

"Sweetly said. But a warning, my dear. The old tabbies won't like it. The cats won't like your quick new marriage or your lack of mourning. They'll find fault with your looks and your manners. Mostly, they will resent your snabbling a wealthy earl before they could get their claws into him." He leaned closer, so close she could hear his corset creak. "Here's a secret. They don't like us, either."

The prince's unpopularity was no secret, although Genie did not think it polite to say so. The newspapers were full of condemnation of him and his profligate ways, and talk from the London servants showed that their masters and mistresses held little affection for their ruler.

"Do not let it worry you," he told her. "That is our advice. We have survived without their approval. And enjoyed ourselves. You will, too."

The last was an order, Genie thought, almost giggling in her nervousness that this overstuffed sovereign thought he could command his subjects to be happy.

Genie was not sure she could obey the royal edict. Nor was she sure that Ardeth would not make a scene if the prince did not return her hand, which was feeling uncomfortably warm even through her gloves. She could not very well tug on a prince's grip or step on his toes, as she would have done with an impertinent corporal in the army. She murmured something suitable and looked toward her husband.

So did the prince. "Besides, Ardeth will win 'em over. Never seen such a chap for persuading people. Don't have to tell you that, eh?"

"He is forceful," she agreed. "And usually right."

"Blame it all on him. That's what we would do. Say he would not listen to reason or some such, what? Rich, handsome gentlemen are always forgiven. The high sticklers might say they despise rakes, but those females would cut off their arms to take your place."

If he did not release her hand, Ardeth might cut off his. Genie tried to back away, to make place for a heavyset woman trying to catch the prince's eye.

She was hard to miss. Of equal girth to His Highness, she had as many gems and jewels dangling from her body—neck, ears, and fingers—as he had medals. She wore peacock feathers in her hair and a turquoise and gold gown, flowing lengths of it except at the bosom, when not enough fabric in all of France could have covered that expanse.

"I think that lady—" Genie began, but she might not have bothered. The female was a warship in full sail, and the prince was the prize. He did not seem to mind, either, dropping Genie's hand to greet the newcomer.

"Ah, Princess Hannah—or is it Hendrika? You sisters are all so magnificent, our mind cannot concentrate, eh?"

"*Ach*, *Liebchen*, it is Hedwig Hafkesprinke of Ziftsweig, Austria."

"Of course it is. Of course. And a great pleasure it is to

see you again," he said when the hefty heiress curtsied deeply enough for him to look down her gown.

Genie curtsied also and started to back away, Ardeth firmly at her side.

"Do not forget to enjoy yourself, eh," the regent called out before forgetting Genie entirely. "Glorious victory, what?"

It seemed the prince was going to enjoy himself very well, *yah*, *gut*.

CHAPTER ELEVEN

"Pompous ass."

Genie looked at her husband, who wore a smile as thin as her gauze overdress. "You do not mean the prince?" she asked in a shocked whisper, lest they be overheard and arrested for sedition. "His Highness seemed very kind."

"The crow is kinder. And smarter."

"Good grief, you did not allow Olive to come along, did you? What if he—you know—on the prince's artwork? Or on the prince!"

Before he could say anything else, the prince's equerry, Sir Kelvin, came to lead them to a knot of gentlemen Ardeth particularly wanted to meet. Genie could not be certain what was placed in the baronet's pocket, but it surely had come from Ardeth's. Perhaps instructions had come from the prince, too. The gathered nobs would not have acknowledged her otherwise, Genie decided. They were polite, if distant, far more interested in

Ardeth's travels, his sudden arrival, and his future plans
than in his questionable wife. How he would vote in Parliament was far more important than how he got leg-
shackled.

Genie did not mind. She took the opportunity to catch
her breath—as much as she was able in the tightly laced
corset Marie insisted she wear—and thank the heavens
that her introduction to the prince was over. She had not
disgraced Ardeth yet. Of course the evening was young.

She watched the men surrounding Ardeth, noting that
none were as tall or as distinguished or as fit looking.
None had his air of distinction, not even the foreign
princes in their uniforms, whom he delighted by conversing in their own languages. She heard one older gentleman say he wished they had Ardeth in the diplomatic
corps or the Foreign Office. Another wished they had him
at the Exchequer's Office, since he had such a knack for
making money. Genie wished she had him back in the
carriage, headed home.

Soon they were herded into a larger room where the
rest of the select few hundred invited guests were queued
up for the receiving line. Genie said another prayer of
gratitude for being spared that ordeal. She did note that
the florid foreign princess in the feathered headdress still
clung to the prince's side and that the men Ardeth had
been conversing with took the opportunity to fade away,
in search of their wives and daughters.

Those females never approached Genie or her husband.

A few military men did come by, and that same petty
court official Ardeth had bribed brought them to the notice of a royal duke who leered, a Russian count who
clicked his heels together, and a marquess who inspected
Genie through his quizzing glass.

Sir Kelvin shook his head, as if to acknowledge his failure in bringing any ladies to the corner where Ardeth and Genie stood, an invisible fence seemingly around them. Ardeth shook the man's hand, another folded banknote passing between them before Sir Kelvin left.

"It is hopeless, my lord," Genie said. "You should have saved your money."

"At least call me by my name here, lest they think we are strangers. They have enough to gossip about without thinking we are at odds."

But they were strangers, weren't they? And one of them, at least, was decidedly odd. Genie took a step closer to him to show the company that they were on intimate terms—ha!—but the closeness made her feel better, too. "Very well, Ardeth. Still, none of the ladies will approach us."

"Then we shall approach them."

"You cannot simply walk up to a respectable female and introduce yourself. It is not fitting. You need someone to present you."

"Have you never heard about the walls of a palace being introduction enough? Come."

Genie tried to hold back, but Ardeth was determined. He handed Genie a glass of punch from a passing waiter, then took two more. He headed for a couple of older women wearing turbans and pearls. They smiled and accepted his offering, his bow, and his introducing himself. They turned to stone-faced seamstresses when he brought Genie forward. They needed to find the ladies' retiring room immediately, they claimed, to repair a flounce. Neither one's gown had a flounce.

"You see? I should leave so you can speak to the influential gentlemen."

Ardeth had hardly begun. He saw a dark-haired young woman standing by herself and towed Genie in that direction. The lady was relieved to have company, but she spoke only Italian. Ardeth conversed, then moved on.

Sir Kelvin found them, with an elderly but diamond-decked duchess on his arm. She smiled kindly at Genie's curtsy, then said, "What did he say your name was? I cannot stand a chap who mutters, even if he is my own nevvy."

She held her hand to her ear as Ardeth loudly reintroduced himself and his wife.

"Oh. I say, there is my husband now. He'll want to go home soon. Done our duty, don't you know." The look she gave Sir Kelvin boded ill for his inheritance.

She left, and again a cleared area surrounded Ardeth and Genie.

"Please, Ardeth, can we not leave, too?"

He could have these wigeons frozen in time and place—at least he used to be able to, in case anyone noticed Death's coming or going. But now he wanted them to notice his beautiful wife, to see she was kind and good and worthy of their paltry approval, even if he had to resort to mental force to sway them into submission.

He could not create a scene, however. That would defeat his purpose. Besides, Genie was looking peaked, almost pained. "You are not going to be sick, are you?"

She thought about claiming her condition as an excuse, but she was too honest. "No. Not that."

"You are not feeling faint, I hope. I heard of ladies swooning in the crush, but I know you have more backbone than that."

She had a whalebone poking into it. "No, I will not swoon." What, and let the scandal sheets claim her frail, besides a member of the frail sisterhood?

He was still concerned. "Dash it, there must be a seat in this monstrosity of a place."

A glare at a pair of fops emptied two chairs against a wall.

"Sit. I will fetch you some more punch."

"I'd prefer lemonade if you can find it. And a biscuit. Perhaps I am just hungry. I ate little, due to the excitement." Panic robbed one's appetite, it seemed.

Genie wished the chairs were behind a palm tree or a column, but she was grateful to be off her feet and out of the center of scrutiny. She watched as Ardeth wove through the crowd, which was growing more densely packed as more guests made it through the receiving line. With the crowds came the heat, so Genie started fanning herself as she kept her eyes on his dark head. She could spot him over all but the tallest egret plumes in ladies' hair.

Many people greeted him; a few gentlemen shook his hand. Some introduced him to their wives. Two women approached him on their own, smiling and batting their eyelashes. Genie plied her fan more vigorously.

No one approached her except Sir Kelvin, whose complexion was turning as green as the ivy vines embroidered on his waistcoat. Ardeth must have paid him to stand guard, she thought, and a lot of gold at that, for she could tell the fair-haired baronet had nothing to say. They spoke of the weather, the heat in the room, and the size of the crowd, which occupied the time until Ardeth was out of sight. Then Sir Kelvin stood silently behind the empty chair, taking another step away, distancing himself from his uncomfortable charge. Genie wanted to dismiss him, but the young courtier obviously had his orders and obviously needed Ardeth's money if that duchess paid his allowance.

Genie thought of finding the ladies' chamber herself, but was afraid Ardeth would worry if she did not remain where he left her. She also wondered if she could find her way back. Then, too, the ladies' coolness might turn to outright hostility in a smaller space, without Ardeth's presence. She recalled her mother-in-law's venom, the names shouted at her in Brussels. At least she was safe here. So she sat, feeling like a weed among the roses, a noxious weed at that.

Ardeth was going to do something to the punch, he'd decided. Otherwise he would have sent that useless fool of a baronet for the drink for Genie. Affecting the beverage meant reaching more of the finicking females . . . if his skills were still working. He could not count on eye contact in this crowd, nor the power of his touch to influence so many, so he was going to resort to pure trickery. That proved he had no real heart, he thought, which meant he was already going to roast in Hell forever. He might as well smooth Genie's way on earth before then.

A woman was standing at the refreshments table, sipping her punch. She was older, with gray hair and spectacles. She was well dressed, but without plumes and parures of gems at her throat. Unlike the other fun-seeking flibbertigibbets he'd encountered, this matron appeared sensible and serious, a harder mind to influence.

Ardeth nodded politely, waiting for her to leave.

Instead she said, "Forgive my impertinence, but you are the newfound earl, are you not? Lord Ardeth?"

He bowed. "Yes, for my sins."

"No, for your blessings. I am Lady Vinross."

He took the hand she held out, perfunctorily bringing it toward his mouth without taking his concentration from the bowl of punch.

"You do not know me."

Now politeness demanded he study the woman. "I fear not. I have met many people in the past weeks. I apologize."

"No offense taken. It is my son you would have met. James Vinross, Captain James Vinross, late of His Majesty's Hussars. He is here somewhere. This is his last official appearance before selling out, thank heaven."

"I met many of our brave fighting men, my lady. If your son returned unharmed, I share your thankfulness."

"No, it is you whom I wish to thank. Jamie told me what you did—not for him; his wound was not a grievous one, although they say he will limp forever—but for his men. He could do nothing but watch them suffer while the army surgeons left them to die, the physicians who could be spared from the officers' care, that is. Only a few surgeons stayed with the common soldiers, and you."

He shook his head. "I am neither physician nor surgeon. And what few medical men were there were sorely overworked. They could not have cared for everyone in time, not if their numbers were trebled."

"Jamie said that, too. But you stayed with the men and saved scores of them, he told me. You helped the ones the surgeons had given up on, the worst wounded. He called your work miraculous. He wanted to thank you, but you left Brussels before he could."

"I did nothing any other gentleman with the necessary skills would not do."

"None did. None tried. I think my son would have been more distraught over those deaths—not the ones in battle, but the ones of neglect and bad doctoring. He came home with a limp, but also scars on the inside. He suffers nightmares, but a disdain for those in charge and those who sent so many to die without going themselves."

"He sounds like a sensible sort. And he must have been an excellent officer, one whose men admired and fought harder for."

"He was. They are giving him a commendation tonight. I had to beg him to come accept the honor. He came, but only in hopes of meeting the one nobleman who acted nobly. The newspapers said you would be here."

"It was my duty. Not to come tonight, but to help the soldiers in need."

"As it is my duty to thank you for giving me back my son. And to thank you for those other mothers whose sons you saved. We all owe you. The government will not offer you a medal, I am sure, nor elevate your title."

"Neither would matter to me."

"I thought not. But someone ought to acknowledge the debt. What can I do to repay you for such a gift to all the wives and mothers and daughters and sisters?"

Ardeth looked at the punch bowl, and then he looked at the love shining from a mother's eyes. Then he looked across the vast room to an empty area where one occupied chair sat in Coventry.

"You can befriend my wife," he said.

Lady Vinross colored. "I, ah—"

"She was at my side most of the time. She could have been with the officers' ladies, winding bandages or whatever they did, but no, she was in the hellhole of an army hospital, holding hands, wiping brows, listening to prayers. And when I asked for her aid, she came forward, helping me perform what you call miracles on the poor lads we could save, bringing ease and comfort to those we could not. If your son saw me, he saw a reddish-haired angel at my side. She deserves your thanks, too. Perhaps more, for I could not have accomplished as much without her hands to help."

"Yes, but—"

"Imogene Macklin gave willingly, despite having lost so much herself. Can you not find it in your heart to forgive what sins of social misbehavior transpired and look to the good she did, the kind and gentle woman she is?"

"A good woman is worth more than rubies, eh? I saw the one around her neck."

"She is worth far more."

Lady Vinross took off her spectacles to wipe them with her handkerchief. "I heard her husband was a cad."

"Her first husband."

She smiled. "Of course. They say he lied to everyone."

"Including Imogene."

"No one likes to be hoodwinked, especially ladies of a certain social standing."

"Snobs, you mean. But of course no one likes being taken in. Resent Elgin Macklin, then, but not his unfortunate wife. She was more victim than anyone."

"Rumor has it that they were never wed."

"I have seen the marriage lines with my own eyes."

"He never claimed her as his spouse."

"He was a fool and a bounder. I claim her, and I claim her as a woman of value, to be cherished."

Lady Vinross settled her glasses back on her nose and looked hard at Ardeth, then said, "As should we all, it seems. So yes, I will do what you ask."

Before Ardeth could thank her, or carry her over to Genie's lonely chair, she said, "I heard that Alice Hadley has joined your household."

Ardeth was not sure what Miss Hadley had to do with the conversation, but he nodded. "Yes, the lady was hired as companion and secretary to my wife, but they have become fast friends."

"Miss Hadley has a good head on her shoulders, despite her unfortunate upbringing. I have known her all her life and I'd swear she would not be taking part in anything havey-cavey. If she is friends with your wife, all to the good, and all the easier our job will be. I am not without influence, my lord, so take me to the young lady and we shall see what can be done to persuade those other ninnyhammers who rule."

"The prince has already acknowledged my countess."

The lady made a rude noise. "The ones who truly rule, my lord. Not our extravagant prince or our politicians. I mean the patronesses of polite society."

There was no way of telling if the change in attitude was due to Lady Vinross's words or the punch. Perhaps enough punch would have soothed ruffled feathers or dulled harsh memories without Ardeth's help. Or perhaps Lady Vinross had enough social clout without any outside assistance. She located her son, who vowed to do his part with the younger ladies, and set to work with the matrons.

When Ardeth returned with a glass of punch instead of the lemonade she'd requested, Genie was ready to beg to go home. She'd sat with no one but the distant Sir Kelvin, and watched women fawn over her husband. Only one castaway colonel approached her the entire time. "Please, Ardeth. Coryn. Admit you were wrong. I can live happily in the country."

"Knowing you were humiliated in London? Never able to return? Your family left to ignore your existence? I cannot live with that. Wait."

So she waited, sipping the punch, which did settle her stomach and her nerves. Then she looked up . . . and understood how the Egyptians must have felt when they saw the Red Sea parting, only in reverse. A flood of smiling women was heading in her direction, almost shoving one another in their hurry to be introduced, not to the earl, but to his heroic wife. She was the angel of mercy who had written to Lady Kincaid for her nephew, had wiped Lady Nevelson's youngest son's brow, had changed the bandage of Lady Haverhill's maid's brother, had taken in poor homeless Miss Hadley.

So she had made an expeditious marriage. Which one among them had not? Which would not have accepted the earl's offer for her own daughter's hand, sight unseen? Now Imogene Hopewell Macklin Ardsley was assisting her husband in good works. She was a countess, with a fortune not to be despised. And she had the prince's approval, for what that was worth, since any pretty female could win his smile. Besides, this was a night for peace, wasn't it? With all the allies celebrating, how could the women of London not welcome one who had done her part in the victory?

Sir Kelvin proved not entirely useless, making note of names for her, invitations, and at-home days. She had more engagements for the following two weeks than she'd had in the past two years. Depending, of course, on her lord's desires about traveling to the country. She was even promised vouchers to Almack's, that hallowed hall of propriety and elitism, for whenever she returned to town. The baby was not mentioned, nor her own family.

Ardeth was actually grinning. When there was a lull in the onslaught, he said, "Now who has to admit she was wrong?"

"What did you do?"

He touched his chest. "I? What could I do?"

"Magic. I have no idea what you are capable of, magic being the least I suspect. You said yourself you knew parlor tricks."

"I believe the ladies simply saw reason, with Lady Vinross's assistance."

Genie raised one eyebrow in imitation of his own superior gesture.

"Or they might have been overcome with an excess of good spirits. The celebration, the punch. You drank all of yours, I see."

"I needed it, against the heat in here."

"Oh, is it warm?"

Now Genie narrowed her eyes. "Do you swear there were no tricks?"

"What, to fool all of these women? Even I would not be brave enough to take on so many self-important harpies at once."

Genie did not believe the punch or one lady's gratitude could have made such a difference. "Then it was a miracle."

"Damme, wife, you don't think I can perform miracles, too, do you?"

"I think I have seen one tonight."

She was about to see one more.

CHAPTER TWELVE

Princess Hedwig of Ziftsweig, Austria, was awesome on her own. When she was joined by two of her sisters, they were an Austrian armada, with artificially bright auburn hair. They were each tall and broad and big-bosomed, like the prow of a ship. Their jewels would have made a dragon drool. If this were not the prince's residence, one might think it was a high-class bordello with ripe triplets as the main attraction, so similar were the sisters in appearance and seeming availability. If not for Princess Hedwig's turquoise and gold gown and the peacock feathers, Genie would not know which sister she had met. She curtsied to all of them when they sailed toward her and Ardeth. The other ladies, Genie's new circle of would-be friends, backed away in the presence of royalty . . . or vulgarity. Genie wished she could, too, dragging Ardeth with her. The princesses were so blatantly set on seduction that no man was safe, not even a recently married one.

This time the Hafkesprinke heiresses were not husband hunting, neither for one of their own nor someone else's. They wanted to talk to Genie, so shooed Ardeth away to fetch more of the delicious punch. He considered for a moment, as if weighing Genie's chances against the flotilla of foreign damsels, then took Sir Kelvin, the baronet's eyes nearly popping out of his head and his tongue lolling to the side, along to help carry. His wife could hold her own, and he'd have the Austrians' heads, peacock feathers and all, if she was harmed. They all knew it.

"You wanted to speak to me," Genie said in disbelief, facing a wall of wealthy, wanton women. She had less in common with the Rubenesque royals than she had with the chair behind her. Yet she'd managed the grandes dames of the *ton* tonight, and Ardeth had left her alone with the sisters. Those two facts gave her the confidence to ask, "Why?"

"Why? Because we hear much of you, Fräulein. *Yah*. We hear from your prince and we hear from your brave officers, much that is good. We hear stories from women when they are in the privy. Not so good. Still, you became a grand lady overnight. We want to know why."

"We have too much curiosity, our brother the crown prince says. But we made him good spies in the war, didn't we, sisters?"

Princess Hedwig scowled at her sibling. "Some of us have too much punch, I think. But, yes, we wonder. Such a man, your husband. He takes no—what do you English say?—no soiled dove. So we ask the one who should know. And get no answers."

Genie still had no idea what they were speaking about, or why.

"We came to tell you that sisters are important."

Ardeth was coming back, thank goodness, followed by a waiter with a tray full of glasses. Maybe he could make sense of the words, even if they were not speaking a foreign language. "Why, yes, I can see that you are a close family."

"Not good to be alone," the sister in puce said.

"We do not believe in feuds." The third princess, the one who admitted to being a spy, was wearing blue, with a walnut-sized sapphire at her throat.

"We might steal a man from one another."

"Or borrow a necklace."

"Without returning it," Princess Hedwig snapped, eyeing the sapphire.

"But we are sisters."

"Sisters," the other repeated.

"Yes, I, ah, see. You are very lucky. And how lucky we all are. Here is Ardeth, with the punch."

The Austrians stepped apart. Genie thought it was to make a corridor for her husband and the servant. Instead they made room for a couple standing behind them: Genie's sister, Lorraine, and her husband, Elgin Macklin's brother, Roger, the current Baron Cormack.

If the chair were not at her back, Genie might have fallen. Then Ardeth was at her side and she felt her heart rate return to almost normal. Princess Hedwig made the introductions, thank goodness, while Genie studied the sister she had not seen in four years.

Lorraine had always been the beauty of the family, their parents' favorite. Older than Genie by five years, she'd had golden hair and blue eyes, a willowy figure, and a porcelain complexion that made her the belle of all the country assemblies. Now, closer to her thirtieth birthday than she would admit, Lorraine's beauty had dimmed. Her hair was merely pale blond, and her blue eyes looked faded and tired. Her cheeks were wan, and her eyes and mouth had the beginnings of wrinkles and shadows. Instead of being lithesome, she was all angles, appearing stick thin next to the substantial Austrians. And she would not meet Genie's eyes.

Genie turned to Roger, a man she hardly knew. The Hopewells and the Macklins were neighbors in Derby, but the age difference, his schooling, his London living, made them mere acquaintances. She could see a great deal of Elgin in his older brother: the sandy hair, the brown eyes, the wide nose. Roger—Lord Cormack, as she must get used to calling him—had none of Elgin's boyishness, no easy grin, no smattering of freckles, no rounded cheeks. He appeared older than Ardeth, with the weight of a barony on his shoulders.

The introductions must have been completed and they were all looking toward Genie, as if it was her turn to speak. Her mind was blank. Was she supposed to greet with affection the woman who had plotted her ruination? Who never answered her desperate pleas? Or was Genie supposed to ask about the parents who had turned their backs on her, struck her name from the family Bible, believing the firstborn, the favorite?

She said the first thing that entered her mind: "Where have you been?"

Lorraine answered with a titter: "Oh, here and about. Mostly London. Grosvenor Square, you know."

"No, tonight. Were you here all night?"

"Here at the assembly? Why, yes, except for the earlier private reception."

Genie thought she heard bitterness in Lorraine's voice,

that a mere baron and his wife had not been elevated enough to be among the chosen guests. How it must rankle her that Genie now took precedence.

Lorraine made her false laugh again. "Such a crush, don't you know."

Too crowded to find the sister everyone was talking about? Too thick with bodies that she could not locate the new earl and his scandalous bride, while Genie sat alone, forsaken, in plain view? "I see," Genie said. "I did not notice you, either, but then I did not expect you to be here." She stepped back, not-so-accidentally treading on her husband's toes. He'd had the guest list, she knew, yet had never warned her.

He muttered a low curse but kept the smile on his face. Genie knew he would support her in whatever she did. She also knew he did not want any scenes, not after he'd worked so hard to see his countess made acceptable. She could not, therefore, and regrettably, throw a cup of punch in her sister's face and tell her to go to the devil, that she was no longer the same innocent girl who could be used for Lorraine's purposes.

"Yes, well, it has been a pleasure to see you again," she said instead. "I suppose we shall meet at some affair or other. Give my regards to your family." She turned to Ardeth, ready to walk out alone if he did not come with her.

One of the princesses stood in the way. "If whole countries can make peace, *Liebchen*, you and your sister can, too. Go find a place to talk."

Genie would not have listened. The Ziftsweig sisters might have crowns, but they were neither her sovereigns nor her mentors. They were foreign and fast and fat and busybodies.

But Lorraine said, "Please."

Ardeth leaned closer to whisper in Genie's ear: "This might be your only chance to have me singe her eyelashes off, but better we do it in private."

That brought a smile to her lips. She nodded, and Sir Kelvin escorted them to a small chamber down a private corridor. The room was filled with chinoiserie, lacquered cabinets, jade figurines, exquisite vases. Genie clutched her punch cup, half-empty as it was, lest she be tempted to toss one of the regent's collection. Ardeth's dynasty porcelains were prettier. Or had been, anyway.

Genie was avoiding her sister, she knew. But Sir Kelvin was directing a servant to bring a tea tray for the ladies and decanters for the gentlemen, who were eyeing each other carefully, like strange dogs. Genie liked that, not that Ardeth was ready to spring to her defense, but that Roger was safeguarding his own wife. After her marriage to Elgin, she had learned to appreciate such protectiveness in a man. Not that she needed to be shielded, Genie told herself. She could fight her own battles. So when the servants had left, she took a chair some distance from the fire, leaving the warmer sofas to Ardeth and Cormack. She gestured toward Lorraine to sit opposite her, if indeed she wished to speak, but then Genie did not give her the chance.

"Why did you not approach me sooner?" she bluntly asked before her sister was seated.

Lorraine smoothed her skirts, then examined a carved ivory horse on a nearby table. "My son would admire this. He is too young for such an expensive bauble, but he does like horses."

Genie cleared her throat.

"Oh, did you need a cup of tea for your voice? I swear,

one had to shout to be heard in the ballroom." Lorraine started to get up, to fetch a cup, but Genie motioned her to stay seated.

"My throat is fine, and I still have some punch, thank you. I still wish to know why you did not seek me out earlier."

Lorraine rubbed her fingers against the flanks of the ivory horse. "I was afraid, if you must know."

Heavens, had anyone else seen him play with fire? "Afraid of my husband?"

"Ardeth?" Lorraine appeared confused. "Why, is he dangerous? He seemed the perfect gentleman to me."

"Of course he is. I misspoke. What were you afraid of, then?"

Lorraine shrugged. "I was afraid of being tarred with the same brush if I associated with you."

"Is your position in society so precarious, then, that your own sister could damage it? I wonder what mischief you have been up to recently. Lying? Cheating? Flirting?"

"Nothing, I swear. I am a respectable matron now, a mother."

"Yet you feared being seen with me?"

"Very well, if you must know, I worried about what you might say. Of what you might tell Roger."

"About?"

"You are not making this easy, are you, little sister?"

"I am not so little anymore," Genie answered.

"No, you are not." Lorraine looked at the ruby Genie wore, the diamond tiara, the gown that must have cost a king's ransom. "You have grown into a beauty, and a countess. So you have to admit, it all worked out for the best."

Genie set her punch cup down, out of temptation's reach. "The best? Tell Elgin that. He is dead, and he never forgave me."

"Why? It was me he should have hated."

"He loved you and would not hear of your treachery. No one believed you sent me out to the garden, wearing your shawl. No one believed you sent our parents out to find us, or that I was unwilling in his embrace when he thought he held you. You did not say anything to restore my reputation or to avert the disaster of my marriage. Nothing, Lorraine. You said nothing."

"Now it is time I said I was sorry."

"Now, because I have been taken to the beau monde's bosom, and you are afraid I will cut you, the way I have been cut? You are afraid of a countess's influence?"

Lorraine shook her head. "It is Roger."

Genie sat back. "I see. He never knew it was you who arranged the debacle, did he? He never realized that you wriggled out of your previous betrothal to Elgin by foisting him on me, and then wept your way into another, more advantageous engagement."

"No. He never knew. He married me out of honor."

"His, not yours."

Lorraine nodded in acknowledgment. "I could not confess and ruin everything, even after you left."

"But surely you expected to see me again. I was wed to your husband's own brother. We would have come to Macklin Manor for holidays when the war was over."

"No, Lady Cormack agreed it was best that you not be invited. She thought—"

"I know what she thought, that I was a doxy who had seduced Elgin. But Roger would have wanted to see his brother. I could have told Roger anytime."

"I hoped he would not believe you if that day ever came."

"So you would have stolen poor Elgin's family from him, too, to keep your secret hidden?"

"No!" Lorraine shouted. Her husband started to stand, but Ardeth laid a hand on his sleeve, so he subsided. "No," Lorraine said in a lower voice. "I never meant Elgin to die in battle or be estranged from his parents. One thing just led to another."

"To protect your lies." Just as she was protecting Elgin now, by letting Lorraine believe he had died in battle. Lady Cormack would never tell of her son's disgrace. Genie sighed and said she understood.

"Thank you. You see, we have had a good marriage. But every time I see the Duke of Eldert's daughter, the one they were touting for his bride, I wonder if Roger is wishing things had turned out differently. I never know if he is truly fond of me or simply too honorable to act otherwise. I do not know if he keeps mistresses or visits houses of convenience. I will never know, and that is agony. I have paid for my sins, Genie, every day of my marriage."

"But not as I have paid for them." Genie thought of the horrid months in Canada, the desperate months in Portugal, or when Elgin told people she was his sister so he could spend more time with his bachelor friends. "No, not nearly."

"Elgin was a good catch for you. He was good enough to be my betrothed, after all."

"A good catch? He was not a trout to be landed on my line! He loved you. And if not for your conniving, he would have married you, stayed to help our father with the lands, then taken them over. He never wanted to be a soldier. He never wanted to follow the army without the comforts he was used to. He never wanted me!"

Now Ardeth looked as if he would intervene. Genie waved him back.

"Ardeth wants you," Lorraine said.

"Ardeth is different. Sometimes I do not think even he knows what he wants."

"Faugh. Look at him watching your every move. The man is head over teakettle in love with you."

"No, he looks upon me as a responsibility."

"Then you are still that foolish little chit, if you cannot see what I see."

Genie ignored her. What did Lorraine know of Ardeth, after all? She could not know that he intended to leave in six months—five now—or that he was planning on giving most of his fortune away. "So why have you let me be in the same room with your baron?"

"To beg you not to say anything. To beg you for forgiveness. I am a better woman now."

"Now that you have what you want."

"Time has made you beautiful, Genie, but it has made you cruel."

"You are right. I have no need to be nasty."

"Please understand, I did not simply want Roger's title. I wanted his affection, too. I will never have my husband's unconditional love. I have accepted that. But I do have my son."

Genie could not resist asking, "How old is he? What is his name?"

"My Peter is nearly three, and more precious than life itself. He is all blond curls like I had, although he has your green eyes, I think, and Roger's nose. He knows some of his letters and can count to ten. He seldom cries and never throws tantrums like some of my friends' children. He is an angel."

He was Genie's own nephew. "I would like to see this paragon sometime. Is he in the country?"

"No, his health is worrisome, so we are in town, where the physicians are more learned than a country sawbones. Not that they have cured his cough."

"I am sorry," Genie said, and meant it.

"Then you do forgive me?"

"I . . . I suppose I must forgive you, since you ask. Every sermon and Bible teaching demands it." Genie thought Ardeth would agree. He had spoken of atoning for sins to win redemption. How could Genie deny another's repentance?

Lorraine looked relieved. Before she could consider the matter closed, though, Genie added, "I can forgive, Lorraine, but I can never forget. Does that make sense? I doubt I will trust you again."

Lorraine brushed aside a tear. "I swear I will never do anything to hurt you. I will put a halt to any rumors, see that your reputation is restored."

"That was already done, I believe, thanks to Lady Vinross."

"But we can be seen together. A ride in the park, sharing a box at the opera."

Both would be more to Lorraine's benefit than Genie's now, Genie thought, still doubting her sister's motives and sincerity. "I have more invitations than I can accommodate."

"Then I shall plead with Papa to acknowledge you and your marriage, and with Mama to write your name back in the family Bible. I will tell them you were innocent, that now I realize it was all a misunderstanding. They will be bound to invite you home on your wedding journey or for the Christmas holidays so everyone in the neighborhood can see what a fine lady you are now, a countess."

"So they will all forgive me for a sin I did not commit?" Genie had ached for her parents' love for her entire life. Their approval now might be satisfying, but would be far too late. None of her friends in the small community had stood by her, and she found she no longer cared for their good opinion. She shook her head.

"What more can I do?"

"You can introduce me to my nephew. I think that is a good start."

CHAPTER THIRTEEN

"Do you believe people can change?" Genie asked while she and Ardeth were waiting outside Carlton House for Campbell to bring their carriage. The night was warm and clear for a change, the air easier to breathe than the overheated, overcrowded, and overly scented rooms inside.

Ardeth looked up at the stars, taking a deep breath. "I live in hope."

"But can someone truly change at heart? What if a woman has been selfish and spoiled her whole life, getting everything she wants? Can she suddenly stop being that way, do you think?"

"I have heard that acknowledging one's faults is the first step toward eradicating them. If a person regrets his or her past actions, then they can try to be better. If they feel no remorse, I doubt they will change. But circumstances can also alter," he reminded her, and himself.

"Yes, Lorraine is a mother now. Perhaps that brings

out the best in a female, considering her child's best interests first. Time will tell, I suppose."

"It always does," he said as he helped her into the coach.

Campbell gave Ardeth a jaunty salute as he shut the door behind the earl. From Campbell's grin, Ardeth gathered that the former soldier had heard of the lord and lady's success, right there on the carriage line. The rest of the household would know as fast as Campbell could drive through the city streets. It mattered to them, for a servant's standing among the other butlers, maids, footmen, and drivers depended on the respect given each of their employers. A valet of a loathsome lord, for instance, no matter how well paid, would be pitied, not looked up to by younger gentlemen's gentlemen.

"Do not rush," Ardeth warned. "The horses can be skittish in the dark."

So could his wife, Ardeth knew. He made sure she was comfortable on the seat across from him, then asked, "Were you pleased with the evening, other than the meeting with your sister? I know you were dreading it, but the party was not all bad, was it?"

"It ended better than it started, of course, but I found the *ton*'s approbation nearly as intimidating as their disdain. Some of the women seemed genuinely kind, not merely swayed by public opinion or spirit-laced punch."

"But you won even the curmudgeons over."

"Again, time will tell. Yesterday I was a wanton. Tonight I am a wonder. Who knows what tomorrow will bring?"

He glanced around, as if to see a light. "Who, indeed?"

"I do not suppose it matters in the end."

"Nothing matters right now but your own opinion of your worth, your own peace of mind."

"Then it does not matter to you if I use the wrong fork at Lady Blessingame's Venetian breakfast or forget which lady goes in first at the Hamiltons' dinner?"

He laughed. "You are asking me about forks when I never used one until—that is, you could ride naked through Hyde Park and it would not make a ha'penny's difference to me."

"Oh. I see."

He could not see her face by the dim light of the carriage lamps, but he knew she stiffened in her seat. "I am sorry. I did not mean to imply that I do not care. In fact, I would not like another man seeing my wife's bare body. I am trying to be generous, but I do have limits."

"Like one of your possessions," she said.

Ardeth heard the chill in her voice and almost shivered, just when he'd been getting used to the London weather. "Anyone may look at my collections. A wife is another matter altogether. What I meant, and should have said, was that I would be proud of you, pleased that we are wed, if you smote Prinny himself to reclaim your hand or knocked a duchess down on your way to the dining room."

"Truly?"

"Truly. I know you went tonight for me, but you showed your true mettle. No foolish conventions could matter more than that."

"And I succeeded, didn't I?" She relaxed back against the leather cushions. "With your help, of course, and Lady Vinross and her son's, and that of the Germanic contingent and the prince himself."

"You did indeed. They all complimented me on what an excellent match I had made. I agreed."

"Thank you. I must admit that I feel better about the

match, too, for your sake. Now you do not have to be ashamed of your countess, or hope I stay hidden in the country. Of course you still deserve a far better wife."

"I was never ashamed. And that was why I wanted you to attend, so you would see your own worth." He laughed. "And if I got what I deserved, I'd be rolling the dice with the Devil. Instead, I am satisfied with our marriage." Well, he was content, if not precisely satisfied. Ardeth feared he would never be satisfied again. Here he was, sitting across from a beautiful woman, smelling the floral scent she wore, thinking about every crass and crude sex act he had ever seen, heard of, read about, or performed—and doing it with her. Genie was his wife, by Hades, his sweet lady wife, whom he'd sworn to protect.

Now she needed more protection from him than from anyone else.

He was grateful for the changed subject when she asked, "What did you think of my sister?"

"I hardly spoke to her. She appeared tired, in body and spirits. I cannot imagine how anyone ever thought she was more beautiful than you. Perhaps the ugliness inside was eating at her these past years and now she can recover her looks."

"I think she was merely concerned about my speaking to her husband, and worried about her son."

"That, too."

"What about Lord Cormack?"

"He did not mention the boy."

"No, I meant your opinion of him. You did spend considerable time with the brother-in-law you never expected to see."

Ardeth had fully expected to meet Cormack at the reception. If not, he would have sought him out tomorrow, to guarantee the baron's cooperation in restoring Genie's reputation. After all, the baron would eventually be head of Genie's family and his goodwill might be a help to her. None of which Ardeth was willing to discuss with Genie. Why dwell on the passage of time when the present was to be savored?

"He seems a nice enough fellow, with his wits about him. He is already making improvements at the mills he inherited from the last baron. I believe I can convince him to make more."

"The whole business about Lorraine's wanting to speak to me, asking the princesses to intervene, even begging for my forgiveness, that was all for him, you know. Or to keep him ignorant, at least. Lorraine wants my silence so Roger never finds out how she trapped him into marriage."

"He knows."

"No, she swears she never told him. I was never allowed to speak to him myself at the time, lest he believe my story."

"I told you, Cormack is not a dunderhead."

Genie was confused. "But then why did he accept responsibility for the loss of Lorraine's betrothal to Elgin? He could have refused to wed her, knowing she was at fault, leaving her with no fiancé, her reputation in tatters instead of mine. Or was he simply acting nobly?"

Ardeth shrugged. He did not know the man well enough to guess his morals or motives. "I suppose he wanted her. Or perhaps he wanted a woman who wanted him badly enough to betray her sister and her lover. Maybe he felt sorry for her."

"But he never told her he knew."

"I say it again. The baron is no fool. Her guilt and uncertainty keep her wondering. Now she will never take him for granted."

Genie thought about that a moment, remembering how Lorraine preyed on the weak. "He sounds as devious as my sister."

Ardeth agreed. "A match made in heaven, but who is to say? What suits one man might strangle another."

They were almost at the corner of their street when Genie's stomach rumbled, loudly enough to be heard over the rattle of the wheels and the hoofbeats, to her embarrassment. Luckily the interior of the coach was too dark for him to see her scarlet blush. "I apologize. I have not eaten in a while."

"Damme, I should have thought you might be hungry. You never did get to the refreshments table, and I forgot all about finding you a biscuit or something."

"Nonsense, it is not your fault. I should have had some toast, at least, before we left. Miss Hadley offered me tea and Mrs. Randolph brought me some soup to fill my stomach, but I did not feel hungry then."

Ardeth was staring out the window, as if he could conjure up a picnic hamper. "I don't think we should go to a coffeehouse, not with you in a tiara and ruby, and me with no armed guard."

Genie thought he could defend a fortress with the strength of his glare, but she kept quiet.

"We could stop at one of the hotels," he suggested. "I hear they serve an excellent meal, no matter what time of day."

"Oh, no. I can find a roll or some cold chicken at home. Only . . ."

"Yes?"

"Only I have a fancy for a raspberry ice. I have heard such cravings are common among women who are breeding."

"I have never had one."

"A craving?"

Those he'd had aplenty, and still did. "No, a raspberry ice."

"I do not suppose you found easy access to ice where you were last."

"Not hardly," was all he said.

"Gunter's makes the best, but they will be long closed at this time of night."

Ardeth tapped on the roof, then gave new directions to Campbell, who efficiently turned the horses, despite a few low-spoken curses.

The confectionary was indeed closed and dark, except for a lamp burning at the back. No, there were no sweets to be had at this time, the floor sweeper told Ardeth, not even a spoonful. Every bit of raspberry ice—and lemon and strawberry, too—had gone to a party at Golden Gollub's house in Kensington. A cit, Mr. Gollub was, born and bred of the banking family. He was celebrating both the peace and his daughter's betrothal, hosting gentlemen who would never be invited to the fete at Carlton House, but who might be invited to pay for it.

Ardeth directed Campbell to head to Kensington.

Campbell cursed some more. The Devil knew how long Marie would wait up for him. He turned the horses with slightly more swaying inside the coach.

Genie reached for the leather strap that helped a passenger keep her balance. "We cannot go to Mr. Gollub's party. We were not invited!"

Ardeth never wavered. "As a matter of fact, I was. I did some of my banking with him. But no, I do not intend to play the aristocrat at his daughter's ball, nor let my wife outshine the bride-to-be."

He could not see Genie's smile, but heard it in her voice when she said thank you. Her voice changed in a moment. "Why are we going out to Kensington, then?"

He laughed at her new, doubting tone. "What, do you think I am going to steal your dessert?"

"Thievery would be better than winkling it out of the house some less, um, ordinary way."

"Silly little goose. I intend to bribe the servants. That is the way things are done throughout the world, throughout history."

And he did, as easily as falling off a log—or finding a footman outside relieving himself. Before Genie could worry, alone in the coach a block away, he was back with a bowl of ice and two spoons.

"One bowl was all the fellow would take for what I had in my pocket. I did not think the diamond stickpin my new valet insisted I wear was a fair trade, not even for your pleasure. I must remember to carry more coins. Bribes are far more costly than they used to be."

Genie was already devouring the cool, sweet confection. "This is so good, I do not care how you got it. Here, taste some."

He moved over to sit beside her, then dipped in his spoon. "You are quite correct. This is worth petty burglary, if not sorcery."

There it was again, the doubt. "Are you . . . ?" Genie could not say the word "wizard" or "warlock." He'd think *she* was the crazy one.

"Am I finished so you can have the rest? If I am a

gentleman, I must swear to be." But he kept filling his spoon, delight on his face.

Genie ate faster, pausing only to worry about the footman when the bowl and spoons went missing. Some households counted the silverware every night.

"We can return the dish to Mr. Gollub's garden if you are worried," Ardeth told her. "They will think one of the diners took a bowl outside to enjoy. I'd wager they find many a champagne glass under the shrubbery, if not a sleeping guest."

After returning the evidence, Ardeth said he would put in a standing order at Gunter's for a supply of this new delicacy.

Genie was glad. "Little Sean will adore it, and Miss Hadley worked so hard to prepare me that she deserves a treat."

When they reached home and had pulled into the carriage drive under the portico, Ardeth did not wait for a footman to come lower the coach steps. He jumped down and lifted Genie out, waving the rushing servant back inside. Campbell drove the coach around to the mews.

By the gas lamps left burning outside the house and the light from the opened door, Ardeth could see that Genie had a raspberry stain on her face. Against his better judgment, he brushed his bare fingers against her lips.

She looked up.

"A bit of the ice got left."

Genie licked her lips, as if that would clean away the raspberry drip. Then she looked back at him, as if asking if she was tidy enough to face the servants inside. She did not want to appear like a hoydenish child after her first grand outing.

"You are perfect."

Then she looked at him as if he'd given her the moon, not just an introduction to the prince and polite society, a bit of confection, and a simple compliment.

Ardeth could not help himself. He could almost taste the fruit on her lips, the sweetness. And why not? She was his wife, and she was willing. More than willing, if he judged that bright light in her green eyes rightly. She was eager for him, and that had nothing to do with the punch, the raspberry ice, or the royals. He bent toward her and lowered his head.

. . . Making it easier for the crow to land on his shoulder.

"Party, pretty? Pretty party?"

"Yes, the reception was lovely," Genie told the bird.

"And yes, Lady Ardeth was a success," Ardeth added, after a word Genie had never heard before.

"Alive?"

Genie reached out to stroke the shiny head. "Yes, we missed Olive, but you would not have liked it there. One lady wore peacock feathers."

"Gawk!" Then the crow turned its unblinking eye on Ardeth. "Alive?"

"Not yet." But there was still a chance, thanks to the blasted bird. He had not carried his wife upstairs, betraying all he'd sworn. He had done no harm.

What was wrong with the man? Genie asked herself as she kicked a stool out of her way in what they were calling the Hourglass Room. He was definitely not like other men. Here she'd been exactly what he'd wanted her to be, a smashing success. Instead of admiring his glittering social butterfly, the earl had shoved her away, back into her dreary cocoon. No, Genie decided, he'd treated her as if she were a slimy, slithery caterpillar to be kicked under the rock or leaf pile it had crawled from. Soon she'd be too big with child, too awkward, too unattractive. And perhaps too uninterested. To the devil with him. She kicked the stool again.

As soon as they'd entered the house, Ardeth had gone to his book room, inviting the crow to share his nightcap, not his wife! Genie was left to chat with Miss Hadley, who'd stayed up late, wanting to know everything.

Genie told her companion as much as she could remember of the actual events: who spoke to her, what they said, which function they had invited her to attend. As for the theoretical part, why everyone had a change of heart, she hardly understood half of it, and none of her husband.

Ardeth raised his glass in a toast. "To honor."

"To being on her," the crow muttered.

"That is my wife, you henwit. Never let me hear you speak so disrespectfully." He slammed the glass of brandy down on an inlaid end table.

Olive immediately swooped from his place on the curtain rod. He perched on the glass, flapping his wings, trying to duck his head down deeply enough to get a sip without falling in.

Ardeth grabbed the stem to keep the fine crystal from tipping, then thought better of drinking from it again. He took a drink from the decanter instead, like old times, very old. Randolph the butler would have been shocked, but Randolph had never seen the manners of a crusading knight. He would not see them tonight, either, for Ardeth had locked the door. That way he would have to think twice before giving in to temptation.

He held the decanter in one hand and the nearly empty

glass in the other, tilting it so the crow could drink. "They say a gentleman never drinks alone."

Olive staggered back, nearly falling off the wooden table.

"Bah, what good are you? Can't even hold your liquor."

"Can—hic—hold a pretty."

"And what do you know of virtue anyway? A crow has no honor. A gremlin sure as hell has no honor." He took another swallow. "*I* must have honor."

The crow eyed his empty glass and Ardeth's full decanter. "Olive must have—"

"That's right. To stay alive, I must have integrity, righteousness, moral principles. You heard Old Nick. Heart and soul."

"More easy—hic—find the hourglass."

CHAPTER FOURTEEN

Genie grew almost too busy to worry about her husband's desires, or lack thereof. Between the morning visits, the afternoon teas, the late-day rides in the park, and the assorted evening activities, she hardly had a moment to herself. She also needed more gowns for such a varied schedule, more staff at home to ensure the comfort of every visitor, and more sleep.

Thank heaven for Miss Hadley. Between them, they had the daily hourglass arrivals under control, accepting them, noting their owners in a journal, then sending them back after a quick perusal by Lord Ardeth. When the earl was too busy, the crow stood sentry as the boxes were unpacked or hand-delivered ones were unwrapped. Genie did not ask—she did not want to know—how the crow understood what Ardeth was looking for, but she accepted his squawked *no*s as enough. Besides, most were too big, too ornate, or too obviously new. She needed no special sensitivity to tell silver from gold, painted tin from precious metal, filigree from the plain base Ardeth had described.

In addition to helping with those clerical duties, Miss Hadley was also invaluable at teaching Genie the niceties of polite behavior. Genie was manor-born, but not to the levels of London's *ton*. Miss Hadley knew everyone in town and their foibles—which dowagers did not speak to one another and which ladies would not attend the same function as their husbands. She knew which invitations were important, which hostesses must not be slighted, and which houses were too disreputable for a woman seeking an impeccable name. With the older woman's assistance, Genie could sidestep half of the pitfalls she had not known existed.

Miss Hadley, together with Marie, also helped add to Genie's wardrobe. Marie's taste was a shade too flamboyant for dignity; Miss Hadley's, too practical to be fashionable. Between them, Genie found a common ground that became her, that gave her confidence she was gowned as befitted Ardeth's wife.

The companion made sure. She knew what was suitable for every activity, every level of social occasion, and she had a good eye for quality. She'd had to when one of her gowns had had to last for years.

No longer. Genie ordered new clothes for Miss Hadley, too, since the older woman had to accompany the countess on most of her visits, while Ardeth oversaw his investments and new projects. He became involved in politics as the best way to effect the most change for improvements, and left the women to their own pastimes.

Genie's new clothes were all in black or deepest gray, but she insisted Miss Hadley wear colors. One of them should look bright and cheerful, Genie declared, lest they bring gloom wherever they went. Miss Hadley looked lovely in the softer tones, years younger in the newer styles, especially with the help of Marie's cosmetic artistry. She wore her hair in a more modern style, and she no longer looked as if her last meal might be her last meal. If she thanked Genie twice a day, she thanked her twenty times, to Lady Ardeth's embarrassment. Genie felt she should be the one thanking the higher powers for sending Miss Hadley. She'd be lost and alone otherwise.

Genie was also grateful for Captain James Vinross. The former officer had joined Ardeth's household as steward or man of affairs or simply aide, whichever suited his mama's notions of the appropriate title for her younger son. Ordinary working for a living was not quite in keeping with her standards, but being an earl's right hand had enough clout to overcome the onus of trade.

Captain Vinross had no such qualms. He was delighted to find real work, helping to write speeches, searching out sites for veterans' hospitals and homes, and acting as escort for the ladies when Ardeth was too busy. As a younger son with no income now that he had sold his commission, James's only alternatives were to be his titled brother's pensioner or live as an idle wastrel in his mother's house.

Instead he was happily living at Ardeth House. Lud knew there were rooms enough for an army, so he did not feel intrusive, and he was away from his doting mother, who coddled his limp and cringed at his nightmares. At Ardeth House James selected the farthest suite of rooms, in hopes that his bad dreams could not disturb anyone else. The notion of waking the newlyweds with his cries almost kept him awake.

Lord Ardeth's hearing must be extraordinary, James

thought, or the man wandered the halls after midnight, which did not speak well of that honeymoon, but the captain would not listen to backstairs gossip about his patron. Either way, Lord Ardeth woke Captain Vinross up the very first night, silently handing him a cloth to wipe off the sweat and tears. The earl spoke softly of his own dreams for the future. Something about Lord Ardeth's voice, or his quiet, calm acceptance of another's failings, comforted James back into a more restful sleep. He had not had a nightmare since.

Genie was no matchmaker, but she thought her companion and the captain were well suited. Both were of a certain age, although the officer may have been a year or two younger. They shared a similar upbringing, except that James's family harbored no drunks or debtors. Both were of serious character, having seen more than their share of ugliness and misery, yet both were pleasant and friendly and willing to work.

So Genie had them keep a joint appointments calendar for herself and the earl, conferring daily to keep their engagements straight. She made sure both sat at the dining room table when they ate at home, and she requested the captain's company at the opera and theater and on their calls, whenever his lordship could spare him. She might organize the seating so that her two new friends were beside each other, send them together on combined errands, and force them to talk to each other while she conversed with Olive, but she was no matchmaker. Of course not. She'd seen what interference could do in her own life, and had no desire to meddle among two intelligent adults. But wouldn't it be nice . . . ?

Of all the new sights and activities, Genie adored the theater best. She'd attended once before in London, when her family had come to town for her sister Lorraine's presentation. Otherwise the only plays she'd seen were by amateurs in her own neighborhood, or traveling troupes of actors performing at the grange or in the largest barn or at country fairs. This was far different, and enthralling to her. The sheer size and splendor of the theater made a visit exciting, no matter what drama or farce was presented. The crowds, the lights, the private boxes, all added to her pleasure. That and knowing she was modishly dressed, with the finest jewels at her neck and the handsomest man in all of London sitting beside her, when the theatergoers turned their quizzing glasses their way.

The opera was made even more pleasant by Ardeth's whispered translations in her ear. Of course she paid more attention to the ticklish, tingly feeling than the music, but Ardeth seemed amused, so Genie was content.

They did not attend balls, public assemblies, or large rout parties. Genie did not care for crowds and would not dance, so what was the point? There were enough smaller gatherings, where good conversation was possible and her unconventional mourning was not as noticeable. Many families who had lost sons in the late war were in similar circumstances and understood, wearing black armbands and ribbons, but living their own lives.

Ardeth used those quieter events to influence votes, to make the wealthiest understand the plight of the poor, in a polite manner, naturally. No one was offended or thought him pushing or radical, not that Genie heard, only a trifle progressive for a newcomer to the scene. And he never played with the fires.

Genie relaxed enough to take the crow with her on a few morning calls. She'd taken him in the park one day, thinking the silly bird had to get over his fear of flying outdoors, especially if they were going to the country. He would not be happy spending the entire journey in a closed carriage. Genie was not looking forward to it herself.

If Lady Pomeroy could have her smelly Pekingese, and Mrs. Smith-Corbett had a spotted cat on a diamond lead, Genie could have a black bird on her black-clad shoulder—atop a snowy handkerchief, in case. Olive was a smashing success, adding to Genie's cachet. So he was invited to pay social visits.

Genie made sure no cats would be present, no canaries, no big dogs, no ladies in feathered headdresses. In turn, she warned the crow that there better not be any accidents indoors.

Olive drank tea from a saucer, took biscuits from eager fingers. He repeated the hostess's name, bobbed in a bow, said "great" and "full" when leaving, and stole only the occasional earbob or shiny key, which Genie promptly returned. He rarely cursed, never pecked anyone, and let the ladies scratch under his chin where he could not reach. He even performed somersaults and circus tricks when the children were brought down from the nursery to see the countess's counting crow. They adored him, and Genie. Few enough adults cared to speak to the infantry or see them, or let their sticky hands touch them. Lady Ardeth did not care. Once a crow had shat on your head, nothing else mattered. Such behavior endeared the bride to her hostesses.

Miss Hadley was already one of theirs, as was Captain Vinross. Now Genie was part of the inner circle of the beau monde, in perfect time. In a few weeks she would be unable to hide her pregnancy or avoid awkward questions about its chronology, but by then the victory celebrations would be over and most of the grand houses would be shuttered, the nobs going to their country estates and house parties. Ardeth would have won over many cabinet ministers and leaders of Parliament to his side, have his finances in order, with trusted men in place to run his endowments, and be ready to leave.

Before that departure, Genie had an important call to make, one she'd been putting off. She did not take her companion, or the crow, not even her maid. She did not invite—or beg—Ardeth to come along, either. This was a duty she had to see through on her own. With only Campbell to drive the coach and a footman to open the door, Genie called on her sister at Cormack House, Grosvenor Square. She chose a time when she knew Lord Cormack was at an important political debate. If she and Lorraine could not converse politely, alone, there would be no more visits, ever. The Dowager Lady Cormack, Elgin's mother, had gone to Bath. Genie would never have come otherwise.

Lorraine was in. Genie had wondered if she would choose to be at home for her sister's visit, and was halfway surprised to be shown immediately into a small, cozy parlor filled with picture books and toys.

"I wanted to thank you for writing to Mama," Genie began after the usual polite pleasantries for the servants' sake were finished and they were alone over a tea tray with macaroons and ginger biscuits. Genie loved macaroons, but she doubted that her sister had remembered. She ate one anyway, while the baroness mouthed empty refusals of any gratitude.

"Once she was apprised of your circumstances, of course she wrote. She is your mother, you know."

And had been the previous years, without as much as a note. Genie swallowed her bite, and her bile. "Yes, I heard from her this week. She sent congratulations on my wedding, as if Elgin and the scandal never existed."

"That is Mama's way. If she does not see it or say it, nothing bad exists."

Which was why, Genie supposed, she and Elgin were shipped out of the country almost before the vicar finished his sermon at their wedding.

"Much of the *ton* behaves that way, if you must know, turning a deaf ear to affairs and illegitimate children."

Genie did not wish to discuss those awkward subjects, either. "She sent a silver epergne as a gift."

"Large, with elephants and monkeys and palm trees?"

"And fruit. It would take up half the dining room table, and no one would be able to see around it to converse."

"I know. Don't you recall the hideous thing taking up a wall in the butler's pantry? She tried to give it to me for my wedding, but I told her I could not accept. Since it had been in her family for so long, it ought to stay with her."

They laughed together—and were aware that they were laughing together.

"I wondered who she would find to foist it off on next."

"Why did she purchase it in the first place? Our mother had better taste than that."

"Oh, I believe the monstrosity came from Great-aunt Loretta to Mama on *her* wedding. There is no way of knowing how many poor brides had to house the horror for decades waiting for another unfortunate girl to dump it on. That is, bestow it on."

"There will not be any more. I am putting it up for auction at the benefit for the widows' and orphans' fund. I thanked Mama for her kindness on their behalf. I added that knowing of her generous spirit, I was certain she would not mind."

"She will be apoplectic!"

"Really?" Genie asked, smiling over her teacup.

Lorraine turned serious.. "How remiss of me. I never gave you a gift, not for your first wedding or your second."

"Yes, you did. You gave me your white muslin gown to wear for my first one."

Lorraine looked stricken. "Oh dear, I was so beastly. How can I hope you will forgive me?"

"Do not apologize again. We are going to take a page from Mama's book and not speak of the past." She took another sip. "Mama says I should visit on our way north."

"Will you?"

"I will wait to hear if Father seconds the invitation before asking Ardeth's wishes. He was not . . . pleased to hear how our parents behaved, and his memory is long. I am not certain I want to have our parents and Ardeth together under the same roof."

"Oh, Mama will be so impressed at having an earl in the house she will be on her best behavior. And Father is growing too absentminded to care. If they should treat you with less than respect, no one can depress pretensions like your husband. I have seen him do it."

So had Genie, which was what was worrisome. She did not fancy seeing him angry.

Lorraine went on: "And I have seen him convince others that he is a saint . . . a very sensuous saint."

"Sensuous? Do you think so? That is, Ardeth is indeed a handsome gentleman."

"Handsome? Why if he were not so obviously moonstruck, you'd have maidens collapsing on your door in hopes he'd pick them up."

Genie recalled how he'd lifted her so effortlessly, how she'd felt sheltered in his arms. "Nonsense. No one would be so forward."

Lorraine laughed at her naïveté. "They'd do worse. Your husband's piercing eyes, his regal bearing, the distant look—they challenge a woman to make him smile, to make him notice her."

"They do?" Genie was feeling like the crow, repeating what she'd heard. She wanted to hear more. "Other women are attracted to Ardeth?"

"Not me, of course. I am quite taken with my own husband, but ladies do talk among themselves, you know. You are considered lucky. And brave."

Genie almost choked on a macaroon. "Me? Brave?"

Lorraine nodded. "Everyone agrees that there is something almost frightening about your husband, something that speaks of confidence and authority."

"Well, he is a commanding figure."

"One no rational soul would chance to cross, although no one can say they have heard him speak harshly. Cormack says he will not take up sword or pistol, yet men tread carefully around your husband. You must have noticed."

Genie shook her head. She seldom watched anyone else when Ardeth was in the room.

"Men might take caution, but women quiver at the hint of danger . . . and desire."

"For my husband," Genie marveled. She thought she was the only one.

"I don't suppose I should ask if his looks match his expertise."

"His expertise?"

"In bed, goose. What else do you think women speak of over their needlework? Not their stitches, certes."

Genie could feel the blush start at her toes. She tried for a countess's contempt. "No, I do not suppose you should ask."

Lorraine burst into laughter. "How well you do that. Who would have thought that my little sister had such nous?"

Genie checked the watch pinned to her gown rather than answer. "I am afraid I must be going shortly. I had hoped to see my nephew."

"I had not supposed you came to see me." Suddenly Lorraine was again the fatigued, ashen figure she'd been. "My angel is not well today. The physician had to bleed him, so he will sleep through the day. Perhaps you could come back tomorrow?" She brightened. "And bring the crow everyone is talking about? Peter would love to see such a sight. He gets out so seldom—the air is too dank and thick for him. He would be thrilled at a new aunt and a talking bird, all in the same day."

Genie agreed. Calling on her sister had not been as terrible as she'd feared, and she still wanted to meet the boy.

When she mentioned the sickly child to Ardeth at dinner that night he scowled, reminding her of what Lorraine had said. He did look intimidating. Luckily he was angry at the physicians who had no idea how to treat a disease except bleeding it out of a body, generally weakening an already-sick patient.

"A child? They would drain his life's blood? How is he expected to regain his strength? Tell them to stop."

"Me? Who am I to tell Lorraine's experts how to treat the boy?"

"You are his aunt. Do it."

So she did. And Lorraine laughed, as Genie knew she would. "I heard your husband had some unconventional notions, and I know Lady Vinross quite sings his praises in the medical field, but the gentlemen who consult on Peter's health have studied in Edinburgh and are considered the finest minds in the nation."

"They have not cured the king, have they?"

"Oh, but that is a mental feebleness, you know. Peter merely has weak lungs."

"Just think about it, because Ardeth makes sense."

As she led the way up the stairs to the nursery, Lorraine paused. "There might be something in what he says, for it does take Peter longer every time to recover. I will ask Cormack to speak with the physicians. But my boy will perk up to see you and your wondrous crow."

Olive dropped the gold-plated sugar tongs. "Dross."

The child was tiny in a large bed, looking pale and thin, but he did smile and try to sit up and bow like a gentleman for his new aunt, whose eyes matched his green ones.

Olive bowed back from Genie's shoulder, then flew down to walk across the bed, eyeing the starched nursemaid hovering at his side. "Pee on her?"

"That's Peter, you naughty bird."

Peter thought it a great joke. He gurgled and clapped his hands—then started to wheeze and gasp and cough and struggle for air.

Lorraine shouted for the nursemaid to fetch the latest prescription, then a footman to send for the physician. She held the choking boy and looked over his head at Genie, through her tears. "I am sorry, but you must go. The excitement is too much."

Seeing a crow? Genie left, because she did not know what else to do. She turned at the door. "Do consider not bleeding him, please. He is so weak now."

"We will ask the physicians."

Who knew no other course of treatment, Genie realized, a great sadness in her heart for the sweet little boy.

"To the park, my lady?" Campbell asked when she stepped into the coach after so brief a visit. He was concerned that the sisters had come to blows and hoped to wipe that gloom from his mistress's face. "No? What about Gunter's, then? We could order more of your favorite ices. Or shopping? You ladies always like shopping."

"Just home, Campbell. Just home." When they were under way, Genie stroked the bird for comfort. "What do you think, Olive?"

For once the bird had nothing to say.

CHAPTER FIFTEEN

Genie could not sleep that night, after a rare evening alone at home. Ardeth had gone out on business, he said. That worried her. She could not ask where he was headed, or with whom, because he was such a private person, and theirs was not that kind of marriage, which also worried her. She was coming no closer to understanding him, although she feared she was way past liking him.

She was also worried about the sickly little boy, her nephew. How helpless her sister had seemed, how frightened. Genie was, too.

The only man who had ever attempted to allay her fears was Ardeth, who also caused his fair share. Drat the man for not being home for her to talk to, not that she often got an answer to any of her questions. She thought of Lorraine's words about his appeal, how the unknown was a challenge to roving-eyed women. Well, his inscrutability was Genie's least favorite attribute in her husband. That and his being gone so much.

She felt like a princess in a tower. The handsome knight had charged to her rescue, forded the moat, stormed the gates, broken the chains of the dungeon, slain the dragon, freed the damsel—and then he had ridden away again. That was not the way the story was supposed to end.

Poor pitiful princess, Genie thought, safe and rich among her diamonds and gold and silks. She looked around her own opulent bedchamber in her own treasure-filled house. How dare she feel sorry for herself? She had no right to complain, not with so much to be thankful for. Nothing like constant companionship had ever been promised to her. In fact, Ardeth had practically sworn to be gone in six months. A sennight less than five months now, so she had better get used to his absence. Besides, she was a strong woman. He'd told her so, made her so. She could face whatever flotsam the Fates tossed her way.

In fact, Genie told herself as she wiped her eyes, she was weeping only because of her delicate condition. Why, she had snapped at Marie this evening for tugging so hard on the corset strings that Genie had not been able to enjoy her dinner. She'd left Miss Hadley and James Vinross alone at the table, claiming a sour stomach. They were concerned, but not enough to interrupt their conversation about some book Genie had never read, making her feel even more blue-deviled. She was glad that they were getting along so well—she'd known they would— but their growing closeness made her feel more of an outsider. What if they married and moved away to live their own lives, without some maudlin pregnant female? She'd be all alone. She'd be glad for them, smug in her successful matchmaking . . . and miserable.

She supposed Ardeth would take the crow with him when he left, too.

Genie blew her nose and gave herself a good mental shake. She would *not* wallow in self-pity. No, she would get something to eat. That was it—she was hungry. Lack of food and company and light could give anyone the megrims. So she put on her slippers and her wrap—not the tissue-thin one from her trousseau, but an old flannel robe in case any of the servants were still about—lit a brace of candles, and went downstairs to the deserted kitchen.

She found a ham, a wheel of cheese, and the last of yesterday's bread waiting to be tomorrow's toast, all right on the wide wooden worktable. Perfect. The pantry shelf held a jar of stewed peaches, a crock of raisins, pickled trotters, candied walnuts, and salted kippers. Yes! She poured a mug of ale because old wives' tales recommended it as healthy for infants.

Eating in solitude was not cheering her up. The kitchen was too big, too empty, with dark corners and strange shadows cast by the hanging pots and pans. The Randolphs' dog could usually be found in the kitchen during the day, but old Helen slept in their son's bedroom, so Genie did not have a four-footed friend to share her meal with. Even two-winged Olive had deserted her, either asleep in Ardeth's book room waiting for his nightly brandy or back in the stable mews, where Campbell and the grooms often diced and drank late at night.

Genie sighed and fixed herself a tray, a heavy tray, she realized when she carried it to her favorite room. With nearly every surface covered by hourglasses, Genie set the tray on the floor. Then she rekindled the fire, pleased to see the light glistening off the polished glass of hundreds of the sand clocks. She'd miss them when they were gone, too, returned to their owners or auctioned off for charity. No, she would think instead of all the good the money would do, paying for schools and teachers and books.

Somehow good deeds were not entirely comforting tonight, either, especially when one was sitting on the floor having a private picnic. What she needed was a book to read, the more boring the better.

First she carried the much-lighter tray back to the kitchen and thought about washing the dishes at the sink: pumping water, heating a pan, disturbing Cook's tidy workplace to find soap and towels. Then she thought about the dessert that she had not touched at dinner.

A small degree of searching found the leftover trifle. Cake and fruit and pudding—and a countess did not have to wash her own dishes, did she? To make less work for the scullery maid in the morning, Genie decided to eat out of the bowl. Only one portion remained anyway. Maybe two small ones.

This time she carried the bowl and a spoon into the library. The room smelled of Ardeth, a bit smoky, a hint of fine soap, his cologne, and leather. The fire was never permitted to go out in here, so the room was warm. That was for the sake of the old, rare books, Ardeth declared. The fire was more for his sake, Genie thought as she untied the sash of her robe.

She sat in Ardeth's favorite wide leather chair and looked at all the books on the shelves, wondering if her husband had read many of them. Most likely he had. She'd been limited to her mother's tastes during her girlhood, then whatever books came her way during the years with Elgin. Books were a luxury she could not afford then, not when money for food and rent were so scarce.

Now she had more books than a lending library, right at her fingertips, and no one to tell her what she ought to read. She'd better start soon if she hoped to catch up with Ardeth, or even Miss Hadley. Then she laughed to herself, at herself. Why, she could not read half the languages on the spines of the books. Still, she did feel better sitting here with Ardeth's books. And with the trifle.

She had not eaten half, or picked up a book, when she heard the door open.

"Ah, what a lovely sight."

So was he, his dark hair slightly disordered, his neckcloth unknotted so the ends hung down his broad shoulders. She felt better already.

"May I have a taste?"

Oh. He meant the trifle. "Of course. I can go fetch another spoon."

"Do not bother. We can share."

Before Genie could move to the sofa Ardeth lifted her, bowl and all, and sat down on the armchair, with her across his lap. She sat stiffly, trying to maintain her dignity with her toes not touching the ground, and too much of her touching the hard planes of her husband. Good grief, her bottom was against his thighs and he was eating trifle!

He pulled her closer, lifting the spoon to his mouth. "You couldn't sleep?"

"No, and I did want to speak with you. But I can wait until tomorrow. I can see that you are tired." His eyes were half-closed, even as he handed her the spoon. "You'll want to find your bed as soon as you finish."

"Not yet. I have too much to do."

"Do you never sleep?"

"Only when I must. Sleep is a waste of time. Sometimes I forget that a body needs refreshing. What did you want to speak of, my dear?"

She swallowed and handed him back the spoon. Instead of handing it to her when he'd had his share, he brought it full to her lips. He was actually feeding her, which had to be one of the most intimate, erotic moments of Genie's life. She could barely remember her name, much less what she'd wanted to ask him.

She licked her lips and shook her head when he offered her another spoonful. Genie needed the time to think, and to think about something other than the warmth where she sat, when Ardeth always claimed to be cold. Where to start? Her toes curling in her slippers? No, no. The easiest place to start was with the boy. While the earl kept eating, she told him about visiting her sister and how she had related Ardeth's warnings about leeches.

"I do not know if she will listen, but the boy was no better. Worse, if anything."

She told him about the child's coughing fit over a silly trick of Olive's, and asked if he had any ideas.

"It sounds as if the boy might be an asthmatic. The condition has been known for centuries, without a successful treatment being found. Odd, is it not, that people know a hundred ways to kill each other, and do so regularly, but they can hardly cure anything?"

She had to ask: "Could you?"

He smiled. "No, I do not have that kind of knowledge, either."

"But you worked wonders with the soldiers."

"Those were wounds. Stitching and sewing, stuffing pieces together."

"But you know so much." She waved one hand around at the shelves that reached to the ceiling. "And you own all of these books."

"I could search them all without finding the cure."

"You are sure?"

"Believe me, if anyone anywhere had discovered an effective panacea, I would know it."

She did believe his statement, no matter how far-fetched. Ardeth was no physician. He did seem relaxed for a change—Genie must remember to tell Cook to make more trifle—so she felt encouraged to ask, "How did you learn so much?"

"I told you, from my travels."

"Many people journey, but few are half as wise."

His lips curved up again at the compliment. "I am not nearly wise enough. I would not hold you on my lap if I had half the wit of an insect."

She started to rise, thinking she was hurting him, but Ardeth held her firmly with one arm around her waist. "I am not stupid enough to let go."

Genie thought she would be wiser to pursue a different tack. "How did you have time to study if you were constantly moving about? Did you attend a university at all?"

"It is too hard to explain."

He did not seem angry or impatient, so Genie persisted. "I would try to understand, to know my husband better."

"I appreciate your efforts, my dear, but much of my past is nearly incomprehensible to me, too." He ate the last spoonful of the trifle and set the bowl aside, obviously seeking an answer to her honest question, so she stayed. Then he said, "Think of a vast place where the greatest minds of all time gather."

"Cambridge?"

He was polite enough not to laugh at her provincialism. "No, bigger. A spiritual space, filled with the knowledge of the ages."

"A monastery?"

"Think larger still, with no walls, no easy answers, only more mysteries."

"That sounds like a magic kingdom out of some fairy tale," she scoffed. "Next you will tell me there are elves and unicorns. No such place can exist."

He rested his head against the back of the chair, his eyes closed. "Oh, it does, somewhere between Heaven and Hell, I suppose."

"Now you are being enigmatic again."

"I told you, it is too hard to explain."

"But you could help my nephew, I know you could. He is a beautiful child, and I hardly got to know him. I fear I never will."

"I cannot. I have been here too long and the knowledge, the power, fades." He flicked his fingers toward the hearth, but nothing happened; the fire still burned.

Genie thought he was teasing. "Surely there are books right here full of magic tricks. But I am not speaking of sleight of hand."

"Neither am I. A man forgets too much. That is his nature, and has to be if he is to go on."

"But you will go back? You will return to this mysterious place in . . . five months?"

"Less now."

"How shall you get there? If you take a ship, I could—"

He touched her lips with his fingers. "It is a different kind of journey. You know that."

"You will die." That was a statement, not a question.

His hand fell to his lap, actually her lap, and idly stroked her thigh while he thought of any other word he could use. He could not find one that made sense. "Yes."

She was only a little distracted by his hand on her upper leg. Somehow his hand was beneath her heavy robe, sliding against the thin silk of her night rail. She refused to succumb to the pleasure, if such was his intent. With Ardeth in an expansive mood, understanding his answers was more important than understanding that the same fiery heat could build in her *other* leg, without his touch. "But you know you will expire at such and such a time? That is impossible unless . . . you do not intend to kill yourself, do you?"

His fingers stopped moving, but wrapped around her thigh in a firm hold. "What, after fighting so hard to live? No, I will not give up until I have to. This"—he squeezed her leg harder, moving his thumb at the same time in a caressing motion that also drew her silk bedgown up higher—"feels too good."

She breathed in. Then out. "You cannot explain more?"

He shook his head and moved his hand to the hem of her gown, now near her knees.

"But you will leave?"

"Unless a real miracle happens. I thought . . ."

He did not say what he thought. "Do you believe in miracles?" Genie asked, thinking there was one at work right now, her bones melting into meringue.

"Oh, I have seen many in my day." His eyes were on the front of her robe, which had fallen open to reveal her bosom, with no stays, no corset, no shift, nothing but a scrap of silk and a line of lace between her smooth, snowy breasts and his hands, his eyes, his tongue, by heaven.

Before he could reach out to lower that neckline, to feast with his eyes the way he had savored the sweet trifle, she shifted around to face him.

He groaned.

"Did I hurt you?"

He could only shake his head, his tongue turned numb and dumb.

"I want to tell you that I understand about your vow of chastity."

She did? Ardeth was having a hard time understanding it now. Harder with every wriggle.

She nodded. So did her breasts, it seemed, the darker nipples rising and falling with her movement, with her breath.

That was good, Ardeth thought. One of them should keep breathing.

Then she said, "Yes, you think marital relations might shorten your life."

That got his heart beating again and his wits back in his brain instead of his breeches.

One misstep might make him Satan's puppet for eternity. If he harmed her or hurt her feelings, if he used her like a harlot, he was finished, hourglass or not. He'd be gone forever, and this time not as a Reaper, either, despite Satan's words. His Grimness would not employ such a defector, and the Devil would not let him go. Ar might end up being a plague bearer or a fire kindler. The Devil loved those catastrophic kills. With so many souls lost, a few more than usual were bound to come his way. A dead Coryn Ardsley, Earl of Ardeth, would have no power to prevent any of it. He would have no will to resist, but enough to know what he was doing. That would be the worst.

As if he felt a sudden chill, Ardeth pulled Genie's skirt

down and her robe closed. He moved his hand to her hair, brushing his fingers through the sunset waves. "We shall not speak of it again. Now rest."

Here, in his arms? In his lap? That must have been what he'd meant, for he pulled her closer against his chest, tucking her robe around her like a blanket. But she was not cold, not at all. Quite the contrary, in fact. And she was still not tired. Well, perhaps she was a little weary. After all, it must be close to four o'clock in the morning by now. And the gentle touch of his fingers on her head was soothing. So what if her husband was an enigma or an escapee from a mental asylum? His arms felt right. His chest made a perfect pillow. His steady heartbeat acted as a lullaby.

The crow flew in an hour later. Ardeth opened one eye at the flapping of the bird's wings at the trifle bowl as Olive looked for crumbs. Then he opened the other eye and noticed that his wife's robe had fallen open, revealing her charms, and that there was a gremlin's grin on the crow's face.

"I didn't do it," he said, meaning he had not lecherously undressed a sleeping woman or nudged her mind into slumber in order to avoid more questions.

"Ar hum ball," Olive cawed.

"I am humble? Well, yes, I have learned humility in the face of my desires, but I have not surrendered."

"Hum ball," the crow repeated.

"You mean humbug? I tell you, I did not tumble my wife here in the library like a libertine."

The crow wiped his beak on the carpet. "Ar. Hum'bird balls."

CHAPTER SIXTEEN

Genie awakened in her own bed the next morning. She did not have to wonder how she got here, remembering her husband's arms around her. She did, however, wonder what Cook had put in the trifle. She had never seen Ardeth at once so talkative and so little in control. Not that he made any more sense than usual. The poor man was deluded into thinking that some dire fate was going to claim him, whisking him off to some metaphysical temple on a specified date, depending on the discovery of a small hourglass. Or maybe Ardeth was still living his fairy tale of a knight in shining armor, with a sorcerer's spell laid on him.

Whether he was deluded or not, Genie was not going to let him go.

She had a kind and caring husband, enough funds that she need never worry. She had friends, family, an almost scandal-free name. Now all she needed, according to Ardeth, was a miracle.

Was it blasphemous to pray for something that sounded entirely heathenish? Genie did not know if her prayers were worth tuppence, since she had lied and cursed and not honored her parents, besides been unfaithful to Elgin's memory. Oh, and she had coveted her neighbor's everything, in the days when she had nothing.

She honestly did not know if she believed in miracles, for that matter. She did, however, believe that God helped those who helped themselves, and she fully intended to help herself to a happy ending. If there was such a thing as a miracle, Ardeth was hers, appearing just when she needed him. Hers to keep.

She was not going to concede defeat, not going to hand the man she loved—she could admit that to herself—over to some evil assassin or wicked wizard, even if they existed only in his own muddled mind. He'd stay, she was sure, if she found the hourglass, or if he loved her enough.

Now who was living a fantasy? The peculiar trinket—if it existed outside Ardeth's imagination—was lost in another country entirely, across the sea. The odds of finding it, though, were better than those of her other option. A man like Ardeth, worldly wise and wonderful—loving silly redhaired Imogene Hopewell? Ha! But she could try.

She knew he cared for her and wanted her happiness, but that was not love. Neither was sex, but it was a start. He already noticed her: her skin, her hair, her lips, her breasts. She was no green girl who could not recognize a man's desire when she saw it in his obsidian eyes and hear it in his ragged breathing. She'd seen it often enough in Elgin, when slaking that desire was about the only use he ever had for Genie. Elgin had not been a gentle lover, nor even a satisfying one—other women had whispered that pleasure was possible for both partners in the intimate act!—but Genie had learned to recognize his amorous moods the same way she watched for his drunken rages or morning-after moodiness. She had also learned to find some excuse to avoid her husband's embrace whenever she could, a headache, the accounts, her courses. Now she was going to use that knowledge of a woman's power to bring a man to his knees, or to her bed, despite whatever foolish notions her husband held. Just let him try to claim a headache, the accounts, his . . . cronies!

That was her plan, to succeed by seduction. She ignored the existence of the scores of women far more beautiful, far more experienced in pleasing a man, and far more dashing than she was. She was his wife.

On the other hand, maybe he could grow to love her mind, which, she admitted, was not a quarter as quick as his. Or her character. She was working on forgiving her sister, and had written a polite thank-you to her mother. Genie knew Ardeth appreciated good deeds, and for every toy and treat and book she sent her little nephew, she sent a dozen to the nearest orphanage, and not just to impress Ardeth. She also went in person to play with the children and read to them, for her own pleasure. Little Peter was seldom well enough for her visits, although he adored seeing Olive perform.

Genie realized she could not do more than look her best and be on her best behavior. But she could try to spend more time with the earl, so he'd be aware of both her physical and mental attributes, such as they were, and her affection for him. According to the novels she'd read and Marie's chatter, liking was the best aphrodisiac.

She sought him out whenever she was not at the orphanage or scouring antiquities shops and jewelers for an hourglass brooch. If there was one such gewgaw, she figured, there must be others made from the same mold. Perhaps her husband could not tell the difference in his addled state.

She wanted oysters; could he take her to dine at the hotel that served the best? The smells of the city were upsetting her stomach; a drive in the country would refresh her. Her father had not written; what did Ardeth advise? Her effort to learn German needed practice, her sketch of Ardeth needed another sitting, and what did he think of the Corn Laws?

To get Ardeth alone meant she had to send Miss Hadley and James Vinross off on other errands. They did not seem to mind. Neither did Ardeth, although he was amused to think she was advancing the other couple's courtship.

Genie took to holding his hand, touching his face, bestowing a good-night kiss on his cheek. He never seemed to mind that, either. He did not offer more, but he accepted her shows of affection, after his first surprise.

Was she making progress? Genie hoped so, for they'd be leaving town soon, and a man could disappear in the country far more easily than among the crowded streets. Ardeth had been studying all kinds of agricultural treatises, she knew, so was liable to immerse himself in his lands once they reached Ardsley Keep. And there would be less than four months left.

Marie lowered the necklines of Genie's gowns. Miss Hadley tutored her singing voice. Cook kept the trifles coming. The Randolphs kept the fires lit. Genie did, too, the flickers of passion she was hoping to kindle.

She held private waltz parties just for him, with a small hired orchestra seated behind a screen. Miss

Hadley and James sometimes joined them, and James's sister and her betrothed, with his mother smiling happily over the lobster patties. Genie suspected Marie and Campbell and the Randolphs danced in the adjoining parlor, so she left the doors open for the sound to carry.

At least Ardeth had to hold her while the music played. She swayed closer, clung tighter, smiled more suggestively—and still the clunch left her outside her bedroom door. A good-night kiss seemed as far as he was willing to go, and not one inch closer.

What in the name of all the saints was a woman to do, beg on her knees? Hide in his bed? Weep? Begging would embarrass both of them, and Genie had tried waiting in the sitting room adjoining his chamber. The man must have extraordinary hearing, or smelled her perfume, or whatever. He never came, not when she was there. As for tears, they were a weakling's weapon. Ardeth would be a comfort, but he would not be aroused.

He liked her. He cared for her. He enjoyed being with her. Genie was certain of those things. She was equally as positive that he was attracted to her. He raised his eyes with effort and manners when her bodice shrank. He swallowed hard when she licked her lips. He never felt the cold when they danced. He smiled more.

And he stayed on his side of the door. Perhaps her burgeoning belly was repulsive to him, or the fact that the babe was not his, despite his avowals. Or perhaps the man was a saint after all.

Genie was plotting stronger measures—accidentally walking in on her husband at his bath, pretending a mouse was hiding under her bed, dancing naked on the dining room table, by Jupiter; she was that desperate—when her plans suffered a setback.

Major Lord Willeford and his wife returned to London after a visit to her father in Cornwall. Her father being a marquess, to say nothing of Willeford's sister's husband being a duke, the pair had an elevated opinion of themselves, and a low opinion of Genie and Ardeth.

Willeford knew better than to challenge Ardeth to his face. The jumped-up foreigner was too popular at the clubs and too dashed dangerous looking to take on head-to-head. One dark glance from Ardeth had younger men fleeing, and older men minding their tongues.

Willeford's own tongue was tied. He could not mention the actions of the earl in the late battle, not wanting his own behavior examined. But he could start asking questions, like where Ardeth's money came from, and where, precisely, his sympathies lay. Here he was, giving money away hand over fist to the poor, just like some revolutionary. Why, he might have been a Bonapartist during the war, supporting the filthy French. After all, no one had seen him before the last victory.

For that matter, no one had ever heard of him or his title. The earldom might have been an ancient one, but no one knew of any Coryn Ardsley, his father, or his grandfather. Where did he go to school? Who were his chums? They had only his vague answers of travel and investments.

Faugh. Now that he was in England, all Ardeth seemed to care about were the lower classes. If he was not a traitor to his country, Willeford hinted, he was a traitor to his class. Gentlemen, especially those who owned mills and mines, began to listen.

Lady Willeford did her part in the whispering campaign. She mentioned to a few of her oldest, dearest friends that she did not care to attend the same gatherings as climbers and fast women. When pressed, she would not name names, but she did hint at a widow bride whose condition was as scandalous as the identity of the child's father.

Soon ladies were staring at Genie's middle, talking behind her back. Her sister defended her, Genie was happy to hear, as did Lady Vinross, but some things were simply indefensible, and harder to hide. Fewer invitations were delivered. Fewer women sought her company.

"How soon can we go into the country?" she asked Ardeth one night after dinner. Miss Hadley and James were singing duets at the pianoforte while Genie stitched at her needlework. Ardeth was reading. He'd be going out later, Genie knew, to yet more political gatherings, rallies in support of workers, meetings with denizens of London's underworld who plied their trades at night. The dangers he faced were yet another reason to leave town. "I thought your work here in London was almost done."

He looked up and smiled to see that she had her feet tucked under her, like a little girl. "Almost."

"Surely you have convinced everyone whose mind is open enough to change. The others will never be swayed to your causes. And I know you have trained assistants ready to carry on when you are gone, so that is no reason to stay longer."

"Why, are you not enjoying yourself?"

"Less every day, I am afraid."

"The social rounds do grow tiresome. I cannot imagine what the fribbles find to speak about, seeing the same people every day."

"They talk about us. There is gossip, I understand, sly whispers that place my new acquaintances in awkward positions. We should leave."

"Concede defeat by running away?"

"It would not be cowardly to go visit my parents. Quite the contrary, but Mama has asked twice now for our visit. No one would think it odd in us to go, especially with so many of the *ton* leaving for their own estates. And it is past time to get your country house in order, too. Those distant relations of yours who live there sent a small pair of candlesticks for our marriage. I took that to be a token of their small regard. I doubt they are pleased to have their places usurped, with a new master and mistress appearing out of the blue. For all you know, they could be robbing the estate blind while we stay on in town."

"No, I thought about the chances for ill feelings and felonies, so I installed stewards who report to me, and other men who report on them. All is in order. Everyone will be amply compensated."

"Very well, but what about the village school for girls I was going to establish, and the pottery for returning soldiers? There is much work to be done."

"You are right, my dear. We should think about going while the weather holds. You will not wish to travel later, and I admit I am curious to see Ardsley Keep."

"It is odd to think of an earl not knowing his ancestral lands."

Sir Coryn had claimed those acres with his sword, defended that castle with his blood. He knew them. "Oh, I have a good idea of the place. But you will want to refurbish it to your tastes."

"And yours. I know you will want to install a bathing room with heating pipes, if one does not already exist."

He smiled at how well she understood his needs, or thought she did. "Yes, we have much to do. Still, I am not content to let one man's ugliness besmear the good we are doing. I have heard the rumors, you see, noticed doubts on men's faces in the clubs and coffeehouses. I do not wish to let James Vinross fight my battles, nor engage in name-calling like a grubby schoolboy."

"You will not challenge Willeford, will you?"

"To swords or pistols? Hell, no. That is, heavens, I am not that bloodthirsty. Mayhap I shall stick Willeford's wagging tongue to the roof of his mouth." He smiled at her gasp. "No, I have one more important meeting next week. I will use the time to decide what to do about the maggot. Then we can go."

Before the week was half-gone, Genie's sister, Lorraine, came to call. Lady Cormack gave her card to Randolph, but rushed past the butler when she heard Genie's footsteps. Lady Ardeth was not the one she wished to see, however.

"Is your husband home, Genie? I must see him."

"Why? Is a mob coming after him?" Genie's words were only half in jest.

"This is no time for levity. I need the man. My son is worse and the doctors have given up. They blame me for stopping the bloodletting, but Ardeth was right—their leeches were not helping the poor angel. He was better for a few days. You saw yourself when he played with the puppet you brought."

"I thought he had better color, more energy."

"And his appetite improved. But last night he suffered another bout of wheezing and took a turn for the worse. I am at my wit's end. What if he cannot recover from the next time?"

Genie poured her sister a cup of hot tea. "But Ardeth is no physician."

Lorraine left her cup on the table. "I have heard wonders. Lady Vinross, and, yes, even Lady Willeford, say that he worked in the field hospital and saved scores of men. Lady Vinross thinks him an angel, while the major's wife swears he is a devil. Either way, he saved lives! He must help me now."

"I do not know if he can," Genie began.

"He can try! I have no one else to ask."

Genie sent messengers around to the various clubs and coffeehouses Ardeth was known to visit. She gave Lorraine fresh tea and honey cakes and handkerchiefs to wipe her eyes while they waited.

In moments, it seemed, Ardeth rushed into the room. He knelt in front of Genie before she could rise and took up her hands. "The footman said there was a crisis of some sort, that I was needed at home. Are you all right?"

"Yes, I am fine. I am not the one who needs you."

As if he'd held his breath the whole way home, Ardeth exhaled. Then he crushed Genie in his arms, rocking her in relief. Any other time she would have been delighted. He really did care for her, in his own muckle-minded way.

"I am fine," she said. "My sister needs your help."

Ardeth noticed the other woman and set Genie aside so he could bow. "Lady Cormack."

Instead of offering her hand, she grabbed his. Without preamble, she said, "My little boy is sick. No one seems to be able to help him. You can, I know it."

Ardeth took his hand back. "Nay, my lady. I cannot help. I am no medical practitioner."

"But I have heard that you know more than those who call themselves doctors, surgeons, or physicians. I have tried herbal women and midwives, priests and apothecaries. Nothing helps clear his lungs, no infusions, no chest poultices, no tisanes. My baby is weaker and less able to recover from the bouts of wheezing. He cannot breathe, I say! Surely you can do something. Lady Vinross swears you have a healing touch. Other women whose sons and brothers were in the war support her. It was your medical skill that opened doors in London to you and Genie."

He shook his head. "My wife already asked about the boy. I am sorry, but I cannot offer any assistance."

"Is it because I was cruel to her?" Lorraine twisted her handkerchief between shaking fingers. "I have begged her forgiveness. I have groveled to Mama on her behalf. I have defended her against gossip and society's disapproval. What more can I do to make up for the past?"

"No, that is not why I—"

Lorraine was crying again. "Would you make my son pay for my mistakes?"

"I swear, your previous behavior has nothing to do with my decision. Without the events of the past I would not have my wife, you would not have your son. We cannot change what occurred anyway. We can only forget and go on."

"Then you have no reason to refuse to help a little child who needs you. I cannot go on without my boy."

Genie was twisting her own handkerchief in her hands. She looked at Ardeth through glistening green eyes. "Please?"

He turned to face the hearth, not his good-hearted, trusting wife. "But I do not know what to do for asthmatics or congestions. I told you, sewing up wounds, cleaning dirt away, digging out pistol balls, those were easy."

"You did more," she softly said. "I saw you."

Lorraine stared between them, pleading written on her face.

"I—," he began.

Genie stepped closer and put a hand on his arm until he turned to face her again. "You gave the men ease, if nothing else. You spoke to them and they rested, so their bodies could recover. I did not understand how, but your touch, your voice, your eyes, all worked as well as any medication or opiate."

"It is gone," Ardeth said on a whisper. He knew Genie meant his skill. He meant his power.

She contradicted him, touching his hand. "No. I feel it in your arms. I feel safe and protected, cared for and un-afraid. I do not doubt you helped me sleep at night."

"That is in your imagination. I do nothing."

He did nothing, all right, but Genie was not going to discuss her empty bed in front of her sister, who now appeared confused—interested, but confused.

"James swears it is so," Genie insisted. "Whatever you did, he no longer has nightmares."

"That was over a month ago. Even if I am still able to give the boy some rest, that will not cure him. Sleep will not clear his chest or strengthen his lungs or open his air-ways. Next time will be worse, and the time after that. Ecod, he cannot sleep forever, and I cannot cure him! Don't you think I would if I could?"

"You can try, dash it! You spend your time and money aiding the poor and unfortunate. You build hospitals and schools. Can't you try to help one little boy? For me?"

Ardeth could not say no. "Very well, I will go, but do not get your hopes raised."

Genie kissed his cheek.

Lorraine said, "I have no hopes."

CHAPTER SEVENTEEN

"I'll just get my bonnet and pelisse," Genie said.

"No, you stay here."

"But I was a help at the field hospital, remember?"

"That was then. This is now. The soldiers had grievous wounds; the boy is sick. There is a vast difference. Besides, you will be too much of a distraction."

She would? So her plan was working, not that this was the time to celebrate. "I'll stay out of the way."

He looked at her as if he wanted to turn her into a tree, rooted to the parlor floor. She did not know if he could. She did know he would not. Ardeth was trying to protect her, as always.

"I promise not to bother you," she said. "Peter is my nephew, too, and I will fret myself to flinders here, not knowing how he goes on."

He jerked his head, but turned for the door without waiting to see if she followed. He called for his horse, leaving her and Lorraine to take the Cormack coach.

Lorraine called after him, "Don't you need your instruments?"

"What, do you think that my flute will cure your son? That weak lungs can be tamed like a cobra is charmed by the pipes?"

He played the flute? Genie never knew. Or that he could tame snakes.

Lorraine had meant medical instruments, of course, the paraphernalia all the experts carried. "Doctoring equipment, that is."

"Why would I have any sawbones' tools when I am not a surgeon?" Ardeth asked. "Do you see what thin fabric you have pinned your hopes on? As thin as air."

"Try," Genie called after him as he mounted the black stallion. "That is all we are asking."

They had no idea what they were asking. Ardeth did, after one look at the boy.

After thanking him profusely for coming, and listening to Ardeth's denials of any skill or knowledge of medicine, Roger, Lord Cormack, took him up to the child's room.

"Here is your uncle, come to help you feel better if he can," the baron said.

"Uncle Elgin is in Heaven," the boy said in a faint whisper, every breath an effort. "You showed me his sword."

"That's right, but this is Aunt Genie's new husband, Uncle Ardeth."

"Uncle Coryn," Ardeth corrected, not liking anything sounding of death to pass through the child's lips, his blue-tinged lips. The boy was as pale as his sheets, thin as the post on his huge canopied bed. He lay as still as one of the wooden soldiers surrounding him. He stirred and struggled to sit up against the mounds of pillows behind him and offered a shy smile. The nursemaid rushed to prop more pillows at his back.

Yes, he had an angel's smile, and Ardeth's own angel's green eyes, but without the dancing flecks of gold and blue. The boy's eyes were dull, droopy. They showed more animation when Olive flapped his wings. The crow flew off Ardeth's shoulder and landed on the boy's, rubbing his head against the lad's cheek.

"Hallo, Olive," Peter said, making a visible effort to raise his hand to stroke the shiny feathers. "I am glad you—"

Then he started to cough, and to choke, and then to wheeze. Lord Cormack was helpless. The nursemaid was helpless. Ardeth was . . . without hope.

He looked at the tiny boy gasping for air in his feather bed, almost lost in his mounds of down pillows, with the blasted bird hopping up and down on his chest, as if that would force the air to go through. It would not, Ardeth knew. The steam from the kettle the nursemaid fanned with damp towels was not helping, nor was Cormack's rubbing his son's back.

Ardeth did not know who was panicked worse, the maid, the baron, or the boy, whose eyes were huge and glassy now, tears streaming down his cheeks. Ardeth pushed the man aside and lifted the frail child to his own chest, stroking Peter's neck and temples with his free hand, whispering words in whatever language came first to his tongue. The gasping subsided as Peter relaxed into drowsiness.

The nursemaid crossed herself. The baron started to mop his damp brow and grin.

Ardeth told him, "Do not celebrate, Cormack. He simply rests between episodes. Nothing has changed. Nothing."

Then, the boy still in his arms, he started to issue orders. "Find another room, one without a feather bed. And no down pillows, either. We need a room with a fireplace for the steam kettle, scores of blankets to lay him on, sheets for his pillows."

"My dressing room will do. My valet sometimes sleeps there on a cot. And there is a small brazier for heating bathwater." Lord Cormack went into the hall to send waiting servants to fetch the sheets and covers, another to bring the kettle and towels.

"And you, get outside," Ardeth told the crow.

"'Awk!" Olive screamed.

"Very well, go to the kitchen."

"Cat!"

"Damn it, I do not have time for your fears and foibles. Be a gremlin, dash it, not a bird with a hollow backbone."

Feathers started to shake and greenish talons started to form from the tip of one wing.

"No, not that!" Ardeth shouted.

Cormack hurried back into the room. "Is he . . . gone?"

Ardeth looked at the bird. "He better be."

The gnarly fingers disappeared. Olive flew to the canopy and smoothed his wing tips. Cormack groaned.

"My apologies," Ardeth said. "The boy is the same. But the feathers are doing him no good."

The baron shook his head. "You mean all these weeks, we only had to get rid of the feathers and eiderdown?"

"No, but doing so might help a little now."

A cot had been drawn up next to the charcoal brazier in the baron's dressing room, its mattress stripped away and soft blankets laid out instead. A stack of folded sheets was at the head, as Ardeth wanted. The copper tub had been shoved into a corner.

Ardeth laid the quiet boy down, covering him lightly, watching.

"What more do you want?" Lord Cormack asked.

"Brandy."

"Will that help him? They sometimes give him laudanum to rest, but he is already asleep."

"The brandy is for me, to settle my nerves."

"You? They say you have ice water running through your veins."

Ardeth shivered, despite the warmth of the new coals. "No. I have fears, like every man." For once he wished he did not have all the emotions mortals endured. He feared he could not save the boy.

The baron went into his bedroom for a decanter and glass. When he came back, Ardeth was sitting on a low stool beside the bed, staring at the boy as if he were trying to read his future.

"What now?"

Ardeth had a drink, then placed a hand on the child's forehead. Next he laid his own head on the small bony chest, listening for a heartbeat, listening to his lungs.

"Your wife will have returned. Now you should go comfort her, and pray if you can. I will stay."

"I will stay with you."

"No, she needs you more. And the boy does not need her laments. He sleeps, but he can hear, I think."

"Will he . . . that is, will he awake?"

"His life is in other hands now."

"But without the fluff and feathers?" Cormack was desperate for something to hold on to, something reassuring to tell his wife.

"Perhaps." Ardeth was not hopeful, not after hearing the crackling, sloshing sounds in Peter's lungs.

"Shall I . . . shall I send for a vicar?"

Ardeth had never been one for empty efforts. "Only if he knows how to cure congestion."

"What will you do?"

"I will wait. I will make sure he sleeps, and I will wait some more. Go to your wife. And mine. Give the crow a bit of brandy, too."

The baron left and Ardeth adjusted the kettle, placing a damp flannel on the boy's chest. None of it was going to make a bit of difference, but at least he was doing something. He smoothed damp curls back from the boy's forehead and wondered what kind of child he would have been. Arrogant as the firstborn, the heir? Spoiled as an only child? Or raised by nannies and tutors like so many children of the upper classes?

The nursemaid came in and saw Ardeth in what she took for prayer. She would have joined him, kneeling on the floor, but he waved her away. She saw the boy's chest rising and falling, and nodded. An earl's prayers must be better than a mere maid's.

Another servant came with a tray of bread and cheese and wine.

Ardeth left them, just waiting.

"Shall I bring more candles, my lord?" the butler inquired still later.

"No. I need the dark." Ardeth shut the door behind the butler and went back to waiting. And waiting.

Finally it came, the light he had been waiting for. He thanked whoever was in charge that he could still see the telltale gleam of an hourglass at its end. A shadow followed the glow, hovering at the boy's side.

"Don't," Ardeth said.

The shadow raised an arm to cast sleep and silence. No

one who lived ever recalled seeing the Alphabet of Eternity.

Ardeth cleared his throat and said, "Don't" again, to show he was wide-awake and aware of Death's presence.

"Who . . . ?"

"I am."

"You are?"

"That is right. It is I, Ar."

The cowled figure tilted his head. "Don't you mean 'I am'?"

"I am Ar, once a fellow gatherer."

"The one who wagered with the Devil and won?"

"I only won a chance. So far."

"Everyone was talking about you, Ar. Some were not happy with what you did. Not good for morale, *comprenez-vous*?"

"My apologies, Monsieur . . . ?"

"*F*, Effe."

Ardeth bowed. Effe bowed back. A duchess's drawing room could not have been more polite. Then Effe said, "A pleasure, *certainement,* but just what are you doing here? I have the boy on my list." He checked the hourglass he held. "Quite on time, too."

"I want you to take him off your list."

Effe laughed, sort of. "You know I cannot do that."

"I know you can, if you wish."

"I can give you a minute or two, *oui*, as a favor. No more."

Ardeth looked at the small shimmering hourglass, the mirror image of the one he used to carry. Only a scattering of grains of sand remained in the top chamber. For an instant Ardeth wondered if he could overpower Effe, steal the hourglass, save the boy, and claim it for himself. Thus saving himself.

No, there would be hell to pay for sure. And the Devil only knew what would happen to Effe.

"I would like to make a bargain with you," Ardeth said.

"Himself would have the catfits."

"His Grimness would not have to know."

"Ha, that's what you think."

Ardeth raised an eyebrow. "Old Grimmy never knew what I was doing all those years. Do you think he keeps track of every death, every second?"

"I never thought about it, *vraiment*. I just do my job."

"And I am sure you have done well at it."

"That is right," Effe said, puffing up his shrouding cloak. "No needless suffering, no more pain. No hysteria, either, if I can help it. I hate that, when they fight."

Ardeth nodded. "You are a good"—not man, not soul, not friend—"worker. That is why I need you to help me now."

"But why? My mishandling of the hourglass will not gain you more months to win your bet."

"I know that, yet I still need him to live. The boy's survival has nothing to do with my own, except in a way you cannot understand. I know I did not use to see. I just did my job, too, until I grew to hate it. Now I have other needs. Tell me, is there no one on this plane you would have me rescue? No wrongs to right, no family to care for? With the French defeated, your descendants might need help. I could make them rich in their own country, or bring them here. With enough gold I could make them part of the new government."

Effe shook his head. "*Non.* It has been so long I do not remember any family or friends or why they might want to be at court. I never followed their progress through the ages. All the Letters agreed it was better that way, I thought. All but you, it seems."

"Then is there anything you want for yourself? No bauble you covet?"

"To do what with?" Effe thought for a minute. "I suppose I could ask for the Devil's lucky bone. They say he was madder at losing it than losing you. You still have it, don't you?"

Ardeth reached into his pocket and held up the relic. "It does not seem to work well for me now, although I am reluctant to test it too far. But, here, you could give it back to him, in return for some favor you wish. You could make another wager like mine."

The hooded figure shuddered, backing away. "I avoid his company whenever I can. Besides, he'd never make another such deal."

"No, I doubt he'd let himself be tricked twice."

"If you must know, everyone thought you were brilliant, and they are all furious that he changed the wager on you. Now no one wants to play in Hell, so Satan is nastier than ever. But no, I would not touch his lucky charm."

So that avenue was closed to Ardeth. Some Deaths were prouder than others. "I do not suppose you would look the other way while I shook the hourglass?"

"I cannot."

"But he is just a boy." Ardeth had heard that millions of times.

Effe gave the same answer. "They all were, once."

Ardeth leaned back against the wall, almost defeated.

"Is there no one, nothing, here that you care about? Is there no one you have met in your wanderings who touched your heart?"

Effe looked as sad as one with no face or features could look. His hood sagged. "Don't you remember, Ar? We have no hearts. No one with feelings could do our work. Maybe that was your trouble. Someone erred at the indoctrination."

"No, I was as cold and merciless as any dark angel."

"Here now, I am not a bad fellow."

"Then help me! Help the child."

"You really do care."

"I do."

"He is not yours, is he? You have not been gone long enough."

"No, he is not mine, but he has a place in here." He tapped his chest, where a man's heart beat. "And I have to try."

Effe thought a minute. "Now that I recall, there was a soldier this morning, right here in London. Poor man came back from war to live with his widowed sister and her five children. He has no money, no job, no prospects. I had to collect the sister."

"I'll make the man a generous gift, so he can hire nursemaids and tutors."

"That won't do. He is a man. Pride, you know."

Ardeth bit back his own. "Then what can I offer?"

"A job, a place to live, a mother for his new children."

"Done. Ardsley Keep needs good men. I can train him to keep the books, clean the stables, whatever suits his aptitude. The children can go to the new school, and my wife likes to matchmake."

"That might do." Effe held the hourglass up. Only

three or four grains of sand were left. "My stop before that was at the home of a miserly old woman."

"What, is her family destitute now, too?"

"No, they were already counting her gold before I left. All but the lady's companion. That poor woman was not even mentioned in the will, so she is left with no home, no position, and no references, with the old bird's heart giving out so suddenly. Worse, she seemed to hold the skinflint in some affection."

"My wife can use a new companion. I'd wager Miss Hadley and Vinross will set up housekeeping on their own soon enough."

Effe ignored him, now that he was remembering. "And the one before that, a shoemaker, left his wife with no sons to take over the business. She needs help."

"Done!"

Two grains were left. The child's breaths were further and further apart.

"Oh, and I did have to collect a vicar whose family will be displaced from the manse by the new occupants, and a flower seller with no one to claim her body for burial. Are you writing all this down?"

"I am memorizing it. I will take care of everyone, I swear. A wife, a position, a home, an apprentice shoemaker, a funeral. What else?"

"The old lady who fell down the stairs worried about her cat."

"Tabby will eat fish for the rest of her life."

"That retired schoolmaster out in Kensington will be lonely without his wife. And then there is the Covent Garden whore who killed her procurer. Self-defense, *naturellement*, but she might hang. But can I trust you? You cheated the Devil, after all."

"I swear on my honor as a man."

Effe was growing pensive and philosophical, now that he had begun thinking. "Did I have any honor, do you suppose?"

Ardeth wanted to shake the bastard as he watched the next-to-last grain of sand fall. "You have centuries more to wonder. But I have enough honor for both of us."

Effe sighed. "I guess I am a gambler after all. I trust you." And he turned the hourglass upside down. The light went out. Effe passed through the wall.

Ardeth started to light more candles so he could see the boy better. Peter was breathing more smoothly, without any rattle. He opened his eyes, looked around at the unfamiliar surroundings and the tall man bending over him.

"Olive?"

"Yes," was all Ardeth could say. Yes, the boy would live.

But Peter was pointing toward the window, where the crow was tapping on the glass.

"Alive?" Ardeth heard him caw.

"Yes."

Olive hopped up and down, flapping against the window. Peter held his hand out.

Ardeth took it, glad to feel the child's grasp. "No, you cannot play with the bird until you are well and strong."

The boy looked at his new uncle with suspicion.

"Soon, I promise."

Peter smiled and went back to sleep, Ardeth's hand in his.

CHAPTER EIGHTEEN

Lorraine was crying, this time in happiness. Her husband was pouring champagne. Their son was sleeping peacefully, breathing easily, after having a bowl of porridge. They were celebrating in the sitting room between the master bedrooms, while the nursemaid watched over Peter in the baron's dressing room.

Ardeth refused a glass. "No, there is no time for celebration. And no telling what the future may bring," he warned as he took another piece of paper from Genie, who was seated at the escritoire while he paced beside the desk. "Take the boy to the country in a few days, where the air is cleaner and easier to breathe. Let him play, but keep him away from feather pillows, maybe cats, and do not put flowers in his room. Then see what happens. Remember, there are no guarantees in this life, but a great debt."

"I owe you," Lord Cormack was saying, after refilling his own glass after another toast to his heir's health.

"No, the debt is mine and your son's." Ardeth was dictating a list to Genie, who did not understand where all these names and addresses came from, each on a separate sheet of Lorraine's stationery. Ardeth had been nowhere but up in the boy's room.

Roger was just as confused, and possibly a bit drunk on champagne and joy. "A debt, you say? Peter is too young to wager," he said, trying to make a joke.

Cormack would be surprised at how much a life was worth, Ardeth thought, surprised himself that the French Reaper had remembered so much. By the time he was finished reciting from memory, Genie had eight names on eight pieces of paper, with addresses. One name was Cat; one address was Newgate Prison. Oh Lord, her husband had performed a miracle, at the expense of his mind.

Lorraine half echoed her thoughts, the marvel part, not the madness. "Whatever the cost of your wonder-working, we will pay it."

Ardeth ran his hand through his hair, allowing more dark locks to fall forward. " 'Sooth, I performed no miracle. I just tried some practical expediencies." When Genie not so subtly cleared her throat, he added, "And an ancient art of soothing, from my travels. And Peter will repay his share of the debt by being a good man."

Roger raised his glass again. "God willing, he will live to see manhood, thanks to you."

Embarrassed by the praise, Ardeth took the last of the cards from Genie and said, "I must go now, with much to accomplish before morning."

"All these people," Genie asked, "we have to find them tonight?" It was already late afternoon.

He ignored her "we" and put the papers in some kind of order. "Yes, they might be gone on their way by daybreak, and who knows where?" He looked at the top address. "Perhaps the river Thames. I will not have another death on my hands."

Genie could see Roger wondering how much brandy Ardeth had taken upstairs. He was not one to let his own debts go unpaid, however. Whatever Ardeth needed, he would get. "I can help."

Ardeth looked at the baron, a pleasant, sandy-haired gentleman with flushed cheeks, a man of the earth who was at home in London, but who would be happy to take his son back to his sheep and hogs. "Very well, there is enough to do for both of us." He reshuffled the squares of paper with Genie's neat handwriting. "Not the cat. Not the five children—that would be too much excitement for Peter." He was clearly talking to himself, leaving the others bewildered. "What would a London swell do with a lonely old schoolteacher or a shoemaker's widow?" He looked at the last two names. "Hmm, the funeral or the jailbreak?"

Lorraine poured herself another glass of wine.

"No, I never get to see the funerals," he muttered, handing the last sheet to Roger. "Here, you must know someone in authority. Or someone willing to take a bribe. There is a young woman in prison for killing a man. It was in self-defense. Go get her out of jail."

Lorraine was choking on the drink. "My husband"—cough, cough—"should associate with a murderess? Chance contracting jail fever?"

Her husband came over to hit her on the back, looking no less horrified. "How do you know she is innocent?"

"I did not say she is innocent, only that she had cause. The man was beating her. Your courts are not known for leniency nor understanding, especially when the murderer is a woman, a poor woman, a prostitute."

"A pros—a pros—" Lorraine could not even say the word. "You want my husband to go bail for a . . . ?"

"Homicidal whore, yes. She will be loaded onto a ship for the penal colonies otherwise, unless she is sent to the prison hulks here in the harbor. Women seldom survive, you know, being used by the convicts and the crew alike."

Lorraine put her hands over her ears.

Ardeth stood over her, glaring. If her eyes were not closed, she would have fainted at the threat in his. "Lady Cormack, you came to me. I told you I was no doctor, but you trusted me with your son's welfare. Now you have to trust me again. This Daisy did not kill for the pleasure of it, nor for revenge. She wanted only to save her own life."

Lord Cormack put his arm around his wife. "We have our boy. We will do what we can for this woman. She will be out of jail and in our keeping before sunrise."

"But what should we do with her?" Lorraine wanted to know. Everyone could tell she was praying not to have the woman in her house.

"Bring her to Ardeth House. I'll leave instructions for the staff. Someone can drive her to the docks and Vinross can get her on a ship to the Americas, if she wants to go where her past will be unknown. But hurry. She deserves better than even one night in prison for ridding the world of the scum she killed." He took another piece of paper from Genie, where she had written *ship, colonies*. "I will take care of the rest if you get her released. It might take a sum of money."

"I have it." Roger kissed his wife and left.

"I must go, too," Ardeth said.

"I am coming." Genie snatched the papers from his hand and grabbed up another stack of blank sheets, plus a pencil. "You need me to take notes, send messages home, et cetera. And you need me to help if you have to accomplish so much in so short a time. You already look exhausted, after staring down death."

"No, I smiled at him."

She smiled, too, at his nonsense. "Well, I am sure your smile is enough to melt the hardest heart. But I already had Campbell come with the carriage to take us home, so you have no excuse not to take me. One of Roger's grooms can walk Black Butch home. Unless you wish me to go by myself to rescue the cat?"

"No, that is in an unsavory part of town. I will go. Lud knows what I am to do with it, since Olive would—"

The crow showed what he would do, on Ardeth's shoulder.

They stopped at home for money, maps, and kippers, with hurried instructions to Vinross and Miss Hadley and the Randolphs. They were to prepare rooms, hire additional carriages, cook more food. He did not know for how many. Oh, and they should plan a funeral.

Then they set out. Genie and the crow drove in the carriage. Ardeth chose to ride his stallion ahead, looking out for danger. Luckily sunset came later at this time of year.

Their first stop was at Lady Wickersham's house at Russell Square.

"But the hatchments are up," Genie said as Ardeth handed her out of the coach. "They are in mourning."

"They are in mourning, but they are not grieving. Furthermore, we are not calling on the family."

He asked for the companion, who came to the drawing room, red-eyed and trembling. "Miss Calverton?" Effe had been right: The fifty-year-old female looked desperate enough to drown herself. "I am Ardeth. This is my countess."

"Yes? If you are here to pay condolences, the family is in the front parlor." Dividing up Lady Wickersham's valuables.

"No, we came to see you. We are sorry for your loss, of course. But some good has come of it. Before she died Lady Wickersham took a chance at the lottery we set up for the widows' and orphans' fund."

"We did?" Genie stared at him.

He stepped on her foot.

"Right, we did."

"She did?" the companion asked, staring at both of them. "That does not sound like Lady W."

"Oh, my husband can be very persuasive," Genie said, rubbing her toes together under her skirts.

"Yes, you might have heard we are collecting money. Anyway, she put the ticket in your name, perhaps out of gratitude for your years of service, for your caring."

The woman clutched her hands to her bony chest. "She truly did think of me?"

"Yes, and you won."

"I won?"

The earl handed her a leather purse, a heavy leather purse. Money did not always cure a heavy heart, though, so he added, "There is also a cottage as part of the prize, near our estate in the north. We will be traveling there within the week, but we invite you to stay at our town house until then."

The faded companion might not have trusted a tall, severely dressed gentleman, but his red-haired wife was smiling and seconding the invitation. They needed Miss Calverton's help, Genie said, in settling all the other prizewinners. "Please come."

"What about Lady W.'s funeral?" Miss Calverton was

expected to be gone from the house, the only home she had had for the last thirty years, an hour afterward.

"We are holding a funeral in the morning," Ardeth told her. "It is not necessarily your mistress's, but you can say your prayers then. She will understand."

The old nipcheese had not understood about pensions or bonuses. Miss Calverton went upstairs to pack. She had so few possessions, she was back in minutes, while Ardeth and Genie were discussing their next destination, the home of the soldier with the orphaned infants.

"Do you like children?" Ardeth asked, handing the companion into the coach.

"Oh no, pesky, dirty little devils."

"So much for Effe's plans to kill two birds with one stone," Ardeth muttered. Olive squawked at the saying, and again when the earl announced they would fetch the cat first.

"There is no help for it." He opened the hamper at Genie's feet, the smell turning her already-uncertain stomach. "Here, have a kipper."

Miss Calverton daintily reached for the fish. He'd meant the bird.

Ardeth rode ahead, out of Mayfair into narrower streets, with houses leaning against one another and garbage in the road. He ordered Campbell to stop at a rickety house at the corner that showed no light, no activity.

"Stay here," he told the women.

Genie did not. Neither did Miss Calverton.

Ardeth found the abandoned, hungry, mewing cat. So did Genie. So did Miss Calverton. They took them all, in case. Olive hid in the folds of Ardeth's cloak.

The retired schoolteacher in Kensington thought the Devil himself had come to call at his one-room flat, with his black cape and crow. He had a hard time believing the fellow was an earl, much less handing him a lottery win.

Genie showed his name on her scrap of paper.

Ardeth showed him the gold. "Your wife must have bought the ticket, but it has your name and address."

"Damn fool woman always was one for taking chances. If she hadn't been such a deuced gambler, I would have my savings still. Serves her right that I can't even pay for a decent funeral. Good riddance, I say."

So much for Effe's concern that the man would be lonely.

"Well, you need not worry about that now. We will hold a service in the morning. Another part of the lottery win is a cottage at Ardsley Keep if you want it. We will be starting a new school there, and need help hiring instructors."

The man collected his books before his cat—a striped one—could lick its ear. He and Tiger took a seat in the coach beside Miss Calverton.

Olive took to shaking.

The shoemaker's widow wept at her winnings. She did not recall her husband purchasing the ticket, but she raised her eyes to Heaven, where the dear man was cobbling for the cherubs, she insisted. Now she did not have to worry about keeping the shop or trying to earn a living on her own. She blessed Ardeth and Genie and Campbell, for carrying her trunks out to the extra carriage Ardeth had hired.

They stopped back at home to deliver the new guests into the waiting arms of the Randolphs before proceeding to the vicarage in Chelsea.

"Gambling?" the widow exclaimed, handing back the leather purse. "Oh, no, my husband would never purchase a lottery ticket."

"Oh, yes, he would, Mother," one of her daughters shouted.

"For a good cause," the middle daughter added. The youngest girl even remembered her father purchasing the ticket.

The widow looked at her three daughters, all of marriageable age, all dowerless, all dressed in castoffs from the congregation, all without a roof over their heads after tomorrow. Then she looked at Ardeth. "Rufus did always say how the good Lord would provide."

Another carriage and wagon were hired, with men to help them move their belongings to Ardeth's house. Meanwhile he asked the two older girls to come along with Genie to help their next and final winner, the soldier who had inherited his sister's five little orphans.

The man looked like he'd rather face the French again. The small flat looked like the French had marched through it. The children were dirty, hungry, and distraught—for the ten minutes it took Ardeth to convince the man that his sister had taken a lottery ticket, that he could hire proper nursemaids (unless he proposed to one of the vicar's daughters) and take up a position at Ardsley Keep, where the children could go to the free school.

Everyone carried an infant out to the waiting hired coach, even Ardeth. His burden, naturally, was the only one not crying. Genie thought he looked wonderful with a babe in his arms, except for the crow she could swear was laughing on his shoulder.

Now everyone was at Ardeth House, including Daisy, the killer, whom the other women avoided. The men did not. They all—except for the children, who were being fed, bathed, and put to bed by Mrs. Randolph and the maids—listened to Ardeth offer them choices. He would

be back to hear their decisions as soon as he completed
two more errands.

This time Genie stayed behind. These people were her
guests, for one thing, and she had no desire to visit the
morgue and morticians, for another. He took James Vinross to help with the details.

When Ardeth returned, hours later, everyone was upstairs, sleeping or counting their coins, except his wife.
He told her about his successes; Genie told about hers.

Daisy wanted to go to Canada.

The young soldier wanted Daisy.

The shoemaker's widow wanted the children, the
grandchildren she never had, so they were all going to the
colonies to start a cobbler's shop.

The retired schoolteacher thought he wanted Daisy,
too, but knew his heart was not up to it, so he chose a cottage, a place at the new school, and the cats. Miss Calverton was afraid of ships, Red Indians, and being on her
own, so she thought she'd keep the cats, and the gentleman, company.

The vicar's wife and daughters decided they would
also teach in the country for a year of mourning, unless
they found husbands with their lottery dowries first.

Everyone was to set out in the morning, after the funerals. Ardeth and Genie stayed up another two hours
making lists and plans, sending messages, issuing invitations. With hard work and a fortune in bribes, Ardeth was
gathering all the dearly departed for one grand send-off:
the vicar, the shoemaker, the soldier's sister, the schoolteacher's wastrel wife, and the flower seller who had no
family that anyone knew of. Only two of Effe's pickups
would not be celebrated in the morning: Lady Wicker-

sham, whose heirs were too arrogant, and Predlow the Pimp, whose demise was too deserved.

"And I could not have done it without you, my dear," Ardeth said as he kissed Genie good night outside her door.

Marie was still working in Genie's room, cutting black ribbons, sewing hems on black shawls, adding a black veil to one of Genie's bonnets for Daisy so no one would recognize her. She helped Genie into her night rail, then left with her mending basket and the promise of a salary increase.

Genie brushed out her hair, thinking about her husband, as usual. She touched her lips where he had kissed her. For once he had been the one to initiate the touch, and not a mere peck on the cheek, either. She wanted more.

This day proved to her what a wonder the man was. She wanted more of him, too. Genie had no idea how he had selected these people to rescue—perhaps he found their names in a newspaper while he sat in Peter's room—but his actions proved his goodness, his strength, his nobility of spirit. This immediacy of giving, of seeing the results, was far more satisfying than allocating funds or selecting architecture, although schools and hospitals would benefit greater amounts of people.

She wanted to help him do more. He'd seen what a capable assistant she'd been, once she caught on. And she had not turned a hair, having a yellow-haired harlot in her drawing room. And it was her idea to hire a band to accompany the funeral procession, which reminded her that she had not asked him about the music, which led to another excellent idea of how she could spend another few minutes in his company.

Without pausing to think, she knocked on the adjoining door and opened it before he could refuse her entry. She stepped in, saying, "I was wondering about the—"

He was half-naked, his back to her, unbuttoning the fall of his trousers. By the fire's light she could see broad shoulders, a narrow waist.

He quickly reached for his dressing robe before turning, slipping his arms in the sleeves, and sashing it closed in front.

Genie sighed.

"About the . . . ?"

"Hymn."

"What him, or whom?"

They were beginning to sound like Olive, who was sleeping with Sean Randolph and his dog, Helen, until the cats left.

Genie forced her eyes away from the vee of curls starting under his collarbone. "Not him, a hymn to be sung at the chapel. Do you have a favorite?"

He was staring at her in her thin bedgown. That one, his baser emotions roared, where he could see the darker nipples through the sheer fabric, and the dark triangle between her legs. This was his favorite. And her hair was down, a sunset all by itself, setting across her shoulders. Heaven help him. "Hymn?" That was all he could manage.

"Do you want me to choose?"

She had already chosen, by coming to his bedroom. They both knew it, and the choice had nothing whatsoever to do with funeral music.

"Genie, you should go."

"But there is so much to be done, and I had a nap before my sister arrived this afternoon. Was it just this afternoon? Goodness, it seems that days have gone by—we have accomplished so much."

Decades had gone by, centuries, eons, since he'd felt this way. He rubbed his neck, to avoid rubbing where he ached. "You should go," he repeated, feigning a yawn.

"Oh, you must be exhausted. Here, let me massage your neck for you."

Before he could stop her, she pushed him toward the bed, then climbed up to wait for him there. Genie, in his bed. Genie, with her hair and her inhibitions all down. Genie.

Jupiter couldn't save him now. He sighed and stepped toward the bed. To protect her sensibilities and preserve his modesty, he lay facedown on the mattress. Genie knelt beside him, tugged down the collar of his robe, and began to knead his neck and shoulders. Oh gods.

Then she bent forward and kissed where her hands soothed and smoothed. He could hear her breathing getting ragged, not as ragged as his, but her breath was burning on his bare skin. Her hair was like lightning, trickling against his neck. Her hand strokes were more urgent, her sighs more mews of wanting. Lud knew who was making those groans of pleasure and pain and passion, him or her.

Ardeth clutched the pillow to him like a drowning man grabs a floating log. He was going under anyway, his hold on his good intentions slipping away with the rising tide of desire. Then he did something he had never thought to do, had never known was possible, to save both of them.

Genie heard him sigh, knew he was surrendering to the heat between them, knew he would turn over and take her in his arms, take her to the stars, take her. She nibbled on his earlobe, waiting. He sighed again. She blew in his ear. He sighed.

Then she realized he was not sighing. Her hero had managed to put himself to sleep and the dastard was snoring!

CHAPTER NINETEEN

"Who's gettin' hitched, one of the royals?"

"It ain't no wedding, you clunch," the driver of an ale cart called back to the drayman behind him on the long queue of stalled wagons. "Can't you see the coffins?"

Now the second driver could see the wooden boxes under all the blossoms. "So who died? Some nabob and his whole harem?"

"I dunno. Maybe royalty after all."

Sure enough, the funeral cortege was one of the finest most Londoners had ever seen, and the most festive. The only truly funereal aspect, other than the black armbands on the men and black clothes on most of the women, was a tall, black-haired rider on a black horse who led the procession. The watchers grew respectfully quiet when he passed by, giving the dead their due.

After Lord Ardeth and the hearses, a band played lively hymns, mourners chatted gaily while they marched, children tossed coins and more flowers to the crowds lining the streets, and elegant carriages drawn by prime cattle made their prancing way toward St. Cecilia's Chapel.

The coffins, the horses, and the children were all covered in flowers, in honor of a lavender seller called Clover by her fellow barrow pushers, just Clover. She had the grandest funeral any poor flower girl could hope for, with most of the Covent Garden market trailing behind. Why not? Their wares were all sold to the earl's men at dawn. Besides, they were promised a ride to Richmond for the burial, and a good meal at an inn afterward.

The cobbler's customers and neighbors marched along, their shoes highly polished. Pupils from the schoolteacher's former academy came to show their sympathy for his loss, as did the congregation of the departed vicar. No one knew whom the veiled woman was bereaved of, but she could not have been terribly grief stricken, tossing flowers to the crowds and kisses to the best-looking young men.

In the carriages rode well-dressed nobs and not-so-well-dressed mourners, a few weeping, a few looking stunned at the sudden changes in their fortunes, and one, a stunning red-haired lady in black lace, fuming . . . especially when the solitary, unsmiling horseman was in view.

The chapel service was dignified, reverent, and short, with the officiating bishop referring to the list in his hand more than once, and to Lord Ardeth and the promised new roof more than that.

The burials took longer. There had not been enough gravediggers in so short a time, so some of the less-affected mourners dug in, literally, while extra hymns were sung. Clover's interment received the same solemnities as the vicar's, the shoemaker's and the soldier's sister's, to the surprise and delight of her friends, who wept as copiously as the bereft families.

Enough bouquets and blossoms were placed at each grave site to cover the fresh earth, so the cemetery looked more like a field of flowers than a final, forlorn resting place.

Ardeth was pleased. Genie was not. Oh, she was happy the hurried plans had gone without much of a hitch—what was a foot or two of dirt?—and no one seemed to feel out of place, the swells and the street vendors reciting the same verses. And she was glad they'd been able to soften the blow of the losses for those who truly mourned.

She was also pleased that her sister and her husband had attended. Their presence meant Peter was well enough to leave behind, and that Lorraine had become less selfish, acknowledging others' needs and her own debts. Lorraine did make certain, Genie noted, to keep Roger away from Daisy.

The supper afterward was more like a country fair than a funeral repast. Ardeth had sent riders and wagons and hampers and caterers to a small nearby inn that could not have managed the crowds on its own. Now all comers were served, inside and out, locals and Londoners, sad mourner and glad free-meal seeker.

Ardeth was host, lord of the manor, and Father Christmas all in one. He consoled; he consulted; he doled out coins. He spoke to nearly every man and woman present, avoiding Genie, it appeared to her, as much as he could. Even the children received more of his attention, as he and Olive performed tricks for their entertainment.

Miss Hadley and James Vinross did their part in seeing that everyone was content, and that the carriages and wagons and drays were emptied of foodstuffs, then filled with weary revelers. They all left well before dark. A few coaches went to the London docks; two headed straight north for Ardsley Keep rather than wait until Lord and Lady Ardeth were ready to leave town. More tears were shed at the partings, it seemed to Genie, than at the burials.

She was weeping herself, her emotions all muddled. She was glad her new friends would have new lives and that she had helped, sad that so many people had to die, and mad.

She knew it before, of course, but now she had a wider appreciation of just how wealthy her husband was, and how devious. But she was a lady. She would never cause a scene, especially amid this group. She watched Lorraine, obviously uncomfortable among the lower orders, maintain her poise and her politeness. Miss Hadley never appeared flustered, no matter how many times she was called upon to keep the vicar's daughters away from the local farmers. Genie watched the shoemaker's widow, how she cuddled the orphans, despite losing her own life's companion. Even Miss Calverton, checking the cats in their crates, kept her composure in the crowd.

Genie could do no less. She would show her husband precisely what kind of female he'd married in so helter-skelter a fashion . . . and so permanently.

Because she was a lady she smiled at the right times. She looked serious at the appropriate moments, gave solace and support when they were needed, and handed out a few coins of her own. She was the countess; everyone looked toward her. They might go to Ardeth for bank deposits and deeds and getting things done, but people seemed to seek her approval, too. Genie stood firm despite the maelstrom in her mind, the butterflies in her stomach, and the anger in her heart. If she was up to the task of rebuilding people's lives, surely she could manage her own. And her husband's.

She waited until they were home.

Miss Hadley retired early, exhausted. She would have a tray in her room later. James was staying with the travelers at a wharf-side inn until their ship sailed in the morning. Genie sent Marie to her own room—or Campbell's, over the stables—as reward for all of the maid's labors.

She knocked on the library door. Then she went in.

She did not wait for him to find an excuse to leave, or someone else to save. If mayhem ruled or he got another hey-go-mad notion, it would have to wait until tomorrow. Now was Genie's turn.

She had not taken her hair down. She had not put on her sheerest, lowest-cut gown. She was not here to seduce the man. Heaven knew if such a thing were possible; the devil knew she'd tried. She was simply going to set some rules of her own.

"Do not," she began as soon as she marched across the room to where he was sitting in the leather armchair, sipping a brandy. He stood at her entry, setting the glass down on the floor. Olive started to drink from it, likely celebrating the cats' departure, if the jug-bitten crow needed an excuse.

"Do not," she repeated in a cold, clear voice, "ever do that again."

Olive flew out of the room.

Ardeth pretended to misunderstand. "I doubt the

occasion will arise that we need to host a whore and a horde of flower girls."

She crossed her arms over her chest and glared at him.

"Would you like a drink?" he offered. "There must be a fresh glass somewhere."

"I mean last night."

For once, Ardeth was without that air of confidence, the certainty that he knew best, that he was in charge, the master. "I, ah . . . um . . . I was tired."

"No man is that tired unless he is dead."

Now that gave him pause.

Not Genie. She went on. "You played your tricks, one of Herr Mesmer's discoveries or whatever it is you do."

He held up his hands, an admission of guilt. "But I did not send you to sleep. I did not touch your mind."

He did not touch her body, either. "No, you ran away. Like a coward."

No one had ever called him a coward, not when he was wielding a medieval battle-ax, not when he was wielding a metaphorical scythe.

"Yes." He had no defense.

"How do you think that made me feel?"

Judging from how he'd woken up, frustrated as hell. He kept quiet.

Genie stepped closer and poked one of her fingers into his chest. "You cheated."

"Cheated? I did not know the rules."

"Liar."

"I do not lie," he swore.

"Very well, do you like me?"

Silence.

"I know that you do. Do you want me?"

Silence.

"I take that for a yes also. You have seen we are well suited, almost partners. You would not treat a partner the way you treat me."

"I have never had a partner."

"And you do not now. I am your wife"—she poked his chest again—"not an audience at a performance. We were in our marriage bed, dash it, not a tent at a traveling magic show. I will not play those games, do you hear me?"

A corner of his mouth was turned up, at seeing his sweet little wife turn into a virago. "I believe the neighbors heard you."

She lowered her voice. "If you do not want to be my husband, say so now and I will leave."

"No."

"No, you do not want to be my husband, or no, you will not answer?"

"No, do not leave."

"Hmph. Well, at least you did not lie."

"I do not lie," he repeated.

"No? And what is that in your breeches, more winning lottery tickets?"

Now he had to smile. "I want you to stay. I want you."

"But?"

"But I do not want to hurt you."

She made another rude noise. "I have seen you hold a frightened cat. For heaven's sake, I have seen you hold a baby. You would never, ever hurt me."

He shrugged. "In the heights of passion, who is to say what might happen?"

Genie made a fist, hauled back, and slammed it into his stomach.

"Oof." He staggered back, more in surprise than pain. "Odso, woman, what was that about?"

"That was for thinking I am some fragile flower. I have thorns. I had to learn to defend myself when there was no one else to do so. You are bigger and stronger, and have . . . odd talents, but I am not without weapons of my own."

He rubbed his stomach. "I see."

"So no more excuses," she said, coming closer to him again. "And no nonsense about a vow. You might have taken an oath to be a better man, and you are fulfilling it a hundredfold. Just look at all those people you helped today alone. But you also made a vow to me, to be my husband. Not my friend, not my banker, not my protector, but my husband, Ardeth."

She was right. Ardeth had wedded Imogene Hopewell Macklin to keep her safe, but her happiness was also in his hands. If the woman's happiness depending on making love, well, he would just have to sacrifice his own concerns and be gentleman enough to oblige. For once, duty and pleasure came together; logic and lust could enjoy the same tumble; philosophy, philanthropy, and passion could all share the same bed. How nice. He would be careful and considerate and how quick could he get her to his chamber? He was not thinking of those scant four months, just the flight of stairs.

"Coryn," was all he said.

"What?"

"Tonight I would be Coryn, not the earl, not the Devil's pawn."

She ignored the bit about the Devil. "Tonight?"

He looked toward the window. "It is almost dark. Dinner will be served soon."

"But what if you find something else to do, someone else who needs—"

"You are right again. I need you, Genie. Now." And he pulled her toward him by the front of her gown, and kissed her the way he had been wanting to do his whole life, it seemed, both lives and what was between them. Now there was nothing between them, between Coryn and Genie, but layers of clothes he was busy unfastening, even as he deepened the kiss, tasted her lips, her tongue. Her tongue answered back, questing, seeking, meeting, melding, melting.

He pulled the pins from her hair so he could run his fingers through it the way he'd dreamed of doing, asleep and awake. He thought he could never stop wanting to touch those fiery curls, not even in the deepest trance.

Genie was helping with the clothes, with fingers that fumbled with the hurry, and because the kiss continued and flowed into many kisses without beginning or end. His jacket was gone, his neckcloth and waistcoat. Her gown was opened, the stays unlaced, so his hands could reach for her creamy breasts, while hers reached under his shirt for the muscles and sinews that strained to hold her closer, close enough to be one.

He trembled.

"Are you cold?" she asked.

"I do not think I will ever be cold again."

"If you are, I will warm you. I am on fire."

"No, this is only a spark compared to what is ahead."

He fanned the flames with his kisses, his touch, everywhere he could reach. Then he bent to kiss where he had touched, and Genie cried out with the pleasure and the agony because the pleasure was not enough, not complete.

She tried to find the fastenings of his trousers but he held her hand back. "Not yet."

"When?" she panted.

"When I have worshipped every inch of you, my magical wish-granting Genie. When I cannot stand the exquisite torment anymore, when I have to join with you or burst."

She touched him anyway.

"Right. Now. But not here. I am not going to make love to my wife on a desktop." He looked longingly at the fur rug in front of the hearth. "Or on the floor."

She giggled, still in his arms. "I thought you were not the dignified earl tonight."

"No, but I am not a barbarian again. I am still a man who likes my comforts, and wants my bride to be happy. Besides, the library door is not locked."

"But I do not think I can walk up the stairs. My bones have melted."

So he picked her up and started to carry her out of the room. Genie pulled her gown up, in case they passed one of the servants. There was nothing she could do about her hair or her reddened lips or her shortness of breath except to urge him to hurry.

Which meant he had to kiss her again, her eagerness more arousing, if possible, than the feel of her in his arms. Before he was ready to proceed upstairs—and that fur rug was looking more and more inviting—he heard voices outside the door.

"I am family. I do not need to be announced," Lorraine was shouting at Mr. Randolph. Then she burst into the library.

She saw Genie in Ardeth's arms and cried, "Oh, you have already heard the dire news."

"What news?" Genie asked, only to be polite. The sooner Lorraine relayed her petty gossip, the sooner they could return to paradise.

"You mean you have not swooned at the catastrophe?"

Genie's senses were swimming, her heart was racing, and her knees were weak, but swoon? Not if it meant missing one delicious moment of her husband's love-making. "No, I am well."

"Then whatever are you doing in Ardeth's ar—? Oh. Before dinner?"

Which might explain, Genie thought in her haze of heat, why Lorraine and Roger had only one son. Genie giggled again, but Ardeth set her on her feet. He kept one hand around her—helping to hold up her gown—and asked, "What news? What catastrophe? We have not spoken with anyone since our return from Richmond."

Out of Ardeth's—Coryn's—arms, Genie could notice her sister's distress. "Is Peter all right?" Genie wanted to know, forgetting about her undress to think of the child suffering a reversal while they were ripping at each other's clothes.

"He is fine. It is my husband."

"What, has Lord Cormack developed a congestion of the lungs? He seemed fit this morning, and the day was clement."

Lorraine smoothed out the handkerchief she'd been clutching and held it to her lips. "He *mph, mph, mrph.*"

"Good grief, he is not dead, is he?" Genie pulled the handkerchief away.

"N-no, but he will be in the morning."

"Explain," Ardeth demanded.

"He went to his club when we returned. That dreadful man Willeford was there. And he was telling everyone that you had gone beyond the pale, turning funerals into festivities, holding parades for poor dead beggars. He even knew about that woman, the murderess. He said that if you were not insane, you were dangerous and should be locked up before you caused harm to someone."

"He has been saying worse."

"Yes, but that was before you saved our son and hosted all those funerals. Now he is saying that Peter's cure was unnatural, when all the physicians could do nothing. He hints that you practice black magic or some pagan religion, that your deeds are unholy, heathenish. He says he saw you light a cigar without flint or matches."

Here was Genie's worst nightmare. She wished she had a handkerchief to stuff in her mouth, too, before she blurted out her own doubts and fears.

Lorraine was going on, explaining to Ardeth that Roger could not stand by and listen to him being slandered. "We are too much in your debt."

"The debt is paid. Cormack had Daisy released."

"No matter. You are still family."

Genie did not mention that until a mere few weeks ago she herself was not considered any kind of kin. "I hope Roger drew his claret."

Both Ardeth and Lorraine looked at her.

"Bloodied his nose. Or darkened his daylights. That's blackened his eyes. You learn a great many new expressions in the army."

Lorraine's mouth fell open, and not just at Genie's use of boxing cant. "What, you think that Roger should have . . . have indulged in fisticuffs at his club? He would have been asked to resign his membership."

"Oh. Then what is the problem?"

Her sister's lips trembled. "He . . . he challenged Willeford to a duel."

"Duels are illegal."

Lorraine ignored that irrelevance. "Willeford chose

pistols. He is a soldier! An officer. His life depended on his skill with a gun. What chance does Roger have against a man like that? All he has done is shoot partridge and rabbits!"

"When?" Ardeth asked.

"Whenever we go to the country."

"No, when is the duel supposed to occur?"

"Tomorrow morning. I made him tell me." She grabbed Ardeth's hand. "You have to do something. It is your fight."

Genie stepped between them. "You are the same selfish girl you always were, Lorraine. You think my husband should die instead of yours? He was not the one who challenged Willeford. Your bacon-brained baron did!"

"But Ardeth is a warrior. He said so, did he not? Just look at him."

She did. He was paler than usual, the glow of lovemaking long faded. And he was cold. Genie could tell just looking at him. She found his jacket on the floor.

He put it on, but said, "I will not fight. I will not kill another man."

"Then put Willeford to sleep!" Lorraine insisted. "You can do that, I know you can."

Genie looked hopeful. Maybe her sister was not such a gudgeon after all.

Ardeth shook his head. "Willeford will wake up. When he does he will be more certain I am in league with the Devil, or making a fool of him. He will still demand satisfaction. Men like Willeford confuse pride with honor, and they can never back down from a challenge."

"Then my son will have no father." Lorraine started crying again, then shouting. "And it will be because of you, Ardeth. Roger's blood will be on your hands, no matter that you do not hold the pistol. You will be the death of him."

"NO!"

CHAPTER TWENTY

He was gone.

Genie was so angry, she left her sister sitting alone in the parlor when she stormed off to the Hourglass Room and her little office next to it.

Lorraine followed her, half out of curiosity and half out of not knowing what else to do. "Will he help, do you think?"

"That depends what you consider help, I suppose. Ardeth will definitely do something."

Lorraine gasped when she saw what Genie was taking out of a lower desk drawer. "What are you doing with that thing?"

That "thing" being a small pistol, the answer should have been obvious, even to one with Lorraine's limited grasp of anything but her own concerns. "I am cleaning and loading it," Genie said.

"Whatever for?"

"Lud, Lorraine, what do you think I am going to do

with a loaded pistol, hold up a coach? I am going to stop the duel, of course."

"But . . . but do you know how to use one of them?"

The answer to that ought to have been equally as obvious by the way Genie was efficiently checking the weapon and handling the powder and ball. "Of course. I told Ardeth—Coryn—that I had weapons of my own."

"He will be furious at you for interfering."

"What, should I sit here with my needlework waiting for Willeford to shoot him? We both know Ardeth is not going to let your husband take his place, even if Roger was cork-brained enough to issue the challenge."

"Roger is a very intelligent man!"

"Intelligent men do not go twenty paces with a braggart and a buffoon." Genie made sure the safety catch was engaged, then carefully placed the loaded pistol back in its leather pouch.

"Are you . . . are you going to shoot Willeford?"

"Or Ardeth if I have to. I will do anything to stop this ridiculous duel, although I doubt it will come to that. Ardeth does not wish to fight any more than I do, perhaps less, because I am so mad I could challenge Willeford myself."

"But women are not permitted at duels, much less allowed to meddle."

"Such rules are as buffle-headed as demanding satisfaction for a social insult with a sword. What do I care if I break a hundred taboos, if I keep my husband alive? You want yours to live past tomorrow, don't you? That is why you came, and that is why Ardeth left. The difference between you and me is that I am willing to do what is necessary, not wait for someone else to step in. Now, do you know where they are meeting and when? I can send our butler to the pubs with a full purse. He'll come back with the information, so you might as well tell me."

"I heard Roger tell his valet Hampstead Heath, near a lightning-struck tree, at daybreak."

"How very dramatic," Genie said, with more than a bit of sarcasm, "and unoriginal. All it needs is fog to be a scene from some dreadful novel."

Lorraine read many of them. "Or a fine mist. That makes it more romantical."

"There is nothing romantic about two jackasses blowing each other to bits."

"But think how affecting it is, with you riding neck or nothing to your husband's side."

"I will take the carriage, thank you, no matter how disappointing to your sensibilities. Why don't you go home?"

"Oh, then you do not expect me to go with you?" The sound of Lorraine's relief was louder than the clock striking the hour.

Genie shook her head. Her sister would be useless, likely dissolved in tears if not her atmospheric mist. "Go, check on your son. Wait for your husband to return."

Lorraine must have felt guilty for leaving Genie alone, because she asked, "What are you going to do until morning?"

"I shall go to the dueling grounds well before dawn. Until then, I shall wait for my husband, the same as you."

"Maybe he will settle everything peacefully?" There was not much confidence in Lorraine's voice.

"With Willeford? Maybe pigs will fly."

After Lorraine left, Genie went upstairs to Ardeth's room. If he came home at all, he would change his clothes before setting out again. She also ordered Randolph to

send for her if his lordship went first to the book room,
and to wake her well before dawn if he did not return
at all.

She lay on his bed, the pistol beside her. Her husband
was not insane, at least no more crazy than the average
earl who wanted to save the world. He was not in league
with the devil or dancing naked around a fire on the full
moon. He knew a few magic tricks, that was all, and
some Eastern spiritual methods for easing the mind. He
was a good man! And she loved him. She could not lose
him now.

Ardeth knew right where to go to find his quarry. His
hours in London's dark side gave him eyes and ears eager
to serve him with information. Those on his payroll of
spies would have supplied hired thugs, an arsenal of
weaponry, even assassins, if that was his pleasure.

For now, pleasure was a distant memory. He wanted
Willeford with a fury he had not known since his
berserker days. The man was threatening to ruin all
Ardeth had worked for, to destroy his chances of staying
past his allotted months. Besides, Willeford had cost him
a night in Genie's arms.

Ardeth had known he would have to deal with Willeford before leaving London, so he was prepared. Maggots
like the major thrived on rotten filth, envy and hate and
fear of exposure. They had to be swept away or squashed,
not merely ignored. Ardeth could guess the man's even-
tual destination, but he would not hasten the journey.

According to Ardeth's informants, tonight Willeford
was at one of the less fashionable clubs that catered more
to military gentlemen than the wealthier aristocracy, instead of at some *ton*ish ball, dancing attendance on his

shrewish wife. He had been at the place for hours, since accepting Lord Cormack's challenge.

Ardeth took a seat, uninvited, at the card table where Willeford gamed with two other officers. The others left, by silent consent, leaving their coins and cards behind.

Ardeth signaled a waiter for a glass of wine, then asked, "You do not think the spirits will affect your aim?"

"My aim will be good enough for Cormack."

Ardeth raised an eyebrow at the man's conceit. "He could get lucky."

"Yes, I might hit just his shoulder instead of his heart."

The muckworm's aim must be good, Ardeth thought. Otherwise someone would surely have exterminated him by now. He sipped his wine and said, "This is not about Cormack, and we both know it."

"Oh, are you volunteering to take his place? I will have my seconds talk to his about the substitution." He gestured to the two men who had moved to a nearby table. "If Cormack is willing, so am I."

Ar did not reply to that dare. "I thought we had agreed that you would not speak of me or my family."

Willeford sneered. "You agreed not to talk of me, then reneged. You must have said something, because there were hints at the War Office. They are not giving me the preferment that I sought."

Ardeth put his glass down, still full. "The rumors did not come from me, but from your men, the same source of my knowledge of events."

"The stories are untrue, all of 'em."

"So we are both victims of unfounded gossip?"

Willeford would not meet his eyes. He shuffled the cards for something to do.

"Ah, I wonder at your silence. Either you are guilty of

what they say, or you truly think I am evil incarnate. Well, let me ask you this: Do you believe in sorcery?"

The cards spilled out of Willeford's hands across the table. "Of course not. That kind of rot went away with the Dark Ages."

"What of curses, then? Do you think a man can place a spell on another man, you know, turn him into a toad, or shrivel his manhood?"

Willeford said no, but without his former assurance.

"Yet you claimed that I practiced black magic. My brother-in-law took objection. Family is like that, I am discovering. They watch out for each other."

"No one else believed I meant it for a minute. We were all in our cups, was all."

Ardeth took out Satan's lucky piece and placed it on the table. Willeford leaned back in his chair, farther away from the small bonelike thing.

"Maybe curses are real," Ardeth said, pondering the Devil's charm. "They say this was from a relic from a saint, or bewitched by a fallen angel. No one knows, but it is valued highly by those who do believe in the Master of Evil."

Now Willeford sat up straighter. "So you admit to having knowledge of pagan ways."

"I have knowledge of many things. I did not know that learning was a sin. Either way, I do not know what this is, manufactured or manroot, or how it works. Who knows? No matter. Are you willing to bet your life against its power?"

Willeford eyed the inch-long desiccated bit. "What do you mean?"

"I mean that if you take the field tomorrow morning, I will use this amulet to lay a curse on you. You will suffer a long, painful life—death would be too merciful, I think." He picked up the relic again. "Yes, small pieces of your person will fall off. An ear, a nose, your toes, your prick. One at a time."

"You cannot do that!"

"Maybe. Maybe not."

Willeford jumped to his feet, ready to dash out of the room. Ardeth laid a hand on his sleeve, just lightly, but Willeford sank back in his chair.

"I do not believe you," he said, his tone not quite as confident as his words. "It is all claptrap."

"What do you call these, then?"

From another pocket Ardeth took out a stack of gambling chits, all with Willeford's initials on them.

Where Willeford was red-faced before, now he went deathly pale. "Where did you get those?"

"From your creditors, of course. I do not gamble myself, you know. I might bargain, but I seldom wager. Most of those you owe were happy to accept my terms of payment. It seems they feared they would never see any of their money otherwise. You've been below hatches for years." He fanned the vouchers out, like playing cards. "Hmm, it appears that you are as poor a gambler as you are an officer."

The sum was considerable, far more than Willeford could pay, and they both knew that. Willeford hoped Ardeth did not know of the other debts, to the cents-per-centers and his wife's family. "I can get the blunt from my relations. You said yourself, kin look out for one another."

"Your family is tired of paying your way. Your wife's family have closed their purses to you. In fact, I believe one of these vowels is from your brother-in-law himself.

He had no compunctions about selling them to me, or the devil. No, you have no resources, and I am calling in the chits. Now."

"But a month is the usual time between gentle—" He paused.

Ardeth nodded. "That is right. I am not a gentleman. Neither are you, it seems, for most of these are far older than a month."

Willeford licked his dry lips. His eyes shifted to the door, to his friends, to the IOUs on the table next to that menacing white piece of the-devil-knew-what. A fox with its foot in a trap could not feel more desperate. "What do you want?"

"That is easy. I want you to call off the duel."

"But then people will think I am a coward."

"You are a coward."

Those words stirred the dregs of Willeford's pride, once he was sure the others had not heard. "Here, now, you cannot—"

"You sent your men to face the cannons alone."

"An officer needs to stay behind the lines to direct the fighting, to issue orders, to sound retreat or advance."

"I believe the word you used was 'claptrap.' And then there is the way you spoke about me behind my back. What is that if not cowardice?"

"Everyone knows you do not fight."

"So you picked on Cormack, a peace-loving civilian with a young family. One you are so confident you can defeat that you do not bother resting or keeping a clear head. I call that cowardice, too."

"It was not like that. I had too much to drink, I told you." His voice took on a whine when he added, "You know how that can be."

"No, I do not know how a man who calls himself an officer and a gentleman can stoop so low."

"Well, I ain't a saint like you. I can't cure sickness and I don't consort with the lower classes." He looked at the gaming chits. "And I don't have the brass to give to charity, even if I wanted, which I don't. Let the poor blighters find work like the rest of us. They could join the army instead of begging in the streets."

Ardeth did not bother mentioning that Willeford's commission was purchased, not earned. "Perhaps I was wrong and you are a brave man. You seem to have no fears about dying."

"Of course I am afraid of sticking my spoon in the wall. What man ain't? I don't want to get sliced apart in battle." He eyed the Devil's charm. "Or die by inches."

"Then leave."

Willeford started to get up.

"No, leave London."

"Right, I can go on a repairing lease. Haven't visited my sister in Cornwall in ages."

"No, again. I mean leave England altogether. I know of a ship weighing anchor for Jamaica with the morning tide. Be on it and you can have these back." He neatened the pile of gambling chits.

Willeford laughed. "Jamaica? Why would I want to go somewhere hot and sticky?"

If he thought Jamaica was hot, Ardeth thought, wait until the dastard got to Hell. Aloud he said, "You want to go to Jamaica because the army has an outpost there, and I own a sugar plantation nearby." He owned property on every continent, just in case. "I will trade the Jamaican estate for your London town house. The property turns a tidy annual profit. The local British society, I understand, is as stuffy as London's, and you can lord it over them all, if I put in a word with the commandant there."

Willeford considered the offer, then shook his head. "My wife would never leave town. She loves being in the thick of the *ton*, shopping all day, gossiping all night."

"I doubt she will enjoy debtors' prison. Do not for an instant think that I am merely threatening you. I can have the bailiffs at your door in an hour." He laid a writ of seizure on top of the gambling debts.

"Oh, God."

"I doubt Himself can be bothered with a sinner like you, but pray if you think it might help. I will not change my mind."

"If I go, then the curse won't work, right?"

Ardeth smiled and tossed the Devil's charm in the air before putting it back in his pocket. "Who knows?" He placed an arm over Willeford's shoulder to lead him from the club, for all the world like convivial acquaintances, not a huntsman and his cornered prey. "Oh, did I forget to mention that the plantation employs freemen only, so you will be denied the dubious honor of becoming a slaveholder? There are lovely flowers, however."

Ardeth could not go home until all the arrangements had been made. He had to roust up the bank owner—it had been an expensive day—to give Willeford and his wife traveling funds. He dragged his solicitor from bed to notarize an exchange of deeds. So what if the man thought Ardeth was both arrogant and attics-to-let, trading a profitable plantation for a small town house in London? Ardeth thought James Vinross and Miss Hadley might take up housekeeping there shortly, or he could transform it into a home for unwed mothers.

He hired carts and porters to pack and move the Wille-
fords' belongings, and another pair of guards to make certain they were ready, between the shrieks and slaps. Then
Ardeth went to the docks to give more money to the captain of the ship, and further instructions to Vinross about
these new travelers.

Later still he called on Roger Macklin, Lord Cormack,
and struck enough fear in that man's heart that Roger
would never make the mistake of fighting another man's
battles, especially not this man's. He dragged Roger to
various clubs to put out the word that Willeford had re-
canted, quit gambling, and rejoined the army abroad.

Then he went home to Genie.

"What do you mean, she has gone to the dueling
grounds?" he asked the butler. "How could you have let
her go?"

"How could I have stopped her?" Randolph asked
back.

Ardeth rode for Hampstead Heath as if the Hounds of
Hell were barking at his heels. Olive flew overhead. At
least the woman had the coach and Campbell. He could
not imagine what force she'd brought to his driver to get
the former sergeant to take a woman to a duel, but Campbell would look after her.

Except . . . wasn't that his own carriage tilted into the
ditch at the side of the road, the wheel shattered, the
horses missing?

Olive learned new curses, not that the gremlin needed
any.

Ardeth found Campbell and the horses at the nearest
inn, but not his wife.

"Demme if she wouldn't hire the innkeeper's son to
take her the rest of the way," the soldier reported. "And

demme if she didn't nearly shoot my head off for arguing. Her ladyship seemed to know which end of the pistol was which, too."

The sun was barely rubbing its eyes when Ardeth found the lightning-singed tree, with a cart parked beside it. A boy was fast asleep in the back, the horse grazing. He tied Black Butch to the rear of the cart and walked along a well-defined path between the trees.

Genie was wondering if she had come to the wrong place. That would be just like Lorraine to get the important details wrong. This clearing looked right for a duel, hidden from inquisitive eyes by a stand of trees, yet level and open where it mattered. But no one was coming, and here it was, almost dawn.

Surely the seconds or the surgeon would have arrived by now, she decided, so Ardeth must have found a way to stop the duel. He'd found an honorable way, she hoped, for all of them. Otherwise Willeford would not concede, only postponing the inevitable. She prayed Ardeth's solution was an honest one, without tricks, lest the rumors of his peculiar skills spread in a wider circle. Lud, what if he'd encountered Willeford in public and made him quack like a duck?

She decided she would leave in ten minutes or so, but then she thought she heard footfalls. She did not want to reveal her presence yet, in case the duelists were arriving. On the other hand, she did not wish to be surprised by someone else, someone not connected to the argument, who was traveling through the woods for his own nefarious purposes. She leveled her weapon in the direction of the sound.

"Who goes there?"

She heard more scuffling in the brush, and the flapping of wings. "Olive! Coryn!"

His tall form strode into the clearing, the bird overhead. He appeared so angry that Genie was surprised the leaves beneath his feet did not catch on fire. She would have been afraid, except she was so relieved to see that he was safe. She lowered her weapon and started to run toward him, but she tripped on a hidden root.

Bang!

Ardeth went down.

"Ar fall. Ar fall," Olive screeched.

Awful? It was beyond dreadful! Genie had shot her husband.

CHAPTER TWENTY-ONE

I n her rush to Ardeth's side, Genie dropped the gun. She shot a tree this time.

This time? But her pistol held only the one ball. So she did not shoot Coryn, thank goodness.

Except if she did not shoot him, someone else had. The innkeeper's son was shouting and running, so she did not worry overmuch that someone would shoot again, not with so many witnesses, people to give chase. Just in case, she threw herself on top of Ardeth to protect him.

Except he was already shot. He moaned.

The crow was moaning, too. "Shut up, you sapskull."

"Sorry. It hurts."

"Not you!" she shouted, rolling off Ardeth. She pulled his cape away, then his waistcoat. No, this was not right. Ardeth never wore bright colors! There was so much blood his shirt was soaked red. "Oh, Lord."

She took off her own cape to press against the wound. She'd seen many bullet holes, thanks to him, and knew she had to stop the bleeding. Clean cloths were better, but her petticoats had been dragged through the damp muddy grass, and there was no time to be particular, not at the rate his life's blood was flowing. She cradled him against her chest so she could press harder.

He stared up at her. "This is not . . . how I wanted to spend the night in your arms."

"You mean you did not get shot on purpose so you could again avoid making love to me?"

She thought he smiled, as she'd intended, but then his eyes drifted shut. "Don't you dare die on me."

He opened his eyes again. "I cannot. My six months are not up."

"If you think that is a comfort, you are crazier than I thought, and you would have to travel a far piece to get there." She was babbling but could not help it. She could hear the boy thrashing through the woods and called out to him to hurry. Meantime, to keep Ardeth's mind—and hers—off his wound, she said, "I did not do it, you know. I thought I had, but my pistol was not the one that shot you."

"I never . . . thought it was. The shot came from behind me."

"It did?" She tried to lift him up, to see. More blood stained the back of his waistcoat. "Oh, my God."

"Not going to swoon, are you, my Genie?"

She felt like fainting, crying, casting up her supper, and running away, all at once, but mostly crying. She would not let herself. Ardeth needed her. "No, I am not going to swoon."

"That's my good wife."

"I think you said it was good when the pistol ball went through."

"Oh, excellent. As long as it did not nick the heart, lungs, or arteries on the way out."

"How would I know?"

"I expect I would stop breathing."

"Can't die," Olive was moaning from atop Ardeth's cape, pecking at the fabric in despair. "Can't die."

"Now is not the time to look for candy, you greedy bird," Genie yelled, worried that the innkeeper's son might not be strong enough to help her get Ardeth back to the wagon.

"No, the twit is looking for a lucky charm. Inner pocket."

Genie could reach the cape while still keeping Ardeth pressed against her, one hand on the wound on his chest. With her other she pulled out a small, hard, white root or something. "It looks like a dried-up turnip sprout. You say this is lucky?"

"Only the Devil knows."

"Do you rub it or touch it or taste it?" She tried to put the thing in his limp hand. "What should I do?"

"Pray. That is called hedging one's bets."

Somehow they got Ardeth out of the clearing and onto the inn's wagon. Halfway back, they met Campbell coming with the earl's newly repaired coach. He drove on, following the boy's directions, to fetch a surgeon.

Back at the inn, the surgeon announced that yes, the ball was out. Of course he had to dig around some to make sure, causing Ardeth excruciating pain, from his curses.

"Most men would have passed out by now," the surgeon muttered as he started to stitch one wound, then the other. "'Tain't proper, your lady wife here and all."

Genie had insisted on staying, along with Campbell

and the innkeeper. Now she told them all to ignore his lordship's vocabulary. She did not understand half the words, anyway, and doubted that Ardeth was aware of what he was saying. If swearing made him feel less pain, then she would curse, too.

The surgeon stitched, Ardeth swore, Genie held back her tears and her fears, and the innkeeper sweated. "Will he live, do you think?" he asked. Dead earls were not good for business, not good at all.

"I expect if he was strong enough to survive that other injury, he can get through this," the surgeon answered. "Barring fevers and infections, of course."

"He will live," Genie insisted. "He promised. What other wound?"

The surgeon pulled the sheet lower from the upper chest he was working on. Genie could see a wide expanse of angry-looking, puckered red flesh. She tried not to gag at the sight.

"Too jagged for a sword thrust," Campbell, the former soldier, stated. "Too wide for a bullet. Might be a piece of cannonball shrapnel. Or a spear. His lordship did say how he'd fought in foreign wars."

"Not even stitched, looks like," the surgeon told them. "See how ragged the edges are? Just healed up on its own, all higgledy-piggledy."

"But, but isn't that right over where his heart is?"

"In every body I've ever seen."

The innkeeper thought the earl must have been wearing some kind of armor, to take the brunt of the thrust.

The surgeon directed Campbell to lift the patient again so they could see his back, and a corresponding scar. "How'd it go through armor? Better question is, how'd he live? I've never seen the like. "

Now Campbell was swearing. The innkeeper was drinking the brandy intended to deaden Ardeth's pain. Genie finally fainted.

The following day, Ardeth was in terrible agony, despite the laudanum he had permitted Genie to pour for him. He tossed and turned, half-aware, tearing open three of the stitches. He had no fever, thank goodness, but he was weak and trembling with the pain.

"Go to sleep, dash it," Genie yelled at him, hoping he could hear from whatever hell he was in. "Sleep can heal you. That's what you told the soldiers."

Glassy-eyed and dry-mouthed, he whispered, "Need to figure it out."

Genie wiped his forehead with a cool cloth. "No, you can rest. There is no mystery to unravel. It was Willeford, of course."

He wanted to talk about it, though, to warn her. He struggled to raise his head, despite the searing pain. "No, can't be. I saw him on a ship myself."

Genie hurried to prop a pillow behind him, then held up a cup of lemonade for him to drink, to ease his parched throat. "Very well, he hired someone to do his dirty work. That would be just like the miserable dastard."

He swallowed, then said, "No. Willeford does not want me dead. I made sure." He tried to smile, but grimaced instead. "I gave back his gambling debts, but I also promised to pay him a yearly competence to stay gone, every year of my life. Great joke, eh? He thinks he will be collecting checks for forty years." The six months, now more like four if Ardeth lived through the week, stayed unspoken.

Genie did not see the humor. "You paid him to leave?"

"That seemed the easiest way to be rid of the vermin. You could regain some of the investment by selling his house if you run out of cash. It comes to you in my will."

Ardeth's will being right there with his life span on the list of topics Genie did not wish to discuss. "Then you do not think he was taking revenge for his banishment?"

"No, I had him watched. He had no chance. Besides, he was going to have to flee London soon anyway, with the money he owed the usurers. He thought I did not know about those debts. I just saw no reason to pay the bloodsuckers. Oh, and I did numb his hand, mentioning that as a symptom of heart failure."

He was exhausting himself, Genie saw, and making no sense, so she said, "If not from Willeford, then the shot must have come from a poacher in the woods. That means there is nothing to worry about."

"No! The wheel."

"The carriage wheel that broke loose?"

"Tampered with. Hire guards."

Genie almost spilled the lemonade. "You mean this was neither Willeford nor a stray shot?" She'd known at heart the shooting was no accident, not in a clearing, not from the back. But to think that someone else was trying to injure her husband was more horrific, even, than the idea of Willeford acting so despicably. Who should she guard him against? Which direction would trouble come from next? "Good grief, who else have you offended, Coryn?"

He tried to smile again. "As many as I could. There are men who do not wish the poor educated, who do not want to see the government spend money on serving the needs of the downtrodden. Why, the owners of some wool mills and mines see their profits diminished if the reforms pass, protecting the workers. They despise me."

"Enough to kill you?"

"Keep your pistol on hand, Genie. Who knows what they might do to keep me from speaking? I did not mean to put you in danger."

"Me?" she squawked like Olive.

"My wife."

"I know that, silly. I just never thought I mattered to anyone."

"You . . . matter to me."

She kissed his cheek, but he winced, so she turned serious again, not sentimental. "Well, you will not be speaking anytime soon. Not until you regain your strength. And you better hurry, for I cannot protect us all from the rest of the world. If you slept instead of fretting, you would do better, I know you would. At least the surgeon would not have to keep coming back to stitch you up again."

"You will take precautions? You will stay indoors? I need to know you are safe."

"I will be fine. Campbell sits outside the door with a loaded rifle. The innkeeper's son has declared himself your savior, so he will look out for strangers. And Olive can cry a warning of any intruders. All right? Can you sleep now?"

"One kiss good night."

He fell into a deep slumber halfway through the kiss.

The surgeon worried he had fallen into a fatal coma, and the innkeeper was near to panic, that a would-be murderer was on the loose, and a would-be-dead nobleman was on his best bed. Genie reassured them both. Ardeth was resting, she said, healing.

She took advantage of his deep sleep to get him back to London. No matter how carefully Campbell drove the coach, Ardeth would have been jostled unmercifully if he were awake. This way he did not suffer for the short journey, and scores of menservants were waiting at home to help him to bed. Others were stationed outside, armed with enough guns and swords and sticks to guard the crown jewels. Ardeth had been looking for ways to employ former soldiers. Genie found it.

She had to take Lorraine and her husband into her confidence, to make up some story about the earl's injury, since they had no proof and no suspects. Rumors flew about town, saying a duel had taken place after all, although no one knew the other combatant. Or Willeford had shot Ardeth before fleeing bankruptcy. Or worse.

Luckily Ardeth still slept, so he could not be troubled by gossip about jealous husbands, errant wives, or, thanks to Willeford's rumors, sorcery gone awry.

Genie decided they would leave for the country as soon as Ardeth was able to travel. They would be safer there, and safer from scandalmongering. He did not develop fevers or chills, and the skin around the wounds looked clean. They could hire extra servants to attend him, and extra guards to ride alongside the carriage.

Genie thought about leaving him asleep during the move to save him pain, but the journey was a long one. Besides, she worried he was not getting enough nourishment in his torpid state. Mostly she worried that he might forget to wake up at all. Wasn't Merlin supposed to be in a deep trance inside some dark cave? Who knew how Ardeth's mind worked? Surely not his wife.

She whispered to him. She pulled on his sleeve and squeezed his hand. She spoke louder. "It is time to wake up, Coryn. The wounds are healing well." She cleared her throat, clapped her hands, and then she set a cup down hard in its saucer. "Wake up, my lord. We have plans to make."

If not for the steady rise and fall of his chest, she would fear he was gone. He was not even snoring. She told Olive to make some noise.

"Meow." That would have woken the crow in a flash.

"Not a cat noise, peagoose."

Olive tried again. "Cockanoodle?"

"Well, that was almost a rooster's sound, so you are doing better. Try something louder, to get him up."

"Naked pretty. Naked pretty."

"Naughty bird," Genie said, glad Ardeth could not see her blushes as she hastily retied the sash of her dressing gown, and glad the bedroom door was closed.

Ardeth slept on.

Genie stroked his cheek, then his chin, knowing he would hate the dark stubble there. She thought it made him look like a pirate or a highwayman, but supposed her sister would adore the untamed, Gypsy look—in a book, not in her bed. "Perhaps I should shave you," Genie threatened, thinking that if anything was going to wake Ardeth up, the notion of a woman with a razor should, "instead of letting your valet do it in the morning. Of course I have never shaved a man in my life, but if you are asleep, you'll never feel the nicks."

She waited, but he did not stir. She thought she saw his eyelashes flutter, although he did not open his eyes, not even when she tugged on the growing beard and told him he looked like a beast.

Then his lips twitched.

Aha! She bent over the bed and kissed his lips. It worked for Sleeping Beauty, so why not for a sleeping beast?

He kissed her back, and reached with the arm of his uninjured side to pull her closer. "Hmm. What a nice way to greet the morning, wife."

Hmm, indeed. Genie was tempted to climb into the bed next to him, now that he was awake, but he was too weak. "Well, it is nice, husband, but the morning is hours away. You have slept for days."

He released her and tested his shoulder, feeling sore and stiff, but without the intense pain. He did not feel good, but at least he did not feel as if he'd been killed again, either. He was even hungry, and not for the thin gruel Genie offered him. "You expect a man to recover his strength on that pap?"

"I expect you to do what the doctor ordered, and listen. We need to discuss some ideas I have had."

Instead of asking his opinions or intentions, however, Genie told him what she had decided, how she would go about it, and what precautions she was going to take. Since the simple act of swallowing—the gruel, blast it—exhausted him, Ardeth knew he was not ready to take back the reins. He could not help teasing her, though. "My, what a bossy woman you have become, my dear. Not at all the little mouse I wed."

"Did you want a mouse?" she asked, not quite accidentally spilling some gruel down his chin.

He tried to reach her hair, to feel it through his fingers, but his arm fell back onto the bed. "I did not know what I wanted. You had not shown me yet."

They left London two days later, going north. They would travel with Lord and Lady Cormack as far as Nottingham, they told everyone, on their way to Ardsley Keep. Lorraine and Roger were ready to leave town, and

s healthy enough for the trip, excited that he
get to ride a short ways in the coach with his fasci-
ng uncle, but not the crow.

Lorraine had demurred at first. If someone was trying
to injure the earl, she did not want her son caught in the
cross fire. Roger had reminded her of how much they
owed Ardeth, and declared they were going, and were
going to make certain he arrived safely. Roger rode
alongside the coach, his pistol close to hand.

Miss Hadley, it turned out, had much in common with
Lorraine, including acquaintances and lurid novels, so
they helped pass the time together, leaving Genie to entertain Peter when his nanny and nursemaid needed a
rest, which was often. Now that Peter was feeling better,
he had all the energy of a puppy, and the attention span to
match. Ardeth helped some, with stories of knights and
dragons, but he slept a great deal, too.

James Vinross was to follow in a few weeks, when he
had more reports from the Bow Street men Genie had
hired, and when more of Ardeth's building plans were fi-
nalized. Genie thought a short separation from Miss
Hadley was good for both of them, to learn their own
minds, now that they were learning each other's.

The Randolphs were staying on in London to care for
the house and oversee the repairs and renovations to
Willeford's place. They were also now in charge of returning hourglasses to their hopeful senders, or shipping
likely ones north to the Keep.

Marie and scores of servants traveled with the cara-
van, which was surrounded at all times by armed riders,
in addition to Lord Cormack. The guards and grooms
were mostly veterans, handpicked by Campbell and Vinross, and sworn to protect the man who had saved their

fellow soldiers. The carriages were inspected at every stop and scouts were sent ahead to inspect the terrain and the accommodations. Genie had traveled with the army long enough to know defensive tactics. She was leaving nothing to chance.

They traveled slowly, for the comfort of the injured, the infant, and the increasing Genie. Ardeth dozed a great deal, recouping his strength, but insisted on walking into the inns at night under his own power. Genie knew he was in pain, but he never complained, not unless the rooms were cold. She slept in adjoining rooms when possible, her pistol under the pillow, while his valet had a trundle bed next to Ardeth's.

After five days, they were all sick of the coaches, the roads, the inns, and one another. "We will be leaving you at the next stage," Genie told her sister and brother-in-law, loudly enough for any interested listener to hear. "To go on to Ardsley."

When they reached the turning for Cormack Woods, the earl's carriage continued north, as planned.

Also as planned, the earl was not in the crested coach. He was riding in a less luxurious carriage that had carried Peter and his nanny, who were now riding with Lorraine, to her discomfort. The elegant Ardeth equipage was filled this time with armed veterans on the lookout for an ambush. Genie was still taking no chances, plotting their route with the care of a general, or an intelligence officer.

What did a woman do when her husband was too weak to defend himself, when she was over four months pregnant and feeling ill herself, when she did not know the enemy, or even if their ultimate destination was safe and defensible? Genie did not know what His Grace of Wellington would do, but she went home, to her parents.

CHAPTER TWENTY-TWO

A countess could count on a welcome almost anywhere. An earl made an enviable guest. Usually.

The Hopewells' invitation, it seemed, was not to a notorious nobleman and his expectant wife. Gossip traveled faster than a summer rainstorm, even this far from London, and the city's scandal sheets still made good reading, only a day or two late.

Despite having sent a note ahead, Genie found her parents' manor house unprepared for any company except the ladies' sewing circle her mother was entertaining. She had not quite expected the fatted calf, but stale toast and tepid tea among coldhearted crones was not the homecoming Genie had imagined.

Her mother's guests were the same sanctimonious females who had heaped coals on the fire of Genie's disgrace, forcing her to marry Elgin and him to join the army. In the days leading to her first wedding, the local gentry women had shown their disapproval by leaving the room when Genie entered, lest they be contaminated with her filth. Those same biddy hens who demanded proper, punctilious behavior in others now showed the utmost discourtesy by staying on in her mother's parlor.

The vicar's spinster sister, a viscount's pensioned aunts, the banker's cousin, and two wives of major landholders all needed to finish their tea and pack up their needlework, a long, slow, careful procedure to keep the threads from tangling. Every one of them wanted a good look at the enigmatic earl to take back to their own neighbors, Genie knew. Before they went home, they were going to tell the linendraper and the butcher and their cooks that Lord Ardeth was too thin, too pale, and not much for conversation. His manners were shabby, too, when he sat down before taking each woman's hand in introduction. Either that or the delicious rumors of his being shot were true.

They were also going to pass around the news that little Imogene Hopewell had grown plump, so the rumors about her must be true, also. My, my.

My foot, Genie thought, removing her shawl. If the ladies wanted an eyeful, let them see the huge diamond ring Ardeth had bought for her, the rare black pearls at her neck, and the fine black silk gown from London's best modiste. Let them see she wore mourning for Elgin, but adored her new husband. She brought him his tea just the way he liked it, and a plate of the remaining biscuits. Then she stood behind his chair, her hand resting on his shoulder next to Olive. Oh, they would chatter about Olive for days.

The only female in the room near to Genie's age was her brother Brice's wife, Mary, a plain girl very much under her mother-in-law's thumb. She and Brice, the heir,

were living at the manor, which was a far cry from the
rooms Mary had lived in over her father's haberdashery,
so Mary could have few complaints. She had been one of
the first of Genie's friends to turn their backs on her.
Genie turned her back now, letting her mother complete
the introductions to the earl, after Genie had presented
him and Miss Hadley.

When the sewing circle biddies finally took their reluctant leave, Genie's mother just as reluctantly told
Mary to call for a fresh pot of tea. Then she informed
Genie that her father was out riding his acres, as usual.
The first visit of a daughter in over three years was hardly
usual, Genie thought, feeling the hurt of his rejection all
over again.

Brice was out shooting, also as usual.

"Crows," Mary added.

Genie tucked Olive in her shawl that she had placed
around Ardeth's shoulders. Now the bird could be warm,
and no one could hear his curses. She'd forgotten how
spiteful Mary could be, and how her father did not permit
fires to be lit at Hopewell Manor until after the first frost.

Her other brother was studying law in Leeds, her
mother reported. And calling on the daughter of an East
India nabob recently settled there. Genie's mother had
hopes of a happy, rewarding outcome. Genie had hopes
they would be shown to their rooms soon, because Ardeth
was looking more peaked than usual and Miss Hadley appeared decidedly uncomfortable. The chill in the room
was not due only to the lack of fires.

As for Ardeth, he was cold and weary from the trip,
but this was his wife's home, her family, and she needed
to make peace with them. Genie also thought this was the
best place for him to recover, so he sank back in an ugly

chintz-covered chair and tried to find a comfortable position despite his doubts. Zeus knew, he was not ready to take on any battles. The bullet wound was healing far faster than a normal man's would have, but at a terrible cost in mental energy. Simply staying asleep had drained what few powers remained to him. He needed to conserve what was left to protect Genie. But damned if he wouldn't use some to start a fire in his bedchamber if he had to. If not for her hand on his shoulder, he'd get a good blaze going right here, starting with the ugly chintz chair. For now, he half closed his eyes and listened. This was her campaign, after all.

When her mother was done catching Genie up on all the news of the neighbors and the distant cousins, Genie recounted young Peter's near-fatal illness, then his recovery. Afterward, Miss Hadley's ancestry was investigated and found to be far higher than either of the Mrs. Hopewells'. Silence fell.

"Well, here you are, Imogene," her mother said at last. "A countess. Who would have thought you'd end up with a higher title than Lorraine?"

Who indeed? Genie thought. Certainly not Lorraine.

Genie's mother looked at Ardeth, then at Miss Hadley, knowing she should not ask in public, but whispering, "And breeding?"

"Yes," Genie whispered back.

"Oh, dear, oh, dear. You cannot seem to stay out of trouble, can you?"

Genie nodded toward her husband. "This last cannot be laid at my door."

"Then it is not Elgin's babe?"

Ardeth tensed and Miss Hadley gasped at the bluntness, but she was used to London's more subtle prying.

Genie had no intention of answering her mother's last question. "I meant the latest contretemps, Lord Ardeth being shot."

"So you wrote in your message. Do you think it wise to drag a gravely wounded man so far from town? We have no good physicians in the neighborhood, you know. That is why Roger and Lorraine had to travel to London with the boy."

"Ardeth no longer needs a physician, just rest."

"In a carriage on a journey? You never did think, did you? Marrying so soon after Elgin . . . but we are not going to speak of that, are we?"

Mary sat forward, perfectly willing to speak about Genie's outrageous conduct. A glare from her mother-in-law kept her quiet.

"I do not see why you had to hurry his lordship from his sickbed. He could have rested in his own home in town"—letting the gossip die down—"before you set out."

"He was not safe in London."

Her mother brushed crumbs from her gown. "Oh, dear. So those tales are true, too. Now you are bringing your troubles home to roost. I do not know what your father is going to say. I so wanted you two to come to terms, but this . . ."

"This is me. This is my husband. Papa will have to accept that."

Or perhaps he would not, which was why no invitation to find bedrooms upstairs was forthcoming.

They did not have long to wait to discover Squire Hopewell's feelings.

Genie's father trudged through his wife's best parlor in his muddied boots, ignoring her tongue clucking. A wide-bellied man with weathered skin, he looked at Ardeth struggling to rise to his feet and waved him back down. He ducked his head toward the middle-aged woman sitting ramrod straight in a corner, and scowled at his niminy-piminy daughter-in-law trying to hide in the blasted cabbage roses on the upholstery. Then he looked at his daughter.

Genie had not expected him to hold open his arms. He had never been an affectionate, demonstrative man, but neither did she expect her father's first words to her to be "Breeding, they say." He did not bother whispering.

"Yes."

"Could be any man's babe, they say."

"They are wrong."

"Shot your own husband, they say."

"Someone else put an end to Elgin's life before I could."

"Not that husband, and do not be fresh to me, girl. This is still my home."

Genie nodded in acknowledgment. "They—whoever *they* are—were not present when Lord Ardeth was wounded."

"There are strange men surrounding my house. I had to tell 'em who I was before they let me come in my own front door."

"I am sorry. They are for protection."

Ardeth started to speak, but Hopewell stopped him. "I do not know you, sir. I will hear what my daughter has to say."

"You never listened to her before."

They all knew what Ardeth was speaking of, and no one wanted to dredge up the past, not when the future was so fraught, the present so puzzling. If Ardeth was throwing down the gauntlet, however, Hopewell would not refuse the challenge. He already had his wife whining, armed men at his front door—and the back, too, he supposed—and the whole parish talking about his family again. He did not like any of it. "I suppose she did not pull the trigger, then, not if you are speaking up for her."

"She is my wife." In those few words, Ardeth expressed both defense and offense. He would defend Genie with every last ounce of strength, and take offense at anyone who insulted her. No one, not even the blustering squire, could mistake the threat in his voice, the danger in his fierce look. They, the ubiquitous and anonymous grapevine, were right about that, at least: The earl's stare could paralyze a man's privates, all right.

Hopewell did not like being set down by a younger man, a sickly one, too, by the looks of him. "In this house, Imogene is my daughter." Still, he addressed both of them when he said, "I do not like this situation, heaping new scandal atop old."

Before Ardeth could answer, Genie did, not wishing to see two stags butting heads until one was bloodied. "We do not like it any more than you do, I assure you. That was one of the reasons we left London."

"Gossip travels on wings, don't you know. And your mother and I live here, not in London. Everyone and his uncle—more like his aunt, the way the women's tongues flap—is talking about how your earl should be in his grave by now."

Ardeth wondered, for the first time, just who was in his grave, where it was, or if he had one at all.

When he did not reply, Genie said, "My husband is strong and healthy. He is recovering, thank you."

"We heard as how he had another wound."

Genie silently damned that London physician Lorraine had insisted they call in to check the surgeon's work. The charlatan had done nothing, but he must have spread the tale to each patient he visited. Ardeth seemed to have fallen into a brown study, so again she answered, "He was in other battles."

Hopewell shook his head. "Word is, it looked like someone tried to put a stake through his heart."

That brought Ardeth's attention back in a hurry. Genie could feel him sit up, just as she could feel her own temper rise. She might have entertained the same thought on first seeing that other ill-healed scar, but only for an instant . . . before she fainted. Anyone else harboring suspicions that Ardeth was some kind of abomination was abhorrent. He might be odd, but he was her oddity. And he was a good man. "I am sure an intelligent person like you, Father, cannot believe such ignorant tripe such as ogres from fairy tales. Superstitions and the like are ridiculous in this modern day. Ardeth was in foreign lands with poor doctoring, that was all."

"I suppose that's why he talks in tongues."

Genie stamped her foot. "He speaks in foreign languages, not some gibberish from a religious zealot. He knows French and German and Russian, Italian, Spanish—" Genie knew there were others, but did not think her father would be impressed with Hindustani and Chinese.

She was right. "Yes, yes, but what has that to do with a man's worth?" Squire Hopewell knew the King's English and that was enough for him.

"If you wish to discuss my monetary worth, Squire," Ardeth put in before either of them forgot he was there, "I can show you my bankbooks and the contract for

Genie's marriage settlements. It is a father's right and responsibility to ascertain a suitor's prospects, so I take no
umbrage at your concern. I do not consider myself a
suitor, naturally, since we are already wed, but for your
information, Lady Ardeth already holds a fortune in her
own name, plus various properties."

The squire had not heard *that* bit of information. He
glared at his wife. "Well, I suppose a countess is always
welcome. Your mother would have my hide if I did not
offer you rooms."

Genie could not resist asking, "But what about a
daughter? Is a daughter not always welcome?"

Ardeth did not wait for Squire Hopewell to answer. He
stood again, holding on to the chair, and handed Genie
her shawl after unwrapping the sleeping crow. He took
her arm, leaning only a little, and said, "Did I forget to
tell you, my dear, that I accepted Lady Cormack's invitation to stay the week with them rather than impose on
your parents? We should be leaving in time to change for
dinner."

Genie happily accepted the reprieve and the lie. "Oh,
dear. I was not watching the time." She bobbed a slight
curtsy to her parents, out of politeness, if not out of respect. "It has been a pleasure seeing you both in good
health. Give Brice my regards, and tell George I wish him
luck chasing his rich bride."

Now it was Mrs. Hopewell who was scowling at her
husband. He cleared his throat. "Didn't mean you wasn't
welcome to stay."

"No? Well, perhaps we will call on our way back to
London next time. I will be sure to send more notice."

Hopewell looked at his wife, then nodded. "That
would be better, then. Family and all."

Which was as much acceptance as Genie was going to receive. "Family, yes. Of course you are always welcome at Ardsley Keep once we get settled there. Is that not right, my lord?"

Ardeth held out an olive branch. "Indeed. In fact, I might need some advice on managing the lands. I did not learn husbandry while studying those other languages."

"We might just do that, maybe when the child is born. M'grandchild and all."

That was the one fact no one could dispute.

Lorraine was not surprised to find Ardeth and Genie and Miss Hadley in her parlor. "I knew how it would be," she said, ordering the fires built up, a more lavish dinner prepared, rooms made ready. "But what about the crow?"

The crow could stay in Ardeth's room away from Peter, as long as he had food and water.

"Wine," Olive whined.

Olive was not half as troublesome to Genie's mind as the Dowager Lady Cormack. Elgin's and Roger's mother resided at the hall, which boasted no dower house, to Lorraine's regret. The senior baroness still believed both Hopewell girls had entrapped her sons. Genie, for one, had hoped never to see the harridan again.

But the situation had changed. Little Peter was healthier, skipping into his grandmother's arms, thanks to Lord Ardeth. The heir to the barony was on Cormack Woods lands, where he belonged, also thanks to Lord Ardeth. Now Lady Cormack the Elder no longer needed Genie's child to assure her husband's succession. She could be generous, if not gracious.

Besides, having the earl and his lady in her house—she still thought of it as hers, also to Lorraine's regrets—

was a coup against Mrs. Squire Hopewell, her archenemy in the war for neighborhood supremacy. That Sophy Hopewell, the mushroom, queened it over the parish despite her lack of a title rankled the baroness. The squire's wife was head of the altar committee, hostess for the sewing circle, chairwoman of the May Day Fair, and in charge of collections for the poorhouse. Besides, her husband was the local magistrate, so the tradesmen gave them better goods at lower prices to win his favor.

But Sophy Hopewell did not have an earl and a countess staying with her! Lady Cormack did.

Unfortunately, after the warm welcome, Genie and Ardeth found themselves in separate chambers of the guest wing across the hall from each other. With all the extra servants, and Peter not sleeping in the nursery until it could be aired and cleared of anything with feathers, Lorraine had had to double up some of the arrangements. Miss Hadley and Marie were to share Genie's room, while Ardeth's valet slept on a trundle bed in his.

Genie was upset. If Ardeth was well enough to dress for dinner, he was well enough to . . . well, enough time had gone by.

"That is all right, my dear," Ardeth told her when he saw her disappointment. "I am not quite ready for sharing a bed with you."

They both knew they would not sleep.

"Besides, the more rest I get, the sooner we can leave and the faster we can travel."

She had to accept that.

CHAPTER TWENTY-THREE

Genie might be disappointed, but Ardeth was dismayed. Not that his valet shared the room, not that they were in possible danger, and not that things had gone poorly with Squire and Mrs. Hopewell. No, he was dismayed that he could not make love to his wife. Not that he would not, not that he should not, but that now he could not. Great gods, what if he had waited too long? He had the body of an able young man. What if he had the manhood of an ancient?

He cursed in far more languages than Genie had mentioned to her father, and he cursed the Devil, whose doing this had to be. That dastard never did play fair. Give a man six months—then make them hell on earth as a eunuch.

Or maybe he was just weak from the gunshot. Yes, that was it. His powers were at low ebb, so it made sense that the rest of him would be at half-mast. It made sense, but it sure as Hades did not make him happy. He was bound to recover, Ardeth told himself. Before too long, he prayed.

If not . . . no, he would not consider the alternative.

Damn, here he was, alive, where he never truly believed he'd be again. Here he was married, again. And this time liking his wife very well. He'd even reconciled desire with dogma. Lust was sinful unless it was for one's spouse. Pleasing her was a duty. He'd thought it would be a delight, done right. He'd even thought that, in his weakened state, he could not hurt her.

He couldn't, unless she broke a rib laughing at him.

Pretty Genie, so sweet, so eager, so naive in her way. She deserved far better. He thought of her, there in the dark, with her hair down and her skirts up. He thought of her with her gown unfastened, so he could touch and stroke and suckle. Then he thought of her out of her clothing altogether.

For once his room was too warm.

He'd thought he was getting closer to finding his true being. He was as honorable as he knew how, harming none, helping as many as he could. He actually enjoyed trying to improve people's lives, not merely performing good deeds for the sake of his own salvation. He was discovering the comfort of friendship, family, children. He was no closer to finding the hourglass, but he'd thought he was nearer to what other men felt.

He needed time, which was the one thing he did not have. Well, time was one *other* thing he did not have.

They spent three days at Cormack Woods while Ardeth rested. Genie played with her nephew and twice visited with her parents and older brother. Lorraine threw a dinner party to introduce them to the neighborhood, and no one refused. The household was supposed to be in mourning for Elgin, so no dancing took place afterward. Miss Hadley played at the pianoforte, with others joining in song.

Genie relaxed. No one asked awkward questions, or gave sideways looks, or whispered behind fans. Ardeth stayed by her side like the perfect bridegroom, looking so handsome in his evening dress, she thought half the women must be imagining him out of it.

He was attentive to her needs, ready to come to her defense if any of the conversation turned personal or ugly. Her mother was before him, and her sister, Miss Hadley, the dowager baroness, and even Squire Hopewell.

"Helped nurse the soldiers, my daughter did," the squire told everyone who would listen. "Got grit, my girl. And saved her husband's life, besides. He could have bled to death without her, according to Cormack. And look at my daughters, the two prettiest gals in the county." He skipped right over his daughter-in-law. "Good men they married." He skipped right over poor Elgin. "Thinking of those without a string of titles to their names. Got honor. Land. Deep pockets." He skipped over peculiar habits, unusual pets, and a tendency to attract trouble, scandal, and assassins. "What more could a father ask for his girls?"

So the visit turned out to be worthwhile in one way, at least.

They left, heading north. With fewer coaches, but with as many outriders, they should have been able to travel faster, except that Genie still suffered morning sickness at odd times of the day. Her discomfort was exacerbated by the rougher roads and the less well-sprung carriage, so they stopped frequently. While she recovered, they admired the scenery, an old chapel, a Roman ruin, a meadow filled with wildflowers. The outriders were less wary now, after all the side turns they had taken. No one could know their itinerary in advance, and the rear guard reported that no one was following them. Campbell sent word back that all was clear ahead; he'd encountered no trouble.

Ardeth was not as weary as he had been, so slept less in the carriage. He even thought of riding the stallion for a stage or two. Genie thought otherwise. He was still weak and a fall might reopen the wounds. Furthermore, no one could keep up with his horse, to protect him from highwaymen or hired assailants lying in wait.

He smiled as he handed her into the coach. "Your nagging sounds just like a real wife."

She looked back and said, "I am a real wife." Then she whispered so Miss Hadley could not overhear, "Almost."

The look she gave him spoke volumes. Chapter one could be titled "If he was well enough to think of riding the horse, he was well enough for another kind of ride."

He quickly climbed into the carriage after her. "You are right. I am not fit for such strenuous activity."

They played cards, read out loud, sang folk songs from various lands, and discussed plans for the school they were going to establish where girls would be educated, too. Miss Hadley pretended to doze so they could converse more privately. Olive grew bored and sat up with the driver. To the crow, the wind in his feathers was almost like flying, without huntsmen or hawks.

On one night of the journey, the inn they chose happened to have enough rooms that Miss Hadley and the servants could each have one of their own. Genie brushed her hair, laid out her traveling outfit for the morning, read a few pages of her book, and repeated her father's words to herself: "Got grit, my girl." She gathered that grit, took a deep breath, and rapped on Ardeth's door after she heard his man say good night.

"Is your room not to your liking?" he asked when he saw her standing in the hall. "Did you have enough supper? Are you feeling ill?"

"Thank you. I am fine. I . . . I was wondering if you were well."

He raised his arm to show that he was getting more use of his shoulder. "I am feeling little pain, only stiffness, thank you."

Her grit was sinking to her slippers. "Um, perhaps you want company, then."

"After all these days in the carriage and nights sharing your rooms, I'd have thought you would cherish your privacy."

"I was, um, worried that you might need someone here with you, in case you required something in the night."

"I have not taken laudanum for a week, and can reach for candles, blankets, or water for myself. Do not fuss, Genie. I do not need a nursemaid."

"Of course. I am sorry. I did not mean to be a nag again. There is nothing I can get you?"

How he wished. "No, thank you."

"Your room is warmer than mine."

"It usually is. Do you want me to build up the fire in your room?"

What for? Genie almost snapped at him. The man was as blockheaded as the bedpost. She was wearing her night rail, for goodness' sake, her hair left unbound the way he seemed to like it. What did he think, she was here to borrow a book or tuck in his covers? She turned to go back to her own cold, lonely room. "I suppose I should leave you to your rest, then."

He did not contradict her, and her heart sank, too, along with whatever courage she'd mustered. He was rejecting her and her protruding belly.

He touched her shoulder, so she turned, hopeful. He kissed her forehead instead of her lips, but placed a hand gently on the mound of her pregnancy. "I am sorry, Genie. I am not ready to share a bed with you, as much as I might want. And I do want. Never think otherwise. I am just not strong enough yet."

"I could . . . that is . . . sometimes Elgin wanted me to . . ."

He held a finger to her lips. "Please, do not speak of Elgin in our bedroom. Even if this is not our own room, I do not want his ghost in here."

She spun around. "Can he . . . ?"

"Metaphorically, I meant."

At least her husband was not seeing apparitions, Genie thought in relief. Who cared if he believed in ghosts? A lot of people did. Then she started to apologize for being forward. A strong man like Ardeth might not like a woman taking the initiative.

"You have nothing to apologize for, my dear. I am honored that you would come to my room. A warm, willing wife has to be every man's dream come true. But I want our wedding night, our own celebration of our union, to be perfect for both of us when it finally occurs. That consummation is more fitting at Ardsley Keep. No one will bother us there, and we do not have to get ready to travel in the morning."

"You are sure it is not me?"

He kissed her, long and tenderly. He could feel her melt against him. He could feel her softness against his . . . softness. He set her aside before she noticed. "I am sure. Now go to sleep. We will be at Ardsley Keep before you know it."

"Soon," she said, standing on tiptoes to brush a butterfly kiss against his lips. "Soon." A plea and a promise.

Now all he had to do was hope his inefficacy ended before the journey did.

Ardeth timed the final leg of their trip so that they would spend the last night at an inn, with only a few hours to travel in the morning. That way they would arrive at his estate in daylight, fresh and tidy, and expected from the note sent round from the inn with one of his own grooms.

"Aren't you worried that you might be alerting an enemy by giving your arrival time?" Genie wanted to know over breakfast before they set out. Miss Hadley was eating upstairs in her room, purposely and politely leaving them alone in the private parlor.

Genie was having plain toast, in hopes of reaching her new home in dignity and style, instead of in a green-complexioned fog.

Ardeth was tasting the inn's specialty, steak and kidney pie. "An enemy at the Keep? I doubt it."

"Tell me who will be there, then, so I am prepared."

He wanted to know, too, so had the messenger speak to the butler there after delivering Ardeth's note. The groom reported back that Miss Calverton and the schoolteacher had moved in, along with the vicar's widow and her three daughters. They were awaiting the allocation of cottages until the earl's arrival.

"I suppose they quickly discovered that the Keep is more comfortable than any empty house on the grounds," Ardeth told Genie between bites, "but we shall see."

Other than the visitors he had sent, the Keep's caretakers were also in residence. Generations of Spotfords had been part of the Keep for ages, managing the properties. The first one had been his first wife's younger brother, left in charge of defending the castle when Ardeth went to war. "They are very distant relations," he explained, "who have always made their home at Ardsley."

"But they are not in line to inherit it?" Genie was looking for motives under every rock.

"No, they are not in the direct line of succession for the lands or the title. Even if they were, the Keep and its holdings are not entailed. The title went into abeyance for a while when some ancient relative died without an immediate heir." Coryn of Ardsley, to be exact. "All of the pertinent documents were unfortunately lost in a fire, and the parish records, too. When an heir was discovered, my great-grandfather, I believe, he was not living in England. Thinking he would return, he petitioned the Crown to reinstate the title, and to rewrite the letters of patent concerning the succession and inheritance. He never lived to see England, nor did my father, either, but the terms clearly remain: If there is no son, the last earl can dispose of the acquired lands as he will, but the original fortress and the title revert back to the Crown. Most of the property has been added to over the years by agents from abroad, with moneys from other sources. They belong to me, to bequeath as I wish. The fortune is mine also, not the earldom's."

Genie knew that rules of succession varied from title

to title. Some could even devolve on the female line in lieu of direct male descendants. "So the Spotfords cannot benefit from your death?"

"Oh, I shall leave them a handsome bequest for their years of service, but they do not need it. They already receive a respectable competence and a percentage of the estate's profits, which they could lose if I die. They also own a parcel of land of their own, although it always made more sense for them to live at the Keep. I suppose they grew to think of it as theirs, but I have sent enough messages and money to remind them of my existence. Our arrival will not be a shock to any of them."

She gave up on the dry toast and tried not to breathe in the odors of the kippers Ardeth was eating now. "Tell me about them, please, as it appears we will all be living under one roof."

He smiled, thinking she was imagining a crowded residence like her sister's at Cormack Woods. He decided to let her see for herself. "I cannot tell you much, because I have never met any of them myself. My agents tell me Spotford is a typical countryman, wed to the earth like your father. He has two grown sons, neither married."

"What of his wife? Will she be upset at losing the keys to the castle?"

"I believe she died in ch—" Ardeth recalled his audience and her pregnant state. "In her late twenties. That was the mother to Spotford's second son. His first wife, mother to his older son, died of a smallpox epidemic. The younger boy manages the home farm and their own small estate. He studied agriculture and is a big help to his father, I understand. Likely Richard will take over the position when his father retires."

Genie looked at the platter of sweet rolls near her

plate, but decided against it, with regrets. "What of the other son?"

"Fernell is more of a charming wastrel, I am afraid. He is well liked in the neighborhood, from what I can gather. All the matchmaking mamas pursue him, at any rate. I assume they expect him to inherit Spotford Oaks. Mr. Spotford pays his expenses, so Fernell lives like a lord. He travels from house party to hunting box. He is visiting friends in Bath now, I understand. The butler did tell my messenger that Mr. Spotford sent for Fernell, to welcome us home."

"He will not like being sent for, like a schoolboy." She changed her mind. A bite or two of the pastry would not hurt her, no more than the carriage ride.

Ardeth passed her the jam to spread on her roll. "Since it is my money supporting him and his profligacy all these years, I daresay he will hide any discontent. Especially since I have the power to tighten his purse strings. There is also an aunt, Spotford's sister, but no, before you work yourself into a fidget, she has never acted as mistress or hostess. An accident in her youth or something keeps her to her rooms."

"How sad. Will they stay on, do you think?"

"That depends on them, and you."

"Me?"

"If you do not like them, they are dismissed. It is you who shall have to deal with them when I am not available."

Genie lost her appetite. "Not available" in his lexicon did not mean busy elsewhere. It meant gone altogether. She refused to think about that. She had enough to worry about now.

He seemed to have had enough breakfast also, eager to

be on the road. "I am hoping they will stay now to advise me and manage day-to-day operations. I know nothing about that, as I told your father."

Once they were on their way, Miss Hadley settled with her sewing, Ardeth staring out the window of the carriage, Genie asked, "How soon before we reach Ardsley Keep?"

"We have been on our land since leaving the inn, I believe. There should be a rise soon, overlooking the house."

He directed the driver to pull up at that hill, off the road, so the other vehicles could pass. The baggage carts, the servants' coach, and most of the grooms were sent on ahead to prepare the house and start unloading. They all thought Lady Ardeth was having another of her spells.

She was not. She was too busy having spasms to have an upset stomach.

Ardeth had helped Genie out of the coach and stood, pointing her in the right direction.

"That is your house? That . . . that castle?" She clutched at his arm, not caring if she wrinkled his sleeve.

The magnificent building, all four stories with numerous wings, scads of chimneys, and two dozen turrets, looked like a palace for a king, no, an emperor. It was huge and sprawling, with windows gleaming, set in vast gardens and wide lawns and elegant stands of trees. Honey-colored stones glowed in the sunshine, with ivy permitted to soften the edges in places.

Genie almost ran back into the coach. What did a squire's daughter, a soldier's widow, have to do with a place like this? Kings and queens ought to live there, or visit, at least. Would she be expected to invite the prince? And how did one keep such a mammoth-sized mansion clean? "Please tell me that is not Ardsley Keep."

"Very well, it is not. That pile of rubble on the hill behind it is the Keep. This building has been built out of the old stones. Do you see that terraced garden? The moat used to be there. And over there, where those cottages are, an entire village once stood to serve the fortress." He pointed east. "They moved the village over there after the fire, just beyond those trees, but the shopkeepers and such still depend on the Keep for most of their trade. Few travelers come so far north, away from populous cities."

"It is lovely."

It was, truly.

This was not the place where Ardeth had been born, not even where he had died. He had never seen the new structures except in sketches from his messengers, and he could not discern anything familiar in the jumble of rocks in the distance. But the lands were his, as far as he could see. He had wedded a stranger to possess this place, then fought to keep it. Ardeth looked over his domain now, the grand residence, the fields filled with crops, the green hills dotted with sheep, and felt his chest swell with pride and a sense of belonging. This was what he had worked for during all those years of stolen moments. This was where he could watch things grow, instead of waiting for them to die.

With Genie beside him, this was home.

CHAPTER TWENTY-FOUR

"Come, wife," Ardeth said, leading her back to the waiting carriage. "Let us start our new life together."

Genie kept looking back. "Are you sure it will not disappear when we get closer, like some mirage?"

"We are not in the desert."

"And you swear you did not simply conjure it all up out of moonshine when we arrived?"

"Your estimation of my abilities never ceases to amaze me. I do not know whether to be honored or insulted." He waved an imaginary wand in the air. Nothing happened. "No, I might produce the occasional coin from an ear or a dove from a hat, if Olive is willing to be powdered, but a castle in an instant? Not likely."

Not by half. Building that edifice, establishing the earldom and all it represented, had taken centuries, document by document in dying solicitors' offices, brick by brick at ailing architects' heart attacks, pound by pound at bankers' bedsides. Making investments, sending messages, having one's wishes known, were deuced difficult for a being who did not actually exist in this world. He had done it. And lived again to see it.

He looked back, too, before closing the carriage door. "Ardsley Keep is permanent now, and it is yours."

"Mine?" Genie repeated with a gasp.

"I told you. It is mine to leave where I wish. You and the child can decide its fate. Stay and be countess, or make it into a university, or an asylum for the insane. It will be yours."

Stay without Coryn? She would have to be insane herself. "Ours," she said. "Yours and mine."

When they got closer to the castle, Genie was reminded of pictures she'd seen of feudal times, all the serfs and vassals come out to welcome their knightly lord back from some feat of derring-do. Men and women lined the roadway, waving and cheering. Children with their faces freshly scrubbed were tossing flowers in the path of the coach. She half expected trumpets to blare, banners to be unfurled in the breeze, great warhorses with pounding hooves to ride ahead of them.

The crowds acted as if they were greeting a fairy-tale princess. All they were getting was Genie.

She smiled and waved out the window, even though she'd rather hide under Ardeth's cape. All of these people were looking to her as their lady? "I feel as if I should be wearing ermine and a crown," she whispered to Miss Hadley.

Ardeth reached across the seats and touched her hair, the strands that curled beneath a tiny black lace bonnet. "This is glory enough. You are perfect."

And so she was, because he told her she could be. Head held high, she properly greeted the army of servants lined up at the castle doors—so that was how the place was kept clean—and even thanked them all for their gracious welcome. She tried to memorize the upper servants' names, and befriended the housekeeper by begging her assistance in finding her way around.

Then they were up the steps and at the door. Ardeth said, "I wish I could carry you over the threshold, my dear, but I doubt that would be wise. What if I dropped you in front of all the staff? They would be so disappointed, we would have to move to China."

She smiled at that, taking his arm to walk through the door of her new home.

"Welcome, welcome," a gentleman of late middle years called out. He was bald except for a fringe of white hair, with white eyebrows and a wide smile. "I am Angus Spotford, and I am delighted to meet you, my lady, my lord. An earl and countess at Ardsley, at last! Come in, come in!"

Genie found herself enveloped in a hug, with a buss on the cheek. Ardeth received a firm handshake and a pat on the back. Then Spotford wiped a tear from his eye. "Forgive me, I never thought I'd live to see the day."

Ardeth was wrong, Genie thought. Mr. Spotford was not at all like her father, more like the father she wished she had. He was open and emotional, and she adored him already, regretting she had suspected this kindly gentleman of harboring ill will toward her husband. He was beaming and bowing, blowing his nose. No one could be that good an actor.

The vicar's widow also adored him, it seemed. Mrs. Newberry hovered at Spotford's right elbow, adding her welcomes. Her daughters appeared to have laid claim to

Richard Spotford, for they circled him like bees on a flower.

Miss Calverton, the former companion, was effusive in her greeting, and her appreciation of the opportunity to be of service, whatever her ladyship needed. Of course she was not trying to displace Miss Hadley, she said with a curtsy in that lady's direction. And a tiny cottage would be delightful, if Lady Ardeth found that Miss Calverton was in the way. Genie doubted she could find the woman in this colossus of a house, much less trip over her.

The retired schoolteacher, Mr. Jordan, thanked Ardeth for the use of his magnificent library, the opportunity of a lifetime for a scholar and an admirer of rare books. He had taken the liberty of beginning to catalog the collection in gratitude, and would like to continue, with his lordship's permission, of course. Now that he had the lottery money, he had no need to work, but this would be a labor of love. He had also been looking over likely sites for a school with Spotty.

Genie looked around for a dog.

"That's what everyone calls me, Lady Ardeth, Spotty. But you might prefer 'Cousin Spotford.'"

"And you must call me Cousin Genie. I find the title is too new to identify me and too ponderous to be comfortable, especially at home."

He wiped his eyes again when she called the castle home. "Then you do intend to stay? I am so glad. As much as I love the old pile, I cannot add those special touches that make it shine. I think of the Keep as a great painting, my life's work, if you will, and my father's before me. But a woman's touch can make it into a masterpiece. We've never had a countess, you see, not that anyone can remember, and my sister's been bedridden these many years. My wives did their bit, but their hearts were not in it."

Most likely because they knew it was not theirs, Genie thought. "I am sure you have done remarkably. From what I have seen, everything is perfect."

"That's because we had the help of Mrs. Newberry and Miss Calverton. I do not know how we would have managed to get ready for you and Lord Ardeth without them. But Ardsley Keep needs a countess and children and company. Not that we have not been merry as grigs since the lucky ladies arrived and our Mr. Jordan. Ah, but I suppose I should not call them lucky despite the lottery, not with them being in mourning, don't you know? Of course you do, my dear." He patted her hand, but a moment of silence was all he seemed to manage. "The village is hoping you'll take a hand in the parish council and the ladies' guild, all that kind of nonsense females take such stock in." He turned toward Ardeth. "And Cousin Coryn—I may call you that, may I not?"

"I would be pleased. It is more like family."

Spotford laughed. "You'll wish for a few less kin soon enough. Be warned that the church needs a new roof, the poorhouse does not have enough firewood for the winter, and the village is without a fire bell, a physician, and a posting inn. I must say everyone but the children is delighted we will have a real school soon, and everyone, including the children, has an opinion on how it should be run and where it should be located. I told them not to bother you your first day here, but I would not be surprised to find the drawing room full of petitioners, all with good cause, naturally, tomorrow. I have been putting them off the last month or so, thinking the decisions should be yours to make. It is your money, after all. Oh, and whenever you wish to inspect the estate books, I am at your service."

"There is no hurry. I know you have done an exemplary job."

Spotford grinned with pride. "Born to it, don't you know? And my boy takes after me."

"Your elder son?"

His smile faded a little. "No, Richard. My firstborn goes his own merry path. He means no disrespect by being late. Nor does my sister. She seldom leaves her rooms."

"None taken. After all, we were not sure when we would arrive."

"We expect Fernell any minute. He's riding hell for leather right now if I know the boy, but he must have stopped off at a mill or a cockfight, unless he met with an accident. He sent his valet on ahead with the baggage yesterday."

Richard Spotford stepped out of his bevy of young girls rather than let his father fret about the absent Fernell. "But I am eager to show you the farms, sir. Whenever you wish."

"Now don't overwhelm his lordship," Spotford warned. "He'll want to rest and settle in before facing more gadding about."

Ardeth disagreed. "I have been looking forward to seeing every square inch of the estate since my return to England. For many, many years before that, in fact, in my efforts to get home. I would have been here sooner, but I had to take care of financial and diplomatic tasks before I could leave London. And I did run into a bit of trouble." He rubbed his shoulder where Spotford had embraced him.

"Heard about that, we did," the older man said. "Country living will fix you up, all right and tight. Mustn't overtire yourself first off, though. The land is not going anywhere." He rapped his knuckles on the paneled wood wall. "Nor this place."

"No, it is not, is it?"

Spotford looked as if he did not know what to make of the earl's question, but he smiled and said, "Well, you are here now. Cook has prepared a feast for later, but I told her to be ready to put a meal on the table in case you missed breakfast. No? Then maybe you want to see your rooms. I was staying in the master's suite like my father and his father always did. No reason not to, eh? But I moved out as soon as word came that you were found. Installed new bed hangings and that kind of thing." He turned to Genie. "I did not refurbish the mistress's chambers, not knowing your tastes, my dear, but the rooms are clean and fresh. The girls—the Newberry girls, that is—have been picking flowers since dawn."

She saw bouquets everywhere, bringing the country inside. No matter what Cousin Spotford said, the house—or castle—was warm and appealing. "I am touched at your efforts," she said. "All of you." She really was. For the first time in her life she truly felt welcome, wanted. She was not her parents' second, less-attractive daughter, nor Elgin's second-choice wife. She was Lady Ardeth, coming home. Her husband looked pleased and proud, adding to her happiness.

"Keep! Keep!" came a squawk from atop a suit of armor in the hall, where Olive had been perched, waiting to see what dangers lurked in the new surroundings: cats, dogs, maids with brooms. His cry drew exclamations, especially from those who had not seen him in the city, but no one complained against a dirty bird in the house or difficulty breathing. Seeing no peril, hearing no orders to sleep in the stable, the crow set off exploring, swooping and soaring in avian excitement, spreading his wings without worrying about predators or wind or obstacles in such vast open areas.

The humans followed him on a tour of the public rooms, which Genie found to be old-fashioned but fitting the character of the house. Cousin Spotford was right about a woman's touch, because the furniture was heavy, the fabrics were dark, and the knickknacks few. This was definitely a masculine abode, except for the bowls of flowers. Some of the draperies and wall hangings could use refurbishing, Cousin Spotford admitted, but he hadn't liked to spend the estate income on rooms that were seldom used. Now she could make the choices. Everyone seemed to be waiting for her opinion. Hers! "Oh, I will not be in a hurry to make changes," she said, "until I am familiar with everything. I like the feel of history to the rooms," which earned her a nod from Ardeth and another grin from Cousin Spotford.

"I was worried, I must admit, that you'd want to decorate in that new Chinese style that's all the kick, or, worse, the Egyptian craze with alligator-leg chairs and mummy cases for end tables."

She laughed. "I doubt my husband would be happy looking at a sarcophagus in the sitting room."

No, he'd seen enough of the damn things.

Spotford was going on: "You'll want to see the nursery. My boys left it years ago, and no one's been in it since. I thought we'd better wait on that, too. Females get fussy about their nests, don't you know."

He winked at her, making no comment about the fatherhood of the child, just expressing happiness that a baby would be in the house again.

Genie could feel tears in her own eyes.

When they had finally seen most of the house—not the attics or the cellars, which were extensive, Spotford promised—the others finally left Ardeth and Genie alone. The tour had ended at their rooms, an entire corridor of their own, with connecting sitting rooms, dressing rooms, bathing rooms, and bedchambers. There was even a small, sunny sewing room and a separate cozy parlor with walls of bookshelves.

"Do you like it?" Ardeth asked outside the rooms that would be hers. He seemed anxious, awaiting her reply.

Genie did not know if he meant her room or the entire house. No matter, she loved it all. And him for bringing her here, although she could not say that, of course. She was so happy that she threw herself into his arms and hugged him, trying to be careful of his injuries. "Not only is the Keep wonderful, every square acre of it, but I have never felt so at home."

"Me, neither," he said, twirling her around as if he had never been wounded. "This is worth everything."

His room, his house, or her in his arms? Genie did not know, which dimmed her happiness when Ardeth set her down on her own two feet. Two things obstructed her view of paradise: a lovable but unloving husband, and his lack of lovemaking. She was sure the second would encourage the first. "How are you feeling?" she asked, trying to be subtle.

"Not damaged by your feather weight."

Perhaps she had been too subtle. "You are not too tired?"

"We only traveled a few hours this morning."

"But we just walked for miles. And then there was the excitement. You did not get too worn-out, did you?"

He gave her a long, slow smile. "Too worn-out for what?" Then he laughed at her inevitable redheaded blush. "I am feeling fit as a fiend."

"Don't you mean fit as a fiddle?"

"Have you ever seen a fiend?"

"Now you are being silly."

He was, and enjoying it. Who ever heard of a silly specter? "Ah, you'd rather have a fiddle than a fiend in your bed?" Then he turned serious. "Or has the day been too much for you, with all the new people and the heavy responsibilities they entail? Being a countess involves far more than wearing the jewels."

"Do you think I can manage?"

"Of course. I would not have brought you here otherwise."

"Then so do I. And I believe I will enjoy the duties, too. As for what I wish in my bed, I think you know that."

"Say it, my Genie."

"You."

After a kiss that shook Ardsley Keep to its foundations, or so it seemed to Genie, he said, "I will be there. Later."

Later got to be much later. Cousin Spotford was so enthusiastic, he kept dragging out maps and charts, drawings and designs, forgetting his strictures to his son about overwhelming the earl. The others wanted to hear Ardeth's plans for a school, and Genie's idea about starting a pottery. After that, dinner was indeed a feast fit for a king—and half his kingdom, it looked like.

Nothing was going to waste, Spotford reassured them. He did not believe in that, wasting good food or the

Keep's blunt. There was to be a party in the barn for the workers afterward, to celebrate the earl's homecoming and how hard everyone had worked to make it a festive one.

" 'Twould be a kind gesture if you popped in for a moment or two," he told them. "There's nothing raucous or wild about it, just high spirits with a bit of music and dancing for the youngsters. Mrs. Newberry's girls are going, half their dances promised already." He looked toward their mother. "I might just try for a jig myself."

"But what about our mourning period?" Genie asked.

"Well, there's been a lot of sadness. We all felt this was a new life, a new beginning, and the girls deserve a chance to be young and carefree. We have never been ones to turn up our noses at the common folks, either, but if you feel that a barn dance is beneath you, I am sure the tenants will understand. Neither my sister nor her maid have ever attended."

"Oh, no. I have never stood on ceremony. I never had a cause to do so."

"Then if you are too tired, people can accept that."

Genie looked at Miss Hadley, who was nodding her approval, which matched Genie's own desires. Ardeth shrugged. He would go if she wanted, his look of resignation seemed to say, although he'd had other, better plans. Later. "We can stay for a short while."

So Genie and Ardeth went out to the barn after a long dinner, to watch their dependents having a good time.

Young Richard danced with each of the Newberry girls, who also made sheep eyes at the shepherds, the blacksmith, and the handsome blond rector of the village church. Marie danced with Campbell, who protested that he was too old for that nonsense. But he'd rather make a damn fool of himself, he confided in the earl, than see her in the arms of the underbutler.

Although she did not dance, Genie spent her time pleasantly. She spoke to the farmers' wives and the dairymaids and the goosegirls while Ardeth talked to as many cottagers as he could, promising to visit with all in turn, to see their conditions and listen to their concerns. He reassured them that he would make no changes without speaking to them, that no livelihoods were in jeopardy if they did their jobs, were honest and loyal—and did not gossip about the lord and lady. If that wasn't enough, he won them over by taking up one of the musicians' flutes and playing a long, haunting tune that no one had ever heard or would ever forget.

Perhaps the song was Russian, Genie thought. Or his own composition. One never knew about her amazing husband. The music reminded her of woodsmoke and Gypsy camps, the god Pan in the woods playing for fairy sprites, fakirs entrancing .cobras—and romance. But then, everything was reminding her of romance: the way his coat fitted so well now that the bandages were reduced, how one lock of his black hair fell across his forehead as he played, how his eyes shut in concentration as he felt the music vibrate through him, as she would feel his heart beat next to hers. Later.

When he was finished playing, Ardeth bowed to the company's applause, then thanked them for coming and for making him and his lady feel so welcome. He would leave them to their revels, he said, and wished them a good night. With his wife's hand in his and the crow on his shoulder, the Earl of Ardeth went back to his home.

He'd said he hated gossip. But was it gossip if one noted what a fine gentleman the new master was, how lovely his countess? The talk from London was hogwash, they all agreed, so there was no use repeating it. He was an earl, so was entitled to any eccentricity he wanted. He was openhanded and good-hearted, even if the man was slow to smile. No one wanted to be in his black books, that was the truth, but he seemed fair so far.

He'd said he valued honesty and hard work. Then he would be happy with his people, they swore, for they each put in a good day's work for a good day's pay. Then they laughed. It was a good thing young Mr. Fernell Spotford was not around, him as never worked and seldom paid his bills. The pretty girls were better off without the basket-scrambler, too, they said, letting their daughters out of sight for once.

That wasn't gossip, either, just fact.

Ah well, the earl would see for himself. They went back to making merry.

Lord Ardeth was just getting started.

CHAPTER TWENTY-FIVE

Like a knight of yore—hell, he was a knight of yore, whenever that was—Ardeth prepared for the lists, his lance at the ready. Praise be to seven saints, his lance was ready. Too eager, perhaps, he worried. He wanted it to last long enough to pleasure Genie. Damn, Ardeth wanted it to last forever. He wanted to give the blessed thing a name, he was so relieved!

Now that everything was working, everything else had to be perfect. He ordered wine and fruit. He had another bath. He deliberated for an hour, it seemed, between dressing again in breeches and shirt, shoes and stockings, which would have to be removed as soon as he could manage, or a brocade robe. He dismissed his smirking valet and donned the robe.

He carefully placed the ring in his pocket. No, his other pocket, where he could reach it more easily. Then he took it out again and polished it against his sleeve.

Damn, he should have had it cleaned by a jeweler. And what if the blasted thing did not fit?

Genie wore the plain gold band Olive had found in Brussels, and the diamond he'd hurriedly bought for her in London to outshine the other ladies, but he wanted her to have a special ring, on this, their private wedding celebration. This ring, of filigreed silver with a ruby stone surrounded by diamond chips, was actually his, not his first wife's or the spoils from some siege, but awarded to Sir Coryn by some warlord for winning a tourney. He could not remember if his opponent had lived or died.

The heirloom without heirs had been in the vault at the ancient fortress and moved to this building when it was completed, the other razed.

Spotford had been amazed that the earl knew the combination to the vault in the Keep's office.

"It was handed down to me," Ardeth had explained, implying from father to son for generations. "I might not have lived in England, but my heritage lived in me, always."

All the prizes of those early years were here, some he did not recall. He did recognize the treasures he'd managed to have delivered more recently, winnings at other games of life and death.

Spotford wanted to show him an itemized inventory of the vault's contents, to prove he had not taken anything except those gems sold at his lordship's agents' orders to pay for more land, new equipment, higher salaries.

Ardeth did not want to look at the pages, not today. If the man were a thief, the documents would be altered and forged anyway. But Ardeth did not think so. Spotford's eyes met his with no qualms, the mirror of a soul without guilt. Ardeth both envied the man and admired him. "I trust you, Cousin. Else you would not be here."

The older man fussed with his papers. "Then you will not be telling me to leave? I do have Spotford Oaks, you know. It is rented right now, but we could move there, my boys and I, if you'd rather have the Keep to your own management. I did not want to ask in front of the others, but now that you are returned, you must have your own plans for the properties."

"Good grief, man, how many generations of Spotfords have lived at the Keep?"

"Since the fire that destroyed the old fort and all the records? Every one of them, with sisters and cousins and in-laws, too. All I have are the two lads now, or I'd be apologizing for another parcel of hangers-on."

"Hangers-on? The place would have gone to rack and ruin without you and yours. Spotfords have been the Ardsleys' right hands since the old castle had a seneschal, I'd wager"—he'd win, but that would be cheating—"when the lord rode off to war. I would not know how to begin, or how to get on without you and Richard. Furthermore, the Keep is large enough for twenty families, if you are thinking of taking on a new wife." He paused. "And her daughters, perhaps."

Spotford smiled. "I am thinking on it. Early days yet."

Now Ardeth looked at the ring on his dresser. Was it too early? Would Genie have had time for her toilet? Had she dismissed her maid? He did not want to rush in like some randy young buck. Well, he did want to, but he would not. On the other hand, he did not want her to worry that he was not coming. A bride, even a widowed one, had enough to fret herself about on her wedding night. Lud knew, Ardeth was anxious enough for the both of them.

He decided to shave again. His valet was long gone with the damp towels and worn linens, likely at the barn with the other servants. Ardeth would not disturb the competent—and blessedly untalkative—man's evening of leisure. He took up the soap and razor.

Olive was hopping up and down, flapping his wings, and screeching something about Ar cutting himself. Like Ardeth, whose powers were weakened with time, the crow was harder to understand.

"Be quiet, you twit. I do know how to shave myself, even if I have not done it much." Sir Coryn had gone unbarbered in his first life except for a hasty trim now and again with a sharp blade. In his second existence, Ar had neither beard nor blood to spill if the razor slipped.

The bird kept cawing about him getting nicked.

Twitchy enough without the confounded grating noise, Ardeth shouted back, "Damn it, if you do not shut your beak, I am liable to cut my nose off." Instead he shut the bird out of his dressing room, to make sure.

He did a fine job, if he had to say so himself, rubbing his hand on his cheek to make certain it was smooth enough for Genie's tender skin.

Just the thought of her soft skin made him harder.

Knowing he could not wait much longer, Ardeth retied the sash of his robe lest he frighten the poor woman out of her wits, and looked for his slippers. His capable valet must have put them somewhere handy, but Ardeth did not have the patience to look. He patted the ring in his pocket, picked up the wine and two glasses, and walked barefoot toward her room.

The connecting door was cracked open. Genie was bending over something, and the sight that met his eyes almost took his breath away. She was wearing a lacy-trimmed white silk bedgown that hugged the curves of her rounded bottom.

Maybe he should have had a cold bath instead of a hot one.

Then, before he could say a word—if his tongue came unglued and if his brain stopped stuttering—she made a noise, a wretched, heart-wrenching, retching noise. His wife, his bride, his would-be lover, was leaning over the chamber pot, he realized now, casting up the lavish meal they'd supped on.

He looked at her; then he looked down. The work of centuries, gone in seconds.

There was nothing for it but to bring her a damp cloth, hold her while she heaved, and half carry her back to her bed. She lay there, limp and worn-out.

"Shall I send for Marie?" he asked.

She shook her head weakly. "I told her I would not be needing her. Heaven knows if she is in Campbell's bed or her own, wherever that is. Or she might still be at the dance, surveying the local prospects."

"Poor Campbell."

Genie sighed at the state of that affair, or her own. "There is nothing she can do for me anyway."

And nothing anyone could do for Ardeth now. He poured out two glasses of wine and offered Genie one. "Have a sip of wine. Get rid of the bad taste."

She took a tiny swallow, while he downed half his glass. "I am so sorry," she said, near to tears.

"It is not your fault." He set down his glass and sat on the bed beside her, rubbing her hands, which still felt clammy. "Try to sleep. You will feel better in the morning."

She sighed again, half a moan. "It does not feel that way."

"Shall I stay?"

"No, I am too embarrassed that you had to see me like this."

"Do not be foolish. You saw me bleeding and unconscious."

Beads of perspiration formed on her forehead. "Just go. I think I am going to be—" She was, missing his bare feet by inches. He grabbed up the chamber pot and supported her shoulders, holding her hair back.

When she appeared to be finished, he asked if she wanted some tea or plain water.

She tried to smile. "No, I had a glass of milk before, to help me relax."

He noticed the half-empty glass on her bedside table. "Well, that did not seem to work."

"It did not taste good. My stomach was already queasy."

"Should I . . . help you sleep?"

"No! I will be fine in the morning, as you said. Or in a few months. That is what Mrs. Newberry told me, anyway."

He put another blanket on her, more because his own feet were cold than because she looked chilled. In fact, her face was flushed and damp with sweat. He supposed he ought to get her into a clean, dry nightgown, but he thought the sight of her naked, now-untouchable body might very well have him in tears, too. He kissed her cheek and said, "I will go get my slippers and a book and come back to stay with you."

"It is not necessary." Her eyes were already drifting shut.

"It is to me."

He went back to his room, then remembered he'd shut

the bird away in the sitting room, the bird that had kept nattering on about him cutting himself. "Ar nick," or something like that.

"Ar nick?" Not a shaving cut? He ran into the sitting room, stubbing his toe on a footstool, and found the crow huddled on the curtain rod.

"Arsenic? Did you mean arsenic?" he shouted.

"Ar'nic." Olive's head bobbed.

"Who? Who?"

Olive tried to turn his head around like an owl.

"No, damn it." Ardeth shook his fist up in the air. "Who did it?"

Olive flapped his wings. "Snell did."

"You smelled it? Damn!"

Ardeth did not take the time to find his slippers or his shoes, but tore out of the room and down the corridor, down the stairs, down another flight, then another. Where was the ability to float through walls when he needed it, the traveling through time and space in a blink of an eye? His solid flesh could do nothing but hurtle down stairs and along dark corridors. He took a wrong turn and had to backtrack through a portrait gallery of prigs in fancy dress who could not possibly have been his ancestors. Who the devil were they, and why did he ever think he needed a barracks so huge? Finally he reached the kitchens. The rooms were empty, as he should have realized, with everyone out in the barn. He opened doors and drawers and cupboards until he found what he was looking for, the cook's stock of stillroom supplies. Yes, the arsenic was there, carefully marked. Every household had some, to get rid of vermin. Some ladies used it in making cosmetics, the morons.

He also found what he needed to counteract the poison. Although arsenic was called the widow maker, he had not had much experience with this end of it and could only hope he had the right ingredients. He tossed the stuff into a bowl, added water from the pump, and then ran back up the stairs and endless corridors, cursing the house, the Devil, his bare feet, and whoever did this to his wife.

She was shivering, and noticeably weaker. "Here, my love, drink this."

"You called me your . . . love."

The woman was poisoned and she wanted to talk about semantics? "What of it? We can speak about that in the morning. Just drink this."

Her nose wrinkled at the smell. "Will it make me feel better?"

He could not lie. "No, but it will rid your stomach of what is making you so ill."

"Then it is not the baby causing it?"

The baby and her poor weak stomach likely saved her life. Ardeth decided he could lie after all, rather than frighten her while she was so wretched. "No, others are sick, too. Something must have been rancid in one of the dishes at dinner."

She drank his potion and was indeed sicker, until he was certain her stomach was empty. Then he gave her a sip of the wine he knew was safe because he'd suffered no ill effects. He did pull the silk gown off her and wrapped her in his own thick robe. He was too concerned to notice her body or his own nakedness. Cold determination doused any sparks of desire, and hot fury kept him warm.

He held her in his arms until she fell into an exhausted sleep on her own. He knew how she feared his trance making, and lud knew, she had enough to fear without that.

When he was certain she would not awaken, he laid her down and went into his own room to dress. A shirt, trousers, his black cape, boots—that was enough. He told the gremlin crow to watch over the lady while he was gone.

"If anyone but I or Miss Hadley or Marie tries to enter, peck out his eyes."

"Eye eye?"

Ardeth saluted back.

He terrified Miss Hadley by pounding on her door. "Good grief, you nearly frightened me to death."

"Death does not do that," he said, then added, "I need you to stay with Lady Ardeth while she sleeps. She is ill."

Miss Hadley noted his boots and cape and thought he was going to ride for help. "But they said there was no physician in the vicinity."

"She does not need a doctor, only a watchdog."

The party in the barn was ending, hurried along by the sudden storm that seemed to reach a thunderous crescendo when the master strode across the packed dirt to Mr. Spotford's side. With the music stopped, everyone could hear Lord Ardeth order Spotty to send the guests home, but to reassemble the entire staff.

"I want to know everyone who was in the kitchens, everyone who brought food upstairs."

Now the servants began to recall those rumors trickling from London of his lordship's madness. If he was this difficult on his first night in residence, they would all be looking for other positions. The tenant farmers and the villagers and the field workers scrambled to leave, in spite of the driving rain. They'd rather face the elements than the wrath of the mercurial nobleman who was kind and caring one moment, raging like the thunder outside the next. And hadn't they heard he'd appeared at that last battle during just such a storm?

Mr. Spotford tried to smooth the troubled waters. "Here, now, Cousin. Everyone has to be up early in the morning for their chores. Whatever questions you have can surely wait."

With cold lightning in his voice, Ardeth said, "You speak to them now, every single one. Find out who brought my wife a glass of tainted milk. You tell them that if any harm befalls her, tonight or till doomsday, I will tear this place down, brick by brick. I will burn whatever is left to the ground, and all the fields and farms. No one will have a job, a home, or a pension if Lady Ardeth suffers. And tell them that no one will benefit from my death, either, for none of you is now or ever will be named my heir."

Those nearby were looking at him fearfully. The vicar's daughters were clinging to one another.

Spotford tried to hide his disquiet. "I say, Cousin, there is no call to be so grim at the party. Neither myself nor my sons ever had expectations of inheriting anything from you. Not in line for the title, by Jupiter, never have been, or for any entailment on the lands. And I am certain no one means any harm to your lovely lady. We all fell in love with her on the instant, didn't we?" He looked around, seeking support, and everyone was quick to nod. "If the milk had turned bad, well, such things happen."

Ardeth pulled the arsenic bottle out of his pocket. "They happen more when someone adds poison to it."

Miss Calverton fainted. Someone screamed and was shushed, so the others could listen. Campbell pushed his way to his master's side, a pitchfork in his hand.

Marie ran forward, crying. "My lady! My lady! She lives?" At Ardeth's nod she crossed herself, then said, "I brought the milk to her myself, monsieur. I poured it myself from the pitcher."

"Who saw you?"

"Almost no one. The kitchens were empty with everyone in the barn."

"And you never took your eyes off it?"

"I left it outside her door in case you had finished your bath, and you and she . . ." She shrugged.

"And you saw no one in the hall?"

Spotford asked, "Who would be abovestairs at this time of night except personal servants like your man and her ladyship's maid? Everyone else was here."

Ardeth's valet stepped out of the crowd, wringing his hands. "I knew I should have stayed after tidying up after my lord's bath instead of joining the frolicking here. I should have been more vigilant."

"Do not feel badly. You would not have seen someone tamper with the glass outside Lady Ardeth's chamber."

"No, but I could have shaved milord."

Ardeth decided to consider a different valet when he had time. "Who else could have been near our rooms?"

He looked around. As far as he knew, the entire staff was present. Every one of them, from butler to knife-boy, looked anxious and curious. No one looked guilty or avoided his eyes. Then someone shouted, "Where's Snell?"

"Who the deuce is Snell?" Ardeth asked Spotford. "I do not recall the name from the introductions this morning."

Spotford was craning his neck, searching through the crowd. "That would be my son's man. Has an elegant touch with a neckcloth, Snell does. He came back with Fernell's baggage, he did."

Ardeth pounded his fist into his thigh. "His name is Snell? As in 'Snell did'? Not 'smelled it'? Bloody hell."

Now they all thought he was demented. Dangerous and deranged, and the devil take him for ruining their evening and most likely their comfortable lives.

Ardeth did not care what they thought. "Find the man. And find him before I do, or he'll be hanging by his own damned elegant neckcloth."

CHAPTER TWENTY-SIX

"I say," came an affected drawl from the barn door, "if you are finished killing the fatted calf for the prodigal's return, Pater, perhaps someone could take my horse."

The young man in the doorway was indeed holding the reins of a fractious brute, scattering the departing cottagers. He was about five and twenty, Ardeth thought, handsome despite being wet from the storm. The rain did not explain his disheveled appearance, his shirt hanging out of his waistcoat, his neckcloth draped around his neck, his hat missing altogether. Perhaps the brute of a stallion behind him explained the mud on his breeches. Or perhaps the fact that he was swaying on his feet, wearing a foolish grin, could account for it all. The man was foxed, and looked like he was going to lead the skittish, unruly horse right into the crowd of guests.

Ardeth strode to the door and took the reins from the gudgeon's hand. In a bare moment, he had the big horse calm and rubbing its damp muzzle on Ardeth's shoulder. The earl gestured for one of the stupefied grooms—the fiddle player—to lead the horse away. Then he turned back to the rider, whose mouth was hanging open. "Mr. Fernell Spotford, I gather."

"'Pon rep, if the tales ain't true," the young man said, belatedly making a bow. "My lord."

Before Ardeth could say another word—and he had several in mind—the elder Spotford had his son's arm and was leading him to an empty corner of the barn where they might have a bit of privacy. "I like gossip about the family as little as you do, Cousin," he told Ardeth.

The earl gestured to Campbell, who still appeared ready to stick the pitchfork into anyone who looked sideways. "Get them all out of here," Ardeth ordered, "and organize a search for that man Snell."

"I say, did you mention Snell?" Fernell said with a giggle. "Old jaw-me-dead will be furious I ruined another suit of clothes." He looked down at the mud and scuffs. "Had to get here in time, though, to greet the nabob."

Richard Spotford came over with a mug of something hot. Fernell made a face at it until Richard said, "You are going to need this, Brother."

When all of the people had left, Ardeth would have hanged Fernell by his collar from a peg on the barn's beams until he had his answers. But one of the dairymen approached, holding his hat and tugging on his forelock. "Pardon, Mr. Spotford, but would it be all right if I brung the cows back into the barn?" He jerked his head toward the door. "Devilish night out there for man or beast. Sure and the milk will be bad in the morning."

The milk was bad enough tonight, Ardeth recalled, outraged all over again.

Spotford started to tell the man to go ahead and bring in the cows, then caught himself. "With your permission, Cousin."

Ardeth nodded, not taking his eyes off Fernell, who was still teetering on his feet. Ardeth pushed him to sit on a bale of hay where the musicians had been standing, before the jackass could fall down. "Where have you been?"

"Why, to Bath, as I told the governor. Deuced boring place. Then I went to Wally Wintercross's place for the shooting. Didn't hit a thing. Meant to get here sooner, but there was a pretty barmaid at the Black Dog, and a cockfight in Upper Rutley."

"You have not been to London?"

Fernell looked up from trying to brush some of the mud off his breeches. "I say, I apologize for not being here to welcome you, Cuz, but that's not a crime, is it, that I should be facing the Inquisition?" He tried to laugh, which was hard with large, strong fingers around his throat.

"Were you in London," Ardeth asked again, "at Hampstead Heath, say, a short while ago?"

Mr. Spotford clutched at Ardeth's hand, trying to loosen his grip on Fernell. "You cannot be thinking my son had anything to do with that duel, can you?"

"There was no duel," Ardeth said, staring into Fernell's eyes before letting go, "only a coward, firing from behind."

Fernell coughed, then held up his hands. "I ain't no good with firearms, everyone can tell you. Just ask old Wally."

"What about your valet?"

"Snell? He ain't invited to go out shooting with the gentlemen. Bad form, don't you know."

"Where is he now?"

"How should I know? I ain't been up to the house. Ask Aunt Frieda. Her maid and Snell are thick as inkle weavers."

"He has not come forward."

"You mean he ain't here?" Fernell looked to his brother for confirmation. "Demme, did my baggage get lost? I had a brand-new waistcoat I was going to wear to-morrow with dragonflies embroidered on it. All the crack, don't you know." He eyed Ardeth's white shirt, with no waistcoat at all. "I suppose not."

Richard answered, "Your bags arrived with your valet. He has become least in sight since then."

"Blast. Who is going to help me off with my clothes and see to my wardrobe tomorrow? And the man had a way with boots. Used twenty ingredients for his special formula to polish 'em."

Ardeth saw Spotford and Richard look at each other, disturbed that their relative's valet was so familiar with apothecaries and chemists.

Ardeth said, "My man will assist you. He might be looking for another job anyway."

Fernell looked at Ardeth's own haphazard dress and wrinkled his nose. "Not up to my standards. The Beau of the Valley, don't you know."

Ardeth turned away in disgust.

"Where do you think Snell is now?" Spotford asked his son. "There's been a bit of trouble and his absence is suspicious."

"How the deuce should I know where valets go when they leave? I'd have thought he'd stick around until I could ask you for an advance on next quarter's al-lowance, so I could pay him."

Spotford shook his head. "You're already three-quarters overspent."

"Chap's got to put up the right appearance, eh? That takes a lot of blunt. Which reminds me, I better go check my luggage, see he did not carry off my snuffboxes or something to pawn."

He stood, but Ardeth pushed him back down. "Why would you want to harm my wife?"

"Harm the woman? I don't even know her. Thought I'd wear my new waistcoat to meet her tomorrow."

Ardeth made a sound like a growl, but managed to keep his hands from the fribble's throat. "Someone must have told the valet to act. Servants do not go around poisoning their mistresses for no reason."

"Poison, you say?"

"In her milk."

"Never touch the stuff myself."

"Why?" Ardeth demanded, as loud as the thunder outside.

"It's catlap."

"Damn you, why would your valet try to poison my wife?"

Now Fernell picked straw from his sleeve. "S'pose I might have mentioned how the purse strings could tighten with you and the countess in residence. No bringing the chaps home for a game of dice, either. She'll be turning the place into a nursery. Building schools, they say. Faugh. Maybe he thought to frighten her off, that's all."

Ardeth was not convinced. Nor was he completely convinced of Fernell's sincerity. The man spoke too clearly for a drunk, and his eyes, shifting from Ardeth to his father and brother, focused too well. Besides, he never asked if the poison had succeeded. No, he was more worried about having his neckcloth properly starched than having a healthy countess.

"Asides," Fernell asked now, "who says Snell committed the deed?"

"Someone saw him."

"Could be someone else trying to shift the blame, eh? Seems to me Snell is too downy a cove to do something havey-cavey in front of witnesses."

"Olive saw him."

Fernell's face lit up. "A new maid?"

"A crow."

The grin faded. "That old, eh? Too bad."

His father said, "No, Olive is Cousin Ardeth's tame bird."

Now Fernell's eyes grew round. "A bird accused my valet?"

"Not just any crow. Very intelligent. Talks a blue streak."

"Great gods, you've tried, convicted, and hanged my man on the word of a carrion eater?"

"No," Ardeth said quietly. "We have not hanged him because we have not found him. Yet."

"I s'pose you're going to banish me to the village inn, eh?" He looked toward his father. "I'll need a bit of the ready to set myself to rights."

Ardeth held up his hand. "You are not going anywhere until we find your man. I want you where I can see you. Do you understand?"

"Glad not to be going out into the night. Thank you, Cuz."

"And your Wally Wintercross had better confirm your whereabouts."

"Oh, Wally's on his way to Scotland. You'll never find him."

"How convenient."

"Well, I don't see what the pother is about. The countess didn't die, did she?" He looked to see his father shaking his head no. "And Snell is gone. All's well that ends well, eh?"

"Until the next time someone tries to kill me or my wife. Spotford, take this sorry knave out of my sight before I am pushed too far."

Fernell called after him, "I say, I hear you can cure sickness. I'm bound to have the devil's own headache in the morning. Can you do something for that?"

"Yes, I can let you suffer."

Fernell was not going anywhere that night, not with one of Campbell's soldiers on guard outside his door. Ardeth went back to Genie's room and told Miss Hadley and Marie to go to bed; he would sit up with his wife while she slept. He built up the fire—damn, would they let the poor woman freeze?—and pulled a chair closer to her bedside, staring across at her by a single candle's glow and the fire in the hearth. Her hair had been smoothed and braided, the bedclothes changed, all signs and scents of illness taken away. She looked like a pale sleeping angel.

He rested his chin on his fingertips, wondering if he could ever forgive himself for putting her in danger. He should have seen the peril and found her somewhere safe. Instead he'd kept her with him, for his own pleasure. What had he been doing but playing God with the female, rescuing her, rearranging her life like some kind of Pygmalion? She was no statue, though, but flesh and blood, far more than he. What right did he have to decide what was best for her?

He'd taken her in because her plight appealed to him. He'd thought feeling protective was an important component of an honorable man. He had helped Imogene Macklin for his own sake, to meet the terms of his own wager. He'd made her a pawn.

He deserved to rot in Hades for the rest of eternity . . . except.

Except he did care about her, more than he thought himself capable of doing. He remembered his fury at the thought of someone hurting her, not because she was his wife, his possession, but because she was Genie and she was precious in her own right, precious to him. He took the ring out of his pocket, the ruby that gleamed like the red in her hair, and placed it on her finger, knowing that Genie herself was the real treasure.

It fit. She fit in his life.

She woke briefly, and he tried to explain why she should stay abed while she sipped a soothing tisane he'd mixed himself. He did not want her to hear of the poison from her maid or Miss Hadley, but she had to know that someone was in the kitchen watching everything being prepared, carried to her room, and put into Marie's hands. She must not be afraid; he would find the man responsible.

"Of course you will," she murmured, holding his hand next to her cheek. She went back to sleep.

Campbell reported that they had searched the Keep from top to bottom—half the night it had taken, too, and all the outbuildings, the villages, and the farms. No one had seen Snell. Spotford's reclusive sister and her maid were fast asleep, and Miss Frieda Spotford had screamed at the men through the door for waking her. She might have thrown a hairbrush, they thought, or a footstool.

Ardeth had Campbell send riders farther afield. Near daylight a messenger came back saying that a drover had seen a man fitting Snell's description at an inn in Upper Rutley, near where Fernell mentioned stopping for a cockfight. Was Snell out looking for the errant Fernell, or had their meeting been prearranged? Ardeth was going to find out, and he was going to drag young Spotford with him, rather than leave him behind anywhere near Genie. Richard volunteered to go with them, half to protect his brother and half to show Ardeth the countryside while they rode.

Campbell wanted to go along, not trusting either brother. Ardeth needed him more at the Keep, guarding Genie.

"But two of the Spotfords together, sir, they could overpower the strongest man."

"I doubt they are stupid enough to do me harm when everyone knows we are together. At least Richard seems to have more betwixt his ears than snuff and shoe blacking."

"Accidents happen."

"Olive will be on the watch."

Campbell's scowl showed his opinion of the crow as guardian.

Ardeth did not give Fernell time for breakfast, but let his own man get the varlet dressed. Ardeth's man was delighted to be of use to someone who truly appreciated his efforts. He was as eager to dress the young gentleman in his embroidered finery as Fernell was to strut around in his unpaid-for apparel.

As they rode, Richard pointed out landmarks and boundaries, fields that needed draining, an empty cottage that might be suitable for the schoolteacher, a plot of land where a school could be. Fernell pouted and nursed his sore head, with help from a silver flask.

They found the inn at Upper Rutley. They found Snell, but they found no answers. The man was dead, killed in an attempt by another scoundrel to steal the heavy purse he'd been toting. Richard went white, Fernell puked, and Ardeth cursed.

When Genie had finally slept away her exhaustion, she awoke to see both Miss Hadley and Marie sitting alongside her bed, one sewing, one reading. Remembering why they were there, she shut her eyes again, taking the time to order her thoughts. She recalled Ardeth kissing her forehead good-bye, telling her he was going with Richard and Fernell Spotford to find the answers to his questions.

Richard was such a pleasant gentleman, she could not harbor suspicions about him. Everyone laughed when they spoke of Fernell, affectionately calling him a charming rogue. He was always under the hatches and always flirting, they said, but no one disliked the man. And she refused to believe that Cousin Spotford had raised a cold-blooded killer. Still, she did not want her husband going off with the two brothers. Ardeth had sworn he would be safe and promised to be back by nightfall with the solution to the mystery. Then they could start their married life all over again. He'd shown her the new ring, a token of his affection.

He had not said he loved her, she thought with disappointment. She was even more disappointed that she would have to refuse him tonight. She still felt drained. Her throat was sore, her stomach was cramping, her back ached.

Then she saw the blood.

CHAPTER TWENTY-SEVEN

Genie's screams brought Campbell rushing into the room without knocking, a wicked dagger in one hand, a pistol in the other. What he saw had him fleeing back out so fast he almost cut off his own ear.

"Get Mrs. Newberry," Miss Hadley shouted. The vicar's wife had borne three girls; she ought to know what to do far better than a spinster.

"Send for the midwife," Marie yelled in French.

"Get Ardeth," Genie ordered. "I do not want anyone else. Wherever he is, bring him back. Now!"

But Campbell had promised Lord Ardeth not to leave the countess unprotected. His lordship had not mentioned emergencies like this. Thankfully, Mr. Spotford said he would go. He knew the area and knew where the men were headed. Besides, he did not want to be in the house at such a time, either.

Spotford found his sons and the earl halfway home from Upper Rutley, with Richard praising the Newberry girls' charms, and Fernell sulking because Ardeth had threatened to make him sing soprano if he so much as looked at any one of them.

Spotford gave his message, explaining the "female troubles" as best an ignorant male could. He offered to trade his fresher horse with Ardeth's, so his lordship could make better time. Ardeth refused. Black Butch had plenty of stamina left, too much for Cousin Spotford to handle. He did not want another life on his hands. And Spotford's mount was not fast enough. The winds of a cyclone would not be fast enough, but the black would have to do.

The stallion was blowing hard when they reached the front of the Keep, enough that Ardeth dropped the reins where he was without waiting for a groom to come. He raced up the stairs two at a time, three at a time. He burst into Genie's room, which appeared filled with weeping, hand-wringing women, and his wife on the bed, pale as the sheets.

Genie told everyone to leave, then she held her arms up to him. "Fix it, Coryn, fix it."

He held her. That was all he could do. "I cannot, Genie. I wish I could, but I cannot."

She pounded on his chest. "You can, I know you can. You saved those men."

"They needed stitching. You saw that. Anyone could have done it, with time enough."

"You saved Peter after you said you could not cure his illness."

"That was sheer luck. This is different."

"No, it is not, and luck had nothing to do with Peter's recovery, no, nor taking the feathers out of his room. I saw him. He was going to die, but he did not."

He took her fists in his hands. "Genie, be reasonable.

I am no magician, no master of life and death. I do not even have what powers I used to. I had to give them up to be here, to be a man."

"To be a man?" she repeated. "What were you before, then, a boy? I do not believe you. I know you can do things other men cannot. Perhaps you pray to other gods who listen better. Then pray, damn you, pray!"

"My prayers will not help, Genie."

"They will," she insisted. "Or your esoteric education. You knew the baby was a boy—you told me so. So you must know how to save him, please!"

"I do not, Genie. I cannot!" For all his experience, Ardeth had none with this. "It is too late, my dear. No one can help."

"No," she wailed. "It cannot be."

"I am so sorry."

Her pleading turned to anger. She pushed him away. "It is because he is not your son, isn't it?"

Ardeth was shaken. "How could you think that? I told you I would claim the child as mine. I have been moving heaven and earth to make it legal. I was going to sign over half of my other holdings to the Spotfords so they do not challenge the birth, so he could be the next earl."

"No, you wanted a son of your own. Every man does."

"I wanted your son."

She was too distraught to listen. "So you killed him because he was not yours, only another scandal. What the arsenic did not accomplish, you did with your potions!"

"I thought only about saving your life, the only way I could. And everyone knows how many conceptions do not succeed, without arsenic or its antidote. No one knows why. Oh God, Genie, I would not have harmed the infant. How could you think I would do such a thing?"

"I do not know how you do anything! I do not understand you and I never have." She took the ruby ring off and threw it at him. "I never asked you for diamonds and rubies. I married you for the sake of my child. Now I ask you one thing and you tell me no. Get out. Leave me alone. You are leaving soon enough anyway. Go now. I hate you!"

He knew she did not mean that. Her grief was talking, not the woman he married. "Please listen."

She turned her head into the pillow, sobbing.

He spoke quietly, but loudly enough that she could hear if she wanted to. "It was my child, too, Genie. He was not of my blood, but he was my future. I know you will not believe me now, in your sorrow, but I am so very, very sorry."

Her muffled cries were like that lance to his heart, bringing pain and helplessness, bringing tears to his own eyes. He slowly left her bedside, hoping she would stop him. When she did not, he went, because that was what she wanted. At least he could do that much for her.

While the countess recuperated, the earl stayed out of her sight. Marie told Ardeth she had orders to bar the door, anyway, so he did not waste his time or try to confront Genie, upsetting her further. She never left her rooms, but Miss Hadley reported she was not ill, only in a decline.

He rode the property with Richard and studied the books with Spotty. He played billiards with Fernell to keep him from the pub, and he played his flute in long, haunting laments, sweet and sad enough to have every woman in the Keep—every woman except Genie—wiping her eyes. A few of the men reached for handkerchiefs, too, when they heard his plaintive tunes coming from the ruins of the old fortress.

He also visited Miss Frieda Spotford in her rooms in the isolated far tower of the modern castle.

Her maid admitted him after he had sent a note asking for an interview with both women. The maid denied knowing aught about Snell, other than that he would do anything for money. She did not admit to any familiarity beyond working in the same household, but her eyes were red-rimmed from crying. She brought Ardeth to her mistress's sitting room door and left as soon as he was announced.

Miss Spotford was older than her brother, and white-haired like him. Her hair was thin where he was bald, pale skin showing where a yellowed lace cap did not cover her head. Ardeth had expected an invalid in a bath chair; Miss Spotford could walk well enough, although she dragged her leg when she stood to examine her caller more closely. One of her eyes was cloudy, but the other was a piercing blue. Her face was scarred down one cheek and through the corner of her mouth, and her neck was held at an awkward angle, as though it had frozen there after whatever accident had befallen the woman.

"I am sorry to intrude, madam," he began.

"I know you," she interrupted. Her voice was a hoarse rasp, likely from damage to her throat.

"That is impossible," he said. "I have not been here before this week and I understand you have not left the Keep in decades."

"I know you," she insisted, fixing him with her stare that was half-blue and half seeing something else altogether. "When I was buried under those rocks, you came. I begged to die; the pain was so great. I begged, and you would not help."

No, it could not be. The system did not work that way. No Reaper arrived if the name was not on his list; no Reaper left without what he came for. Ardeth ignored Effe and the boy, Peter, as a once-in-a-lifetime—or Death's-time—occurrence. That meant the woman was not ailing; she was insane. No wonder Spotford kept her in this tower. "I assure you, no one ever saw me," he said. "That is, I have not been in England before."

"And now you think I tried to kill your countess."

Her bluntness was as shocking as her claims to have been denied by a Final Ferryman. "No, I merely come to you for information."

"I have none. I know nothing about poisons or I would have taken some years ago to end this hell of my life."

Ardeth looked around. The rooms were airy and comfortable, with a beautiful view, if one accepted the ruins as picturesque rather than a sign of time's passage. Beneath the window was a private terrace that led down to a walled garden. "I cannot know what pain you suffer, but your surroundings are pleasant."

"What do you know? I cannot go to the village, not even to church."

"I do not see why not." A keeper could follow her about to make sure she did not wander off.

"What, let people see me like this?" She rubbed at the scar that pulled her mouth down on one side. "Sometimes I drool. Should I have them say I am the local freak, knocked in the cradle?"

"You could wear a veil."

"The pain is too much."

Others suffered and went on with their lives, but he did not say so. "Laudanum might help."

"Bah. Then I have terrible dreams. Of you."

"No. That is only your imagination and dread."

She pointed one trembling finger at him. "I know you, I say. You came back, didn't you, to torture me more?"

"I came back to England, yes. For my soul."

Her finger touched his chest, right where he had been killed the first time. "You. Have. No. Soul."

He would get no answers out of the woman, and nothing else he wished to hear, so he left her presence to find Miss Spotford's brother.

Spotty did not think the woman was a danger to anyone. She was full of talk, he said, weird, rambling speeches everyone ignored. She hardly left her tower, so how could she care who owned or ran the Keep? Frieda might be missing a few cogs in her cogitations, but she played a decent hand of piquet when her mood was right.

"It was the accident that did it." He pointed in the direction of the old Keep. "No one's fault, because she wasn't supposed to play there, but she lay trapped under a pile of rubble for hours before someone found her. Never been the same since."

Ardeth found a woman to act as companion to Miss Spotford. One of his tenants had left his widow with nothing but debts and no way to pay the rent. She was strong and willing to do anything rather than face the poorhouse. Live at the Keep with nothing to do but watch a batty old woman and her sneaky maid? And get paid for it, to boot? She moved in that afternoon.

Ardeth left it to Spotford to explain to his sister. "Say it is for her health, to help her get out more. But she must not be alone, like a spider in her web, nursing imaginary grievances. I do not know if she hired Snell or if someone else did. He might have acted on his own, then stolen the money. I will find out, believe me."

Spotford was relieved Ardeth did not appear to suspect Fernell any longer.

"Your son says he was out shooting by day and passed-out drunk by night. And he thinks he spent half of one week at a bordello he cannot recall, leaving Snell to his own devices. I will find that out, also, if it is true."

"The boy lives a wild life, that is all. No harm in him, I swear."

"Your boy is a man, full-grown, and will act like one. If he is behind the attack, I will send him to India. If not, I will find him a post somewhere. I will not have a man drink himself to death on my land, on my wine, or litter my neighborhood with his bastards. I already had to threaten him with the antipodes for taking one of the Misses Newberry into the gardens."

They both knew Ardeth had threatened far worse than that, having to do with Spotford's hopes for grandsons.

"Fernell did not mean anything by it. He was just flirting."

"And the young ladies are too young to understand that. I consider them my wards now. I will not have their reputations ruined for a rakehell's pleasure."

"I thought he was partial to the eldest girl. I was hoping he might marry her and settle down. The chits have comfortable dowries now, and pleasing ways."

"He will have to prove himself worthy of her before I let your scapegrace son play suitor."

Ardeth wanted to talk to Genie, to ask her opinion. He wanted to discuss the plans for the new school, too, and see if she approved the site and the architect he was thinking of hiring. They were supposed to be partners and he missed her intelligent questions, her ways of looking at things from different angles than he saw.

She refused to see him. She did not come to meals with the family and she did not accept visitors, claiming her indisposition.

Ardeth could have forced her to see him. There was not a door on earth that could have kept him out, lost powers or not, but that would only make her hate him more, he feared. She needed time. Which was running out, with less than three months left.

He decided to go back to London to trace Snell's whereabouts, taking Fernell with him to help. None of them would be truly safe until the details of the duel were uncovered, nor would Fernell's name be cleared of involvement. Despite himself, Ardeth actually liked the younger man, when Fernell was not foxed. He was not stupid, and had a cheerful personality and a fine tenor voice. The earl thought he might interest Fernell in politics or finance in London, anything besides gaming and whoring. At the least, he would see him patronize a better tailor. Besides, he would not dare leave him here, not with the Newberry chits batting their eyelashes at him.

If Snell had acted alone, Ardeth considered that he was safe with Fernell. If he discovered otherwise, his mood was so foul he might just reconsider his vow not to take another life.

Genie was safe. While she kept to her rooms, what could happen to her? Maybe she would go out once he was gone. She needed walks and fresh air to recover her strength and her spirits. Perhaps she would visit with the cottagers, take interest in the school again, make friends with the women of the neighborhood, or plan renovations to the Keep. Anything, he hoped. He also hoped she would become her own woman, find the independence she would need when she was on her own, instead of turning into a hermit like Miss Spotford. He prayed she learned her own worth. He prayed she learned not to hate him.

He was gone. Better sooner than later, Genie tried to tell herself, and good riddance. Coryn, Lord Ardeth, had not intended to stay. He'd warned her, but she had not truly believed him. She believed him now. He never meant to see her child, the son who would never see the sunlight. She had the drapes kept pulled and took laudanum to let her sleep and help her forget.

No one would let her.

Miss Hadley read Genie a letter from her mother. According to Mrs. Hopewell, Genie's loss was for the best. No one needed more scandal broth served up if the child were born far too soon to be Ardeth's. And what was Imogene thinking, letting such a handsome, rich gentleman go off to London on his own? Hadn't she learned anything about men from Elgin and his wandering ways?

Genie's sister wrote that since Genie had conceived once, she should have no difficulty becoming pregnant again, despite Lorraine's own failure to do so. As if that would make Genie feel better now.

Marie said it was God's will, and practical Miss Hadley said something was most likely wrong with the babe, that it could not have lived anyway.

Mrs. Newberry was the most comfort. She had lost three babies herself, so she could share Genie's grief. One infant was stillborn, one was miscarried like Lady Ardeth's, and one died of whooping cough within a month. That one was the worst, the vicar's widow said, because she got to hold the babe and suckle him. A mother never forgot any of them, but the world did not end. Mrs. Newberry had had a husband and other children to care for, a whole parish depending on her to visit the ill and the aged. She could not build a cocoon of sorrow to hide in.

If she was chiding Genie for indulging herself, Mrs. Newberry did not come out and say so. According to her, everyone faced such a loss in his or her own way. A body had to stop mourning at one's own pace, but life was for living.

Genie thought Cousin Spotford was helping the vicar's widow get over her loss a bit sooner than she might have, but Mrs. Newberry's words made sense. Besides, Genie was bored, lying abed day and night.

So she got dressed in her prettiest dark gowns and had her hair cut in a new fashionably short style, befitting a new life. She took meals with the family and guests, and she drove around the property with Cousin Spotford. She called on the neighbors, attended church, and established an at-home day for company. This was where she lived now. It was time to put down roots.

Everyone was kind and made her welcome. No one mentioned her loss or her husband's absence. She had enough funds to make donations in his name, and enough authority to make decisions, too. She approved the site for the new school and was working with the architect, the retired teacher, and the village council to find the best design for the most children. She worked to overcome all of the gentlemen's prejudice against educating the girls as well as the boys. Yes, they would be taught sewing, but females needed to learn their letters and numbers as well as the boys. A woman could not, must not, always depend on a man. Genie was proof of that.

James Vinross arrived from London with instructions,

signed bank drafts, and orders for everyone to defer to Genie's opinions in all things.

So Ardeth did trust her, despite the terrible things she had said to him. That was something, anyway.

Oh, how she missed him, and how she still loved him. Which went to prove that the poets were right: Love was a madness, without rhyme or reason. It just was, like Ardeth himself. Inexplicable, infinitely worth the pain.

She worried about him, too, alone with Fernell Spotford. The Newberry sisters assured her the young gentleman was everything pleasing. Genie was not pleased. James said the earl took Olive everywhere with him. Genie was not satisfied. They were tracing Snell's steps, James told her, and discovering that the valet did have ample opportunity to get to London without Fernell's knowledge, so perhaps that whole trouble was behind them. James also reported that his lordship was locating other "lottery winners," so Genie could expect more houseguests needing cottages, work, or comfort.

James did not ask why the earl stayed away now that the mystery seemed solved, but he and Miss Hadley had their heads together, so he must know. Everyone knew Lady Ardeth had thrown her husband out of his own castle.

He would not come back unless she asked, she knew, not out of pride, but out of respect for her wishes. How many days before that departure he'd warned her about? What if she never saw him again, never got the chance to say what needed to be said? She could not live the rest of her life wondering if she might have changed things, if she might have stopped him from leaving. Even if he did eventually go, she could have the remaining weeks with the man she loved. Wasn't that better than nothing?

So she sat down and wrote him a letter. She apologized for the dreadful things she had said. They were not true. He was an admirable man, she wrote, but only a man. She ought not have demanded he perform magic or miracles, then grown angry when he could not. She did not blame him for her loss. How could she, when he had given her so much?

He did not want her gratitude. She ripped up the letter.

She wrote about the plans for the school, the new furnishings for the parlor, the progress of the various courtships at the Keep: James Vinross and Miss Hadley, Cousin Spotford and Mrs. Newberry, the middle Newberry girl and Cousin Richard, Marie and Campbell, Marie and the underbutler, Marie and the architect. Lud, he'd think she was running a matchmaking service! What man wanted to get involved in that? More shreds of paper hit the floor.

She wondered if he was interested in establishing a horse-breeding operation. Campbell would be in heaven, and perhaps Fernell could learn to manage it, which would please the eldest Newberry daughter. Bah, that sounded like she was putting forth a business proposition.

He had to be interested in Miss Frieda Spotford and the woman he had hired, so she wrote a page about that, how the older woman was getting out more, although she ignored Genie entirely. No, he might agree she was ignorable.

Eight torn pages later, Genie gave up. She scrawled two lines, sealed the note, and put it in a messenger's hands for the quickest possible delivery. *Dear Coryn,* she'd written, *I love you. Please come home.*

CHAPTER TWENTY-EIGHT

Ardeth must have retained some extraordinary skills after all, for no mere man could get from London to Ardsley in so short a time. He left Fernell in the dust on the first day. He would have lost Olive on the second, except for tucking the bird inside his greatcoat. He changed horses at every chance, paying for the best mounts even if he had to buy them. He slept only when it was too dark to ride on without becoming lost or injuring the horse. He ate when some innkeeper thrust a wedge of cheese in his hand, or a street vendor held up a meat pasty. He drank when he remembered to fill the water bottle in his saddlebag.

Genie loved him. Nothing else mattered. That's what he'd learned, what he had to tell her, so he rode on, and on.

She was waiting for him in the carriage drive. He did not question how she'd known he'd arrive three days before he should or how he'd known she would be there, her arms open to him. She loved him; that was enough. He jumped off his horse and ran the rest of the way, lifting her off her feet and holding her against him—Olive jumped out of his pocket in time—kissing her cheek, her hair, then her sweet, soft lips when she raised her face to his. So what if half the servants were watching from the front door, the gardens, and the windows? Genie loved him, and nothing else mattered.

Well, perhaps the visiting bishop mattered. The elderly man cleared his throat, loudly.

"I love you," Ardeth whispered before reluctantly setting Genie on her feet, a short but respectable distance away.

Her cheeks flaming scarlet, Genie curtsied and said, "Welcome home, my lord. We missed you."

"As I missed you," he answered for the bishop's sake, without trying to liken his missing her to an eclipse of the sun. "Are you well, my lady?"

"Quite, thank you."

Then they had to go inside. Ardeth needed a bath and a change of clothes. Genie needed to get her feet on the ground. He loved her!

In honor of the bishop's visit, a lavish dinner was planned for the noonday meal. They were celebrating the donation of a new roof for the local church. Genie was celebrating her husband's return.

Ardeth was wishing them all to the devil, even as he chatted politely with those nearest him. Who the deuce invited so many people to sit between him and his wife down the long table? He barely recognized half of them, but supposed they were the latest London rescuees. He should have sent them all to one of his other properties. In Constantinople.

At last it was time for the ladies to withdraw. The host could not, blast it. Ardeth sat through toasts, boasts, and belches as long as he could, then hurried the bishop on his way, saying he feared a coming thunderstorm. He told the others he would be at their service to discuss the school, the farms, the horses, tomorrow. The ladies had been alone too long, one in particular.

"Would you care to take a walk, my dear?" he asked Genie when he reached the drawing room.

"What about the thunderstorm?" she asked, then said, "Oh." The sky was now cloudless, a bright autumn afternoon. "Yes, thank you. I would like that."

He made arrangements, sending servants scurrying, while she went upstairs to fetch a shawl. Then she took his hand, trusting him to find somewhere private where they could talk. And kiss.

He led her around the back of the castle, near Miss Spotford's tower, and through the walled garden there, where Spotford and his sister were playing at cards. The new companion was visiting her niece on her half day off, Genie explained. Spotford smiled and waved them on, bringing more blushes to Genie's cheeks at his knowing look.

At the garden's outer gate, Ardeth headed toward the ruins of the original fortress, his Keep.

"Is it safe?" Genie asked. She had not ventured here, not after hearing of Miss Spotford's mishap.

"Where we are going is. I spent time here before I left for London, making sure."

"You played your flute there."

"I felt closer to the land here, closer to the heavens, when I asked for forgiveness."

"You had nothing to atone for," Genie said, apologizing

again for her tirade. "You are only a man, and I asked you to be a god."

"No, I am a monster beyond your imagination, with sins enough before I ever met you. I wanted so badly to be a man, I would do anything. I thought if I tried to be better than most, living with honor, doing good deeds, that would be enough to make me complete. I was wrong. Nothing could make me feel whole except your love. I realize that now, my dearest. And I am sorry for not telling you so. I did not know how. I did not know what love was, until you showed me. Being without you was like being without . . ."

"Your own heart? I know. I felt it, too. I was living in shadow until you brought back the light."

He held her arm as they climbed a few low fallen stones into the center of what had been his great hall, away from the crumbled walls. Grass was growing there, and a few late wildflowers. The servants had brought pillows and blankets and wine at his direction. They also brought his flute, knowing of his past habit of playing in the ruins.

"Will you play for me?" Genie asked. "A happy tune this time?"

"Later. First I would play a different composition, a different instrument. We can create the music of life together, if you are willing."

She was already arranging the pillows. "No one can see?"

"Olive will warn us. And he will keep his back turned if he knows what is good for him," he said in a much louder tone of voice.

After he helped Genie spread a blanket over the bed of pillows, he brought her a glass of wine. "Oh, before I forget, I must warn you that you will need a new companion. James asked permission to pay his addresses to your Miss Hadley. I know they are both of age, but I said I would consult with you. James is going to stand for the House of Commons from this borough. That way he will be able to continue the work I have begun with the reforms. I thought we could give them the Willeford house for their wedding present."

She quickly agreed, happy for her friends. "But what will you do for a secretary?"

"Cousin Fernell is going to take over as my assistant in London, now that he is sober. The Randolphs will keep an eye on him at the London town house."

"Fernell?"

Ardeth shrugged. "He has a knack for locating the lottery winners."

"But there is no lottery."

"There is now. So you shan't mind parting with Miss Hadley?"

Genie set down her glass. "You are the only companion I will ever need."

"Ah, Genie, your sweetness touches me to the core."

She touched him elsewhere, too, stopping his conversation, almost stopping his breathing. She did not care if he hired Attila the Hun as his henchman, not now. They kissed, a homecoming and a promise. They kissed, with their tongues and their sighs and their caresses.

In minutes they were on the blanket on the ground, on his ground, with his black cape like a blanket over them. He stroked her lips, her eyes, her hair, trying not to hurry, trying to memorize every detail of his beautiful bride. He let her new curls slide through his fingers, watching the sunlight catch the fire in the red and gold.

"I cut it."

"I see. Now you look like a naughty cherub, my own angel."

She showed him she was no angel, with impatient hands untying the knot in his neckcloth. "Will you mind," she asked, wriggling out of her gown and stays as he unfastened them, "that your bride is no virgin?"

He kicked off his shoes and pulled his shirt over his head. "What would I want with a virgin? Bridal nerves, shyness, and pain?" Which reminded him: "You are fully recovered?"

"It has been a month." Genie tugged at his sleeves, showing her eagerness.

When his shirt was off, Ardeth raised a ribbon from around his neck, dangling the ruby ring. "Will you wear this now?"

She let him put it on her hand while he recited, "With this ring, I do thee wed."

"You may now kiss the bride," she said with a smile.

He did, until they were both so warm, they pulled off the last of their clothes, stockings and all, and lowered his cloak so they could admire each other. Genie had to kiss the recent wound on his shoulder, and the lower one on his chest. He had to kiss her breasts in turn, holding them, fondling them, feeling their weight, memorizing the wedding gifts he'd just received. "So beautiful, my love. But you are certain you are ready for more? I would not hurt you for the world."

She rubbed her body against his, her bare breasts against his bare chest. "Perfectly."

Perfectly certain or a perfect fit? He groaned. "I want to be tender and slow for you, but I have waited so long, wanted you so badly. I do not know if I can hold back if you keep doing that."

She did that, and more, pressing against him. Now they were touching from tip to toe, reveling in the bare skin, the hard length of him, the soft roundness of her. "We can have tender and slow the second time."

"No, you deserve more. You should have a far better man than I, and a more patient lover."

He was loving her very well right then, his hand sliding between her thighs while he kissed her breasts, her throat, the ticklish spot on the side of her ribs.

"Oh, my. Elgin never—"

He stopped her words with a kiss, then said, "Remember, Elgin never enters our bedchamber."

She had to laugh, looking at the sky and the broken walls, the flowers and the sea of grass. "If this is our bedchamber, then poor Elgin is not welcome anywhere."

"Exactly." Then he showed her exactly how a woman's body should be worshipped and adored. He was not her first lover, but he was the first to introduce her to a woman's pleasure. He taught her how lucky a woman was, to be able to reach ecstasy until she was limp with satisfaction, and once more.

"But what of you?" she managed to gasp.

"I am enjoying myself as I never thought possible. Just hearing your sighs, feeling your body tremble, seeing the glory on your face, brings me more pleasure than anything I have ever done. I might never need to complete the act."

She touched the evidence of his own desire. "Hmph. And here I thought you never lied."

Her touch made him forget every principle he ever had. "You are right. I want to be inside you more than I want to take another breath of air. I do not care if I die tomorrow, I would have that now."

It was her turn to stop his words with a kiss. "There will be no talk of death in our marriage bed, my lord. No talk of leaving."

"You are right, my lady. There should be only love between us now."

She stroked him more firmly. "Now, Coryn, come to me now. I need you. All of you."

He was glad enough to obey her wishes before his body betrayed them. While that might not have been the longest lovemaking of his life, it was the most thrilling, the most complete, the most earthshaking.

"I never knew . . . ," she began when he rolled onto his back, pulling her on top of his chest.

But the earth shook again before she could complete the sentence.

Then Olive cawed.

Genie tried to make out the words. "He is afraid of something."

"No, he is saying 'Ar, Frieda,' not 'afraid.'" Coryn jumped to his feet to see the crazy woman atop the wall of rubble, hurling rocks down on them.

"Get down, you fool," he shouted. "That whole pile will collapse."

"And bury you! The same way it buried my future, my life! Your stones did it, and your family never noticed. My father should have been lord of the Keep, not yours, who never came home. My family took care of the Keep for all these years. You cared for nothing! Now you come here with your doxy and desecrate the very ground."

Ardeth started to roar out a reply, but a boulder under the lunatic's feet was dislodged. It came tumbling down, stirring the smaller rocks beneath. Ardeth threw himself on top of Genie, protecting her, as he felt the stones bounce and fall, striking his bare back, the ground, and Genie.

"No!" He yelled, shoving rocks away from her. Blood was everywhere, his or hers, he could not tell. As soon as the rocks stopped falling, he gathered her limp body in his cape, in his arms. "Genie, talk to me, dear heart." He brushed back the short curls and saw most of the blood was flowing from a gash on her forehead, right near the temple. "Oh, God, no!" He told himself that head wounds bled copiously. They were often not as bad as they looked. He grabbed for his discarded neckcloth to blot at the wound, unmindful of his own nakedness, his own injuries.

Then he saw the light, that telltale, unmistakable light, and cried out again, this time in anguish.

The cloaked figure appeared, as if from the dust of the stones, hourglass in hand.

"No, you cannot take her," Ardeth yelled. "Take me instead!" He pressed Genie against him, as if to hide her.

The voice that whispered through his mind sounded disappointed: "You know it does not work that way, Ar."

"But I have two months left!" Two months to heal Genie and give her a new life to carry. "I cannot go yet!"

"I am not here for you or your wife. It is the madwoman whose time has come."

Ardeth looked around. Now that the dust had settled he could see that the last remaining wall of the old fortress had fallen, burying Spotford's sister under it. This time there would be no rescue.

This was not Genie's time. He could breathe again. Ardeth neither put her down nor relaxed his grip on her, but he did stare at the cowled figure. He could not recognize the physical form, which seemed larger than most of his former associates'. But the voice, that murmur in his mind, seemed familiar.

"Do I know you?"

"You ought. You are one of the few who ever cheated Death, you know."

Himself? Ardeth almost dropped Genie after all. "I—"

"You cheated and lied and swindled your way back here. You broke every rule, Ar. You took every advantage of your position."

Ardeth could not protest his innocence, not when the evidence against him was in his arms.

"You even gambled with the Devil, my my."

Ardeth waited for the thunder to roll and the lightning to come, striking him dead. Instead, he heard, "Good job, Coryn of Ardsley. Well done. Do not tell any of the others, but it was high time Old Nick met his match."

"Then you are not going to take me back?"

"A rogue like you? I should say not. Besides, you won your wager. Today you are a man, if that is what you want."

Ardeth looked down at Genie, still unconscious in his arms. "It is."

"Then so you shall remain until your sand runs out. I so decree. Of course you will not remember any of this, but I will."

He reached out an invisible hand to lay on Ardeth's forehead, but Ardeth stepped back. "What about the hourglass? I never found it."

The cloaked figure moved his hand to Genie's wound, which stopped bleeding. The edges of the wound closed up, with no stitches, no bandages, no sticking plasters. "I'm afraid it will leave a scar."

Ardeth wiped the dried blood away, using his neckcloth and his tears. Under the curls, over a swollen spot, was an *X*, with both the top and bottom closed in. An hourglass. "Thank you."

"You are welcome. People so seldom thank the Grim Reaper, you know. It was my pleasure. But you can do me a favor. I'd appreciate the Devil's good-luck charm. One never knows when one might need to strike a bargain with Old Nick."

Ardeth found the bone in his pocket and tossed it into the air. It disappeared, along with all of his memories of another life.

Genie groaned right then, even as he heard Mr. Spotford shouting for more help, other men running, calling for horses and ropes.

She opened her eyes and looked up at him. "You are here, after all. I dreamed you had left."

"Of course I am here. I would never leave you, sweetings."

"Never?" She touched his cheek, staring into his eyes, looking for the truth.

"Never, I swear. Why would I go anywhere without my love, my heart, my soul? Till Death do us part, remember?"

EPILOGUE

Death ignored the crow. Without instructions, Olive figured he'd live as long as Ar. And if not, the earl's children and Olive's nestlings would grow old together, generation after generation. Olive would teach the chicks how to talk, and how to watch out for the children of the man who had pulled a gremlin from Hell. Yes, that would make a good bedtime story.

Oh, and he would teach them about love, too.

"Alive! Alive! I love. I love."

BARBARA METZGER
Ace of Hearts
Book One of the *House of Cards* trilogy

Never did Alexander "Ace" Endicott,
the Earl of Carde, imagine himself to be
thrice-betrothed against his will by the doings of
three desperate debutantes. So he escapes London
for his property in the country, where he follows
through with his father's last wish—to find his
long-lost step-sister.
But the search takes a detour, leading him to Nell,
and forcing him to wonder if two
mismatched lovers can make a royal pair.

0-451-21626-1

ALSO AVAILABLE
in the *House of Cards* trilogy

JACK OF CLUBS
0-451-21805-1

QUEEN OF DIAMONDS
0-451-21867-1

Available wherever books are sold or at
penguin.com